FORGED IN MOONLIGHT

S.F. HENNE

First Paperback Edition December 2024

ISBN 978-1-964791-02-9 (Paperback Edition)

Published by Ink & Magic Books

Cover Designed by Trif Book Design

Developmental Editing by Craft Better Books

Formatted in Atticus

ALSO BY S.F. HENNE

The Lunar Order Chronicles

The Last Lunar Witch

Forged in Moonlight

Sworn in Twilight

Eclipsed in Darkness - *coming soon*

From the Academy: Cursed Curriculums and Lessons in Lore Anthology

Shield by Duty

Dedicated to the one who is always there when I need them the most . . .

My microwave

Whenever I forget about my tea or coffee you are always there for me.

Content Disclaimer

There are several darker subjects that come up within this novel, including PTSD, traumatic flashbacks, death, as well as brief mentions of torture, murder, and child harm. While the general level of violence is similar to book 1, this is a darker time for Nyssa, and the story's tone reflects that. If you have any questions or concerns please feel free to reach out to me at sfhenne@sfhenne.com

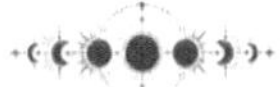

Nyssa's struggles with PTSD are a large part of this novel and I hope this story can shine a light on the issues many people face.
If you are struggling, just know there are always those around you to offer you support and strength when you need it.

Never give up hope. Do not suffer in silence.
If you need help please reach out.

You are NOT alone.

Pronunciation

Nyssa Thornheart – niss-ah thawn-haat

Tobin Thornheart – tOH-bihn thawn-haat

Voren – vaw-ren

Zola – zOH-lah

Indra Terral – IN-druh t-uh-r-EH-l

Rynac Terral – RYE-nak t-uh-r-EH-l

Carmen – kaar-muhn

Danika – DAN-ick-ah

Kaelan Renatus – KAY-lan Reh-NAH-t-us

Nathaniel Einheri – nuh-thAEN-yuhl in-HAIR-yee

Astrid – AST-rid

Thaddeus Flamebury - thAE-dee-uhs flaym-buh-ree

Selene – suh-leen

Aelia – eye-lee-uh

Terrarum – teh-ruh-rum

Trutina – tru-Tee-nah

Arkirith – Ah-k-ear-ith

The World of the Lunar Order

Realm - Trutina

Aelia, Goddess of the Sun, creator of witches, twin of Selene.

Gaelithra, Goddess of the Earth, creator of nymphs and the realm.

Selene, Goddess of the Moon, creator of the shifters and the moon-blessed.

Witches, blessed with solar magic from Aelia. Known for their powerful magic and bright hair, they live in isolated communities.

Shifters, blessed with lunar magic from Selene. Known for their ability to shift into an animal form and skills with alchemy.

Nymphs, blessed with nature magic from Gaelithra. Three distinct types: dryads of earth and flora, oreads of stone and mountain, and naiads of water and wind.

Moon-blessed, gifted with lunar magic after accepting Selene's offer to save them from death. Granted a second life, they retain small amounts of their original magic and now dedicate themselves to the moon goddess and protecting the realm.

Realm - Terrarum

The dead god who once ruled the realm, creator of humans.

The demon lords who now rule the realm, creators of erebian.

The archangels who remain silent, creators of nephilim.

Humans, once blessed by their god, they now despise magic. They live in isolated cities, creating technology for their new home.

Enhanced, who were once human but were altered by wild magic. Disowned by their own kind due to their magic, they now look for a new place to call home.

Nephilim, blessed with holy magic from the archangels. Known for their wings and ability to fly, along with their arrogance and ability to sway those around them with magic.

Erebian, cursed with infernal magic from the demon lords who created and then enslaved them. Known for the reddish skin and horns, generally distrusted due to their magical powers to glamor.

Organizations

United Magical Council (UMC) - A diplomatic and political organization that represents all races, and is intended to maintain peace and security, ensuring the safety of all races and beings.

Magical Enforcers of Arkirith (MEA) - The police force that protects and serves the city of Arkirith.

The Lunar Order - A secret organization of moon-blessed who work to protect the realm from demonic forces and threats to the veil.

Inquisitors - A special task force of witches, sanctioned by the witch council to hunt down those of their kind with dark or volatile magic and turn them in for judgment.

The Story So Far...

Nyssa Thornheart was a witch with broken magic. Desperate to fix it, she left her witch-only community for Arkirith, a vast city where all magical races lived. She struck a bargain with her parents: if she stabilized her magic and established an alchemy business within a year, she could stay. Failure meant returning home, sacrificing her power, and abandoning her true passion—alchemy.

A month into her stay, with money dwindling and no progress on her magic, Nyssa snuck into the Alchemy Guild's restricted library and stole a tome. The tome's was unreadable but when a cobalt fox appeared, she found an enhancement potion to help control magic. Struggling financially, she took a trial baking shift at Divine Coffee, where a magical mishap earned her a job. There she befriended two enhanced enforcers, Rynac and Indra, while still seeking a potion contract to secure her business.

When demonspawn attacked Rynac, Nyssa drank the potion and rushed to help. On their way to a healer, they were cornered by thugs. Nyssa summoned a shield but lost control of her magic. The veil separating Trutina from the demonic realm of Terrarum tore, and the thugs twisted into thralls. Though Nyssa held off the enemy, the backlash from her unstable magic struck her down.

Upon waking, Nyssa discovered the fox—Danika—was her familiar, and that Nyssa carried both solar and lunar magic. After an interrogation with nephilim from the United Magical Council—Kaelan and Nathaniel—she learned her magic had damaged the veil itself. Crushed with guilt, she wanted to bind her powers, but her friends urged her to master them instead.

When her shifter friend Ruby vanished, Nyssa confronted the dark witch, Carmen, who sought to fully awaken Nyssa's powers. Surrounded by demonspawn, Nyssa battled Carmen but was hit by the lunar energies stolen from Ruby. Only the nephilim's intervention saved her from Carmen and the Inquisitors.

With the aid of the third nephilim, Astrid, Nyssa discovered her solar energies had clashed with her lunar magic, causing the instability. Astrid trained her to harness her powers, and with a runed band to contain her solar side, Nyssa could wield her lunar magic freely. She also learned she was moon-blessed, chosen by the goddess Selene, and that the nephilim belonged to the Lunar Order.

When her friend Voren was kidnapped by Carmen, Nyssa joined shifters and enforcers to mount a rescue. They freed the captives but were ambushed by demonspawn. Nyssa used her new power to shield her allies from a warlock and seal a tear in the veil, only to be captured by Inquisitors for wielding dangerous magic.

Before they can strip away Nyssa's magic, her allies rescued her. But Carmen's horde soon captured Indra and Rynac, intending to use them to manipulate Nyssa's power. With the nephilim's help, Nyssa agreed to surrender herself in exchange for her friends. Kaelan, fearing for her life, gave her an angelic protection rune.

Tricked by Carmen, Nyssa was bound in a spell array, unable to save her friends. Carmen revealed that Nyssa's magic was the key to breaching the veil and opening a portal for a demon lord. Desperate, Nyssa disrupted the array from within, channeling both magics at once. She destroyed the spell, and even though Carmen escaped, Nyssa emerged with more allies and a renewed purpose. Accepting her place as a lunar witch, she pledged herself to Selene and prepared to face whatever came next.

Chapter One

With the dappled afternoon sun streaming through the trees and the gentle rustle of leaves whispering around me, this could've been the perfect place to rest and enjoy the scenery. But that illusion shattered with the deep thrum of magic resonating through the ground, saturating the air and setting my nerves on edge.

Danika, my cobalt vulpine familiar, waited beside me—a strong, steady presence, ready if I needed her. Sharp eyes took in everything, but she never commented. Not on the small beads of sweat breaking out over my skin, my struggle to keep my breathing even, or the way my nails dug into my palms, leaving crescent-shaped marks as I fought to maintain control.

Just a few paces away, the powerful wards thrummed as they contained the potent magic that crackled behind them. Goosebumps prickled over my arms. Deep within me, my power swirled in recognition of the lunar magic I'd unleashed here.

Almost two months had passed since that fateful night, two months of dreams—nightmares—about that depthless pit. My heart skittered in my chest as I took another half-step forward, every instinct in me screaming to turn and run.

"You don't have to do this," Danika said in my mind. But I did. I needed those nightmares to stop haunting me. To prove to myself this was all in my head, and reconnect with my magic.

Stupid, I thought. *Why was I so stupid?*

"Nyssa," a voice called out. I whirled, but it was only Lainie, the tall, graceful shifter, jogging towards me. I shoved my fear down, locked it away, and forced a pleasant smile, stuffing my hands into my pockets to hide how they shook. "We're going to check on the northern wards. Want to join us?"

The shifters, along with the MEA—the Magical Enforcers of Arkirith—had worked together to secure this location. After I'd shattered the warlock's spell array, it unleashed the magic he'd gathered, a surge that flooded the area, saturating it with energy that still resonated today.

We had no idea how long this echo of power would last. For now, both groups maintained their wards, shielding it from any that might misuse it, and monitoring the fluctuating magic levels.

"I think I'll stay here," I said, somehow keeping my voice even. All the while, whispers filled my head, warning me not to turn my back to the power churning behind me. The nape of my neck prickled, as if something watched me.

Lainie gave a brief nod, then turned on her heels and joined the others. They'd asked if I wanted to help when they created these wards, as part of my training to master my lunar magic. But just the thought of returning here had left me in a cold sweat.

Frustration gnawed at me. I'd poured everything I had into mending my magic, sacrificing so much, only for it to turn stagnant.

I thought I'd finally found my path, the way forward that would make it all worth while. But with each attempt to train, every effort to slip back into my regular life, it crumbled before me. Even the simplest of spells defied me, my magic rebelling and slipping out of reach.

I hissed out a breath through clenched teeth, a mix of frustration, fear, and annoyance boiling within me. I spun around, directing my glare at the invisible wards that surrounded me, as if they were the source of my failures.

That was why I was here. To confront what was wrong with me. Facing this place, the memories lurking in the shadows, would be the key to fix this. It had to be. Otherwise . . .

I took a step closer. *I can do this.* It was only my imagination. I just needed to overcome it, to silence the doubts that clawed at my mind.

I sat down and unpacked the supplies from my bag, laying them out in a neat row before me as if I could ignore the magic looming over me. My grimoire, the pages filled with all my spells, *The Lunar Codex*, the book that had given me the potion recipe to awaken my magic, and last, my vial of ink and brush.

My fingers trembled as I set them down. *This is why I'm here*, I reminded myself once more. But, as I uncorked the ink and dipped in the brush, my hand shook, and I bit down hard on my cheek to regain my focus.

Without the runed band spell, I was useless. Even though I'd awoken my lunar magic, I was still a witch, still blessed with the solar energy of my Goddess. This rune was essential to contain my solar magic and prevent it from flaring up and disrupting the spell I cast. Otherwise, things would turn volatile, and I'd be back at square one.

Ink the rune, I told myself.

The brush hovered just above my skin. My gaze locked on the white line that snaked from my knuckles down past my wrist. The scar that marred my hand.

I dug my nails into my thigh, fighting to steady my hand as I drew the first line of the rune. My world narrowed to my hand, the scar, and that rune. Every ounce of my restraint focused on drawing the next line.

Pain sliced through my scar, a vicious wound opening, blood pouring down and dripping onto the ground. A clawed hand closed around my throat, pressing tighter, cutting off my air.

Someone shouted my name, but I could do nothing but stare down at my ruined hand and gasp. A mocking laugh, one I knew too well, filled my ears and drowned out everything else.

"Nyssa!" Reality slammed back into me, the world once again full of light. A soft breeze brushing my sweat-soaked skin. *"Breathe."* I sucked in a shuddering breath, following the command.

I needed to get out of here. The magic of the woods pressed down on me, stifling, until I thought I might suffocate.

Shoving to my feet, I ignored the ink that tipped over and splattered across the ground. The sight of the black liquid twisted my stomach. Too reminiscent of the blood of the thralls, of the bodies I'd seen lying in that alleyway, of the remnants of the demonspawn I'd killed.

My vision swam as I stumbled away. I couldn't breathe; couldn't get enough air.

"I'm fine," I hissed before Danika said anything. "Just need some fresh air." Which was a stupid thing to say, given that I was in the middle of a clearing. But she didn't call me out.

I just walked and walked, letting the trees close in around me, as if I could outpace my own nightmares.

Not that Danika left me alone. I sensed her presence following me, close enough to offer support but distant enough to give me space, lending me her strength when I was so empty and hollow.

A trickle of magic prickled at my senses. I blinked, realizing I'd wandered deeper in the forest than I'd ever ventured. I knew I should head back, but all that waited for me there was failure.

Curiosity surged within me—anything was better than confronting my new reality. The shifters patrolled this area of the forest to keep animals from stumbling across the warded section. But this magic felt different. So, I followed it, with nowhere I needed to be, no one depending on me.

Movement caught my eye.

A dark figure crouched between the thick trunks, shadows clinging to them. My pulse thrummed in warning as I took one step closer.

I squinted, trying to make out more details, but the shadows seemed to sway with their body, and then I realized they had a hood covering their face. Beneath, a mask gleamed faintly in the dim light, giving no hint of the person behind it.

Warning bells blared in my mind, and my gaze dropped to the churned soil at their feet. There was something marked there. Not just something, but a rune. A demonic rune.

Terror speared through my chest, and I flinched back. Their head snapped up, eyes hidden behind that mask, yet somehow they pinned me in place. My mouth opened but all the words stuck in my throat, choking me, my thoughts turning sluggish as if a thick fog swept through my mind.

The figure straightened, tall and imposing, their presence seeming to warp the space around them, the very air shrinking away.

Magic shivered over me, then burrowed underneath my skin, leaving a prickling numbness in its wake. My body refused to respond. The figure seemed to blur and dissolve as the shadows grew larger.

Danika! I called out, but even the voice in my head was barely a whisper. Where was she? She'd been right behind me. Darkness wrapped around me until I was drowning in it. No escape. No end.

My blood froze. Ice seeped into my very bones. A thick band squeezed the breath from me as a pair of soulless eyes held me in place.

Red irises against wholly black eyes. Shadows snaked from the ground, wrapping around the figure's body, devouring any light that touched it. The air grew stagnant, and an oppressive silence fell, as if the figure's very presence had snuffed out all sound and warmth.

A smile slithered over Carmen's lips, satisfaction gleaming as her gaze fixed on me. Savoring my terror as if she tasted it. I couldn't move. My body refused to respond as my mind screamed.

I was weak. Helpless. At the dark witch's mercy, yet again.

How had she found me? Why had I let myself be isolated like this? After months without a single demonspawn sighting, I thought it would be safe. Thought *I* was safe. Stupid. Foolish.

Phantom nails dragged down my arm; the wound throbbed. A dull ache at first, but it grew with each beat of my heart, until I had to bite my cheek against the pain. I feared if I looked down, blood would be dripping from my hand.

Alone. I was all alone. No one was here to help me. And if she took me, no one would ever find me.

I couldn't even look away. Trapped like snared prey. Her eyes brimmed with the promise of all the pain she would inflict on me as she drained every last drop of my magic. Of the torment she would exact upon me for destroying her attempt to open a portal and flood the city with demonspawn. Pleasure widened her grin as if she read my every thought, as if my fear sated her hunger.

Carmen lifted her hand. Bright red blood dripped from her fingers as she crooked one of her black talons to beckon me closer. My legs locked. I refused to go. Not again. I couldn't . . .

The shadows deepened around us, the sun overhead long forgotten. I ripped my gaze from hers and scanned the darkness, eyes darting between the trees, torn between the need to know and the fear of what I might discover.

How many demonspawn had she summoned? Sulfur clogged my nose until I wanted to gag. Memories of their needle-sharp teeth, their savage claws, filled my thoughts until I couldn't breathe. Would I even leave this place alive?

A buzzing filled my ears, my body trapped in limbo. I refused to comply with her, yet I knew I wasn't strong enough to resist. Not powerful enough to fight. I reached for my magic, but it slipped through my fingers like I was trying to grasp a moonbeam.

A sharp bark cut through the air behind me, and I flinched. Wait. That wasn't the sound of demonspawn.

Carmen's features darkened, a savage light filling her infernal gaze. She stepped towards me. She would snatch me up, drag me away. I was helpless. Useless. I deserved this.

How many innocent people died because I brought Carmen to this city?

How many lunar magic users suffered to fuel her dark spell?

All because of me.

"It's not real," Danika's voice rattled through me. *"She's not here."*

A blur of blue launched through the air, slamming into the ground in front of me. Danika's growl reverberated in my chest and I blinked. Light had returned, bright enough that I winced. The area was empty, save for me and my familiar.

Danika spun, searching for the threat. Carmen wasn't here. It wasn't real.

All at once, reality caught up to me. Whatever force had pinned me in place lifted and my legs gave out. My knees slammed into the ground as I sucked in a shuddering breath.

Wrapping my arms around my stomach, I pressed my forehead into the cold dirt and squeezed my eyes shut.

Magic skittered across my skin, but it was familiar this time.

"Are you hurt?" Danika asked. I opened my mouth to say I was fine, but my lips trembled, refusing to form words. *"Help is coming."*

She curled up next to me, her warmth doing nothing to stop my shivering. Why was I so cold?

Memories of demonspawn pierced through the mental walls I'd erected in my mind. Acid churned in my gut, bile burning my throat.

"You are safe." A soft, soothing magic pulsed within Danika, and I wrapped my arms around her. *"I am here."*

How many times had Danika whispered those words into my mind over the last few months? How many times had she curled up beside me after waking me from yet another nightmare, when I was covered in sweat and shaking? But she never complained.

Shifters spilled into the area, on high alert. How had Danika called them? I wasn't sure, but I didn't have the strength to ask, my mind still too numb.

Only one shifter approached us. Her pure-white hair twisted into a knot, her kind silver eyes creased with concern as she took me in. Her sharp gaze noted the failed rune on my hand.

"The area is clear, but we'll keep searching," Nan said.

"Thank you," I croaked. When did my throat become so dry and scratchy? As if I'd been screaming. Wait? Did I scream? "They drew a rune." I pointed, my lips protesting each word. Nan nodded, ordering the shifters to search the ground. I pushed myself up, holding Danika tight against my chest, not wanting to be here if they didn't find a rune. If it was just another nightmare my mind had conjured.

"I've sent a runner to prepare the car," Nan said. I almost sagged with relief that she didn't ask what had happened. "We can head back to the den—"

"Home," I muttered. I wanted to be alone. To forget about all of this, not have to face yet another failure. But most of all, I needed to escape the way the shifters gazed at me as if I were a hero.

The truth was, I was more broken than ever before.

Chapter Two

When I entered Divine Coffee the next morning, the familiar warmth embraced me. The sentient coffee shop's magic seeped into my skin, reassuring me that I was safe here.

The invigorating, earthy aroma of freshly brewed coffee swirled around me as if Divine knew what I needed, and the tension in my shoulders eased.

My eyes fluttered closed for a moment as I savored that wonderful smell, before red eyes flashed through my mind and I jerked back.

To say I was exhausted was an understatement.

Dreamless sleep potions no longer worked; the others I'd tried had only trapped me in my nightmares, unable to move. And now, if being plagued by nightmares wasn't bad enough, I'd one while awake. Just what I needed.

I scrubbed my face with my hands and willed the coffee to brew faster. A heavy silence had filled the entire car ride after my "incident", but Danika hadn't probed or prodded.

Her presence at my side had been the only thing holding me together. Strength and reassurance pulsed through our bond, doing more than words could at that moment, my sweet little fox knowing I wasn't ready to talk.

We'd cuddled on my bed in silence, but sleep was elusive, nothing more than a phantom that haunted me. Just like Carmen's eyes that seemed to lurk behind my eyelids.

After hours of tossing and turning, I gave up and headed to work early to get a head start on the day's baking. It also helped that I knew I was protected here, that Carmen couldn't reach me when I was within these walls.

Danika nestled into her spot, a nice little nest at the base of a bookcase. One day when I'd come to work, Divine had kept the door open after I entered, a silent invitation. Danika hesitated for a moment before following me in. There was little doubt Divine had created it.

I slipped into the familiar routine of prepping for the day's business, checking supplies, and starting on the first batches of baked goods.

The front door jingled, despite there being no bells—Divine's way of alerting us about a visitor—and I glanced at the clock, surprised how much time had passed.

"Hello?" a tentative voice asked, in something akin to a low rumble.

"Come on in," I called, not hiding my smile. It reminded me far too much of my first shift at Divine.

Back then, I didn't know the shop was sentient and thought someone had broken in, and I'd been jumpy after running head first into a demonspawn.

I shuddered, pushing thoughts of those creatures from my mind before they could unlock memories I didn't want to deal with right now.

Pyrah pushed through into the kitchen, and I smiled again. For an oread they were pretty shy. A nymph of stone and mountain. Their skin was almost translucent and reminded me of quartz. Oreads took after specific minerals—how that all worked was still a mystery to most of the magical community.

Wordlessly, we fell into an easy routine, as if we'd been working side by side for months.

I tried to keep myself busy, refusing to slow down, but in the few quiet moments a heavy weight settled in my stomach. A creeping sensation crawled over my skin like the feeling of unseen eyes watching me from the shadows.

My phone rang, jolting me from my thoughts. I cursed under my breath, irritated that the stupid thing had given me a heart attack. I pulled it out and swore again when I saw the caller ID—Dad. What in all the hells had happened now?

"Hi, Dad," I answered, forcing a cheerful tone despite my heart bouncing against my ribs. "Is something wrong?"

"Why do you always think that?" he replied, though I could hear the smile in his voice. "I just wanted to check up, to see how you were doing."

"And remind me again that you are visiting in a few weeks." Because everything had to be perfect when Mum came to visit, she was taking time off, blah-blah. Yeah, how could I forget? I'd been dreading it since the moment my brother, Tobin, had first mentioned it.

This would be the first time they visited me since I left home—and since my magic awakened and I discovered I was a lunar witch.

Worst of all, I still had no idea how to confront them about it. Did they know about our lunar heritage? That I bore a moon-blessed mark? Why was I the only one to inherit both solar and lunar magic?

Each question felt like a lead shackle wrapping around my limbs, weighing me down until I couldn't move.

"I also want to know how you are doing," he said. "How are things in Arkirith? Pretty quiet?"

You mean now that the demonspawn, warlock, and dark witch are gone? I thought ruefully.

There was little doubt my parents knew about that incident because of their high-ranking positions in our government. But they couldn't know I was involved, or they'd have dragged me home.

"Things are getting busy," I said. "It's tourist season. But I still should have enough time off to come for the summer solstice," I added before he could harass me about that again.

It was the holiest witch holiday, after all, the longest day of the year to celebrate Aelia, the Goddess of the Sun who gifted witches their magic. And somehow I would have to interact with all those witches, hoping they didn't notice what I really was.

And if you run into an Inquisitor?

Right. I'd never sorted all that out, either. The Inquisitors had arrested me for the use of wild magic and endangering lives. Then they'd almost severed my connection to magic. But after I escaped and disrupted the demonic ritual, they'd arrested the warlock and chased after Carmen.

I hadn't heard anything and guessed I was no longer a suspect. But I needed to figure that out before I willingly walked back into Myrite.

The Inquisitors must've stayed silent. Though it was more likely due to their distaste for the UMC—the United Magical Council who oversaw all races—than keeping the knowledge from my family. The Inquisitors were a powerful organization, but going up against my coven was not a smart move.

Another thing that wasn't easy to bring up: *Hey, Dad, can you ask the Inquisitors if they still have a warrant out for my arrest?*

"Good, your mother will be so pleased," Dad said. A weighted pause hung between us, and I braced myself for what would come next, knowing I wouldn't like it. "And how about your alchemy? I know it's not even halfway through your year, but I just want to hear how it's all going."

My shoulders sagged. "Running into a few snags, but nothing I can't handle." The false brightness in my voice left a bitter taste on my tongue.

I'd made a deal with my parents to allow me to move here and set up my alchemy business. If, after a year, I could prove I was self-sufficient—and didn't have any incidents with my magic—then they would let me stay. I'd sorted out the magic part—mostly—but opening my alchemy shop was another matter.

I was almost there—all I needed was a location for the store, but either the rent was too high or they didn't want an alchemist with no credit history.

"It's bound to happen. Opening a business isn't easy. But I believe in you." Well, at least one of us did. "And if you need any help—"

"Dad," I groaned. The whole point of our deal was to do it on my own, not just to prove it to my parents, but to prove it to myself. That I was an adult who could handle whatever life threw at me.

"I'm sorry. All I want is for you to be happy. I've got to run, sweetie. Talk to you soon."

Staring down at my phone, silence pressed in around me. There had been so little time to brew potions, too many other things demanding my attention, and I missed it. Alchemy was the slice of peace in my life.

If I could just get all of this sorted, then I could get back to brewing and maybe . . . *Maybe I could find my happiness again?*

After ending the threat of the warlock, I'd thought life was starting to look up. I couldn't have been more wrong.

When was the last time I felt happy or excited for the next day?

Flipping the switch, I turned on the large mixer as I started the sponge cake and my eyes followed the paddle in its hypnotizing turns. My mind was the same, churning through all the worries and troubles, mixing them together until they became one coagulated blend of anxiety.

How could I even begin to deal with my family when I didn't even know how to handle the ceremony tonight? What if I couldn't channel the magic? And what if my vision of Carmen from earlier was a warning?

What if this marked the moment the dark witch was going to strike again and—

The mixer turned off, and I blinked to find the concerned dark gaze of Beylin watching me.

"Nyssa, are you alright?" he asked, in that ever patient voice. Just what I needed, to catch the notice of my dwarven boss.

"What do you mean?" I said, taking a step back. Just how long had I been staring? And then I noticed the lights above were pulsing and the dry ingredient bin's lids were clacking in agitation.

"Your magic was fluctuating and Divine's worried about you."

"Oh, sorry. I'm fine, just a lot on my mind. Didn't sleep well." I flashed him a smile as if that would prove it, but his eyes saw right through me.

"You're not in any kind of trouble, are you?" he asked, his voice low enough not to be overheard.

I didn't know if I should be offended that he thought I was getting into trouble again, but after what I'd gone through back then, could I blame him?

And Beylin was the one to take care of me when my lunar magic was unstable; he'd been nothing but supportive. Even when I'd been arrested by the Inquisitors, he'd joined the enforcers to free me.

I knew I could trust him, that he was looking out for me, which made my mouth taste all the more sour when I said, "No, just an important meeting with the shifters tonight."

He nodded, though I didn't think I'd convinced him. The urge to tell him about the vision bubbled up, but I quashed it down.

These were my problems to deal with. If I couldn't figure them out on my own then I didn't deserve to succeed.

Chapter Three

I sipped on herbal tea as I clocked out; caffeine had little effect when I was this sleep deprived. And though I was dead on my feet, a genuine smile graced my lips when I noticed the two shifters waiting at a table.

Jade leaned back, cradling Danika in her lap, her grin wide as she ran gentle fingers through the fox's fur. Ruby, her older sister, sat nearby, phone in hand. Her amber eyes bright against the contrasting colors of her silver hair and twilight complexion.

"What are you two still doing up?" I asked Jade as I joined them. Shifters were nocturnal by nature. Ruby offered me a nod in greeting before returning to her hushed conversation.

"More errands before tonight," Jade huffed, but bounced in her seat at the reminder of tonight's ceremony, which only made my stomach twist. "Are you still nervous?"

A lie danced on the tip of my tongue, but I swallowed it down. "How could I not be, when it's such an important ritual?" I said. This would be my first time participating in the ceremony, and I wasn't just attending—I was at the heart of it.

Every full moon the pack held a ceremony to honor Selene, the Goddess of the Moon, to bask in her glory and strengthen the pack's power. Despite my protests, there was no backing out. It was an honor I couldn't refuse.

After everything I'd done to restore the stolen magic and protect the city from the warlock, they believed I was the best person to conduct the ceremony. My connection to the lunar energies embedded in the ground from that final battle with Carmen made me the ideal conduit for the power—it should recognize me.

"What else can you tell me about it?" I asked. The shifters had explained my part, but were vague about the rest. "Or at least what is it like when you don't have . . . ?" I gestured to myself, not willing to say "lunar witch" aloud.

We were pretty much beings of myth, which I never even believed could exist. The solar magic from Aelia and the lunar from Selene didn't play nice with each other, turning volatile inside us, which is why witches like me were so rare.

Not to mention that I was also a moon-blessed witch, that Selene had saved my life, and marked me as one of her chosen.

"Sometimes," Jade said, "important people from the other packs come to lead the ceremony, but that doesn't happen often. For the winter solstice, we usually go to a high priest's pack to make our bonds stronger. But there aren't as many priests now. Oh, I'm not supposed to talk about that."

"Don't worry, I'm great at keeping secrets," I said with a wink. Jade smiled and ducked her head.

The ability to wield magic was a touchy subject for all the races, and we tended not to discuss it with others. The witches were one of the last races to have full access to magic, though that had begun to decline.

It used to be that every witch born would manifest magic on their thirteenth birthday, but now it could take several days, if at all. Though the number who never manifested was low, I wondered if it was more than the witch council let on.

Witches knew that the number of magic users among other races had dwindled, which the council claimed was why they kept us isolated.

The loss of magic appeared to have no clear cause, but it was a sensitive topic. Our Goddesses were the ones who granted us magic, so if magic was fading, did that mean the Goddesses were turning their backs on their people?

Whatever the cause, I doubted the gods would tell us. Perhaps it was just part of the cycle.

"Under the full moon," Jade continued, "we say our prayer to the Goddess. When a magic user leads us, they help guide the pure magic into the spell circle we stand in."

I flinched at the words, but Jade didn't seem to notice.

Danika's awareness shifted to me and I did my best to keep my mind blank. As much as I loved my familiar, I didn't want to cause her any extra stress and worry about me.

But the idea of being within a spell array with others . . . I banished the memories. But it would've been nice if the shifter pack had mentioned that part.

"We get to wear fancy clothes too." Jade's grin was infectious. "We wear the prettiest white clothes . . . I want to wear mine all the time, but they say I'll get them dirty."

"Oh, white is hard to get stains out of, but I've a special formula if you ever need it," I said in a stage whisper to Jade, and she giggled.

Potions and formulas had been my life for years. I'd learned everything I could, hunting for a wide variety of creations that could be useful. Even for the mighty witches, stains were a problem.

"But yours is the prettiest I've ever seen," Jade said with wonder in her eyes. I had to smile—at least someone was excited.

With a heavy sigh, Ruby hung up her call. "Another dead end." She didn't have to say more, and I tried to offer her a reassuring smile, that it didn't feel like a knife in the gut.

Jade's shoulders drooped. Just another failure as I tried to sort my life out.

At least demonspawn aren't hunting me down. I wasn't bitter or anything . . . I know, I'd roll my eyes at me too. But it was hard not to be cynical.

After so many years of reaching for that dream of my own shop, it cut even deeper when it seemed fate worked against me. Like everything I strove to grasp came with too many strings attached.

I gained the magic I always wanted but couldn't do anything with it besides channeling it, crafting a shield, or summoning moonlight. Anytime I tried something harder where I needed the rune band . . . the magic within me turned to lead.

Then I'd earned great alchemy contracts, but they were only enough to keep me afloat. No matter how hard I hunted, I couldn't find somewhere to open a store. Without a shopfront I could only brew with contracts, I couldn't sell individual or one-off potions.

If I could just open a shop, things would return to normal. I'd have a steady income, a permanent place within Arkirith, and I'd be living the life I wanted. Safe. In control. Normal.

"None of the people I approached will take anything less than two s of rent up front," I said.

"There is one more," Ruby said, trying to hide her grin, but her excitement sparkled in her eyes. "I'm going to meet with them tomorrow. I wasn't planning on saying anything, as I didn't want to get your hopes up."

"Really?" I said, my heart fluttering. But I tamped down on the hope. I knew better.

Ruby had become my unofficial partner, helping me to drop off orders, preparing the reagents, and scouting for new contracts. After all, she ran errands for her pack and knew just about everyone in the city. But she had a way with people, she could put them at ease and chat with them like they were old friends.

Which was probably how she convinced me to let her help. She desired to support herself and Jade, and though the pack would offer assistance, she wanted to stand on her own. A sentiment I understood all too well.

Since the incident where Carmen had attacked Ruby and stolen her lunar energies to force them upon me, we'd become great friends. I'd feared she'd hate me, blaming me for getting her wrapped up in the events, but instead, a bond had been forged. And Jade was never far behind.

They'd lost their mother several months before we met. After Ruby had been left unconscious from the attack, Jade refused to let her sister out of her sight.

For someone so young, Jade had a knack for reagents, and I was more than happy to give her a safe place to stay when away from her den.

Shifters, like witches, tended to isolate themselves and only interact with their own kind. But since I moved to Arkirith, I'd learned that it was actually more of a hindrance.

The other races had so much to share and teach—while I used to think that our differences were walls that stood between us, the truth was the opposite. They were a chance for us all to learn and grow together.

"It's not a sure thing," Ruby said, "but it might be a good lead." Her phone rang again and with a grumble she answered and stepped away.

"You'll find somewhere," Jade said. She stared down into her hot chocolate; she hadn't even touched it yet.

"Well, either way, we can just keep hanging out at my place," I said, hoping to brighten her spirits. My issues didn't need to be passed on to the kid.

"I'd like that, and I know Ruby would too. It's much more fun to be around you. Ruby really wants to get your shop going and become your assistant."

I sipped my drink as my stomach dropped. "I think you both would make fantastic assistants, but I don't know if I'll earn enough to pay you two. At least not for a while." Wait, I couldn't hire a kid, there had to be laws against that.

"I'm happy to become your apprentice," Jade said with a bright smile. The hope burning in her eyes made my heart twist. "That way, I can help Ruby out. I know I just get in the way some days; she works so hard to support us."

"You're not a burden, if that is what you are thinking. Family always looks out for each other."

"That's what the pack's meant to do," Jade grumbled.

"Is there something going on at home?"

Jade pressed her lips together. I knew I shouldn't pry into pack business, but I couldn't stop myself from wanting to help the girls out. "She doesn't get along well with some of the elders. She always has to take the lowest-paying jobs, and it makes it harder when I get in the way."

"Why is that?"

"They don't like her because she doesn't have magic," Jade whispered, her eyes downcast. "They say those without magic just weigh down the pack."

Ruby didn't have magic? My heart stuttered. Was that my fault? "They want to kick her out because of that? How could they blame her when it was because of me her lunar energies were stolen?"

Jade shook her head. "She never manifested, she's never had a wolf form."

I didn't even know that was possible. Magic was declining, but I thought all shifters still had access to their animal forms. I doubted it was something they would make public. It could make them look weak, make their pack appear vulnerable.

But that didn't mean a person was worthless. Ruby had been an enormous help to me. Without her, I never would've earned the brewing contract with the pack. Nor would I've been able to keep up with the demand for my potions.

No wonder she'd been trying so hard to help me open the shop; I might be her chance for freedom.

I'd moved to Arkirith for the same reason. And the fire in Jade's eyes when she said she wanted to be my apprentice, it was the same strong desire I'd felt when my magic was all mixed up.

"We will find a place to open up a shop," I said, squeezing Jade's hand. "And I'll make sure that both you and Ruby have a job. I can't let my apprentice be stolen away."

Jade giggled, the sound imprinting on my heart. I didn't know what I would do, but I couldn't let her or Ruby down.

Magic or no, everyone deserved a fair chance in this world. Before I'd fixed my magic, I'd been treated like those with none. Dismissed for something I'd no power over. Just because the Goddesses decided not to share their gifts with all of us didn't mean we were less.

Ruby rushed back, needing to run another last-minute errand for tonight's ceremony. I waved goodbye and headed home, knowing I should sleep, but the idea of giving in to my dreams filled me with dread.

How was I going to get through the ritual, standing on the other side of the wards this time?

What if that vision was a warning? The rune the figure had drawn was demonic, I was sure of it. What if Carmen knew? What if she was waiting for me to go back and—

Magic flared in my fingertips, and I cut off my thoughts. Danika's gaze settled on me, but I kept my eyes fixed on the ground.

I'd been doing so well, my life almost felt normal again, so why did I have to see Carmen? Was my mind working against me?

I shoved all thoughts of Carmen back down into the darkness where they belonged. Hopefully, one day I could forget it all.

That was what I wanted, right?

As I trudged up the stairs of my apartment building, I could sense Danika's attention was fixed on me.

"Just spit it out," I said, too tired for this.

"Do you want to talk about yesterday?"

"No," I snapped, and she flinched at the harshness of my voice. "It's just—" I shook my head, fearing if I started talking then I'd never be able to stop. All of my fears and doubts would come tumbling out for all the world to see. "No."

"She wasn't there. Not really."

"So you think I made it up?"

"No—"

"I know what I saw."

"I'm not doubting you," she said, the pain etched into her words cutting into my heart. *"I'm just trying to help."*

"I'm sorry," I said, kneeling down and rubbing her head. "I shouldn't lash out at you. It's just . . . remembering that feeling again. All that I've tried to forget . . ."

"You need to talk about it. I'm always here for you."

"What do you think it was then?" I asked, trying to ignore that twinge in my chest at her words. "Do you think magic was involved?"

It'd felt so real, but that didn't mean much. Once before, I'd accidentally performed divination and the scene it showed me felt far too real.

The flames that had surged around me . . . I'd swore my skin was about to melt off. Feeling real and being real were two very different things.

"In an area like that, with so much potent magic, it is likely that it has a mind of its own. The wolves believe it could be doing many things to the forest."

"Even with the wards in place?"

"The wards will keep people out, but there is little we can do to contain magic that powerful. It could be that the energies are attuned to you. That they latched onto your emotions and enhanced them."

Lovely. But that was still better than the truth that I feared. That Carmen was coming for me again. She'd escaped before the MEA and the UMC forces had arrived. Evading capture even though a large force pursued her, including the Inquisitors and the nephilim from the Lunar Order.

A lump lodged in my throat, and I banished all thoughts of the three nephilim. I'd thought we'd become friends, or at least something, after what we'd been through. They'd returned to the Lunar Order, had said they would visit, but I'd heard nothing from them.

That stung more than anything. Abandoned once I was no longer useful. Just a means to an end.

Chapter Four

Butterflies swirled in my stomach as I tried to control my breathing. I stroked Danika's back while she lay curled up in my lap. Fox hair be damned, I needed something to calm me.

Jade and Ruby worked on my hair, ignoring my protests. They both wore beautiful flowing dresses, stunning in their simplicity. Silver jewelry adorned their wrists, with charms shaped like the moon and stars, and made the sweetest tinkling sounds as they twisted my hair back.

My dress was gorgeous. As the leader of the ritual, I wore silver, a color meant for elders or respected leaders. It flowed in soft waves around me, leaving my arms bare. But I didn't feel the chill of the evening—one perk of being a witch. Even with my weak solar reserves, it was enough to keep me warm, just not in freezing weather.

"You will do an amazing job," Danika said, not even opening her eyes.

I'm glad you're so confident in my abilities.

"I will always have faith in you, and I know you've the skills and power to do this. Plus, if you forget the words, I can whisper them to you."

I chuckled, thankful she'd stuck by me. Danika nuzzled my hand as she sensed my thoughts.

The curtains parted and Nan entered, her flowing silver ceremonial robes adorned with intricate patterns; she exuded a graceful yet commanding presence.

Tonight, her pure-white hair was intricately twisted and braided back, accenting her face lined with the deep creases of a life well-lived, full of laughter and wisdom. Her silver eyes sparkled with a hint of mischief, a reminder of the spirited soul within.

"I have something for you," she said, offering me a wrapped bundle.

Danika shifted to the side, her head tilted, and whatever was inside called to me. The lunar energies in my chest swirled in response, and I sucked in a shuddering breath as she placed it in my hands. Even without touching it, I sensed the power emanating from it.

My fingers trembled as I pulled back the cloth to reveal a fine circlet nestled inside. The thin silver twisted into an intricate crown, with tiny star charms hanging down. But it was the stone at the center that tugged at me. The silvery gem shone in the soft light, and my fingers itched to touch it as power pulsed within it.

"What is this?" I said, somewhat breathless. What was it about this item that twisted my energies into a frenzy?

"The Circlet of Selene," Nan said as she settled it on my head.

Power rushed through me and I gasped for air. The gem thrummed against my forehead. Such lightness filled me I thought I might float away. Danika pressed against my side, and the sensation subsided just enough to clear my thoughts.

Thank you, I whispered to her. All of that power was too much for a novice witch like me.

While I'd been studying magic for years, that was with my solar energies. I didn't realize that lunar magic would be so different, which seemed silly now that I thought about it. Solar and lunar energies were literally like night and day—while some spells were the same, the way to apply your energies differed.

When I started training with the shifters, I'd been excited, but besides my astral shield and moonbeam spell, I struggled to learn others. It didn't make any sense to me.

When I'd learned those spells, I'd been struggling to understand the balance between my energies. My solar powers disrupted many of my spells because they were annoyed I wasn't using them. That's why I needed the runed band.

"This is an artifact that our pack has protected for many generations," Nan said, interrupting my thoughts. "It will help you focus your energies and channel them into the array."

"Thank you," I managed to say. None of them appeared to notice how unsettled I was as the sisters wove my hair to incorporate the circlet. *I don't deserve this.* The words snaked through my mind. *Unworthy.*

"We're ready when you are," Nan said, before wrapping her soft hands around mine. The warmth seeped into my skin as she held my gaze. "I'll be next to you the whole time. We all have confidence in you, even if your own wavers. Thank you for blessing our pack."

She patted my hand and left without another word. But I hadn't even done anything yet. What if I messed up? What if I failed?

Jade was bouncing on her feet, and I realized I hadn't heard what she'd said. She pushed a mirror into my hand, beaming at me with such pride. Unable to disappoint her, I lifted the mirror. Was that me?

My coral hair had been curled and twisted into a crown of its own, while the rest fell free down my back. But it was the circlet on my head that I couldn't tear my eyes from. The gem seemed brighter now, as if I could see the power that I sensed thrumming within it.

"Ready?" Ruby asked. And I realized I hadn't said anything.

"Thank you, it looks beautiful," I said. Jade practically squealed.

Ruby tugged her sister towards the curtain. "We need to find our spots, but come out when you are ready."

If that was the case, then I doubted I would ever leave. But I sensed the full moon rising, something that I'd become far more attuned to. It was an odd sensation, as if a piece of me was contained within the moon and when it grew closer, I could sense its presence.

Danika curled around my legs as I pushed to my feet, her large sapphire eyes staring up at me, awaiting my command. I nodded, not trusting my voice, and stepped outside.

Soft orbs of light bobbed nearby to illuminate the path and my guide, a young shifter. They'd erected tents within the thick oak trees so that we were able to prepare in peace, away from the pack.

The shifter guided me along a twisting trail, the trees thinning until the hum of magic mixed with the rumble of voices.

My guide waved his hands, parting the wards, and I stumbled the moment I crossed. Power pressed in against my skin as if it were a torrent of water rushing in.

The surge swirled around me and I stepped away, ready to run, but Danika brushed against my legs and her magic crackled through the air until the power eased. It was still there, a heavy weight on my skin, but no longer threatening to suffocate me.

My guide paused, looking back when I didn't follow.

"I've got you," Danika said. *"The power here is more potent, drawn to the full moon. It will not harm you, it just senses your magic."*

I nodded, more to Danika than the shifter, but he resumed. The last of the trees fell away and my heart skipped a beat as I took in the wide open area filled with people all dressed in white.

Watching my step as we wound down towards them, I realized why they looked so odd—there at their feet I caught the glimmer of it. A spell array for the ritual, marked out in shimmering crystal, and the shifters standing along the edge of the outer circle.

I'd never witnessed something like this. The rituals the witches held were always within the temples.

The gem on my forehead thrummed in time with my heart, each beat growing stronger as we approached the cluster of respected leaders.

Despite being all garbed in silver, I didn't feel like I belonged here with them. I hadn't earned my place through years of hard work and leadership. I'd just been a witch in the wrong place at the wrong time, and I'd fallen into that catastrophe with the shifters.

The elders nodded as I passed, with warm smiles and bright eyes. I returned the gesture, though my smile was weak.

Who was I to lead this ritual? I'd been the one to cause all of this potential magic to linger in the area. If this was the best way to help disperse the energies that could be used for terrible deeds, then who was I to question it?

The magic clearly responded to me, recognizing my energy. It was as if it knew that I was the one who had commanded it, the one who ripped it away from the spell array meant to open a demonic portal.

Nan waited at the front. She smiled and waved me closer as my guide slipped away. The weight of the entire pack's gaze pressed against my skin as I stopped before Nan, swallowing hard. I dared to look up.

Oh, that was a bad idea. So many expectant eyes, hopeful gazes fixed on me.

Towering trees surrounded us, forming a natural amphitheater. Moonlight filtered through the canopy, casting shadows over us but it would shine down unimpeded in a few minutes. I inhaled a deep breath of the crisp night air that mingled with the scent of pine and earth.

"I believe in you," Nan whispered. "Have faith in yourself, Nyssa."

"Thank you," I whispered back, my voice cracking. Off to a great start, it seemed.

"Nyssa Thornheart," Nan spoke, her voice carrying out to the far reaches of the spell array. "As the full moon rises, will you lead our pack into embracing the light of our Goddess? Will you lend us your strength and guide us as we celebrate Selene?"

"It would be my honor," I replied, and stepped forward into my spot at the top of the array.

The power within my chest thrummed, a vibration that filled my body before I even called to my magic. The moment I summoned it, energies pulsed through me, as if electricity coursed through my arms and up into my forehead.

A wave of vertigo washed over me; memories of feeling this powerful flickered through my mind, but I pushed them away.

I tried not to think about that intoxicating sensation as I commanded all the power within that other spell array. As if I were the Goddess herself.

A dangerous thought; seeking power like that—power beyond my own abilities—was a perilous path. One that led many to sign pacts with demon lords, corrupt their own magic, and become warlocks or dark witches like Carmen.

It wasn't just that, such thoughts felt like blasphemy. Though Selene wasn't as vengeful as her twin Aelia, I wouldn't put it past either of them to strike down anyone who dared to compare themselves to the divine.

Nan stepped back, breaking me from my worrying thoughts. Now really wasn't the time for such things. I had a ceremony to conduct.

My gaze lifted to the sky as the full moon crested the trees, her silvery glow washing over us. I stepped up to the array.

Today, I was its conduit. Closing my eyes, I inhaled a deep breath, taking in the crisp evening air to settle my nerves and gather my power.

"Goddess of Moonlight, hear our call," I said, finding my rhythm. The ritual words flowed from my lips, as if they'd always been a part of me.

The moonlight answered my call, streaming into the array with a steady, silver glow. Its power flowed along the lines, filling each curve and angle with an ethereal light. The very ground buzzed as the power grew, but I guided it, keeping it balanced. It needed a firm hand to keep it in check; raw power did as it pleased and was difficult to control.

Centering myself, I took another steadying breath and sensed Danika shift closer. This would be the hardest part, and I would need her aid when I first tugged upon the lingering energies.

I teased out a thread of my own lunar energy, and then gathered another thread from the magic that lingered in the air. Twisting them together, I guided them into the rune at my feet.

Magic pulsed through me as the power filled the inner lines of the spell array. I wove in more of the surrounding magic, increasing it until my power was only the thin line within guiding the potent magic.

The gem pressed against my skin warmed. Faintly, I was aware that the magic never faltered, never wobbled, which wasn't typical for me. Only when I was infusing power into a potion did it feel like this.

What did I expect with such a powerful artifact on my brow? Of course, the shifters wouldn't have trusted me without precautions already being in place. That'd just been my own self-doubt gnawing away at my confidence.

The words of the ritual swelled as the rest of the pack joined in. The power around us responded; I could almost feel it gathering around me as if it wanted to be channeled into the array, as if it couldn't wait to join in the spell.

All other thoughts fell away. I was just the conduit of power. Moonlight poured over me, tingling over my skin.

For one glorious moment, I stood cloaked in power, as though Selene's light itself shone down to guide me.

I floated there, the words of the ritual wrapping around me until they became a wordless song that carried me away.

My magic stretched wide, as if I was spread across the entire array. And then the tiniest of flickers ignited.

Small blooms of lunar energy sparked within the shifters around me, like the stars blinking into existence in the inky night sky.

Magic shivered through me, different from the energies I called. This was sentient, and it vibrated through me. My moon-blessed mark throbbed and a torrent of magic flooded my body, drowning the solar magic before it could even flare.

My mind fractured, splitting into a thousand different pieces. The ground beneath me disappeared, and darkness swallowed me.

Chapter Five

Panic constricted my throat as I tried to call out, it squeezed at my chest as my heart thudded harder. Then a reassuring thrum resonated through me, and despite my fear, my heart calmed.

Darkness still wrapped around me, but I was no longer falling, rather it seemed as if I was floating through the air.

A tiny pulse of light blinked in the distance, my magic matching the beat. Soft at first, before growing until it pounded through my body with each thump of my heart.

The silvery, ethereal light wrapped around me, then dimmed to reveal an object that called to something deep within me. It looked like a small box, the size of a tome. Silver filigrees ran over the surface and it shimmered, the colors appearing to change and shift the closer I moved. Almost opaque, silvers changed to tranquil blues, luminous white, then a flash of purple . . . the box was a never-ending kaleidoscope of colors. Mesmerizing. Hypnotizing.

Magic tugged within my chest, wanting to connect with it. A burning need to touch it. To find it.

I reached, my awareness brushing against it. For a moment, there was a peaceful tranquility. Relief. Hope. Like returning home after a long time away.

Images flashed before my eyes, too many to comprehend. But my mind snagged. A rune etched into stone. Stairs that descended into the darkness. A pulsing heartbeat at its core, but too far for me to reach. A doorway that opened under my touch. It was there, waiting.

Waiting to be reunited. Waiting to be wielded.

A bone-deep loneliness ached through me.

It would help me. Protect me. This box. This relic.

It filled my mind again. I could almost see myself holding it. The runes etched into the surface sparked to life, flickering like the stars in the sky.

Find me, it seemed to pulse.

Heat pressed against my forehead and the gem within the circlet thrummed in time to the same beat. Darkness swept around me until shapes emerged from the shadows, indistinct and obscured.

Figures moved in my periphery, their faces hidden. Runes glowed on the ground, flickering and shifting before I could decipher them. The air crackled with an oppressive energy, and a chill ran down my spine as a deep sense of dread filled me.

The circlet pulsed, and the images sharpened. Bound forms, their eyes wide with terror. Dark silhouettes chanted and gestured over the indistinct shapes on the ground. Blood pooling out, only to sizzle when it touched a rune, which blazed brighter for an instant before fading.

My heart pounded, trying to make sense of these fragmented scenes.

The acrid stench of burning hair shoved up my nose and coated my tongue. Haunting screams echoed through my mind; I pressed my hands over my ears, but it did nothing to silence them.

Magic lashed over my forearms, cutting deep into my flesh. Terror clawed at me, filled me until I would drown in it.

Too much, my brain couldn't keep up. I gasped and tumbled backward, falling into my own body once again. The lunar magic of the ritual swelled, pressing against me as if to stop me from collapsing.

My eyes flew open, staring at the moon, but the vision didn't fade. My fingers squeezed into fists until my nails bit into my palms, but even the pain couldn't snap me from whatever spell had ensnared me. More images assaulted my mind, as if in some frantic, desperate plea.

No, it wasn't a plea. It was a demand. Angry. Furious.

The overwhelming emotions swelled inside me, burning molten hot. Outrage. It seared my throat until I wanted to scream.

A hand wrapped around my own, and the vision started to fade. One last image flickered through my mind: a storefront that glowed faintly under a moonlit sky. Delicate patterns of whorls and moons framed the windows and seemed to shimmer with a soft light. The deep cobalt-blue door stood open, almost thrumming with an unspoken invitation. Curled, silvery letters above the doorway read *Edrik's Curiosities*.

The power that had gripped my mind eased, and I sagged.

"Release your hold," Danika commanded.

My energies faltered, and I withdrew my connection to the spell array before it pulled the rest from me.

"You can let go, Nyssa," Nan said. Concern and worry clouded her silver eyes. Hands wrapped around me, keeping me upright, but I couldn't think, not as the images continued to flash through my head.

"Thank you all for being here," Nan called out. "Nyssa needs to rest; the amount of power she commanded takes a toll on the body. There is no need for concern."

Her words faded away, and the steady sway of being carried lulled me enough to let my eyes flutter closed.

Screams of terror cut through the air and I jolted upright, fighting against the restraints, against the people trying to push me into that spell array.

"Nyssa! You're safe." Danika's voice drowned out the screams. I blinked, attempting to figure out where I was. White walls surrounded me and I lay on a cot. The tent from before the ceremony. Knowledge flooded back into my mind, grounding me in the real world once again.

I dropped my face into my hands, the visions still lurking behind my eyelids. It was a struggle just to breathe.

Too many thoughts swirled through my head. What was I meant to make of those images? What had I seen? My fingers lifted to my head, but the circlet was gone. Relief washed through me though my heart mourned the touch of its power.

My body was sluggish from the toll of channeling that amount of magic. I shied away from the intense moonlight. The colors of the world, even at night, were too bright.

A paw pressed into my thigh, and I straightened to look at Danika, concern brimming in her gaze.

"What happened?" she asked, and it was impossible to miss the worry in her voice.

"Did you see it?" I feared that I might have forced it upon her, but hoped she'd seen it so I wouldn't have to explain.

She shook her head. *"A vision?"*

"I don't even know. It felt so real. I didn't think visions were meant to be like that." What I'd heard, smelled, and sensed had been as if I lived it. And the terror that gripped me. I'd only experienced that once before.

"Nyssa, can I come in?" Ruby called out in a pinched voice.

"Yes," I called, and tried to sit up.

"Are you alright? What happened?" Ruby asked as Jade rushed in after her. "Jade, I told you to stay behind!"

"But Nyssa might've been hurt."

Ruby sat beside me and Jade gripped my hands, her bright eyes brimming with unshed tears.

"I'm okay," I lied, not wanting to worry them. "It was just overwhelming. I've only done something that powerful once before. And then I was asleep for days."

"I'm sorry," Ruby said. "The elders shouldn't have asked you to do that."

"I wanted to. It was probably my own fault for pulling too much magic."

Ruby just nodded, her eyes fixed on the floor.

"It felt amazing," Jade said, wonder filling her gaze. "I've never felt anything like that before. Is that what magic feels like?"

I chuckled, her awe rubbing off on me. "It did feel pretty amazing for me—well, for the first part at least. I just hope I did things right."

"You did," Nan said from the entrance. "Can I join you?"

I nodded. These shifters had supported me over the last few months, been the solid foundation so that I could start my life over again, I didn't know what I would've done without them.

"You did a wonderful job leading us, Nyssa. I've not felt a ceremony like that for . . . well, far before any of you were a twinkle in your parents' eyes."

"What does that mean?" Jade asked.

"It means a long time ago," Nan said with a chuckle. The full weight of her gaze turned on me, worry and concern creasing her features. "I wanted to check you over, make sure that there was no harm from overexerting yourself."

Nan ushered the girls from the room and started pulling out her healer equipment. Enhanced items that aided in diagnostics, both magical and mundane, and anyone could use them.

As she waved an item around me, I closed my eyes and turned my focus inwards. My training contained a lot of meditation and introspection as I learned to become aware of my power, how much I had and if I'd damaged it.

It was a valuable thing to know, so that a magic user didn't overexert themselves, but today I hadn't even sensed I was getting near my breaking point.

"You had a vision," Nan said, catching me off guard. She didn't look up from the device in her hand, and even though it hadn't been a question, I answered.

"Yes, though I've never experienced one like that before. How did you know?"

"I sensed you were somewhere else, and with the full moon and connection to such powerful latent magic, I thought Selene might have offered you a vision. I didn't want to put you on the spot, as visions are for the one who witnesses them." Nan wrapped a soft, warm hand around mine and squeezed. "We didn't mean for this to happen to you. The circlet, as I said, is a lunar artifact, though its true purpose has been lost to the ages. We have used it in our full moon ceremonies since before I was born, but I've never heard of it being anything more than ceremonial." She shook her head as if trying to banish whatever she'd been thinking. "I would've never forgiven myself if it'd harmed you in any way."

"I'm just drained," I said, wanting to reassure her.

Nan nodded and patted my hand. "As long as you are feeling fine, that is all that matters. It doesn't seem as if you were injured—all my readings just say your body's energy is low. You've done us a great service today, boosting our connection to Selene and empowering our pack so that we can protect ourselves."

Eventually, I knew I would be proud of what I'd achieved today, but what I'd seen had stolen that away for now.

But why did I see a vision? I'd only ever had them before when I asked for guidance. Memories of my first vision barged their way into my mind. That was one vision I hoped never came true.

When I was thirteen, I asked Selene to show me who my soulmate was. Instead, she showed me a vision of fire and hate-filled eyes intent on destroying me. I didn't believe in soulmates, but teenagers will be teenagers.

And ever since, I hoped with everything I had that soulmates were not real. How could one be destined to love someone who hated them with every fiber of their being?

As if sensing my darkening thoughts, Danika nudged my arm before settling next to me, offering her strength and warmth.

Nan moved over to the bag she'd brought with her and pulled out a white cloth, unwrapping it to reveal the circlet I'd worn. Energy pulsed through it, enough to make the air tingle. The silver gem at its center gleamed, its surface swirling in hypnotic patterns, like smoke caught in moonlight.

It didn't look like that before, I said to Danika.

"No, it changed during the ceremony."

"Why did you bring that here?" I demanded as fear rose. She wasn't going to make me wear it again, was she? Force me to have another vision?

"This artifact has been dormant for a very long time. But you awoke it," she said, staring down at the circlet.

"Is that a bad thing?"

"No," she said slowly. "It's the first spark of hope we've had in far too long. Lunar magic is dying."

Chapter Six

Her words hit me like a knife in the heart. "What?" I choked out. Nan's shoulders sagged as she sat down beside me, her gaze heavy with pain and sorrow as she stared at the circlet.

"It's been fading for a long time," she murmured. "Shifters were the first race to feel it—their connection weakening. While some packs suffered more than others, now many have lost all but their ability to take on their animal form. And even that is slipping away."

Like Ruby.

A realm where shifters couldn't even shift—how had it come to that? The pack's desperation, asking me to lead this ritual, even performing it here . . . all the pieces started to fall into place.

I frowned, trying to make sense of it all. "But then, how do I have lunar magic if it's dying?"

"Because you're chosen," she said with a sad smile, as if that explained it all. But that didn't seem fair. They were the children of Selene—why would she impart her magic to me and not them? There had to be more to it. "Lunar magic was the first to suffer, and it was hit the hardest. The fact that our power helped end the great war, that it's the strongest against demons, could hardly be considered a coincidence."

Did you know about any of this? I asked Danika, who'd been unusually quiet.

"Parts," she replied after a long moment. *"Just . . . not to this extent. It's deeply concerning."*

"These artifacts have been dormant," Nan continued, "which is why we don't know what they do. We were certain that it was possible to awaken them, but despite the attempts, no one has ever succeeded until today. Which brings new worry."

"Was it because of all the latent magic here?" I asked.

"It's more than that," Nan said. "While the energies here might have played their part, I believe the real catalyst was you. Even before the ceremony, I could sense the difference within the artifact the moment I gave it to you." Before I could voice my protest, Nan pushed on. "Selene has blessed you, and her touch still lingers. Why else would she offer you another vision?"

I wanted to argue that the shifters were blessed by the Goddess too, and yet her words rang true.

"If you don't believe me, take the circlet." Nan lifted it towards me and my hands itched to touch it again. Magic crackled as I brushed my fingers over the fine metal, and when I picked it up, the gem at the center began to glow. That pulse of need thrummed in my chest, to find the item I'd seen. Another lunar artifact. How I knew that, I wasn't sure, but as I held the circlet, I understood it with certainty.

"I think that the vision showed me a different artifact, like it wants me to find it."

"Then you should follow its guidance." Her gaze held such a fierce determination that it was impossible to look away. "Since the magical explosion that resulted after you destroyed the spell array, we've monitored for other relics and artifacts. And I believe you might've awoken the one you saw. Though I fear that it might alert many unwanted people, that its powerful magic calls out to them."

"Why me? Why hasn't your pack sought the others?"

Nan paused. "We have been searching, but the magic of our pack isn't strong enough to connect to them. But now you've forged a connection, and your vision makes it clear this is the path Selene has chosen for you."

Rubbing a hand over the moon-blessed mark on the back of my neck, I shook my head. I didn't feel chosen.

The moon-blessed were those who'd been about to die, only to be saved by Selene in exchange for a second chance at life. She would grant them her blessing, infusing the person with lunar energies and charging them with protecting our world.

And yet those I'd met from the Lunar Order—who said they'd come back—had been silent. Was I no longer important to them? Once I'd attempted focused on the connection that I shared with the moon-blessed nephilim; the mark had tingled, but I'd sensed no response on the other end.

I'd no idea how the Order worked—for all I knew, they could be away on the other side of the world for a mission. I dashed away those thoughts. A fool's hope.

The circlet pulsed in my grip, as if annoyed that I was ignoring it. There was a yearning deep within me, urging me to reach out and connect with that power again.

Something else lurked beneath, a need to protect, a need to find the other artifact. But those emotions made no sense to me. Was this the moon-blessed mark? Was this the purpose Selene wanted for me?

Each moon-blessed had their own roles to play. While I might not be worthy of joining the Lunar Order and becoming a protector of the realm, maybe this was my path.

But dread coiled within my stomach. Visions only meant something bad was coming. I couldn't get entangled in that again.

My gaze met Nan's, an apology on my lips, but when I opened my mouth I found myself saying, "I saw something, a shop called *Edrik's Curiosities.*"

Nan huffed, a sound very unlike her. "Of course *he* has one."

That startled a laugh out of me. Nan had been nothing but a sweet grandma around me, but it turned out she'd a grumpy side too. "It's here in Arkirith?"

"Yes. Edrik is like a greedy dragon when it comes to magical items. He has great skill in acquiring them and knowing the value behind them. We have approached him many times, but he always claimed he never had one, nor would he help us locate any. So either he was lying, he didn't know he had one—which is unlikely—or he was linked to it in another way and refused to assist. Which is why you should approach him."

"Me? Why would he talk to me?"

"You are a curiosity," Nan said, and then chuckled at my less-than-amused expression. I mean, sure I know I was, but hearing someone else say it . . . "He doesn't want anything to do with our pack, but the Goddess has chosen to put you on this quest, so there will be a way forward."

I shook my head, letting go of the circlet. After everything that happened, it was clear I wasn't cut out for that kind of life. "I . . . I don't have time for this. I've so much going on right now, my alchemy and working at Divine."

"It's your choice, Nyssa." Nan gripped my shoulder as she stood. I searched her silver eyes for disappointment or anger, but they just shone with understanding. She wouldn't pressure me into anything I didn't want to do, but knew what choice I would make! If lunar magic was dying, I wouldn't refuse. I'd fought so hard for my power, I wasn't about to give it up even if I was struggling. "Oh, and keep the circlet."

I jerked back. "What?"

"I think that you are meant to have it," Nan said with a knowing smile. "You're the one who woke it, and if you choose to follow the visions and all else fails, let Edrik see it and I'm sure he will be more than eager to help."

I shook my head, words failing me. How could she just hand over a powerful lunar relic, one that had been with their pack for generations?

My fingers tightened around the circlet at the thought of handing it back to her. I couldn't accept it, but when I looked back up to say so, Nan was already gone.

Chapter Seven

The rich scent of roasted beans with hints of vanilla and cinnamon embraced me as I stepped through Divine's doors. I would've wrapped that feeling around me like a blanket if I could.

The cafe buzzed with activity, even though the new day was just a swirl of pinks and oranges on the horizon.

Thayna and Pyrah hustled around the kitchen, trying to keep up with demand as the next influx of tourists arrived in Arkirith.

Divine Coffee was located away from the popular tourist spots, but its reputation for high-quality coffee and pastries spread, attracting visitors who wanted a more authentic experience. At least, that's what I'd overheard from a bunch of loud tourists from the other continent.

As I tied on my apron, there was no need for talk or orders. Thayna and I had worked together long enough that we knew our duties and could've opened the shop in our sleep. I found my station already prepped with the laminated stack of recipes, along with the equipment and supplies I needed for my first bake.

The stack of muffin tins rattled on the stainless-steel top as I glanced over the recipe.

"Pushy today, are we?" I said to Divine, who just rattled the tins again, either telling me to hurry up or excited I was there. Or possibly both.

The connection with Divine and their employees was an odd one when I thought about it too hard. But over the months of working here, I'd become more in tune with the sentient coffee shop. Almost as if I could sense the intention behind their magic, feel their mood the moment I passed over the threshold.

It was a symbiotic relationship, as creepy as that sounded. Divine seemed to thrive off people—the emotion and magic they brought—as if they found joy in satisfying their customers and caring for their employees.

Despite their insistence, I was more than happy to dive into my work. Even now, I still felt the buzz from the ceremony, as if my magical reserves were filled to the brim despite my night of endless brewing.

Mentally I'd been exhausted from, well, all of it, but the energy flowing through me wouldn't settle down. Sleep had been the only thing on my mind, a way to escape the memories of the vision and the weight of Danika's gaze as she waited for me to talk to her.

Half hoping to siphon off some of the energy and half to avoid *that* conversation, I'd started brewing. Yet even though I'd picked the most demanding brews for the shifter pack and for my contract for the MEA, I didn't feel a dent in my reserves.

That or they are so full because I haven't found any new spells to practice.

I growled at myself. I didn't need a reminder of my failure on that front. Before, my alchemy was sufficient to drain my wild magic before it turned more volatile. But in the weeks after I'd awoken my magic, it took me longer to use it up.

At first, the training with the shifters had been enough, until we tried something more advanced. I'd inked on the rune for my solar magic, and everything had locked up. My mind. My magic. Now I even struggled to ink the rune.

With nothing to test my powers on, it began building up until my skin was too tight, like I was ready to burst.

My hands moved automatically, measuring out the ingredients and requiring little focus. My thoughts circling back to the fragmented visions, playing out over and again in the back of my mind. Dread curled tighter until my grip on the jug of milk slipped and it crashed to the floor, spilling its contents everywhere.

Bright red blood pooled over the floor, seeping out from the—I jerked back when a hand gripped my arm. Thayna stood before me, a worried look on her face.

"I'm fine," I said, not sure if she had even asked. My gaze slid past her, but the floor was clean, Divine's magic having already cleared up the mess. "My hand slipped." I couldn't even muster a weak smile, but Thayna nodded.

"Your thoughts are eating away at you," Danika said. I wanted to snap back a retort, but that realization was like being hit with a splash of cold water. My familiar was a part of me and I a part of her. She would always be honest and open with me, and yet I wasn't doing the same. A knee-jerk reaction, because her words exposed a truth I didn't want to admit. *"You need to talk to someone. If not me, then what about Rynac, or Indra?"*

My friends were back in their former home for the first time in three years. They had too much going on for me to bother them with my issues.

A denial was already on my lips, but I swallowed it. Why didn't I want to tell Danika? It wasn't like me to hide these things from her, so why was I resisting?

No doubt Danika knew there was more to all of this, but she was offering me the chance to reach out when I was ready.

Someone cleared their throat, and I realized I'd just been staring at the now clean floor. Beylin stood at the base of the stairs watching me. Without a word, he nodded for me to follow.

I trailed after him, knowing better than to ignore my boss. Beylin led me into the familiar sitting room with its plush couches and small kitchenette at the back. I settled into the couch next to Danika, raising an eyebrow at her.

"Is this where you've been hiding?" I asked. My little fox was nestled in a large, fluffy blanket, and I wondered if it was Divine or Beylin who had put it there for her.

"Tourists are too noisy and nosy," she huffed.

Beylin came over, setting a teacup in front of me and another for himself. He stroked Danika before taking his seat.

I sniffed at the tea before taking a tentative sip. Usually, when I wound up here, Beylin would give me an awful dirt-flavored water. A great painkiller, if you could get past the taste.

"I'm not sure if I should be offended that you think all of my teas are like that," Beylin grumbled as he took a long sip. "Now, would you like to tell me why you've got both Danika and Divine agitated?"

I glanced at my familiar, but she just burrowed her head so I couldn't see her. My first instinct was to make an excuse, but I stopped myself. Beylin and Danika had been there for me whenever I needed help, even though both of them had barely known me at the time. They'd offered me strength and support when I faced unknown threats, like the dark witch and her horde of demonspawn.

"I had another vision." I forced the words out past the lump in my throat. Dread seeped from my heart just at the thought of explaining what had happened, like black tendrils oozing out until they coated my insides, making me want to shrink away. Forcing out a heavy breath, I let the words flow out of me: the ceremony, the vision, Nan's encouragement.

"But?" Beylin prompted.

I paused, searching for the right words. "What if this is something bigger than me, than all of us? What if I'm getting myself entangled in dangerous situations again?" Fear squeezed my throat closed, cutting off the rest of my words. Memories of the vision clawed at my mind.

"You fear what happened with the dark witch," Beylin said, not even needing to read my thoughts.

"Yes." The word rushed out of me, nothing more than a whisper. What I wanted to say was that I didn't think I could endure that again, but I could never tell them that. Danika shifted, pressing herself against my side, her reassuring warmth seeping into me.

"If this was a vision sent by Selene, then she knows that you are strong enough, Nyssa. Trust in that." Danika's cool words slipped into my thoughts. I tried to take comfort in them, but the gnawing doubt refused to release me.

"So then don't act on it," Beylin said.

I shook my head, unable to explain it. "Every time I tell myself that, my gut twists. What if not acting makes things so much worse?"

I hissed out a breath through my teeth, squeezing my eyes closed for a moment. I knew I needed to give them more.

Both Danika and Beylin watched me, their expressions open and reassuring, yet I feared how they would change if they knew what was going on inside me. How would they look at me if I told them about that living nightmare I saw of Carmen, about the person I'd seen but no one could find?

And what if the shifters found out? How would they look at me if they knew that their savior was just a scared little witch? They would see me differently, treat me differently. If they saw me for what I really was, they would believe that I wasn't strong enough to help them.

"I saw other things," I began, my voice trembling. "Dark things after I felt that pull towards the artifact. The images were hard to untangle, but I know they were a warning that people would be hurt. Knowing that, how can I go and look for this if that's what I'm going to bring about? My friends suffered when the dark witch had her sights set on me. I can't do that to them again."

"You were not to blame for the dark witch's actions," Beylin said gently. "But I understand your hesitation. You said that this item wanted you to find it. How do you know that it showed the future and not what might happen if you don't look for it?"

"Visions are always open to interpretation," I replied, something I knew well. Though some of my visions had left no room for guessing about what they meant.

"There is no way to know what your future holds," Beylin said. "Even if the Goddess has granted you a vision, that does not mean it will come to pass. There are too many factors to know for sure. Trust your instincts, Nyssa. They have guided you well so far. You might dismiss your role in the defeat of the dark witch and her plans, but you were crucial in it, no matter if there were mistakes made."

"What does your gut tell you?" Danika asked.

"The thought of forgetting about the artifact I saw, about not trying to find it, twists me up inside." At least that I could say with honesty. The dread of not acting was almost as bad as the fear I felt when I thought about the visions.

"I believe you are right and that it needs to be in safe hands," Beylin said. "But just because you are searching for it does not mean you have to keep going, especially if things get dangerous. One step at a time."

I nodded at his words, trying to let them absorb into my heart to shield me from the dread. "I also fear that what the vision showed me is what will happen if I don't act."

And the truth was, when I thought about it, that terrified me even more. A choice between putting myself in danger to find this artifact versus not doing anything and letting other people suffer?

I knew which option I could live with and which one would haunt me for the rest of my life.

Beylin smiled as if he knew the choice I made. He patted my arm as he passed by. "I've got work to do, but I'm always here if you need help."

Danika's warmth pressed closer, her presence a silent promise of support. *"We're in this together,"* she whispered. *"No matter what happens."*

"You're not angry with me?" I asked her. "For not telling you about it?"

"Would you be angry with me if I kept something from you?"

"No, because I know you would either have a good reason or didn't want to burden me with it," I answered without hesitation. Danika just stared at me, waiting for the realization to hit me. "Oh."

"Exactly." She sounded far too smug for my liking. *"You hold yourself to far more rigid rules than others. That's hardly fair. Relationships are two-way streets."*

I huffed, but wrapped her in a hug.

"Is it that annoying when I'm right?"

I rolled my eyes, but I wouldn't want any other familiar by my side. Giving her one last squeeze, I straightened. "Let's go to Edrik's." And though unease swirled within me, I knew in my heart I'd made the right choice.

Chapter Eight

The quaint little shop seemed to hide, squished between the two buildings beside it. In my vision, it'd called to me like a beacon, but now that I saw it with my own eyes I could see the flaking paint on the sign, the dim interior, and the dusty displays.

None of it invited people to come in and visit, but maybe that was the point. When dealing with powerful magical items, it required a lot of money and even more expensive wards and protections. This way only those who had something of true worth would enter, or those who heard of it through word of mouth.

The circlet felt like a lead weight in my bag, trying to drag me down into the depths of the ocean. There was something unnerving about having such an item entrusted to me. I'd tucked it away into my warded drawer, along with my most potent potions and *The Lunar Codex*, but I'd still checked it was there every five minutes.

I swore I could feel it watching me. How does an artifact with no eyes or sentience watch someone?

Neither of my roommates had commented that they sensed anything. I'd felt bad keeping it a secret, but I wanted to avoid getting them involved with lunar magic problems again. I liked this new apartment, and though the events a few months ago hadn't ruined my friendship with Zola or Voren, I didn't want to test it.

After the Inquisitors had ransacked my old apartment, I no longer felt safe there. Everything reminded me of that terrible time in my life when I'd not only been targeted by the dark witch but also hunted by the Inquisitors. They were witches who tracked down other of our kind with wild or dark powers and severed their connection to magic—which would've been me, if my friends had arrived a few minutes later.

Not that I was the only one to have their life and home disrupted. To lure me in, Carmen had broken into my friends' apartment and kidnapped Voren while Zola slept in the next room. The two had understandably moved out.

What was more surprising was their offer for me to become their roommate. I was the reason the erebian had been taken, yet he didn't hold it against me. I'd only started moving in last week, but it had finally felt like a home. Or at least somewhere I was safe.

Getting used to roommates would take me a bit, but it was nice not to come home to an empty apartment with only Danika for company.

Yet here I was again, getting involved in something that might lead me to danger. They didn't deserve to be put through all of that just because they were friends with me.

"You're going to grow roots if you keep standing there," Danika said.

I rolled my eyes. "You've been spending too much time with Zola." But it still brought a smile to my face.

To say Danika liked my new roommates was an understatement. She adored both of them, probably because they gave her treats far too often and the dryad talked to her, even though she could never hear the vulpine's response.

I wove through the morning traffic and bit down hard on my lip before I could turn back. A bell chimed as I opened the front door, the sound not nearly as welcoming as Divine's, more as if it was questioning why I had come here. I asked myself the same thing as I pushed myself inside.

The protection wards around the entrance were so thick they squeezed my chest. I popped out on the other side, a tad short of breath and slightly disheveled. Well, I sure as the seven hells wasn't doing that again in a hurry.

Once inside, the magic permeating the shop became even more palpable. The air itself seemed to hum with energy, a subtle vibration that tickled my skin and made the hairs on my arms stand on end. The musty scent of antiques hung heavy in the air, while the shop floor appeared far too small, cramped with all the "stuff" packed in there. Shelves and display cases lined the narrow aisles, filled with trinkets and artifacts, each holding but a pinch of magic.

But judging by the wards on the entrance, this shop was hiding much more than it appeared to display to the common customer.

No, all the good stuff would be on the other side of the wall behind the counter. With every step closer to it, the magic grew stronger until it thrummed through the air. Just how many wards did one need? And they were so obvious.

Was that intentional, to dissuade anyone from attempting to steal? Or was it so that only those with enough magic to sense it would know that they were in the right place?

A male shoved aside the heavy curtains dividing the store and strode in, his expression dripping with sheer annoyance. Long dark hair framed his face, and his sharp, calculating eyes flicked over me, sizing me up in an instant.

He wore a crisp, buttoned-up shirt and tailored dress pants that looked like they'd been custom-made. The sharp lines of his outfit made me feel underdressed, as if I were stumbling somewhere I didn't belong.

No wonder this place was empty. The scowl alone would send most customers running. Then again, maybe that was the point.

"Yes?" he said, as if I was the biggest inconvenience in his life. There was no way this—I squinted—*person* was going to give me any information if I just asked him about a random lunar artifact I'd seen in a vision.

"Remember, confidence."

His eyes flicked down to Danika as if he heard what she had said to me. For a moment, interest and curiosity sparked in his gaze, but as they darted back to me, they were once again full of contempt.

I bit down hard on the inside of my cheek. Familiars were rare in the witch community, and even more so outside of it. I'd wanted Danika to stay out of sight, but she'd argued—and, obviously, won—that we needed every advantage if we were going to extract the information from him.

"I assume you are Edrik?" I asked. His lips turned into a flat line as if I was wasting his time. I took that as a yes. "I'd like an evaluation on an item," I said, hoping that I sounded confident.

Edrik sighed. "Let's see it, then."

No one else was in the shop, so I pulled out the circlet, still covered in cloth, and set it on the bench between us.

Edrik's eyes fixed on it with such an intensity I knew he could sense the power within. Then again, if you dealt in magical items, you probably had to have a good instinct for such things.

"And you want to sell?" he asked, far too casually. Did he think I was that stupid?

"No, I just want it appraised. I heard that you have extensive knowledge about artifacts, the best in all Arkirith." Okay, maybe that was a little much, but I wasn't above using flattery. If it led to discovering the other artifact's location, it would be worth it.

Edrik eyed me for a moment longer, then his gaze slid past me to scan the streets before he nodded. "Come in the back, then."

I scooped up the circlet before he could grab it, not trusting that he would give it back. Danika kept tight next to me as we stepped into the back room.

I did a double-take, feeling as if I'd walked into a fancy hotel. The difference between front and back showed that my intuition had been right—the shop front was to drive off those he didn't wish to deal with.

Edrik motioned us into a side room with a large, dark wood desk that dominated the area, with intricate runes carved into the surface. All around us, energy thrummed, the sheer weight of the wards pressing down on me. The air felt thick, the power heavy and suffocating.

I winced, sitting in one of the polished leather chairs. Danika ignored the extra chair and jumped into my lap. The pressure from the wards went down a few notches, but my familiar's ears were pressed against her head. I guess both of us weren't having fun.

The sensation of being on a small boat in the middle of the ocean, rocking back and forth with no way to stop made my stomach protest. Urgh, I didn't need to think about deep water right now. I'd enough going on without adding more to it.

When my gaze lifted, I found Edrik watching us with more curiosity than anything else. "Is your fox alright?" he asked.

"Peachy," Danika snipped.

"Vulpines are quite sensitive to magic," I said. "I believe the massive amount of wards is affecting her."

"I see," he said, but I really didn't think he did. He seemed far too interested in that information. I narrowed my gaze. I wouldn't let him touch my bonded no matter what he offered.

Edrik noticed my scrutiny and smiled; it was all teeth and did nothing to reassure me. He waved a hand over what looked like a bare wall, but I felt the wards withdraw, or at least not pressing in so tight.

Danika's ears flicked around, but she made no move to leave my lap. I placed the circlet on the table to draw Edrik's focus off Danika.

"So, tell me about this item," Edrik asked.

"I'd hoped you'd be able to do that for me," I replied, my voice clipped. Why did this feel like such a bad idea? The shifters hadn't said anything bad about Edrik, but then again, they hadn't said he was trustworthy either. "Isn't that your job?"

His smile stretched far too wide. "May I?" he asked. I wanted to say no, some possessive instinct rearing up in me, but I nodded. "Quite curious. You came across it recently?"

I remained silent, which seemed to amuse him. He slipped on a pair of white gloves and picked up the circlet, twisting it this way and that, running his finger over the intricate markings.

"This artifact was forged close to five hundred years ago, by expert smiths. It has the markings of oread blacksmiths, but the gem within it is the most intriguing aspect. If I'm correct, it contains a moonstone." Edrik didn't seem to notice my reaction, thankfully. Moonstones varied a lot in their classification—the more power they stored, the more expensive they were. The stones offered stability and represented balance—I'd used the crushed powder in spells before, and they could be used as an offering to enhance a spell array.

"And what does it do?" I prompted.

"This gem is attuned to lunar energies; it can act as a repository for lunar-attuned magic. These artifacts could do many things depending on the purpose they were created for. Without testing and research, it would be impossible to know its full capabilities." He paused for a moment, weighing something behind his dark eyes. "As you're a witch, this item would be useless to you. I'd be willing to purchase it for around four hundred thousand dollars."

He said it so casually, but a heavy stone dropped in my stomach. That much money for a magical item? To think what I could do with that kind of money . . . I could easily open my shop wherever I wanted and even hire staff.

"That seems low," I said, hoping I sounded cold. "But the item is not for sale."

"Eight hundred thousand then. That is my final offer."

"No." My voice was steady, despite the fact my head was spinning.

"Then why did you come here?" The harshness in his voice made me want to snatch the item from the desk, fearing he would run off with it.

"For your knowledge of the item." I sensed a tingle of magic emit from Danika and she locked her gaze on Edrik. Whatever was going on, I wasn't sure what to make of it.

"He has lunar energies," Danika said.

I didn't want to doubt her judgment, but everything about him set off alarms to be wary. Carefully, I unfurled my magic, which I'd withdrawn to lessen the weight of the power in the air.

Like a gentle breeze, I stretched my awareness out until it brushed over Edrik. A spark flickered in my chest and a weight pressed against the back of my neck.

My eyes snapped to Edrik's left forearm, knowing on some deeper level what was hidden beneath the fabric of his shirt.

"You're moon-blessed," I blurted. Edrik tensed, but smoothed his expression into practiced annoyance. Before he could kick us out, I pushed a drop of power into my own mark and pressed it through the connection.

Edrik's eyes widened, and he unbuttoned the cuff of his shirt. He rolled the sleeve back until he revealed a mark on his forearm. It was much smaller than the few I'd seen, but the runes formed a moon shape.

Without realizing, I reached out, a shiver of magic slipping from my fingers as they hovered over the mark. The tattoo brightened, almost shimmering against his skin. I jerked my hand back as a jumble of emotions washed over me. Curiosity. Intrigue. Heartache.

I shook them off, but Edrik didn't seem to notice. He was staring intently at his mark. I guess that wasn't normal. He dragged his gaze away and met mine—shock pooled in them for a moment, but then it disappeared as Edrik straightened himself. He cleared his throat, buttoning his sleeve.

"What are you?" His attention darted between Danika and I as if he could see the magical bond that tied us together. "Why are you really here?"

"There is another artifact that I'm looking for, one that has recently awoken. I've been tasked with finding it."

"By whom?"

"Selene," I replied. If I said "a box", he might just kick me out for being crazy.

His gaze narrowed. "Not the Order?"

"No, though I'm acquainted with a few members." Which was technically true, and I couldn't help myself when I asked, "Do you know the team that was here a few months ago dealing with the dark witch?"

"I don't deal with field operatives. I'm an acquirer, so I only have minimal contact." He assessed me for a moment longer. "When you find what you are looking for, what will you do with it? Give it to the Order?"

"Keeping it safe is my only priority." The truth was, I hadn't got that far in my planning, and Selene hadn't given me a hint of what I was meant to do after I found it.

Edrik looked far from convinced by my answer. "Why do you think there is another relic in the city or that it has awoken?"

Brushing my finger over the circlet, I pushed a thread of magic into it. The runes burst to life, shimmering over the metal before the magic faded. "Because I awoke this one, and it gave me a vision to come to your shop."

There. That was the truth of it. Now it was up to Edrik if he believed me. He stared at the circlet, his eyes wide in wonder, and I remained silent.

He let out a small huff as a half-smile pulled at his lips. "I can aid you in locating it," he simply said.

I quashed down the flutter of excitement. "And how much will it cost?" We might have just met, but he gave the vibe of someone that didn't do anything without being paid.

He waved off my question. "May I see your mark?" His serious voice dropped at the question, becoming something like an excited child unable to contain themself. He bore a moon-blessed mark, so I shouldn't fear showing mine to him, but it seemed very intimate.

I twisted around, pulling my hair aside to expose the back of my neck. Doing my best not to think, I pushed a dash of magic into the moon-blessed mark. The slight prickle of power danced over the nape of my neck where my mark would appear, an intricate design of a crescent moon.

Edrik made a noise, but I couldn't see his face. Was there something wrong with my mark?

"I think you caught him off guard," Danika said, a smile in her voice.

I dropped my hair and twisted back, hating feeling so vulnerable. Edrik's expression was hidden behind his mask by the time I faced him. A bell chimed and his features darkened. My stomach clenched, the room suddenly feeling far too small.

Edrik's head snapped toward the front of the building. His gaze narrowed as if he saw through the walls. "You need to leave."

CHAPTER NINE

"Now," Edrik said, his voice hard. He pulled a card from inside his jacket and held it out for me. "Call this number once you reach the street. Let it ring four times and then hang up."

"What?" I stared down at the card, the phone number in neat writing.

"I believe it is best we do business away from prying eyes. Come," he said, standing, his gaze still focused somewhere else.

Danika's ears flickered around as we stood and headed toward the door.

Edrik paused and looked back at us. "You should put that item back in your bag to shield it," he said, gaze dipping from the circlet in my hand to my bag.

How in all the hells did he know it had warding? The shifter's enchanter had added it to my bag, to hide the energy signature within, in addition to those to protect the contents from damage.

"I think it is best if you use the side door; head left after you exit and it'll take you out onto Grayite Street. My wisp will guide you."

With that, he pulled open the door. A ball of white mist formed in his raised palm, then bobbed down the hall the opposite way from where we'd come. Edrik waved towards it before rushing back to the shop front.

The door swung open. The bright light from the front pierced the surrounding darkness, and through the narrow gap, I caught sight of the customer.

It was only a glimpse, but it stopped me cold. The figure loomed, rigid and foreboding, dressed in dark clothes. Their hood cast deep shadows over their face, revealing only a sliver of a featureless mask—one I'd seen before.

A creeping sensation burrowed under my skin and, for a moment, the world seemed to tilt as I recalled the clearing, the masked figure, and then those chilling red eyes.

Red eyes? But I'd seen a mask covering their entire face, and that magic . . . Carmen had never been there. Both Danika and the shifters confirmed it.

My heart pounded in my chest as I strained to see more, but the door closed behind Edrik, cutting off my view. The shadows seemed to deepen around me, and an icy dread settled in my bones. I couldn't shake the feeling that the dark masked figure had followed me here.

I glanced down at Danika, unable to voice what I'd seen. A whisper of strength curled around our bond and she dipped her head, understanding passing between us without the need for words.

The dark halls were even more creepy with nothing but the wisp to guide our way, but if it meant getting away from that person, I didn't care. The magic pressed against my skin, a tangible weight. But just what was all this magic for? It could hardly be only for the privacy of the clients, or wards to protect the "curiosities" he possessed.

My head kept telling me that I could not trust Edrik, that he would turn on me the moment he had the chance. And what if he was working with that person? But if he had a moon-blessed mark, that had to count for something, right? And it was real. My magic could sense the truth in that. But then again, could my magic be tricked?

Edrik had been doing this for longer than I'd been alive, let alone the few months that I'd been learning to use my lunar magic.

The wisp stopped and a strip of light bloomed on the wall, growing until it formed the edges of a door. It swung open and for a moment the sunlight blinded me as I stepped out. The door snicked shut, and when I glanced back, there was nothing but a solid brick wall behind us.

I wanted nothing more than to investigate, to reach out with my power and figure out if it was an illusion, or magic that created a door that wasn't always there.

Danika tugged at the mental bond between us, and I reluctantly followed her down the narrow alley. The unease from the encounter with Edrik melted away and, even though I knew I should be cautious, my body seemed lighter. Then again, nothing about me made much sense these days.

The alley came to an end, and those rushing along the adjoining street didn't even seem aware of us. When I reached out, there was the faintest shimmer of magic that blocked off this alley.

Does Edrik have a warded exit route from his store?

"*It would seem so,*" Danika said, slipping out in between the gaggles of people.

Just what kind of business is he running to need such a thing?

"*Judging by whomever entered the store when we were there, my guess is he deals with very powerful people, either in terms of their magical abilities or status. When there is money and power at stake, people can go to great lengths to get what they want.*"

And just who had that person been? I pulled out my phone to follow Edrik's instructions, but paused when I noticed a message from Zola.

Dread coiled around my stomach—she and Voren were heading to the airport soon to pick up Indra and Rynac and were wondering where I was.

I hesitated—what should I say? My excitement to see them again warred within my churning stomach. I'd hoped this meeting with Edrik would take longer, so I'd have an excuse to miss it.

I squeezed my eyes shut as if I could fight off the memory, but it was branded into my mind. Indra and Rynac kneeling, bound and gagged, surrounded by demonspawn. Bruised. Bloodied. At the mercy of Carmen. Their eyes pleading as they stared at me. It was my fault they'd been taken. That Carmen had hurt them, all to get to me.

And what would happen when the dark witch came for me next time?

My fingers trembled as I punched in Edrik's number. It was better if I didn't go to the airport—it might hurt their feelings, but wasn't that preferable than causing them physical harm?

"You said you'd go," Danika chimed in, as if sensing my hesitation. *"You could try talking to them, you know they'd be there to help you—"*

"The last time I let them help, I almost got them killed," I snapped. Danika flinched, and regret stung my heart. I bit down hard on my cheek and walked faster. It didn't make my words any less true.

My thoughts circled in an endless war against each other until I pushed into my apartment.

"You're here!" Zola called out in her musical voice, and rushed over. Her sage-green skin was slightly flushed and a few pink flowers bloomed in her myrtle-colored hair. "Voren has been fretting over his outfit all day. I can't get him out!" She huffed, then gave Danika a scratch under the chin.

I hesitated, regret and relief clashing in my chest.

"Is everything alright?" Zola asked, and I had to look away from the warmth and concern shining in her gaze.

"Of course," I said, shoving away my thoughts. I didn't need to get Voren or Zola mixed up in my personal issues. Not when they'd welcomed me into their home and offered me a place to live. I'd disrupted their lives enough. "I'll get Voren."

In my room, I changed in record speed, tucking the circlet away into the drawer and activating the protection wards. I hesitated, a handful of excuses to stay home swirling through my mind, but I shoved them aside. Not going would only draw more attention to me, more questions, and that was the last thing I needed.

Voren's room looked like a natural disaster had hit it and I failed to hide my smile. He checked himself out in a mirror, his white shirt standing out against his dark reddish skin. He grumbled and stripped off the shirt, adding it to a growing pile.

"Pick the black one," I suggested, even though it lay in the discarded heap. Voren huffed at me, hands on hips, but then snatched it up.

Voren had been getting moodier with each passing day that Rynac was away. It had been hard not to poke fun at him. Neither Voren nor Rynac had mentioned much about whatever was going on between them.

I'd set the two up on a date, which sounded like it went well—not that either would give me any details, which was rude—but after Rynac had dropped Voren off at home, Carmen had kidnapped him.

My fault.

At least I hadn't completely ruined things, but I'm sure that put a dark cloud over the whole first date. Not that I'd know. Dating and I didn't seem to mix.

And I don't have time for that, I snapped at myself. I didn't need anyone coming into my life and messing everything up. Not when I seemed to be doing a first-class job at that myself.

"Not even a certain someone with emerald-green eyes?" Danika said, and I jumped.

Get out of my head! Heat burned my cheeks, and my heart thumped frantically as those very eyes flashed through my thoughts.

Danika snickered. *"You think loud enough I can hear you blocks away."* Well, that was embarrassing. I hoped the only mind reader around was my familiar, or I was in trouble.

And no, I thought back to Danika, *I don't have time for him, as he definitely doesn't have any for me.*

"I'm sorry." The weight of her regret seeped through our bond.

Don't be. I sighed. *It's not your fault they've been pretending I don't exist.*

Against my better judgment, I pulled out my phone and tapped on the name. No new messages. Not that I expected any. Why had I thought that there had been something there?

Four weeks ago, I'd broken down one night and messaged Kaelan. Nothing serious, just a "Hi, how are you?" but it was still on unread.

Maybe he lost his phone?

With a huff, I dashed the thought away. I'd been forgotten.

For a week, I'd checked my phone damn near every hour. Several times my finger had hovered over the delete contact button, and each time I chickened out, because whenever my phone chimed, my heart leaped, hoping it was from him.

My fingers trailed over the skin just over my heart where Kaelan had drawn an angelic protection rune moments before I faced off against Carmen. The skin was bare. No sign the rune had ever been there, but I swore I sensed a flicker of magic every now and again.

I'd been foolish to think there had been something between us. He'd just been doing his duty, but it'd saved my life. I guess I'd read more into it than I should've.

"They're not worth it," Zola said as she joined me. I shoved my phone back in my pocket. "If they can't make any time to get back to you, then you shouldn't waste your time either."

"I know," I mumbled. My brain knew, but my heart was another matter. I rubbed at my chest and I could have sworn something tingled.

"How do I look?" Voren said, buttoning up the black shirt. His riot of bright red curls fell around his ears, despite the clear attempts to tame them, but only just hid the horns that poked through.

"Good enough," Zola said, grabbing her keys and heading for the door.

"I'm not going for 'good enough'," Voren snapped, but I grabbed his arm before he could pull it off.

"You look wonderful," I said, tugging him towards the door. "And you know Rynac has a thing about being on time. You want to make a good impression, right?"

Voren grumbled, but let me guide him out the door. Danika was hot on our heels, ready to nip our ankles if we didn't hurry up.

Fear bubbled up, burning like acid in my throat, as I watched my roommates. Were they going to be harmed again because of me, because of what I was?

Chapter Ten

The bustling noise of the airport enveloped us, a cacophony of rolling luggage, chattering voices, and the faint crackle of announcements overhead. Danika weaved between my legs, her magic cloaking her from sight as she dodged the feet of rushing travelers.

I pushed through the crowd, carving a path to the arrivals area, with Voren and Zola close behind. We hurried toward the gate, passengers already spilling out into the terminal.

Then, through the sea of strangers, I spotted them. The siblings were almost opposites of each other. Rynac with his short-cropped hair and broad shoulders. His steely blue eyes, piercing and unyielding, as they scanned the surroundings with a sharp intensity. In contrast, Indra's long hair was braided back, her soft blue eyes were calm and commanding as she strode through the crowd.

Without thinking, I rushed forward and threw my arms around them. The familiar warmth of their presence grounded me.

My logic caught up to my excitement a moment later. Was I being too clingy? What if they hadn't missed me as much as I missed them?

But my self-doubt melted away as they both squeezed me back just as fiercely.

"I'm so happy you are back." My voice came out muffled as the siblings were far more vertically blessed than I was. I took a step back, far enough to look both of them over.

"Shouldn't we be the ones to check that you're still whole?" Rynac said. "You have a knack for getting into dangerous situations."

I pursed my lips, but Zola answered before I could. "Don't worry, she's stayed out of trouble."

With a chuckle, Indra hugged the dryad, who appeared a little taken aback by the affection. The two had only started to become friends a month ago, but I was more than happy to see them growing closer.

"How did it go?" I asked.

"Better than we hoped," Indra said with a half-smile, but sadness still lingered in her eyes.

The airport wasn't the best place to catch up, at least not for this delicate matter. Indra and Rynac were both enhanced humans, altered after exposure to volatile magic following the death of a dangerous warlock. Last week marked the third anniversary of the massacre of East Vale, where thousands of humans and magicals had perished, where the siblings had survived but lost their mother.

Humans in East Vale and other human-only cities despised magic and the magical races. Not only had the siblings' lives been thrown into chaos due to the physical changes, but shortly after, they'd been forced to leave the only home they'd ever known. This was the first time they had been allowed to come back, to mark the anniversary and visit their mother's grave.

But it was the hostility towards enhanced humans that I'd feared would hurt them the most. Setting foot back into a place you loved, with the people you grew up with, and to be met with aggression, disdain, and anger.

"I'll grab our bags," Rynac said, nodding to the baggage claim.

"I can help," Voren quickly added, trotting after him. They walked side by side, not close enough to touch but far closer than strangers, as if something pulled them together.

"Huh," Indra said as the three of us just stood there watching them. "When did that happen?"

Oh no. Had he not told Indra? Then again, he hadn't even told me much—life had been a whirlwind after the demonspawn flooded the streets. "I might've set them up on a date," I said sheepishly.

"Really?" Indra said. I had to blink a few times as it was joy lighting up her face.

Indra had tried to set Rynac and me up when we first met. I didn't know how she felt about Rynac dating not only a male but an erebian at that.

Humans had far more stigma around such things than the races native to my realm. Humans and nephilim tended to have far more rigid views on sexuality and relationships.

Nephilim. Urgh. Why did I've to think about them?

"So that's who he's been texting all this time?" Indra said.

"You're okay with it?"

"Of course, I haven't seen him that happy in years."

"Voren has been insufferable," Zola added with a huff. "I knew there was a reason behind it, just not like him to be secretive."

"I don't think they've figured it out yet," I said, a smile growing on my lips. What right did they have to look so adorable together and be so clueless at the same time? Bags in hand, Rynac and Voren rejoined us, and we did our best to pretend we didn't notice the blush creeping across their cheeks.

Indra linked arms with me as we headed to our ride home. "How have you been?" Her voice was low enough that only I could hear it.

"Fine," I said with a smile, knowing what she meant. Her intent gaze burned into me, assessing every inch, and I stiffened, fearing she would be able to see through my facade. I needed to give her something else, a tidbit to latch onto that wasn't about me directly. "Still no update on finding a storefront for my alchemy; I swear the world is against me opening a shop."

I rambled about everything that had happened, enough to fill the silence and avoid other subjects, like how some days I felt on the verge of fracturing into a thousand pieces.

The ride back to the city was too short. But for twenty minutes I laughed and chatted with my friends, and could forget about everything that was wrong with my life.

Arriving back at the apartment buildings where we all lived, Zola and Voren headed to ours, but the siblings insisted I stop by theirs.

"I call first dibs on the shower," Indra shouted the moment we walked through the door, and set off running as if Rynac was going to fight her for it. Instead, he just huffed and flopped down on his couch.

"I can head out. You look beat," I said.

He waved me off. "No, I'm fine. Come sit."

I swallowed. There was no getting out of this. "I'll put the kettle on." At least I could buy myself some time. I veered into the kitchen. "How are you doing?" Just looking at Rynac, I could sense a bone-deep weariness; this was more than just exhaustion, but fatigue in his soul.

"It's been a lot," he huffed, raking his hand through his hair. "Everything felt so familiar, but different at the same time. Though I guess it's me that's different. Like reliving a memory that isn't your own."

"And the memorial?" I asked as I made our tea. I didn't want to admit I'd worried about them throughout their entire trip.

"It was rough," was all he said. I set the mugs down on the table and wrapped Rynac in a hug.

"I can't even begin to imagine," I said, my voice muffled by his shirt as he squeezed me back.

"Everything came crashing back, all the memories, what we lost." He paused, and I knew his thoughts had turned to his mother. "But even though it was one of the hardest things I've been through, it was good in other ways. Like a weight that had been clinging to my soul was lifted. Closure, I guess."

The earlier unease evaporated from Rynac as he began telling me about where he grew up and all the changes. I was more than happy just to sip my tea and listen to him, but his words faded as my eyes fixed on the thin scar trailing down his cheek. Carmen's laugh echoed through my mind as her clawed hand scraped across Rynac's face, bright red blood trickling down.

"Nyssa?" Rynac's voice cut through my trance and I blinked, my eyes darting back to his cheek, but there was no blood. "How have you been? I know it's hard to talk about things in texts, but I'm here now."

I cursed myself for being so obvious. "Oh, you know, same old," I said, forcing myself to smile. As if I could just pretend there wasn't anything wrong with me, as if I didn't close my eyes at night and witness his death at the hands of Carmen. "Divine has been as busy as I've ever seen it, and there aren't enough hours in the night to get all my alchemy brewed." I rambled on about everything I'd been doing and thankfully Rynac didn't prod again, just nodding along to everything I said. It was better this way, to keep them at arm's length, to keep them from being hurt because of me.

"Have you talked to your family yet?" Rynac asked, and I tensed. He fidgeted with the ring around his thumb. "I know family isn't always the easiest thing to deal with but . . . visiting my mother's grave made me realize how important it is. I don't want you to have all this stuff between you and those who care for you."

"All this stuff" being the fact that I was a lunar witch. I might've never heard of lunar witches before, but if the reaction of the Inquisitors was anything to go by, we were not popular.

Those traitors? Inquisitor Flamebury's mocking voice played in my head. While I might not be the target of the Inquisitors any more, or at least not top of their list, I'd no clue what the rest of the witch community thought about what I was.

"See," Rynac's voice cut through my thoughts and he tapped my forehead. "All those thoughts clogging up your brain. You can't keep them all inside. It's not good for you. Not knowing is the worst, and our head likes to make this far worse than it actually turns out to be."

"Yeah, yeah," I said, waving off his words even as they struck true. It wasn't anything I didn't know already. Fearing that my family might reject me was not doing wonders for my mental health. Yet every time I tried to bring it up on the phone, my lips froze, the words trapped. I needed the truth, but feared it all the same.

"I'm always here if you want to talk."

My phone chimed, saving me from conjuring a response. I rushed to open the message from Edrik.

8pm. Building C Apt 1337 Aspen St Groves.

I blinked a few times, waiting for another message, but that was it.

"Who's texting you that has you rushing for your phone?" Rynac said with a playful smirk.

"Just an alchemy contract," I blurted. "An important one."

"Sure," he said, clearly not believing my terrible lie.

"I need to get to bed," I said.

"It's way past your bedtime," Indra said, toweling her hair dry. "We'll catch up tomorrow."

Waving goodbye, I headed out, but Rynac's comments swirled through my mind. I knew I needed to be honest with my family, and

I wanted to know the truth about it all. Only that scared me just as much as revealing the change to my magic.

I heaved out a sigh as I started up the stairs to my apartment. Would it hurt more if they knew about lunar witches and never told me? That I'd struggled with my magic for nearly ten years and they never thought this might be why?

And if lunar witches are so special, why didn't the Lunar Order take more interest in me?

Urgh. I swiped that thought away. I didn't want to join the Lunar Order, where I'd have no choice but to be thrown into dangerous situations. That's what I'd said to Astrid, at least. Alchemy was what I wanted, this little slice of life I'd created here. And yet . . .

Too late to change your mind now, I scolded myself.

The Lunar Order didn't care about some witch with mediocre lunar magic. The nephilim from the Order weren't interested in being friends with me. And after all the death and destruction Carmen had wrought to fully awaken my powers, she too had cast me aside after I didn't live up to expectations.

What is wrong with me? That was a good thing. If I never saw Carmen again it would still be too soon.

I swiped a hand over my face. I was overtired. My thoughts made no sense. It was better to just blend in with everyone else. To be normal.

CHAPTER ELEVEN

Excitement buzzed through me at the thought of meeting Edrik. Indra and Rynac would be on duty, and Zola and Voren had other plans, so I didn't have to make up an excuse about where I was heading.

Ruby and Jade were still going to swing by after, as they wanted to know how the meeting went. I didn't know if they knew about all of this, but it was impossible to keep secrets from them.

Danika trotted beside me, tail swishing as she sniffed the cool evening breeze. The last hints of the day were swirls of pink on the horizon.

As fun as summer was, the long days meant shorter nights and less time to brew my potions. Usually I'd spend this time preparing the reagents, but with the help of the sisters, I wouldn't have to worry about falling behind.

My phone chimed, and I read the text from Edrik. "Weird," I muttered. "It's just a bunch of numbers." It wasn't a phone number or a date; maybe he'd accidentally messaged me.

I tightened my grip on my bag as I eyed everyone walking down the street. Could any of them sense the powerful circlet within? Did they want to take it from me?

I'd packed my bag with potions, and even worn my special potion belt that the siblings had commissioned for me, though it now had a rune etched into the leather that would conceal it from sight.

It felt weird carrying around all my potions, as if I was inviting danger. Though for weeks after the incident with Carmen and the warlock, I'd carried a fully stocked bag. But when the last of the demonspawn fled the city, I'd reduced the number. I still kept a few, because carrying none seemed like holding a sign saying *Easy target right here!*

Maybe if I trusted my magic more, I wouldn't feel this way. Potions were reliable. I knew they'd always do what they were made to do, only user error would mess them up. But my magic . . . it seemed stupid that I didn't trust it, but after eight years of fearing it, of keeping a tight grip to ensure it didn't get out of hand, it was hard to break that mindset.

I might be able to throw up a shield, but if I couldn't do anything else, I'd still be in danger. Would my shield last long enough to escape? What if there was no way out? Then I would just be biding my time while draining all my energy.

"Nyssa," Danika's voice sliced through my spiraling thoughts. *"Take a deep breath."*

Breathing in through my nose, I banished what I'd been thinking about. I'd been getting too stuck in my head—without Danika to snap me out, I don't know what I would've done. Probably lock myself in my room and never leave.

The back of my neck itched again, and I caught myself before I reached for it. My gaze scanned over the crowd. Ever since we left the apartment, I'd had that same sensation. As if someone was watching me.

Is anyone following us? I asked Danika. No one on the street seemed shady, and I didn't spot anyone lurking in the shadows.

"Do you sense something?"

Just this weird feeling, I said. *It's nothing.* I couldn't trust my emotions. Ever since that encounter with the vision of Carmen, I'd been unsettled. Sometimes it was the sensation of being watched, other times just an unease that swirled in my stomach.

Not to mention that—as per usual these days—my sleep was anything but restful. Though the dreams had been different today and I didn't know if that was a nice change or a worrying turn of events. The truth was, I'd far too many nightmares to choose from. I didn't need to be adding to them.

Oh, and I forgot the best bit, the fact that this last one felt far too real. That part I remembered. Usually they slipped away until I could only recall snatches. Chains around my wrist. The moon hidden behind clouds. Silver eyes watching me. So many eyes.

A shudder crawled over my skin and, with a huff, I raked a hand through my hair, but my tension clung to me like a thick ooze. Warmth wrapped around my heart and whispered that I was safe. My lips quirked as I whispered a "Thank you" to my bonded. Without Danika's connection, I would've gone crazy, jumping at shadows.

The foot traffic thickened and we were forced to weave around them, then the crowd compacted until we moved at a crawl.

A passerby knocked into my shoulder in their haste, and I stumbled, trying not to step on Danika. My heart kicked up a notch as I realized just how many people surrounded us and here I was trapped in the middle.

"Work your way back," Danika said, her voice cutting through my panic before it could grip me. *"I'll look for another way."* She took off, darting between legs as I spun and elbowed my way back the way I'd come. Relief washed over me when I spotted a narrow alley between two of the buildings, thankful to have space to be able to breathe.

I found an alley. I'll meet you on the other side.

"On my way. There was an accident and enforcers are blocking the way."

I headed down the alley, but my steps slowed when I realized how dark it was.

A chill ran down my spine. I could see the end of the alley, with cars and the pedestrians passing by. All I had to do was walk there.

This was silly. There were all these people around. I was just letting my fears get to me. After all, I didn't have the best track record with alleyways.

I picked up the pace but a presence brushed against me and I stumbled to a stop. Eyes wide, I swallowed around the lump forming in my throat and looked back over my shoulder.

A figure stood just on the edge of the deep shadows. Unmoving. Gaze locked on me.

The breath rushed out of me. *Carmen.* A pulse of warning cut through my mind, urging me to move. I spun back, stumbling away from her as I shoved a hand into my pocket. My shaking fingers gripped my conduit and squeezed until sparks erupted from the tip.

My legs wobbled beneath me as I sprinted, uncaring as I splashed through questionable puddles.

Danika's concern pressed against me. Our connection pulsed, and I missed a step as my awareness split between me running down the alley and Danika flying down the street.

I skidded, crashing to a halt at the end of the alley before I ran head-long into the pedestrians, earning myself a few harsh looks. Others cursed, dodging out of the way as Danika barreled around the corner.

"Where is she?"

I whipped back around, searching the shadows. I didn't see her anywhere.

That unsettling feeling of being watched still burned across my skin, but she wasn't here. I slumped against the wall, sliding down it as my knees gave out.

Covering my face with my hands, I shook my head. "I don't know." My voice wobbled, nothing more than a whisper. "It felt so real." I pressed my palms harder as my eyes prickled. I'd been so sure. But the alley was empty. No one was there.

The breath rushed out of me and I really didn't want to have a breakdown right now. There wasn't time.

Time. Right, I've an appointment to make.

Danika was silent as we set off again, but I could sense her attention on me. I pretended not to notice. Though I knew once this appointment with Edrik was over, there was no way she was letting me out of explaining what was going on inside my head.

The apartments towered over us, their sleek glass facades reflecting the last rays of the day. The clean lines and modern design were impressive, each building seeming larger and more luxurious than the last. These were places meant for comfort and style, and far above anything I would ever own.

The main door for Edrik's building swung open for me and we stepped into what looked like a hotel lobby.

There were crowds of people milling around, and before they could notice me, I ducked down to one of the side elevators. As I waited for it to arrive, I couldn't help but chuckle as I noticed Danika was no longer in sight, though I sensed her there.

I wish I could do that, I said, only a little jealous. Cobalt vulpines were a rare sight, but one who followed a person around could draw unwanted attention.

"You know, we could try to share the spell. You could lend your magic to mine and then we could both run around without anyone seeing us."

Sounds like a spell I've needed my whole life. Do you think it's possible? My thoughts turned to my failed attempts at learning other spells. This seemed like it would be even harder.

"There is no knowing how far our connection can go, or how much we can share," Danika said.

She continued to talk about bonds and what others had been able to do. We entered the elevator, and I nodded as she chatted, realizing she was trying to distract me.

When the doors opened on the thirteenth floor, I walked out feeling disoriented. The hallways branched off, each one looking identical. It took me a moment to find the right one before we headed toward Edrik's apartment.

Excitement swirled inside me, but I tried not to get my hopes up. It was invigorating to have something to work towards, something that I might actually be able to accomplish when everything else in my life seemed to be flopping.

I turned the last corner and came up short. Two doors down, a tactical response team of enforcers waited in silence, guns at the ready as they crowded around a door.

Chapter Twelve

The officers wore heavy tactical protection, helmets with visors down, weapons out, while two held battering rams.

One of the officers kneeling nearest me rushed over and I could only blink, feeling like I'd walked into a movie set.

"You need to get back," they ordered, but my mind was too slow to process everything. A heavy thud reverberated through the air and I flinched.

The battering ram hit the door again, and I stumbled back a step as my magic recoiled. "What's going on?" I hissed, my eyes locked on the door. My feet refused to move, the magic within me whispering that something was wrong, half willing me to run, the other half pulsing in warning. But what it was trying to warn me about, I didn't know.

"Move back to safety," the officer repeated. "We will handle the situation." The battering rams pounded against the door. Every logical brain cell ordered me to back away, yet deep in my bones, I knew something was wrong.

Danika, what do you sense? I asked. Was it just me, or was there something utterly wrong going on?

"Power," she whispered. I sensed her moving closer, and I realized she'd turned invisible again. *"It appears linked to the wards around his door."*

His?

"This is Edrik's apartment."

The battering ram crashed into the door, the wood fracturing. I gasped as potent energy slipped through the cracks—not since I'd been back in my home city had I felt raw power like that.

The wrongness shivered over my skin. Even if his door had been heavily warded, power shouldn't escape like that when the wards were damaged. There should be a failsafe to dispel the latent energy, that was if it followed standard laws.

More power crackled free, and whatever words the officer was hissing were lost on me.

"The only reason power would slip free—"

". . . was if it's designed to." The words fell from my lips as I darted around the officer. "Stop!"

I raced towards the enforcers, Danika beside me. A few moved to intercept me and I didn't even think as I summoned a shield to deflect them as they tried to grab me.

The power was building behind that door, sizzling against my awareness like a cork ready to pop. I didn't need to understand its intent to know it would do severe harm to anyone close, magically enhanced gear or not.

Time seemed to slow. My gaze locked on the battering ram as it sped towards the door. Wood splintered and power crackled. I threw myself in between the officers and the door, hands outstretched as my shield bloomed to life.

The world exploded.

Blinding light seared my vision. A thunderous roar ripped through the air and crashed into me, hurling me backward as the door shattered. I collided with bodies, then slammed into something unyielding. Pain throbbed through me.

Hands seized my shoulders, and I blinked, forcing my eyes to clear. An officer crouched in front of me, visor lifted. Her mouth moved, but all I could hear was the piercing ring in my ears. I tried to concentrate, my arms trembling.

"Release the spell." Her words cut through the haze. My gaze slid past her to take in the devastation. Officers lay scattered across the ground, many groaning, but they seemed more disorientated than severely injured.

There was now a gaping hole where the door had been, the walls and floor blackened by the explosion as smoke curled through the air. The blast had torn through everything—chunks of brick and splintered wood lay strewn across the hall.

But the most unnerving sight was the shards of debris suspended in the air, embedded in my shield. My spell hadn't been enough to absorb the full force of the explosion, but it'd kept the worst of the shrapnel from tearing through us.

"Oh." I dropped my arms and released the spell. The debris fell to the ground as I slumped back against the wall. "Danika?" The officer gave me a confused look.

"Outside," she said, her voice somewhat strained. *"Need somewhere safe to discharge the energy."*

"My familiar," I explained to them. "She absorbed a portion of that blast." I winced as I tried to sit up, my head throbbing and my muscles protesting.

"Stay put," the officer said. "Medics will be here in a moment." She eyed the destruction, the injured officers around us, but whatever thoughts were running through her head were locked away behind her emotionless mask. "When your familiar returns, can you extend a thank you to her?"

My brow furrowed. *Thank you?*

"If it hadn't been for the two of you, I fear I'd be filling up body bags rather than stretchers. Thank you for protecting my unit when our magic failed."

Words escaped me. But as I took in the area and my brain rebooted, I finally began to comprehend what had just happened, and what might've happened if we hadn't acted. I opened my mouth, feeling as if I was meant to say something to that, but I closed it again.

The officer beside me groaned, and she rushed over to him, shouting for the medics again.

"Special Agent Lyra," a voice barked, and the officer was on her feet again in the blink of an eye, cursing under her breath.

She stepped towards the approaching group. The skin on my chest heated and fear seeped into my heart, urging me to run. The emotion was so overwhelming that I squeezed my eyes closed against a wave of dizziness. It didn't make any sense, the threat was over. Or was my brain just catching up to almost being killed in a magical explosion?

"Lieutenant Einheri," she replied, and I almost shivered at the ice in her voice.

"Report," the lieutenant barked, and my head protested the sound.

"I don't report to you," she said, this time covering any emotion. "Where are my medics?"

"Nyssa, what's wrong?" Danika asked a moment before she pressed against my side. I stroked a hand down her back, her presence grounding me as I shoved the dregs of that odd reaction away. But I stilled my hand after I opened my eyes, realizing she was invisible again. If the medic saw me patting the air, they might assume I'd hit my head a lot harder.

Just this unsettling feeling overcame me. Must be from the residual magic. Racing feet approached and a cluster of enforcers from the medical unit rushed towards us. More officers were filling the hallway, but they weren't being allowed through.

Special Agent Lyra stepped aside as the lieutenant pushed past her and all the heat rushed out of me.

Even just the sight of the pair of white wings was enough to make me freeze. But then my gaze dropped to the familiar ice-blue eyes and the scowling face of Nathaniel.

I wanted nothing more than to disappear. He marched forward with all the swagger of a nephilim and I could barely breathe.

His gaze swung to me and his magic shivered over my skin, a sensation that made it crawl. "And what is a witch doing here?" His voice dripped with venom. "Name," he snapped.

I blinked, searching his face as the silence stretched. There wasn't even a flicker of recognition. "Nyssa Thornheart." *But you know that,* I thought. Something shifted behind his eyes; his gaze turned distant as his brow furrowed, but then the expression disappeared.

"A civilian," Special Agent Lyra interjected.

Nathaniel's lip curled, but then his head whipped towards the shattered remains of the door and he turned away.

"The crime scene has not been secured," she snapped, but Nathaniel just waved her off.

She spun, hissing to one of her officers, but my attention was fixed on Nathaniel. He paced around the apartment, his eyes searching. I didn't know what for.

Who was this person? It couldn't be the same nephilim I'd met all those months ago.

I shoved to my feet. The wrongness of this whole situation was making my head spin, but I was determined to get answers. Nathaniel's head snapped up, fixed on something out the window.

My gaze followed his, and perched on the balcony of the apartments across the street was another nephilim.

His two black wings spread wide as if signaling to Nathaniel. From this distance I couldn't make out his features, but my heart stumbled as I swore he looked directly at me, and then he dove off the balcony.

"Sir," one of the UMC soldiers called to Nathaniel. "We spotted Renatus." But Nathaniel was already moving, sprinting as he tucked in his wings and crashed through the glass.

Chapter Thirteen

"He jumped out the window," I said, stunned, as the rest of his unit rushed after him.

"Bloody nephilim," the special agent said, rolling her eyes as if this happened on a regular basis. "Barging into my crime scene and then possibly destroying evidence."

"Nyssa?" Indra's voice cut through the fog of disbelief. Worry etched into her features as she hurried towards me, scanning me for injures.

"I hope there is a good reason," a deep voice said from behind my friend, "as to why my alchemist is at an active crime scene."

Reluctantly, I looked past Indra to find Captain Everson, the head of this division of the MEA and the one who contracted me to craft potions for his officers.

"Saving lives," Special Agent Lyra said.

The captain's lips turned into a thin line as he eyed me. "Yes, that sounds like something she'd do." His voice was far too hard to think that might've been praise. "Please escort Ms. Thornheart to a secure room. I'll be there shortly."

We walked down to the end of the hall into an apartment the MEA had turned into a temporary office. Indra led me into the empty bedroom and closed the door behind us.

I tensed, feeling like I was about to be yelled at, not that I'd done anything wrong. Turns out the silence was worse. I stared out the window, as a jumble of thoughts crashed through me, my mind trying to make sense of . . . whatever the hell just happened.

The door clicked open, jerking me from my thoughts as the captain strode in. As always, his face was unreadable as he fixed his stare on me.

"Please tell me you have good reason for stumbling into this crime scene," he said. "I sincerely hope that this was just a coincidence and not a repeat of the warlock incident."

"She can hardly be held accountable for that," Indra interjected. "The dark witch targeted her. It wasn't like she was looking for trouble."

The captain dismissed Indra's words and turned his hard gaze back to me, waiting for an answer. As much as I didn't want to discuss what I was doing, I'd no reason not to trust the enforcers for all that they'd done for me. The MEA trained for this kind of danger, yet that didn't make me feel any better about all the officers who'd been killed or injured when Carmen attacked.

"I had a meeting with Edrik, the person who lived at the apartment that exploded. Did something happen to him?"

"Why were you meeting him?" he asked, and my gut twisted at my ignored question.

"We were going to discuss this." I pulled out the circlet. "Edrik studies magical artifacts, and I went to his shop this morning. He wanted to meet somewhere private." I gnawed on my lip, trying to decide how much to tell him. But the captain had already stuck his neck out for me. He deserved the truth, at least part of it. "It's a lunar relic, a very valuable one, and it recently awoke."

"Do you know anyone who would wish harm upon him?"

"I literally just met him earlier today for the first time. He texted me his address to meet again."

"Can I see the message to verify the time?" the captain asked. With a nod, I handed my phone over.

"What is the code in the text for?" he asked.

"I don't know. I just thought it was an accident."

Captain Everson frowned, then headed out of the room, calling to someone.

"Where did you even get this?" Indra asked. Was there accusation in her voice or was I just hearing what I feared?

"The shifters gave it to me as a thank-you gift after the full moon ceremony." My tongue burned with the half truth, but how could I tell her I'd had another vision? Dread snaked through me. Visions always led to bad things, and now I was standing at a crime scene.

The captain strode back in; the door clicked shut as he assessed me. He offered me my phone. "The timestamp on the second message was just before the emergency calls. Are you sure you don't know what it means?"

"No, it doesn't make any sense to me."

He watched me for a breath before nodding. "I hear you saved the lives of several enforcers." It was a statement, but I could hear the question hidden within it.

"I turned into the hallway just before they attempted to breach the apartment. Energy was leaking from the door, it was unstable, and I knew if they tried to break it down—" I cut myself off. Saying it aloud, I realized how foolish I'd been. "Obviously they wouldn't listen to a random person telling them to stop. I cast a shield trying to minimize the damage."

The captain just nodded, but it was the intense gaze from Indra that seemed to bore into me. I met her eyes, waiting for anger or to be shouted at, but instead she stepped closer, turning me this way and that to inspect me. "Were you injured?"

"Just bumped my head on the wall." I was trying to reassure her, but my words had the opposite effect. Indra squeezed my hand tighter.

"You should sit down. Are you sure you're alright?" She searched my gaze as she pulled me towards a chair.

"I'm fine," I said, a tad more forcefully than intended. Why did she treat me like I was made of glass?

"We will need a full statement later," the captain said.

"Nathaniel doesn't smell right," Danika's voice said in my mind.

Is he coming back? And what does not smelling right mean?

"He was chasing after someone, so it was hard to get close. There was a heavy knot of magic around him. It wasn't nephilim or lunar magic."

Do you think that's why he acted like we had never met?

"Hard to be sure. It could just be protections laid over him, but it seems fishy."

But you love fish.

Her laugh filled my head, and I smiled, only to realize the two enforcers were watching me. Shit, had they been talking to me?

"There was a nephilim here," I said. "He talked to the special agent. Lieutenant Einheri."

Captain Everson scowled. "Yes, he popped up at our last few crime scenes, trying to take over the investigation. But the UMC has no jurisdiction here."

"And before that?" I asked, but the captain shook his head. "He was here with the other two nephilim and helped me after I escaped the Inquisitors. But today, he acted as if we were strangers."

"Is that unusual?" the captain asked.

"It wasn't that he was just pretending, but it was as if he didn't remember me at all. The Lunar Order might be secretive, but what reason would they have for pretending they didn't know me? If they wanted to keep things on the down low, wouldn't they have at least mentioned it to me?" Didn't I at least deserve that? I shook my head. "I know it sounds silly, but it just didn't feel right."

"Except that the nephilim have been ignoring you this whole time," Indra added.

I shot her a glare. *Like I need a reminder?* "Danika also sensed unusual magic on him."

"Who is Danika?" the captain asked.

"Her familiar," Indra answered in a rush. "Why does she think that?"

Captain Everson's brows knitted. "Familiar?"

"Yes, the blue fox that follows her around." She waved off the captain, her gaze fixed on me.

"She isn't sure," I said. "Nathaniel was chasing after someone. But she said there was a heavy knot of magic. She was around him a few months ago, so I trust what she says."

"Who was he chasing?" Indra asked.

I hesitated, I couldn't be certain about what I'd seen and yet . . . Nathaniel and Kaelan were part of a team. If one was in the city, there was a chance all of them were.

"His prime suspect for the murders," the captain answered.

The word sent a chill down my spine. My brain shuddered to a stop and then rewound. "Is Edrik dead?"

The captain was silent for a moment. "This is an active crime scene, and the investigation is still taking place—" He cut off at a sharp look from Indra. "There is no body but signs of a struggle. We received several calls about a disturbance and a sighting of armed intruders, which would mean this would be a missing person or kidnapping. But as the UMC showed up, even though we didn't call them, we assumed it was linked to the others."

My mind tumbled, no body meant he could be alive but . . ."The others?"

"There have been several murders over the last six weeks—that we know of. We have nothing to connect the victims, but the way that they were killed seems to be similar. There is a good possibility that they are targeted, not just picked at random."

Who were they targeting? My heart kicked up a few notches as all my fears began rattling around in my head again. It was far too much of a coincidence. The vision sent me to Edrik and now he was gone.

Captain Everson studied me for far too long. Despite working closely with him, I still felt unsettled by that stare. I guess being one of the main suppliers for potions suitable for his enhanced officers wasn't enough to win me any points. "The nephilim from the dark witch attack have not contacted you, correct?" he asked.

I nodded, hating that the truth stung so much.

"Good," the captain said. "Report it, if they do."

"Why?"

"Because the UMC's prime suspect is Kaelan Renatus."

Chapter Fourteen

I flinched—his words were like a slap across my face, but there was no sign of deceit in the captain's expression.

My gaze swung to Indra, and she winced. She knew. Knew and didn't tell me. That stung. My mouth opened and closed, unable to find the words I needed.

But how could it be Kaelan? My heart kicked up a notch. No, it couldn't be him. That didn't make any sense at all.

How well do you really know him? a voice asked. I wanted to tell it, *Well enough,* but the truth was I'd known him for what, a few weeks at most?

Why would his friend and the UMC hunt for him if they didn't have solid proof? The thought made my chest squeeze, but I couldn't dismiss the logical part of my head that had to agree. The evidence was stacked against him.

At least he'd a good reason for not contacting me, I thought with a wry twist of my lips.

"Did you tell them about how we left Edrik's?" Danika asked, and I cursed myself for leaving that out. I'd tried to brush it off as my paranoia, but now, with all of this going on, was there more to it?

"When I first went to Edrik's shop this morning, he sent us out the back door when someone came in; he seemed concerned and a bit annoyed. I only got a glimpse of them, but everything about them felt wrong. Just looking at them unsettled my magic." It wasn't much to go on, but I had to do what I could. No matter how little I knew Kaelan, I couldn't believe he was a murderer. He was part of the Lunar Order—Selene's blessing had to mean something.

So why is another moon-blessed hunting him?

"We will have someone check into it," the captain said. But whatever he uttered after that was lost when Danika's voice filled my head.

"Nyssa. I think I know what that code is for."

One moment I was sitting in front of the captain and Indra, the next I was low to the ground, sniffing in a dark room. A cool, crisp scent surrounded me, like silver and frost, and I wanted nothing more than to lean into it. But a soft glow pulled at my attention, and there, in the shades of gray, sat a small safe with a keypad.

I blinked, and a wave of vertigo washed over me as I was back in my own body again.

Indra gripped me as if to keep me from falling, her face pinched with concern. "Are you alright? What was that?"

"Danika just showed me something, what the code might be for."

"Where?"

"Somewhere in Edrik's apartment."

"How is the fox in the crime scene?" Captain Everson demanded.

Oops. "She is very sneaky," I said with a weak smile. Danika snickered.

The captain was silent for a long moment. "I'll have my officers finish up and see if I can get the UMC to step away. Not that there is much for them to catalog. You can look around—just don't touch anything without asking." He left before I could answer.

I looked over at Indra, who just shrugged.

"Is that normal?" I asked.

"From what I know, we've been hitting dead ends with these murders. So if there is a lead or a way to connect them, I think he is willing to take the risk."

"You know about them?" I couldn't help my morbid curiosity. The siblings rarely talked about work. I wasn't sure if that stemmed from their reluctance, or if they were trying to protect me from all the terrible things happening in the city.

"Only what I hear from the other officers. The first few we didn't realize were linked until later. However, a killing occurred right before we left for East Vale. It was—" Indra stopped, shaking her head as if she could banish her memory. "It looked like a ritual of some kind. Runes and an array."

"A ritualistic killing?" My throat tightened. That was something out of ancient history.

The incidents we learned about at school were to demonstrate that there were always better, more advanced approaches. The majority had been archaic ways of transferring magical energies, whether to cast a spell or to imbue an object with power.

Carmen's spell array had been built on those same principles. She'd placed me in the sacrifice circle, the name coming from those old rituals, though most tended to use small magical animals rather than people. The essence from within would be extracted and used to fuel the spell.

Although never safe, it aimed to deplete the person's magic, but excessive drain could prove fatal.

On the other hand, sacrificing someone's life essence was barbaric, but that hadn't stopped people before. I was intrigued, but my mind not so subtly reminded me that people were dead. The curiosity soured in my stomach. Why was I like this? I needed to go back to my baking and alchemy.

"Let's go," the captain called from the doorway. I was quick to follow, Indra sticking close beside me. "The detectives were not that happy, but if they have a breakthrough in these cases, then they will shut up."

"And the UMC?" I asked as we headed out into the hallway, now empty except for the lone enforcer waiting by the door.

"They stepped out for a bit to contact their higher-ups, no doubt to get their orders in place so that they can take over. So we need to be quick."

"Are you doing okay?" Indra whispered, tugging my hand until I stopped. "I know this can't be easy for you." Concern pinched her features, her eyes intent.

"I'll manage," I said, hoping I was giving her a reassuring smile. She nodded and stepped away. Relief washed through me that she'd believed my lie, that she thought I could handle this.

But you can't, a voice slithered through my thoughts. *You're haunted every time you close your eyes. Now you're adding more fuel to the fire.* The voice cackled, sending a shudder down my spine. I clenched my fists, nails biting hard into my palm as I strode forward.

A ripple of magic washed over me as I stepped past the scattered debris that'd once been Edrik's door, and I jerked away.

"It's keeping everything in place while we catalog," Indra said, noting my reaction. "We don't need people interfering with evidence, but the effect will only last for a few hours."

I admonished myself; I should've known that. Since when did I let a little bit of magic unsettle me?

I pressed forward, but came up short again once I was fully within the apartment and frowned. The way they'd been talking about it, I'd been expecting . . . well, not this. A few chairs had been overturned, some papers scattered, but that was it.

"This doesn't look like a murder scene," I said slowly, my gaze darting over every surface, trying to figure out what I was missing.

"Right now, it's just a crime scene," the captain answered. "The other confirmed scenes didn't look like this. The only reason we assumed it was another murder was the presence of the UMC and the lieutenant. Otherwise, it might be a kidnapping, or at least an assault on law enforcement." He finished with a gesture to the door.

"Did any of your detectives figure out what kind of security he had on the door to cause that explosion?" I asked.

"From what we could tell, it wasn't primed to explode, it was just the basic wards that came with the apartment. Our enforcers are used to disabling traps that try to keep us out, but they only detected regular wards, which they were shielded against. The initial investigation suggests too much power was funneled into them, which made them unstable."

"That doesn't sound right at all," I said, mind racing. "Even from only meeting Edrik once, it was clear that security was a top priority. His business had wards so thick it was hard to breathe. Why would his home be any different? And there are minor wards over the rest of the apartment, enough to keep things in place. To overcharge the wards . . . it would've been intentional."

"Though," Indra added, "that doesn't mean it was targeted at the enforcers. Just whomever tried to break down his door."

"You think he targeted Nyssa?" the captain asked.

"No, she was invited here. If he planned anything nefarious against her, it wouldn't be in a way that directly linked to him."

"You think he knew someone else was coming for him?" I asked. Hoping. Edrik targeting me didn't make any sense. Especially given the fact he knew both Danika and I could sense lunar energies. *And that's why he left you a clue.* "Can we check the other room?"

With a nod from the captain, the three of us headed to where Danika sat in a doorway. She let out an annoyed sigh when we finally joined her.

The room appeared to be a study, or more accurately, a treasure trove of magical artifacts and curiosities. Shelves lined the walls, crammed with an eclectic assortment of items: ancient tomes with gilded spines, glass vials filled with shimmering substances, and enchanted trinkets that glowed.

A large, ornate desk dominated the center of the room, cluttered with papers and books, and even a half-empty mug of black coffee.

The air was crisp with the scent of old books, mixed with the faint tang of magic. Despite the disaster of a desk, which the captain glared at it as if it personally offended him, the room appeared untouched. As if Edrik had stepped out and would return at any moment.

Without needing to be prompted, Danika trotted over to what I assumed was the couch. The small green seat might once have been used for its intended purpose, but it was now being used to house haphazard piles of papers and books.

Fearing one wrong move might make the whole thing come toppling down, I crouched and peered underneath. And there, deep in the shadows, was the safe.

"Do you sense anything?" Captain Everson asked as he pulled out a flashlight.

"Nothing besides a faint pulse of lunar magic."

The captain reached under and pulled the safe out; it was small, likely for securing jewelry or a few watches, so why was it under here? I extended a hand, hovering it over the surface of the safe.

The faint thrum of magic tickled my skin. Without a thought, I called to my power, summoning a lunar orb of light. Its soft glow washed over us, and sections of the safe shimmered.

"What is that meant to be?" Captain Everson asked.

I rubbed the back of my neck. "It's for me," I said, staring down at a drawing of my moon-blessed mark, a crescent moon surrounded by seven stars.

Whatever was in here, Edrik wanted me to find it. I punched in the code from my phone, and it clicked open to reveal a stone and a scrap of paper.

"That's it?" Indra huffed.

I was almost as disappointed, but the stone pulsed with lunar energies as I picked it up. As I twisted it, the surface shimmered with a cascade of colors, shifting from white and light blue to purples and silvers. Tiny iridescence flecks danced, resembling distant stars twinkling in the night sky. It glowed with an ethereal light that seemed to come from within, while lunar energies pressed against my skin from within the gem.

"It's a celestial opal," Danika said.

I choked, almost dropping the it. "You're certain?" I didn't want to doubt her, but I knew how expensive the dust was for my potions. But a whole gem? I could afford to buy an apartment twice the size of my current one and still have plenty left over.

The opal was also said to be a conduit of lunar energies, though I hadn't known if that was myth or truth, but holding it in my grip made it clear enough.

Danika sniffed at it, her ears twitching. *"It contains a trace of Edrik's magic. Those opals can be used to store lunar energies."*

I explained to the others what Danika had told me. "Why would he hide this away? How is it meant to help us?" I asked, but no one had any answers.

"What is this?" Indra said, picking up the scrap of paper. It looked like it'd been torn from the edge of a notebook, and scribbled on it was an image of a shield and two crossed blades.

"An insignia of some kind?" Captain Everson said, frowning down at it. "We can check it against our archives, but we should head out before the UMC comes back and takes over," he added, then shot me a pointed look. "Keep that safe. It might be against protocol to let you take it, but the victim wanted you to find it. I just trust you will come to us when you find anything."

I nodded, following the others out. Danika and I ducked down a stairwell before anyone spotted us. Only when we were back out on the streets, far from Edrik's apartment, did I slow to a walk.

What was I meant to do with this opal? I squeezed it in my grip, as if willing it to tell me what I needed to do, but nothing happened.

Reaching out with my awareness, I let my magic wash over the gem, probing to glean an inkling from it. A jumble of emotions that were not my own whispered against my skin. I closed my eyes, focusing on the feelings pulsing from the opal, trying to tease out the sensations.

Desperation was the strongest; it coated my tongue with a tang of bitterness and left it dry. Urgency was next, making my heart speed up, and I pushed it aside, digging deeper. The sensation of the next was less tangible, as if the very wind was whispering a warning. And then I sensed a growing shadow, looming, ever present but impossible to find.

A weak image flickered through my thoughts . . . fuzzy like an old memory. The edges were blurred and hard to make out, but there was little doubt what I was looking at. It was the artifact I'd seen in my first vision, and next to it lay a celestial opal.

I released my magic, sucking in a deep breath. Edrik knew where it was. Had seen it. A spark of hope glimmered in my chest. They might've taken Edrik, but I'd just have to get him back.

Chapter Fifteen

Too many thoughts swirled through my head, too many questions popping up, ones that neither Danika or I could answer. I hailed a taxi in a rush to get home faster. My hands squeezed into fists as if that could stop them from shaking.

Everything was too much. Too overwhelming. How had I stumbled into all of *this* again? I didn't want anything to do with looking into murders, and yet, what choice did I have? Someone had taken Edrik, but why?

The nagging thoughts chased me all the way to my apartment. I slipped inside, whispering a thanks that the living room was empty before legging it to the safety of my bedroom.

"Are the people that took Edrik after what I'm hunting for?" I said, more to myself, as I slid down my door until I was in a heap on the ground. Without hesitating, Danika curled up at my side, her reassuring presence warming me.

"We can't know for sure, but vulpines don't believe in coincidences."

I huffed at that. "You sound like my dad." A warmth pulsed from Danika, one I'd learned was her version of a smile. "But why would they take him? If the artifact has been sitting around for years and Edrik knows about it, why would they only target him now?" A heavy sigh escaped me and I pulled out the opal. The magic within it thrummed and heated in my palm as I stared down at it. "Right, not the time for a breakdown. We need to try to locate Edrik before . . ."

I wasn't sure what I was going to say, but it was better not to finish that thought. With a groan, I pushed myself up and gathered the supplies I'd need for a tracking spell. We headed for the open garden terrace we rented, where I brewed my potions under the moonlight.

Stepping out onto the terrace, a wave of calm washed over me as I took in the soft luminescence of the moon that cast everything in a silvery light. The small open deck jutted out from the side of our apartment building, in the perfect position to soak in the moonlight all night, at least during the summer months. The other option, the balcony attached to our apartment, faced the wrong direction, so I'd only get moonlight when it was setting.

A beautiful garden now embraced one side, Zola's labor of love. A variety of plants flourished in the space, their leaves and petals glistening under the moon's glow, casting delicate shadows across the wooden planks. The air was rich with the perfume of the blooming flowers and earthy scents.

With Zola's enchanted touch, she'd helped cultivate plants that I could use in my alchemy, and at the center was my Starlight Tears bloom. Its magical properties encouraged the other plants to grow, not to mention it'd been a key ingredient in the potion that had unlocked my lunar magic.

I brushed my fingers over its soft leaves as I did every time I passed and pushed a small trickle of lunar magic into it as a thank you.

After clearing away the patio furniture to open up a space to draw the array, we got to work. *The Lunar Codex* thrummed beneath my fingers as I selected the runes I needed. I would've almost called it excitement, but it was a book, and they didn't have emotions.

When I first discovered this tome and rehomed it—it hadn't been stealing, the book wanted to come with me, okay?—I hadn't been able to read anything but the title. Over time, the pages had changed from illegible to words I could read, and it'd offered me several spells that had aided me in awakening my lunar magic.

Since then, it'd revealed more to me, mostly detailed descriptions about lunar energies and how they differed from other types, but of late, nothing new had appeared. No matter how many times I flicked through the pages, the same words would stare back at me.

Then again, my magical growth seemed to have stalled as well. Unlike during my childhood, when my magic battled itself, now it felt like a block that stopped my magic from emerging. The passive magic and my shields were fine, it complied with spell arrays, but when I tried to learn more spells to protect myself, it was as if the flow turned to lead.

Was that all my magic was good for?

I admonished myself for complaining. It was more than I hoped for when I first moved to the city. All I'd wanted was to save my alchemy, and I'd done that and more.

My magic no longer surged or threatened to overwhelm me or burn everything around me to a crisp. I'd become stronger in my brewing, able to tackle larger and more complicated potions. I could cast astral shields, not that I needed such a spell any more—no more running from demonspawn or shielding myself and my friends.

It saved the lives of the officers today. And for that, I was thankful. I was content with my life, using my magic to help others, but I didn't want to rely on it daily. I didn't want danger to be stalking my steps. It wasn't like I was going to go and hunt down this serial killer on my own; I'd do what I could to help the MEA, and that was all I wanted. Being an enforcer wasn't for me.

Or a moon-blessed warrior.

So why did that thought still sting?

Danika hummed as she paced around the edge of my spell array, inspecting it for any fault. The waxing gibbous moon hung heavy just above the horizon and I was thankful not only for its brightness but as an added component to the spell.

Despite the limited nature of my power, it didn't seem to ebb and flow with the phases of the moon, something the shifters thought was fascinating.

The question still gnawed at me though, why did my magic remain the same?

The moon-blessed nephilim hadn't seemed to struggle either, but then again, it was clear I didn't know them at all. No, that was stupid. I might not have known them well, but I couldn't accept Kaelan was a mass murderer. I wasn't that terrible at judging people's characters.

Blowing out a breath, I did something foolish. I pulled out my phone and hit call. It rang once before it beeped, telling me the number was unavailable. I tried Astrid. Nothing. Nathaniel. Nothing. Okay, I was kind of relieved about the last one, but what did it mean? Then again, if Kaelan had answered, what would I say? *Hello, you never called me but also are you a murderer?*

"Looks good to me," Danika said, cutting off any more self-pitying thoughts about being attracted to criminals.

With a nod, I pulled out the last few reagents that would help to empower the spell. My fingers brushed over something cold within my bag, and magic vibrated through my hand and up my arm.

The circlet peeked out of the cloth I'd wrapped it in. Even through the fabric, magic seeped through as a soft melody floated through my mind, soothing and oddly familiar.

I hesitated. The shifters had given it to me, and they'd said that it was an amplifier of lunar energies—it seemed foolish to ignore an item that could aid me.

Someone had kidnapped Edrik, and not only did I need to find him, but I needed to know whatever he was going to tell me tonight. It was too much of a coincidence—that person at his shop, the vision—that Edrik was taken just before I could get to him.

And yet . . . a shiver wracked my spine, and I covered the circlet back up.

"Do you fear more visions?" Danika's quiet voice whispered in my head, but I still jumped. *"Or did it show you more than you revealed at the ceremony?"* There was no accusation in her voice, and yet guilt stabbed my chest. Why had I been hiding the visions from my familiar? The one being who would always stand by my side.

"It was a jumble, but yes, there was more to it." I paused, fearing saying the words aloud, but they'd already proved to be true. "I saw fragments of what I think were the murders they mentioned, glimpses of the runes in the spell arrays and the . . . bodies." A twang of hurt resounded in my heart, but then it was gone as if I'd imagined it. My gaze lifted to Danika. Her head hung low—the hurt was not mine but hers. I'd sensed it through the bond before she could suppress it. "I know I should've mentioned it earlier, but . . ." But I just wanted to forget, pretend I'd never seen those terrible images. Danika already worried about me and my nightmares. I didn't want to add more to that.

"You know you can share your burdens with me," she said, trying to hide the pain in her voice. My heart squeezed—again, my actions were harming her. I sat down before her, my arms aching to wrap around her as if that would convey how sorry I was, but I gave her the option to approach.

"I'm sorry." The words whispered from me as I forced them out. "I guess I was trying to protect myself, but only hurt you in the process. And—" My mind churned, wading through my thoughts to find the truth. There was an "and," one that I tried to even hide from myself. "And I was afraid of what it meant. I haven't had a single vision since . . . the incident. The fact I'd another one made me fear that more bad things were coming, and I thought that if I didn't speak of it, maybe it would go away. I barely survived last time, and knowing that I'd have to go through that again, I—" My voice wavered and I bit down hard on my cheek as my eyes prickled.

Why was this happening to me again? My life was finally starting to get back on track and I'd been ignoring the dark shadow that always lingered in the back of my mind. But now I'd had another vision that could only mean things were about to go bad again.

There was a serial killer in the city and I'd got myself entangled with that. Why was I seeing these things? Why were they being inflicted on me after everything that'd gone wrong last time?

"I don't want this," I whispered.

"So why did you go to Edrik's? Why did you tell Nan about your vision?"

I opened my mouth to tell her that they'd asked me to do it, but that wasn't true. I'd chosen to follow the lead, to go where the vision had shown, and ignored what I'd seen of the ritualistic killings.

"The shifters see me as some kind of hero, but I'm not."

While I wanted them to appreciate me and to help them, I didn't deserve the admiration they gave me.

"I didn't confront Carmen to rescue the shifters, but to save Indra and Rynac. And I was so terrified. Afraid I wasn't going to survive, but I fought to keep you and my friends safe from suffering from my mistakes." I swallowed hard around the lump in my throat. If my failures had cost the lives of those I cared for, I couldn't have lived with myself. "I want to be worthy of the way the shifters treat me. I . . . just want to matter, to make a difference in people's lives. But now Edrik is caught up in whatever all this is."

"I don't think Edrik's involvement has anything to do with you."

I swiped a hand across my face, the weight of everything pressing down on my shoulders. "I should've ignored the visions. Now that I started to follow them, I'm only leading myself towards disaster. It was foolish of me to think using the visions would bring about any good; they only ever bring about destruction and pain."

"Seeing these visions does not change the course of the future. You're already walking down the path. The visions only offer insight or warnings so you can make your choices."

"But why does she offer them to me? There have to be people far more qualified to handle these situations than me, like those from the Lunar Order."

Danika tilted her head back and forth, her version of a shrug. *"Selene believes in you."*

A sigh escaped me. I'd just have to trust in everyone else's faith in me, whether terrified or not. I'd made a vow to Selene, devoted myself to her. And if she asked me to find this artifact and save lunar magic, I'd give it everything I had.

Chapter Sixteen

Danika's eyes glittered in the moonlight as she watched me. Certainty solidified in my chest, not just because she would be at my side, but that we were doing something important together.

In that moment, our thoughts aligned—no need for words or explanations. She brushed against my leg, a silent promise that she would follow me wherever this led.

Her presence filled me with a calm, steady assurance, the kind that settled deep in my bones. For the first time in a long while, I wasn't second-guessing myself. Our bond pulsed with clarity, a shared purpose humming between us like the rhythmic beat of a heart.

I smiled down at her. We were more than a witch and her familiar. We were bonded. Ready to face whatever came next. Together.

An odd sensation prickled over my skin, like unseen eyes were watching me. I paused and scanned the twinkling cityscape, and my gaze landing on the apartments across the street. Deep shadows clung to the terraces on the top levels—unlike our building, the upper floors had their own private areas rather than just balconies.

I shook off the feeling. Nothing was moving over there, and the building hadn't yet opened to residents. *Just my overactive imagination yet again.*

Before I could hesitate, I snatched up the circlet and placed it on my head. The moment it touched my skin, the gem warmed. A soft pulse of magic brushed against my awareness, and if it hadn't just been jewelry, I might have thought it was happy that I was using it.

Last, I palmed the celestial opal and nodded to my familiar that I was ready. I couldn't help the smile on my lips—for a moment I could forget my worries, the murders, and my fears, and allow my power to mix with Danika's.

The air vibrated around us as I closed my eyes, enjoying the soothing ebb and flow of our magic pooling into the spell array and activating the runes. There was a weight to the moonlight, and I tilted my face towards the moon, allowing it to fill me with its energy.

The gem in the circlet heated, not to a painful level, but enough for me to focus on it as I whispered the words of the spell to locate Edrik. The opal pulsed in my grip, and I teased out a thread of its power and imbued it into the array.

Each word fizzed on my tongue as if my voice was laced with magic. The potent spell was a tangible weight pressing against my skin, and my head began to ache as the gem pulsed with insistence.

Opening my eyes, I jerked back when I took in my surroundings. Where was I? The dark world around me seemed to ripple, as if I was staring at it through a pool of water.

I was about to take a step backwards when Danika's voice cut through my mind. *"Focus. What do you see?"*

My heart pounded in my chest, and it was an effort to suck in a deep breath. Thick magic surrounded me, but I could still sense Danika through our bond. It told me she was right beside me, yet when I looked down I didn't have legs, or a body. I waved my hand in front of my face, or at least that is what my body told me it was doing, yet I saw nothing but the damp, shadowed room around me.

I don't know, I thought back to her, not sure if I could talk or how I would deal with the fact that I might no longer have a voice. *It's dark, I'm inside. That's about all I can tell.*

"Your body is still with me," she said. *"Focus on Edrik. You need to find him."* The urgency in her voice sharpened my thoughts, and I refocused, summoning Edrik's face into my mind as if I could will him into existence.

A noise clattered behind me and I whirled around. I tried to keep my physical body still, but my movement sent more ripples out, distorting the world, until I couldn't see anything but gray shadows.

Magic pulsed on my forehead, the gem trying to tell me something. I took a deep breath to settle my nerves and relax my mind and body, allowing the magic more control. The vision around me sharpened. In my mind, I looked around but kept my physical form still.

The unsettling sensation washed over me, like I'd fallen into a dream but with more awareness. Only when I concentrated on my surroundings would they come into focus, while the edges remained blurry and unformed. It was too dark to make out much, but I pushed myself forward without moving my real body.

Solid walls pressed in around me, more of a sixth sense than what I could actually make out. A damp earthiness clogged my nose as a slight metallic taste coated my tongue. Not the taste of blood. *Rust?*

A soft scuffling made me pause, and I tilted my head, trying to pinpoint the direction it'd come from.

Where are you, Edrik?

My stomach lurched forward as if there was a rope tied around it and the surroundings shifted. Weak light filtered in, but when I looked up there was only darkness.

Frantic footsteps echoed and scraped over the concrete floor and I spun to face the sound. My heart bounced off my ribs with a fear that was not my own. The need to escape, to get away, seeped into my skin and it took every ounce of restraint to push away the thoughts that were not mine.

Reassurance pulsed through my bond with Danika and I steadied myself; it was all in my head.

A figure shot out from the shadows, scrambling on their hands and knees. Their frantic pants were too loud. They shot a desperate look behind them and whimpered as I pushed myself forward.

"Edrik?" I called out, but I'd no voice here. Their face turned towards me. Grime coated his skin, a pair of wide terrified eyes scanned the area, but it was Edrik.

The shadows shifted and coalesced behind him as another whimper spilled from his lips. Edrik whipped around as the shadows formed a body and reached for him.

He fell backwards, scrambling away as a shadowed arm lunged towards him. "No, no, no." Edrik's fear snaked around me and squeezed.

I pushed myself closer as if I could shield him, but the moment my awareness touched him I was tumbling, falling into never-ending darkness.

A scream cut through the air, and my mind jerked to a stop. I hissed in a breath as my head spun, but the world appeared more real. Solid.

Concrete walls surrounded me, plain and blocky, unfinished. That wet, earthy scent assaulted me again as I pushed myself in the direction the scream had come from. Working my way through the endless maze of blank corridors and rooms, I slowed at the sounds of murmured voices.

I inched closer to the doorway, peering in to see several figures all clad in black, as if the very shadows wrapped around them.

My breath hitched as I saw Edrik—he looked unharmed, but bound to a chair. His eyes were shut, and his face contorted in that same frightened expression I'd seen earlier. One figure had their fingers pressed against his temples while another was bending over and whispering in his ear.

What were they doing to him? I drifted closer without even realizing, as if something within me was connected to Edrik and was pulling me in. But how could I do anything to help him? I didn't even know where "here" was.

I tried to resist the tug, fight against it, as I realized it was going to pull me into the figures surrounding him, but nothing I did slowed my progress.

I flinched as it pulled me right into one of the people blocking my path, their features hidden by black clothes and a hood pulled over their head. My breath caught, and an unsettling sensation washed over me as I passed through their body. The figure shuddered and shifted away, but said nothing.

Blood splattered Edrik's waxy skin, a small trickle from his hairline, but nothing life-threatening. His fingernails dug into the arms of the chair, his body taut, but I could sense his energy was waning.

"Edrik," I said, my words muffled. "What do they want from you?" I hovered inches away from his face, the tug relenting. Beneath his eyelids, his eyes darted frantically, and his jaw was clamped shut. "Who are these people that have you?" No matter how hard I tried, my head refused to turn to look at the figures who held him. But with their faces covered, I doubted I would glean much anyway. "Where are you?" My voice was a pleading whisper.

I lifted a hand that didn't exist in this form and reached, pressing my awareness out to Edrik. Energy jolted through me and I was tumbling.

Images flashed around me and I squeezed my eyes shut, not that it did anything to stop the images within my own mind. I pushed out with my magic, as if I could grip the world around me to keep it from moving, and the images slowed enough to not be a blur. They flickered in my mind too fast to take in the details.

A magical tome. Then a dark room. A figure entering his shop. The opal. A construction site at night.

The images began to slow. No, not images, memories. Like they were flicking through a photo album.

It changed again, and I recognized it as Edrik's back room. There was no sound, but he stared at a woman with bright hair, her features blurred. But a smudge of blue in her lap caught my eye. Realization jolted through me. That was me and Danika.

The memory shook and faded, replaced by the glowing artifact. Shrouded in darkness, a silver light pulsed within it.

A force shoved me out of Edrik's mind and back into the dark room. The figure behind him jerked their head up, the mask covering their face hovering a breath away from mine. I flinched, falling backwards as their voice cut through my mind. "Who are you?" they demanded.

I stumbled back, my legs tangling, and I landed hard, the pain jarring me back into my body.

"You are safe." Danika's voice grounded me as she pressed her body against me. My fingers sunk into her fur as I wrapped my arms around her until my heart calmed and my breathing evened out.

"Did—" My voice cracked, terror that was not mine still gripped my throat.

"Yes," she said. *"I've no idea what that was. That wasn't a normal vision."*

"No," I croaked. "Some was reality, the rest was like a living nightmare only it wasn't mine."

"A nightbane." The fur on Danika's back shivered. *"I've only ever heard of it in a few terrible stories that I thought were only myths. They claimed it could trap a mind and induce great terror."*

"There are some poisons that have similar qualities." I hunted through my memories, anything to forget what I'd just seen. "They can invoke hallucinations and paranoia, but why would they do that to Edrik?"

"They want something from him. I'm sorry you had to go through that, but I recognize the building."

"Well, at least we have a lead." I scrubbed a hand over my face and huffed a humorless laugh. "We should head out before the trail goes cold."

"Indra and Rynac should be off duty in a few hours—"

"No," I said, too sharply, as something cracked in my chest. "I don't want to waste any time. We are going." My words were a command. Danika dipped her head, and I hated myself for that, but I had to keep the others safe.

Her gaze burned into me as I gathered up my belongings. Removing the circlet, I wrapped it up and tucked it away. What did I say to Danika? How could I even begin to explain?

"We are just going to look. If we see anything of note, we can call them. This is their first shift back. They are going to be exhausted, and I don't want to drag them out there for nothing."

Tell her the truth, a voice urged, and I bit down hard on my cheek.

"The last time they were involved—" my voice wobbled, and I swallowed hard. "—they were used against me. It almost cost them their lives. I can't—I couldn't—" My breath caught in my chest.

"Okay," she said, soft and soothing. *"Just you and me tonight."*

"Thank you." I rushed to get everything cleared away.

The sooner we left, the better. I locked the door and we raced down the stairs. I pushed my legs faster, as if I could outrace my own thoughts. Out race my feelings.

I rubbed my palm into my chest where that ache still lingered. The very thought of dragging Indra and Rynac into danger once again was like a knife in my heart. This was the only way to protect them.

The consequences of my actions would fall solely on me.

Chapter Seventeen

My bag bounced against my hip as Danika and I jogged through the near empty streets. Although Arkirith had a sizable nocturnal population, this area wasn't one of their hot spots.

What had once been an older, more rundown area, was now being transformed as the population expanded. Nearly a million inhabitants lived within the city, and that wasn't including any of the magical creatures or the beings who didn't take part in the census.

Just thinking about that sheer number of people around me made me shudder. Arkirith never seemed overwhelming or crowded, but considering the city I grew up in had only a quarter of this population, it sounded too large for one place.

The shadows deepened as we ran closer to our target, and my gaze flickered from one to the next, unable to shake that unsettling sensation of being watched.

Too many memories from when demonspawn stalked the streets emerged in my mind, escaping the box I'd locked them in.

The current street was a smattering of rundown office buildings, many barely standing upright, while others were in various stages of demolition. Others were deep holes in the ground, next to new buildings that had begun construction.

My grip tightened on my conduit as I scanned the darkness. I flexed my left hand, all to aware that the surface of my skin was bare.

How much magic would I be able to use without containing my solar energies? I'd told myself I was just going to scout, that I didn't need the runed band, but . . .

"*What do you think the rest of the vision was?*" Danika asked. I clamped down hard on my emotions, wondering if she'd sensed my unease and was trying to distract me.

They were his memories, I thought to Danika, panting too hard to be able to talk. *As if someone was flipping through a book of his memories and hunting for something. One was us.*

"*Yes, I recognized that too. But it seemed like he was trying very hard not to think about it. Though he could just be trying to keep his clientele anonymous.*"

I think it's more than that. My stomach churned knowing the truth. *The last object was the same one I saw in my vision at the full moon ceremony.*

Only the sounds of our footfall filled the silence. When Danika spoke again, it wasn't what I expected her to say. "*Then we are on the right path. All of this is connected; we just need to find a way to unravel it. If that item is important and might fall into the wrong hands, then we must follow the guidance offered and act as Selene's chosen.*"

Do you really think that? It was impossible not to doubt that I wasn't just making this all up in my head, that my desire to be part of something larger was making me create connections that were not there.

"*Why else would Selene intervene and grant you a vision?*" Her words were so matter-of-fact, as if there was no way to dispute it. I thought I'd just been holding onto the foolish hope that the visions granted to me meant I was important. That I could make a difference.

We slowed, cutting through a narrow accessway between two large buildings that gave me the creeps, and paused in the shadows across from the building site.

Is this the right one? They all looked the same to me, and there was nothing here to show that anyone was around. All the streets were empty, no vehicles or people—it was unsettling how quiet it was. Even the distant sounds of the busier parts of the city felt muted. Detached.

"Which is what makes this the perfect location. The few others that come to mind have night construction crews—this one hasn't had workers for weeks."

We watched the site for a while, each minute dragging by, but nothing changed. The entire area felt abandoned.

"We should take a closer look."

I nodded stiffly as dread crept down my back. Icy fingers scraped over my skin before sinking deep into my bones.

My mind screamed to just turn and run. That I wasn't strong enough, good enough, but I shoved it away. I had every potion I could carry, my shield, the circlet, and Danika. What more did I need? I'd been through worse with far less.

"Nyssa?" Danika's concerned voice broke through my thoughts. *"We don't have to—"*

"Let's go," I hissed aloud, as if saying it would give me back the courage that had abandoned me. This was my duty. I'd awoken the artifact they were after. Selene had granted me the vision. So it was my responsibility to carry this out.

Danika gave me one last look before padding forward, keeping close to the shadows clinging to the walls.

Releasing the tight hold on my magic, I let it unspool around me. It seeped into the ground and into the air around me, becoming an extension of myself.

Not that I could send it out far, but even this small amount might alert anyone paying attention. Though that was preferable to going in blind.

Memories scratched at my mind, of demonic runes scrawled over the walls, traps hidden in the darkness just waiting to ensnare their prey. I'd always been cautious, but the harsh reality of the dark side of magic users was one I wouldn't forget.

These people had kidnapped Edrik and might be linked to all the killings; there was no knowing what they were capable of.

I swallowed hard as I followed Danika through a gap in the chain-link fence, just wide enough for me to crawl under on my stomach. I'd wanted to come alone, to prove that I could do this by myself and to keep the others far from danger, but doubt gnawed away at me.

No, I could do this. I'd taken on a pack of thralls, fought demon-spawn, and faced down Carmen and her horde.

My fingers dug into the dirt as I crawled over to hide behind a pile of boxes, long forgotten by the construction crew. I needed to do this alone. How else could I prove that there was nothing for the others to worry about, and that I was absolutely fine?

Selene had given these visions to me, and it was my duty to follow her guidance, no one else's. This was my chance to prove to the Goddess that I was worthy of her blessing.

I nodded to Danika, and she slipped between the shadows, weaving her way closer to the building. Too bad I was far bigger and far less agile on all fours.

Acknowledgement pressed against my mind as Danika signaled the all clear. Over the months we'd been training to strengthen our bond, learning to communicate without words, both mentally and with visual cues.

Keeping my movements smooth and measured, I crept my way over to the first shadow large enough to hide me. This would've been far easier if it hadn't been a gibbous moon overhead—the moonlight was usually my ally, but not tonight.

If there was a way to use my magic to persuade the moonlight to conceal me, it wasn't a spell I'd found within the shifters' tomes. I'd have to ask them next time; it hadn't occurred to me that I might need such a spell. No, I'd never considered the shadows anything but darkness that could conceal a lurking threat.

Unbidden memories resurfaced of the dark night at the sports field, how the area had been empty until Carmen's massive horde of demonspawn poured from every slip of darkness until they surrounded me. The reek of sulfur assaulted my nose. I shuddered at the sound of their talons scraping across the ground.

My foot caught, my ankle rolling. Fear spiked through me as my arms flew out to brace myself. Something gripped my ankle. I whipped around, wide eyes darting around, hunting for what had grabbed me. But only moonlight and shadows haunted the area.

"Nyssa?" Danika's concern wrapped around me, enough to ease my frantic thoughts. By my feet lay a hunk of concrete that I must've tripped on.

Slipped on something, I replied, then scolded myself, *Not the time, Nyssa.*

Over the last few months, control over my thoughts seemed to have waned. How many times had I found them going in a direction I didn't want them to? Dredging up memories that I didn't want to remember? But it had been worse of late, after whatever the hells that had been at the explosion site.

It's all in your head, I told myself firmly as I started moving again. Why wouldn't my brain just let me forget all of those things? What good did it do me to think about terrible things in the past that I'd no control over?

I doubted anyone from the Lunar Order would've had their own memories turned against them. No, they were stronger than that. They put their lives on the line every day, faced demonspawn and other terrible creatures and never balked.

And you'll never be one of them, a voice hissed in my head. The words struck like a knife in my gut.

After what felt like an eternity, I reached Danika's spot against the solid external wall of the building. Cold from the bare concrete seeped through my back where I pressed against it, stealing the warmth from the balmy summer night.

Her ears twitched, keen eyes scanning the area ahead, and I inched forward to peer around the corner. The vacant doorways and windows revealed nothing of the interior, only filled with a yawning black void that seemed to swallow the light. I glanced at Danika, her presence a small comfort in the oppressive darkness.

She turned her head in a signal to follow. My heart pounded in my chest as I trailed after her, stepping cautiously around the corner.

The shadows cast by the skeletal structure loomed over us until they blocked out the moonlight, and I tried not to shudder, but I already missed its soothing touch. The deeper into the shadows I moved, the more a growing chill enveloped my body, constricting my heart with fear.

I wanted nothing more than to retreat back to the safety of the moonlight, but I forced myself to keep moving forward. We paused by a doorway that led inside, but the inky darkness revealed nothing of what lay beyond.

Do you see anything? I asked as my hand dropped to the potions on my belt until I found the one that would enhance my night vision. It would only last about fifteen minutes, so I didn't want to waste any time.

"The shadows lie heavy on this area."

I reached out with my awareness until it brushed over the darkness. A faint prickling sensation ran over the back of my neck. *Magical?*

Danika hummed in my head. *"I can't tell if it's active or just the lingering remnants of magic. Do you want to wait until morning?"*

Let's keep going. It appears empty, so if they left, then their trail might already be fading.

I uncorked the potion and downed the contents, the sharp flavor of starlit frost tingling over my tongue and down my throat. I blinked as my vision adjusted—that taste was new. Was the potion going bad? I hadn't needed any of my potions of late, but I didn't remember it tasting like that last time.

Danika padded inside, leaving me no option but to follow after her unless I wanted to lose her in the darkness. The air inside was cooler, damp with the scent of concrete and something metallic. The familiar scent was unsettling. This was the right place, or did all construction sites smell like this?

No sign of light or life was evident. Relief and disappointment warred against each other, relief that the enemy had gone, but disappointment that I'd lost the only lead to find Edrik.

If the enemy had been here, what would I have done? I wasn't a fighter. I'd a few potions that might subdue them if I was lucky, but my abilities weren't enough to take on those four beings I'd seen in the vision.

The darkness was almost complete, broken only by the faintest slivers of moonlight filtering through the gaps in the wall. Each slow step felt heavier than the last, as if the darkness itself was trying to hold me back.

I kept my gaze fixed on the outline of Danika as we slipped down a hallway, allowing her sharp instincts to guide us through the maze of concrete and shadows.

To ground myself, I trailed my fingers over the wall. My eyes flicked down, shadowy tendrils were curling over my feet. I froze.

My magic hadn't sensed anything and yet I could see it. Living shadows. What other unseen horrors lurked beyond the wall of darkness?

Danika nudged my leg, bringing me back out of wherever my mind had been spiraling. The shadows that'd covered my feet were gone. Only the regular darkness remained.

I took a deep breath, reassuring myself that as soon as we knew the area was empty, I could cast as many orbs of light as it took to banish the darkness.

We moved deeper into the building, each light step still echoing in the cavernous emptiness. Thin slivers of moonlight pierced through the unfinished floors above, offering small areas of sanctuary, though without my potion they wouldn't be visible.

I needed to find that larger room I'd seen in the vision where they'd held Edrik. A growing sense of dread pooled in my chest, threatening to overwhelm me.

Something within me tugged to the left, and I squinted. I caught sight of a doorway hidden in the darkness.

There, I whispered, fearing my thought might echo in the absolute silence.

Danika didn't hesitate as she set off towards it, her quiet determination keeping me moving forward. A surge of hope mingled with the fear as we approached. When I stepped inside, a chill ran down my spine. This was the place. This was where they'd held Edrik, where I'd seen those people holding him. Knew it deep in my bones.

The air felt thicker here, charged with an unseen energy. Danika's fur bristled, and she let out a low growl. We weren't alone. Something, or someone, was here.

Without a second thought, I pushed energy into my palm; in the blink of an eye, I'd molded it into an orb of light and tossed it into the air. My fingertips brushed over my potion belt, ready to pull them out in a heartbeat.

I braced myself as the soft moonlight of my orb washed over the room. But under the silvery-blue light it was as empty as the rest of this place, just a lone chair lying toppled on its side.

Movement out of the corner of my eye snapped up my attention as a shadow shifted unnaturally.

"Your fears are so thick they coat the air, I can practically smell them." The voice coiled through the silence, echoing off the empty concrete, making it impossible to pinpoint its source.

Magic crawled over my skin, making me shudder. I spun around, but couldn't trace its source. Fire flickered in my chest, unbidden it flared and slithered through my veins.

My breath caught, fearing I was about to lose control, but instead, the whispers of shadow pooling over my skin evaporated like the morning sun burning off the fog.

Do you sense them? I pushed the thought to Danika, hoping to hide the magic of our connection.

"No." The desperation in that single word wrapped around my throat. My mind hissed to run, but the burning need to protect my bonded steeled my heart.

"Where is Edrik?" I demanded as I gathered more magic into my hands, ready to cast a shield in the blink of an eye. But I didn't want to show my hand too soon.

My solar magic flickered in my core, but to help or hinder? The back of my left hand throbbed, phantom pains jolting through my scar.

More shadows seemed to shift, my eyes darting from one to the other. How many of them were there? How did they hide in the shadows when I only felt a trickle of magic? My gaze landed on one to the left, larger than the others, but it shifted less. Some instinct within me whispering that it was that one. That they hid there.

"For someone with so much fear pulsing through them—" the voice called again as if I hadn't spoken; was it coming from the right or were the echoes playing tricks on me? "—you resist their pull admirably."

I spun the other way, convinced it came from behind. *Danika?* I asked, swallowing hard as I scanned the way we'd come. What had I missed?

"You brought me a present," the voice said, and I could hear the wide, sinister smile on their lips.

I almost stepped forward, every fiber of my body telling me it was coming from that direction. My energies swirled within my chest and I called to them, finding that flickering spark within me as I cast it out, a beam of moonlight shining down on us.

And then I sensed it. The presence directly behind me, the brush of their breath on the back of my neck. I whirled around.

A figure of darkness loomed before me. My moonbeam brightened, revealing one of the people I'd seen in the vision, their face covered by a mask, and a hood thrown over their head. But it was the sight of the circlet still wrapped in the cloth in their grasp that jolted me into action.

I lunged as the figure jerked backwards, but my hands snaked out and grabbed the exposed circlet. The metal was far colder than any other time I'd touched it. My solar magic flared against my palm as the metal turned to an icy bite.

The figure reached for me, their shadow-shrouded hand shooting for my face.

I darted to the side, yanking the circlet out of their grip. The cloth fluttered to the floor, the circlet shimmering in the moonlight like a beacon.

The figure's head snapped to the circlet and the shadows thickened. I pushed more magic into my moonbeam and the shadows flinched away, but my energies wavered—I couldn't keep this up.

Danika yelped. My focus broke, and they lunged. Their hand wrapped around the circlet and a jolt of energy surged through me.

Power built in the air, pressing down around me; in vain, I tried to summon a shield, but I was dragged into an abyss of darkness.

Chapter Eighteen

The air thickened with an oppressive magic, heavy and suffocating. I stumbled forward in the utter darkness, heart pounding, as a pulse of dread washed over me.

"Danika?" I yelled, but my voice came out so muffled that I barely heard it.

Weak moonlight filtered through the thick clouds overhead and I could just make out the brick walls on either side of me. A narrow alley littered with debris and broken crates.

The stench of rot permeated the air, and murky puddles reflected the faint light from above. Shadows clung to every corner, and my eyes darted to each one, my heart racing as if I'd been running.

Rusted fire escapes zigzagged up the walls, out of reach. The distant drip of water echoed in the narrow space, amplifying the sense of dread that pressed in.

A faint light glowed at one end of the alley, the other nothing but darkness. But when I took a step towards the light, a shadow detached, moving with a fluid, predatory grace.

Demonspawn.

It stood hunched, its sinewy body covered in mottled, leathery skin that glistened in the moonlight. Its elongated limbs ended in razor-sharp claws, each one clicking against the ground in a rhythmic threat.

Glowing red eyes pierced the darkness, fixating on me with a hunger that sent shivers down my spine. Its mouth, filled with rows of jagged, yellowed teeth, twisted into a grotesque grin as it advanced. The creature's breath came out in hissing gasps, releasing the foul stench of decay that surrounded it like a shroud.

A jolt of fear pierced my chest. I spun on my heels and ran. The alley seemed to stretch endlessly. No matter how hard I ran, I never made it any closer to the end.

Behind me, the guttural growls of the demonspawn grew louder, closer. My breath came in quick, panicked gasps that burned my lungs.

The uneven ground beneath my feet threatened to trip me with every step, but I forced myself to keep going. My pulse echoed in my ears, drowning out everything but the demonspawn behind me.

"Keep running," I urged myself, the terror giving me fleeting bursts of speed.

I darted around broken crates and leaped over puddles, every muscle straining with the effort. The sound of the demonspawn's claws scraping against the ground grew louder, closer, urging me faster, despite the growing fatigue and fear threatening to consume me.

I glanced back once; its eyes glowed with malevolent intent as it closed in, spurring me to push harder, but as my head whipped back a stack of crates blocked the way.

Unable to stop, I crashed into them, pain blooming in my arm and shoulder that took the brunt as I crashed to the ground. Scrambling to my feet, I reached for my potions, but my fingers grasped at empty space. Panic flared in my chest. They were gone.

Reaching deep within me, I called to my magic, but there was only silence. The demonspawn lunged. I flinched, waiting for the pain when hot liquid splattered on my face, burning my skin.

I blinked. The demonspawn lay dead at my feet, an arrow protruding from its eye.

"Really, Nyssa?" A voice sliced through the darkness, dripping with mockery. My gaze snapped upward, heart lurching, and I saw Astrid standing on the roof above me, bow in hand. Moonlight cast shadows over her face, but I couldn't mistake her. My breath caught. She'd come back.

"Astrid?" I choked out as I stared, fearing she would disappear if I looked away. Relief surged through me, a desperate jumble of emotions, but it evaporated the second I noticed the disdain curling her lips.

"You can't even handle a single demonspawn without your precious potions?" she sneered, each word a knife to my chest.

Before I'd a chance to reply, movement flickered on the roof across from her. Kaelan stepped forward, his expression a mix of disappointment and contempt. "I thought you were stronger than this," he said, voice low and cold. "But you can't even kill one without help?"

I wanted to call out to them, to demand an explanation, but my throat closed up. A hollow ache settled in my chest.

Nathaniel appeared, leaning against Astrid. His usual smirk twisted into something cruel. "Pathetic. We thought you were one of us, but you're just a scared little witch."

The ground swayed under my feet, my world unmooring. A harsh, guttural growl broke through the haze, and my head snapped to the demonspawn.

It crouched low, claws digging furrows into the earth as it crept closer, eyes fixed on me with a hungry, predatory gleam.

"Please, help me," I whispered, my voice cracking with desperation, but they only laughed.

Kaelan's eyes, once so familiar, were distant as he shook his head. "We need someone who we can trust to have our back. You would only be a liability."

"You're a burden, Nyssa," Astrid said, staring down her nose at me. "I don't know why I wasted so much time helping you."

Nathaniel's smirk grew sharper, his eyes glinting with cruel amusement. "Face it, you're useless. All you can do is brew potions and cast a shield. After all these months, we thought you'd be able to do more." He shrugged, already turning away. "I guess we made the right choice to leave you behind."

My chest tightened, breath hitching as the truth of their rejection slammed into me. More demonspawn emerged from the shadows, slowly stalking towards me. Their snarls echoing in the silence as the nephilim disappeared from sight.

I opened my mouth to call out, but I couldn't make a sound. Tears blurred my vision as the demonspawn closed in.

Desperation clawed at my chest. I had to fight back, had to prove them wrong. But my limbs felt heavy, my strength sapped by their abandonment.

With a final, desperate cry, I lashed out at the nearest demonspawn, my boot connecting with its jaw. It didn't even flinch, just bared its fangs, and I knew I was finished.

As the demonspawn lunged, I closed my eyes, bracing for the end.

The moment stretched, and when I dared to look, there was only darkness and my familiar.

"I've searched my whole life for my bonded," Danika said, an aching sadness in her gaze, *"and this is how you treat me? I tried to be everything for you, but you won't even trust me."*

My heart ached, the weight of her disappointment pressing down on me. "I'm sorry," I whispered. Guilt needled me. I knew it was selfish, but I reached for our bond and pushed more magic into it.

Understanding vibrated back through the connection and I latched onto it, clinging to it as if I was drowning in an endless ocean and it was a lifeline.

"I don't want you to see how scared I am. You didn't ask for any of this. I . . . I don't want you to leave me, but you deserve a better witch."

"I could never, nor would ever, leave you, Nyssa." Her voice sounded more distant, as if we were talking underwater.

"You don't deserve to bear my burden."

"I've seen deep into your soul. I've seen the witch who devotes herself to her friends, to her work. The witch who treats everyone as equals, who fights for those she cares for. I've seen the witch who was ready to sacrifice herself to protect innocent lives, even though she was terrified. I'll always be by your side."

"Even though I'm terrified Carmen will come for me, that she will hurt all of you to get to me? Even though I'm not strong enough to protect all of you? I don't want to fail you again." My own words pounded in my head.

A small spark flickered in my chest. I'd failed my friends once, but I wouldn't fail them a second time. I gritted my teeth and pushed to my feet. Danika was out there somewhere, while I remained trapped here.

Nightbane. The word echoed through me. It had to be. Danika's fear seeped into our bond, but I also sensed her determination. A heavy weight wrapped around my limbs, but I forced one foot forward and then the other.

The darkness shifted, and I found myself deep in a jungle. The harsh tang of blood lay thick on my tongue as I pushed through the tangle of vines and leaves.

Blood and gore turned the green forest a sickly red, and my stomach revolted. Chaos and destruction enveloped the area where a group of black-clad fighters fought against a horde of demonspawn. But there were other demonic creatures, far more intelligent and powerful in their ranks.

Where was I? There was nothing to identify who the fighters were, but a warning flared in my chest not to trust them.

"We can't hold them off forever!" someone shouted over the din. Screams filled the air as one of the large demons speared a fighter through the chest with an obsidian sword.

Shadows seethed around another figure who launched themselves at the demon, shadows that were far too familiar. Despair that was not my own weighed down my limbs and I tried to push it away.

The circlet. I pushed out with my awareness, but every surface was coated in magic. The circlet was doing this. Just like it had shown me the visions, now it was doing this. But why?

Pain stabbed into my head and I fell to my knees; the world around me fractured.

"Why do you allow yourself to be so weak?" The voice slithered around me, chilling me to my core.

No. The word just a whimper in my mind as Carmen stepped closer. Red and gold blood dripped from her clawed hands as she crouched before me. Resting her chin on one hand, she looked down at me like a teacher at a young child who wouldn't learn their lesson.

Carmen shook her head. "I guess I was wrong about you. You don't have the strength to do what needs to be done, don't have the strength to claim the power that should be yours. The spark of greatness is wasted on you. Soon everyone will see it and they will turn their backs on you."

"I'm not weak," I snarled back. Carmen's lips quirked in amusement.

"Is that why you can't even admit to your friends how terrified you are of shadows? Why you hide the truth from your familiar that you're still just a scared and broken little witch? You don't deserve your magic."

The dark witch loomed, her cold laughter piercing through me. I sensed the pull of her magic, my own power twisting and slipping away.

Panic rose as I tried to resist, every fiber of my being fighting against her control. My limbs grew heavy, my will sapped, until I was nothing more than a puppet in her hands.

"You don't deserve this power." Her voice burrowed under my skin and turned my bones to ice. "You couldn't even use it to save those you cared for. The same friends you put in harm's way. One by one, they will fall."

The darkness, a living, tangible thing, writhed around me, then drew back. Dark splotches pooled on the ground. My gut twisted, my mind refusing to name it. But I knew. Deep down, I knew.

The shadows slinked back like the receding tide and a hand emerged, then an arm.

No, no, no. I opened my mouth, but no sound came out. I could only scream inside my head for it to stop.

Rynac's skin was pale, splattered with blood. His sightless blue eyes stared at me. And then Indra. Their hands still clutched each other, their bodies too still.

More bodies appeared; every way my head turned, more dead lay scattered around me. Zola. Voren. Beylin. Ruby. Jade. The shadows wouldn't stop pulling back, more and more.

My fault.

The deep crimson pools that surrounded them trickled towards me, like tendrils of blood that reached for me. My nails dug into the solid ground as if I could escape from the bindings around my arms. I thrashed as the blood spilled closer.

I flinched as the cold liquid touched my fingers, pooled under my hands, coagulated and thick. Panic rose in my throat, knowing that this blood would drown me. I squeezed my eyes shut, scrambling for my magic. I had to get away.

"You think you can escape?" Carmen's voice taunted from the darkness. "Only sheer luck and desperation allowed you to walk away with your life last time. But that won't save you again. No one will come to save you. You've driven them all away. Just accept your fate, Nyssa. Let me drain your magic. You were never worthy of it. How could someone who failed everyone she cared for be worthy? How could someone who failed two goddesses be worthy?"

Desperation clawed at my throat. I wanted to scream, to break free, but my strength was gone.

Each one of her words rang true, each one another weight around my neck that pulled me deeper down. Bit by bit, my magic drained away.

The silence was deafening, the loneliness crushing. Faces of my friends flickered in and out, their expressions unreadable. The visions all swirled around me, an unending loop of terror.

My breath came in ragged gasps, my mind teetering on the edge. I wanted to wake up, to escape this nightbane, but the magic held me fast. I wasn't strong enough.

Ice stung my palm, and I jerked my hand back. My head ached as the room spun, a blur of darkness and shadows.

"Nyssa!" Danika's desperate cry cut through the haze as she bounded towards me.

I lay on the ground, back in that room. Was this reality? The figure across from me shoved to their feet. My gaze snagged on the glint of a gem in the weak moonlight.

The circlet, gripped by the figure. I struggled to my knees, reaching for it, but I flinched away as slivers of my nightbane flickered through my mind. *Not worthy*, it seemed to say.

The figure caressed the circlet. "Thank you for this prize." Their voice plain now it had no echo of magic. Danika growled as she took up a defensive position before me. Fighting off the lingering cobwebs of those visions, I swayed to my feet. "It found you wanting, but now it has a worthy master. But that doesn't mean I'll let you live."

Before I could even fumble for a potion, the figure pulled a gun from the shadows and trained it on me.

I froze, mind going blank, not even a whisper of magic stirring as they squeezed the trigger. A sharp crack split the air as something heavy barreled into me, slamming me to the ground.

Agony ripped through my arm as a bright flash seared my eyes. The skin on my chest burned white-hot.

Feet scuffled, another gunshot cut through the air, followed by a grunt, then a heavy thud as the now two figures slammed to the ground.

But it was the sight of the black wings on the new arrival that felt like a gut punch.

CHAPTER NINETEEN

Magic crackled across Danika's fur, throwing long blue shadows across the room. Nausea roiled through me and the pounding in my head grew, but it was the ice-cold realization that froze me in place.

Nephilim.

Wide-eyed, I could only stare as the two fought each other. The gun skittered across the floor as shadows twisted closer, winding their way towards those fighting. I flinched back as one snaked past me.

He was here.

Real.

"We need to run," Danika hissed, head butting into me as if she could hoist me to my feet. The gun fired again. *"Nyssa, run!"* Danika's voice was a sharp command in my mind, enough to snap me out of the paralysis, but my body was sluggish as I pushed myself upright.

Carmen's laugh echoed around me as I spun away, chasing after the weak glow of Danika. *Not real. Not real!* I chanted to myself, praying it was true.

The oppressive magic grew thicker, suffocating, as I fought my way through it. The darkness pressed in around me, twisted faces emerging from the walls, clawed arms swiping at my legs.

"Weak. Pathetic. Useless." The taunting words from the nephilim hit me like physical blows as memories from that nightmarish vision seeped into the world around me. I reached for the power that thrummed in my core, but it was silent. Empty.

I lifted my hand, desperately willing an orb of light to form, to cast away all these shadows. To banish all the lies. My magic sputtered, scorching my hand.

Footsteps pounded behind me, but I didn't dare to see who it was. My heart lodged in my throat, and on instinct, my fingers dropped to my potions.

Pulling one free, I sent a warning to Danika a moment before hurling it against the ground and I squeezed my eyes shut. Bright light flared and something hissed in pain.

I blinked away the afterimages as we spilled out of the cursed building, my legs churning up the ground as I followed Danika.

She veered off to the right to a larger gap in the fence and I slowed only enough to half crawl, half slide through it. My wounded arm protested as I clawed my way through, the sharp metal gouging into my back.

Shoving back up onto my feet, I tore across the road as if I could outrun all those whispered words. Adrenaline and fear swirled through me, pushing the pain down and urging my legs to run faster.

We stumbled out the end of the alley and into an overgrown garden, the wild bushes large enough to hide us from sight. My legs gave out beneath me, the night air swirled around us, and the shudder that wracked my body had nothing to do with its cool touch.

Darkness threatened to pull me under again as the voices swelled, and I closed my eyes, trying to will it away. I sensed someone else, far too tangible to be another nightbane, his feet making deliberate noise to signal his approach.

And I hated that. Loathed it. Prayed that it was another nightbane so that I didn't have to face the truth, that I didn't have to deal with the jumble of emotions knotting inside me.

But the weight that'd been pressing down on me, threatening to crush me, lifted until I could take a deep breath, and I hated that all the more.

My gaze fixed on my fingers as they clawed into the soil, as if that act could ground me in reality. I refused to look up, knowing what I would see. Who I would see.

The inky black wings, the bright green eyes that seemed to glow with magical light, a face I wished I'd been able to forget. A voice I never wanted to hear again. I knew it deep in my bones, had known it the moment I'd seen his wings, felt it as the skin on my chest burned with power.

"Are you hurt?" His voice was soft, haunting, and I squeezed my eyes closed for a moment. He crouched down when I remained silent, and I flinched back when he reached out. In the blink of an eye, Danika took up a defensive position in front of me. "You are not safe here. We need to move."

Too many thoughts battered through my head, too many words danced on the tip of my tongue. Worst of all was that tiny spark of hope I hadn't been able to quash, that now flickered brighter, because he was *here*.

I glared up with all the hurt that'd festered within me over the last few months. Feelings that I'd tried so hard to deny. At being abandoned. Forgotten. Unworthy. Crafting my anger into a shield to protect me from the truth.

"Why are you here?" I demanded.

Kaelan didn't even have the decency to flinch. The weak moonlight that filtered through the trees overhead cast his features into sharp relief, his green eyes duller than I remembered.

"To protect you. You were in danger," Kaelan finally said, as if that was answer enough.

"And so I'm ignored for months because I wasn't in danger?" Somewhere in the back of my mind, I knew this wasn't the time. The sharp tang of fear still coated my tongue and my hands shook, no matter how hard I squeezed them into fists.

His head snapped up, though there was nothing but more trees. "The enemy is regrouping."

"We need to move," Danika said, her concern cutting through the maelstrom in my head. I forced myself to my feet, my body trembling with a mix of exhaustion and rage.

"I know somewhere nearby that is safe," Kaelan said, body half turned away as if he were talking to the plants and not me. He started off without waiting for an answer. Stubbornness kept my feet rooted to the spot.

Danika took a few steps after him, but paused when I didn't move. She urged me forward, tugging on our bond.

A twig snapped somewhere behind me and all the memories of the visions I'd just seen crept into my mind. My heart raced as I glanced back into the shadows, the fear clawing at my resolve.

My anger still burned, but the terror was stronger. I pushed myself into an uneven jog, hoping that for now, it was enough to survive. I would get my answer, even if it meant suffering his presence for a while longer.

Kaelan moved swiftly, his silhouette cutting through the darkness with familiarity. Ice pierced my chest—how would he know this area unless he'd been here? Kaelan had been in Arkirith and never once tried to contact me.

Danika stayed close by my side, her small form a comforting glow in the oppressive night. We twisted and turned through the labyrinth of streets, the sounds of distant activity breaking the silence as we headed closer to more populated areas. Still too far from my home—my legs wobbled at just the thought of carrying me that distance.

After what felt like an eternity, Kaelan led us into a personal storage facility. As the heavy metal door slammed shut behind me, I flinched.

The dim lights cast long shadows across rows of cold, unmarked metal units stretching down each aisle. A metallic tang filled the stale air, our steps echoing on the concrete floor. I was over creepy buildings today.

The shadows lay heavy on this area and I slowed, ready to refuse stepping into the darkness. Kaelan paused, glancing up and down the aisle, before opening a roller door that only made the slightest noise. Darkness shrouded the interior, and I hesitated, dread seeping into my bones.

Danika went first, her soft glow lighting up the tight area. Having no other choice, I followed her. I glanced around just a few steps inside—though all I could see were stacks of boxes. Something struck me as odd.

The door rumbled shut, cutting off the little bit of extra light and I couldn't help but flinch again. My eyes darted to the shadows lingering in the corners. Then, as if she sensed my thoughts, Danika grew brighter, banishing the deepest shadows.

The unit was small, filled with an assortment of boxes as well as other items I'd expect in storage: skis, two mountain bikes, various camping supplies. A sleeping bag was unrolled in one corner, with a small lantern, a first-aid kit, water bottles and ready-to-eat meal packets.

A safe house. But this couldn't be Kaelan's storage unit. He'd told me he lived in Orillian, or at least the Order was based there. No, this looked more like he'd gathered supplies from what was available in this facility. The perfect place for someone being hunted as a murderer to hide.

"You can rest here," Kaelan said, not moving from his position at the door.

Then again, there wasn't any room with the three of us, and I wondered if he ever found it cramped in here, unable to stretch his wings.

I remained standing with my back to him, my legs shaky, like they might give out at any moment. The adrenaline that'd kept me going was fading, replaced by a bone-deep exhaustion.

"Why are you here?" I demanded again, hating that my voice trembled.

"Because you were in danger," he repeated simply, and that made my anger boil even more. Too many words tried to spill out. "I'll leave you to it."

"What?" I snapped, whirling around to face him. His hand was already on the door, ready to run away all over again.

"It's safe in here," he said, as if that even mattered.

I stormed across the two paces between us, refusing to let him disappear again, jabbing my finger into his chest. "You're not going anywhere until I get answers." I glared up at him, but his eyes dropped to my arm.

"You're bleeding."

"Don't change the subject, Kaelan." I refused to back down.

His brow knitted, not even seeming to register my fury, which only made it bubble up faster.

He blinked twice, his gaze turning distant for a moment.

"You know my name." It didn't sound like a question, nor did it seem to even be directed at me.

"How could I forget?" I'd wanted to snarl, but hurt laced each word. This wasn't how I'd imagined meeting Kaelan again. "I've been waiting months to hear from you, and instead I get absolute silence. And now you just randomly turn up and expect everything to be fine?"

"Months . . ." His voice sounded weak, and he swayed ever so slightly.

"What in the hells is going on?" I demanded, jabbing the light switch on the wall beside him.

Light flooded the room, and I winced at the sudden brightness. I opened my mouth, ready to demand my answers, but it snapped shut as I took in Kaelan.

The darkness had hidden most of it, but now under the light, the stark reality crashed into me. Bruises and cuts marred his exposed skin, all in various stages of healing. The black t-shirt was torn in places, splattered with what I first thought were various shades of mud, but then realized it was blood. The dried gold blood of the nephilim and the red blood from who knew, too dried to be the assailant from the construction site.

My healer's eye assessed every inch of him, only now noting the tightness in his features that signaled serious pain. The way he favored his left leg and stood hunched, as if his stomach or ribs were causing him pain.

"What happened to you?" I whispered, my hand reaching out on instinct before I could snatch it away. "Who did this?"

A new anger boiled in my chest, but no longer directed at Kaelan. No, this white-hot fury was for whoever had done this to him.

Nephilim blood allowed them to heal faster than the other races, so the injuries had to be recent.

Lunar energies swirled in my chest and I gathered them up. I wove a thin strand into my moon-blessed mark that connected us, hoping to offer him some strength. His eyes fluttered closed as my energies flowed into him.

Kaelan gasped, hands clutching his head as he stumbled, and then his body went slack.

My arms wrapped around him, but my five-foot-seven against his six-foot-two, all muscle and a pair of wings, was a losing battle. I could only hope to keep him from cracking his head on the wall as we unceremoniously crashed to the ground.

"Nyssa!" Danika cried. *"Are you hurt?"*

"I've been better," I grunted, trying to wiggle my way out from underneath the unconscious nephilim.

By the Goddess, he was heavy. Untangling myself, I pressed a hand against his neck, my fingers trembling as I tried to find his pulse.

For several long moments I held my breath, waiting for that soft thrum against my fingers to remind me he was still alive, to reassure me I hadn't imagined it.

His breathing was slow and steady and I slumped back. My ribs protested at the movement, likely bruised from the fall, but it didn't feel right to complain, not after seeing the state Kaelan was in.

Who'd done this to him?

Panting, I sat on the cold concrete, not having the energy to get up. Danika rubbed against me and I wrapped her in a hug. Just what in all the realms was going on?

"What do we do?" I asked, my voice halfway between a hysterical laugh and a terrified cry. "There is no way I can carry him anywhere to get medical attention. I doubt I could even get him to the sleeping bag."

Too many questions swirled around. Why hadn't Kaelan healed? Even a regular doctor could've sped up recovery so the bruises would barely be visible, but the state the wounds were in made it clear they'd not been treated.

I needed to call for help, but who? Rynac popped into my head first, but how would I explain this? That I'd gone out alone on a dangerous mission and not said anything to him. Which also ruled out Indra because I wouldn't be able to handle either of their questions, and they'd never trust my word again. Nor would I be able to contact any of the healers at the MEA, fearing they would let it slip to the siblings.

"Call Beylin," Danika said.

I chewed on my lip, hating that he was likely the best option. Not only did he have knowledge of healing—he'd tended to me up a few times before—he also had a fully kitted-out medical room and still hadn't explained why.

That and he knew all about the nephilim, the moon-blessed, and the Lunar Order. If there was one person I could trust to keep this quiet, it was my boss.

CHAPTER TWENTY

Beylin answered on the first ring. "Just what mischief have you been getting up to now?"

"I need help," I choked out as the reality of everything crashed down around me. The nightbane, the shadowy figure, losing the circlet, Kaelan appearing.

When a bright white light shone around the roller door, I thought I'd accidentally fallen asleep, that I was tumbling into a nightbane again.

Before I could even panic that someone was outside, the roller door lifted to reveal Beylin. I squinted, then rubbed at my eyes. Behind him wasn't the storage facility but a richly lit hallway filled with doors. Maybe this was a dream.

"Well, this looks like a right party," Beylin grumbled, but as soon as he took in my form, his gruff expression softened. "Come on, then." He offered me a hand, all my aches and pains reawakening as I stood. Pins and needles coursed through my legs, my ribs still aching something fierce.

"What?" I looked down at my phone and hung up. "How did you get here already?"

Beylin smirked, then poked Kaelan with a toe. "Next time you knock someone unconscious, try to do it somewhere more convenient. Can you manage his legs?"

I didn't think I could even stand on my own, but if it meant getting out of this tiny box I'd find the dregs of energy. I nodded. Danika brushed against me, and a small burst of energy rippled through our connection. I sent her a soft smile and thanks.

Beylin bent and scooped under Kaelan's armpits as I grabbed his ankles. I wasn't sure how this was going to work. Kaelan's wings outstretched would stand taller than the dwarf, but as we hoisted him up, Beylin muttered a word, and the body beneath my fingers lightened.

I stumbled along down the halls, realizing we were now within Divine Coffee. When I looked back over my shoulder, the door snicked shut, a faint tremor of magic rolling through the air.

"This way," Beylin said as we turned down a familiar hall and into the small medical examination room that I'd unfortunately been in before.

We lifted Kaelan higher; somehow, he rose as if he barely weighed anything, his wings folding in before we settled him down on the table, which shifted to accommodate them. The longer I stared at the table, the more my head started to hurt.

"You'll break your brain doing that," Beylin chuckled. "Sometimes it's better not to know how magic works. Trust me."

Under the harsh lights in this room, I saw the full extent of Kaelan's injuries. I'd never seen anything like this before, and it stole my breath away to know he'd been suffering so much.

"Care to explain what happened?" Beylin asked as he set out medical supplies. "Most of these don't look fresh."

"I don't know," I replied, feeling pitiful, like I should have known what happened to him.

"Is this one of the Nephilim from—"

"Yes," I interjected. "I was out . . ." I started, not sure where I was going with this or how much I was going to tell him. Did it even matter? "I . . . got myself into some trouble, and Kaelan appeared and helped me escape."

Beylin shot me a look that was half reprimanding, half worried.

"We got somewhere safe, but he didn't seem right. He didn't seem to remember me. He was surprised I even knew his name. And then I saw all these bruises and cuts. I tried to connect to him with my magic, but I did something wrong, and he passed out."

Beylin was silent for a long while as he began his assessment of Kaelan, but then he looked me over.

"You're hurt," he said softly, and I could only comply as he guided me to a seat.

I wanted to brush it off, but my arm was aching and all the stress and magic use caught up with me as fatigue washed over my body. My mind drifted as he bandaged up my arm.

"All patched up." Beylin's soothing voice brought me back to the room and the slab where Kaelan lay. "I'll need help with him. Are you up to that?"

"Yes," I said with enough determination to convince myself.

And I knew what to do. I'd done this before, shadowing the healers and learning how to treat wounds as part of my alchemy training. While we weren't healers, we were adjacent to them and needed to understand how healing worked—how our potions would affect the patient and how to dose them.

I followed Beylin's instructions, clinging to the tasks, trying not to let my mind wander. Far too thankful for how bright this room was, that it banished all the shadows.

But how long would I be able to keep them away?

I dumped the dirty water and refilled the basin, helping to wipe away the crusted blood that still coated Kaelan's arms. Beylin grunted as he tried to remove the vest Kaelan wore.

It was a black tactical vest, something I'd seen my father wear—something the military used, with all its pockets and straps.

As I put my hands on the other side to help pry it off, I saw the extent of the damage the vest had endured. Splashes of blood covered the dark surface, along with slices and cuts—some clean, likely made by a blade, while others were jagged, and I couldn't help but picture claws. Where in all the hells had Kaelan been to suffer this?

We pried it off, having to cut the last bit, not quite figuring out how he'd gotten it over his wings. Then again, I never knew how any of their clothes worked—my guess had always been magic.

I laid the torn vest out on a different table, my fingers searching through the pockets for any hint of what had happened to him. But they were empty.

My thumb trailed over something, and a faint whisper of magic caught my attention. I tilted the vest until I could see the insignia stitched there, black on black, so it'd be hidden among the darkness. My mouth went dry. A shield with two crossed blades, the same one Edrik had drawn.

"Do you know what this is?" I asked, showing it to Beylin.

A shadow crossed his features as he looked down at Kaelan, assessing him. "Are you sure he's part of the Order?" Beylin's voice was a growl.

"Yes, he was here with Astrid." Just what was going on? I swiped a hand across my face and explained to the dwarf about when I'd seen Nathaniel—the oddities there as well.

Why did neither of them act like they knew me? No, it wasn't an act; there was no recognition in either of their faces when they saw me—no one was that good at acting.

Beylin frowned as he took in everything I said. I tried not to shudder at the snip, snip, snip of the scissors as they cut open the black shirt Kaelan had been wearing.

The breath rushed out of me as Beylin peeled back the remains of the fabric, and I swayed, gripping the table hard to keep myself upright. Kaelan's chest was a mess of amber and brown splotches—bruises in various stages of healing, cuts both fresh and old.

Grabbing a wad of gauze, I pressed it over one cut that'd reopened, the small trickle of golden blood pooling on the table.

What had he been through? The question whispered through my mind as I stared down at his face, which, even in rest, seemed pained.

"That symbol," Beylin said as he set to work cleaning the wounds, "belongs to a group named Aegis. I don't have enough words to explain what I think of them, but 'terrorists' would be the closest. Fanatics who will stop at nothing to return this realm to the way it was, with only the races born of your goddesses.

"They claim they want to protect Trutina from the threat of demons, but they'll go to any lengths to ensure it. They also want to shove the other races back to their home realms, no matter the cost, no matter how long they've lived here, no matter that the governments of this realm offered them refuge."

"You can't think he's part of that," I said, ignoring the fact that he was wearing clothes with their insignia.

"I don't know what to think. From what I last knew, they didn't accept anyone from Terrarum. We'll just have to ask him when he wakes up."

I was silent for a long while, the two of us working in tandem to clean Kaelan's extensive injuries, but my mind refused to be quiet.

"What do you think happened to him to get all these wounds?" I asked, needing the answer, yet fearing it all the same.

"Given the nephilim's enhanced healing, I'd say he's been fighting for weeks. But . . . most of these wounds were made when he wasn't wearing any kind of protective equipment."

My gaze returned to the vest lying behind me. The fabric was thick, strong enough to deflect a blade, and the damage showed it'd fulfilled its purpose.

So why hadn't he been wearing it if he was fighting? None of it made sense—too many questions and no answers, not until he woke up.

"There's a good chance," the dwarf said, snapping me out of my thoughts, "that this was done to him." It took me a moment to understand what he meant, and then an icy chill rolled over me, the hairs on the back of my neck rising.

"Torture?" I choked on the word.

He gave a noncommittal grunt. "Given that he's having issues with his memories, it's likely. I want to prepare you for when he wakes up."

Questions clawed at the edge of my thoughts. Who could have done this to him? What cruelty had driven them to such an act? How much had he endured?

My hands trembled with the spiraling thoughts that burned through my mind, but I shoved them aside. Kaelan needed a healer right now, not my worried thoughts.

Another thought nagged at me—why did Beylin know such things? Just what had he lived through before he became the owner of Divine Coffee?

Beylin finished the last dressing on Kaelan's torso, and I provided another fresh bowl of water.

"I can manage the rest," Beylin said. "You look dead on your feet. Why don't you try to get some sleep?"

I opened my mouth, ready to protest—it was my fault Beylin had all this extra work to do. Then I realized the only part left was Kaelan's lower half.

Heat prickled against my cheeks, realizing Beylin might be trying to spare me—or perhaps Kaelan—the embarrassment. I wanted to insist that I could be professional, but I fumbled with the bowl and almost tipped it onto the ground.

"Divine will prepare a room for you," Beylin said. I mumbled a thanks and headed down the hall.

A door on my left swung open, revealing a small, immaculate room. The warm glow of the overhead light illuminated the soft cream walls.

A simple, perfectly made bed stood against the far wall, the crisp white sheets and plush pillows inviting, almost like they'd been freshly laundered moments ago. The comforter was a deep, calming blue, contrasting with the light walls.

Danika curled up atop the pillow, her breathing steady, with the blanket tucked around her. The room, though modest, radiated a sense of calm and care, a sanctuary.

"Thank you, Divine," I murmured as I stepped in. The light above brightened for a moment in satisfaction, and I had to smile. No one would call Divine a bad host. Padding over to the attached bathroom, I stripped off my clothes, not wanting to get the sheets dirty.

Before I could see my reflection, I opened the medicine cabinet and pulled out a washcloth and soap. Turning on the faucet, I let the cool water run over my hands before splashing it on my face, trying to wash away the fatigue clinging to me.

The sweet scent of lavender from the soap eased some of the tension in my shoulders as I cleaned off the last of the grime.

I reached up to close the mirrored cabinet, and the lights above dimmed, casting long shadows across the room. My heart skipped a beat as red flashed in the mirror. Behind me, Carmen stood. Her crimson eyes bored into mine, a cruel smile playing on her lips.

A wave of fear crashed over me, freezing me in place. My breath caught in my throat as I stared at her, my pulse pounding in my ears. The light above flared, and I spun around, clutching the sink for support, but the room was empty.

Rubbing my palms into my eyes, I let out a humorless laugh. Jumping at shadows. I really was broken.

Sleep dragged at me, but I feared what would lurk behind my eyes. Danika peered up and shifted to make room for me.

With reluctance I complied, tossing on the clean oversized shirt Divine had laid out for me and then slipping under the covers. The bed was gloriously comfortable, and I sank under the blankets.

As I closed my eyes, the nightmares lurked at the edges of my mind, but Danika nestled against my chest, her presence holding them back for now.

Chapter Twenty-One

I woke with a start, my heart pounding as if I had been yanked from a nightmare. The rune on my chest pulsed with magic, hot and insistent.

The bed beneath me rattled, and I realized it wasn't just me—Divine was trying to wake me up. I lurched out of bed, nearly tripping over the covers in my haste. Shouts echoed down the hall, and I didn't waste any time.

Running on instinct, I bolted down the corridor. The walls blurring as I raced toward the source of the noise. My breath caught as I skidded into the medical room, where the sight stopped me cold.

Kaelan was in the corner, covered in bandages, his chest heaving as his eyes darted around in panic.

The metal table in the center of the room slid across the floor, blocking his path every time he tried to move. Divine was trying to contain him. Beylin stood with his hands up, palms out, trying to placate him, but Kaelan was too far gone to notice.

A flicker of gold on his chest caught my attention, and I blinked down to find the angelic rune was glowing through my shirt.

I feared that the moon-blessed mark might hurt him again, and pushed a thread of magic into the rune, then let it flow towards Kaelan. I focused on calming him, sending waves of reassurance and comfort.

The glow of the rune on my chest intensified, and I could feel the energy weaving between us, a bridge in the chaos.

"Kaelan," I called, my voice steady despite the turmoil in the room. His wild eyes snapped to mine, and I poured everything I had into that connection—trust, safety, a promise that he wasn't alone. "We are here to help."

Slowly, the tension in his body eased. The metal table stilled its screeching grind across the floor.

His breathing slowed, and the panic in his eyes dulled, replaced by something softer, something closer to recognition.

"Where am I?" His voice was rough and uncertain, but he was coming back to himself.

"I brought you to Divine Coffee for healing," I said, cautiously walking over towards him. "Do you remember who I am?"

"No," he whispered, as if it pained him to admit it. His eyes tracked my every move, but he didn't appear like he was about to bolt.

"Do you remember your name?"

"Kaelan." He paused, brow furrowed. "At least, that's what every-one seems to call me."

I halted a few feet in front of him, summoning my most soothing healer voice. "Can you please sit back down so that we can tend to your wounds? We are trying to help you."

Kaelan remained motionless, his gaze narrowing in on Beylin be-fore it dipped back to me. I managed what I hoped was a reassuring smile, which was not easy when this massive warrior before me was wound tight like a coil.

"I will not hurt you," he murmured.

I cursed myself for letting my fear bleed into my magic enough that he sensed it. But Kaelan sat down again, not on the examination table but on an empty workbench. *Close enough, I guess.*

Kaelan's gaze darted around the room as if assessing every exit point, every threat. Beylin took a step closer, and Kaelan's attention snapped to him.

"He's the one who treated your injuries," I said, putting myself in between the two. "I trust him with my life."

Kaelan's lips turned into a thin line, his shoulders tightening, but he settled back down.

"Will you answer some questions for me?" I asked, attempting to draw his attention. His gaze shifted from Beylin to meet mine, and then offered me a small nod. "Do you know what city you are in?"

"Arkirith." His gaze went distant for a moment. "They brought me here."

"Who are 'they'?"

"Aegis." He spat the name like a curse. "They held me, did this to me, until I escaped."

Beylin exchanged a glance with me before asking, "What did they want with you?"

"Information. But I can't remember." Kaelan winced, a flicker of pain crossing his face. "They just kept digging and digging with their magic." Anger flared in his voice, his hand clawing into his hair, and he gritted his teeth as if he was living through it again.

"Kaelan, it's alright, you're safe here." My voice shook as I gripped his arms, afraid he would hurt himself. His breath came in gasps, but he let his arms fall back down as he shook his head.

"Scouring the mind is dangerous magic," Beylin said, his tone careful as he moved a step closer. "Especially if it's resisted, it can cause great damage and instability." He held my gaze for the last part, as if trying to warn me to take great care.

"Do you know what you are?"

Kaelan's hand went to his neck, fingers brushing against the skin as if searching for something that wasn't there. "A member of the Lunar Order," he said, uncertainty clouding his features. "But . . . things are murky. It's hard to recall what is real and what they put there." His confusion tugged at my heart.

"You are," I said. "You're a moon-blessed warrior and your mark is on the side of your neck. I could show it to you, but that's what I tried yesterday and it caused you to pass out." He nodded, as if trying to remind himself that he knew that.

"It's likely joined to memories that Aegis was trying to find or connections they broke," Beylin explained. "You will need to be careful what you think about until I can run some diagnostics. There is a chance they left traps or triggers behind that could do you harm."

"From what I recall about them," Kaelan said, his lip curling as he stared down and flexed his hands, "that's likely, judging by the lengths they went to secure us."

"Us?" I asked, my heart leaping into my throat.

"My team. Nathaniel. Astrid." His brow furrowed, eyes going distant before he shook his head.

"How did you escape from Aegis?"

His eyes flicked away from me. "You were in danger. Nothing could stand in my way to reach you." The conviction in his voice sent a shiver down my spine.

It was the first real hint of the nephilim I had known, or thought I had known. Where was this coming from? If he had cared about my wellbeing like he said, then where had he been for the last few months? Why had he never contacted me?

Or did Aegis have him all this time?

A heavy stone sank in my stomach at the thought. And here I'd been cursing his name, upset he'd forgotten about me, and yet—what if he hadn't? What if he'd been held against his will, locked away, and forced to endure terrible things?

Beylin's eyes narrowed, considering. Then he asked the question that had been gnawing at me since this all began. "Why do you feel the need to protect Nyssa?"

Kaelan hesitated. For a moment, I thought he wouldn't answer, but then he looked up, meeting my eyes with an intensity that made my breath catch. "I'm sworn to protect her," he said, his voice low but resolute.

I blinked, the weight of his words settling in. "That's news to me."

"It was how I knew you were in danger." He shook his head, wincing. "But I couldn't get to you in time. I'm sorry for failing you."

"Failing me? If it wasn't for you, that person would have shot me." I looked down at the bandage. "Well, shot somewhere more vital." Beylin frowned at me and I gave a weak shrug, realizing I might've forgotten to mention that part to him.

"No, not then, four days ago. It took me too long to escape Aegis. You were safe when I reached you, so I've been watching over you since."

"Watching me." The thought was unsettling, but at least explained some of that odd feeling I'd sensed of late. When I was walking through the city, or up on my terrace, had that all been Kaelan? "Wait, four days, that's when—" My throat closed up. When I'd seen the first vision of Carmen. "But how did you feel that? How did you even know where I was?"

Kaelan tapped his chest, my rune flaring to life. "It is my duty to protect you, and this rune will guide me." Unable to resist, I pulled my shirt down enough to see my skin, and there the golden rune shimmered in a mesmerizing pattern.

"What rune?" Beylin demanded, turning me towards him. His eyes widened as he took in the rune, and his gaze shifted back to Kaelan, a storm brewing behind his eyes. "You marked her with an angelic rune?" His voice was sharp, slicing through the air with an edge I had never heard before.

I flinched back at the fury in his voice, thankful it wasn't currently directed at me. Kaelan remained silent, his expression unreadable, offering no defense, no explanation.

"What's wrong?" I asked, peering down at the rune again, trying to understand what had caused such a reaction.

Not once in the time I'd worked here had I ever seen Beylin angry; grumpy, yes, but never furious like this. And that was including the time I'd tried to work my shift after being attacked by thralls. How could a single rune provoke such a response?

"Do you know what it is? Did he even bother to explain?"

"It was to offer me protection," I said, more to myself than to anyone else. "I was about to walk into Carmen's lair, up against a dark witch, warlock, and a horde of demonspawn. I was desperate."

Beylin's scowl deepened, his eyes narrowing as he shot a glare at Kaelan. "And you took advantage of that desperation," he snapped, his voice like a whip.

Kaelan finally moved, his eyes meeting Beylin's with a cold intensity. "The burden of the rune is on me," he said, his tone firm, unyielding. And then the clarity in his gaze faded. "But I don't remember that moment, so I can offer no other explanation."

Tension crackled in the air, and my gaze darted between the two of them. Absently, my fingers traced over the rune. I couldn't understand why Beylin was so angry. Sure, inscribing a rune onto skin was risky, but I'd been heading into certain death and needed every advantage I could get.

And if I was being honest, there was a good chance that if I hadn't had the rune, I might not have walked away from our fight with Carmen.

Kaelan's offer had meant far more than I could ever express. A nephilim offering a witch angelic protection? Unheard of. Sworn to protect them? Maybe when the sun burned cold.

Too many thoughts crashed through my head when my phone chimed, scattering them all. I reached into my pocket for it, only then realizing I was wearing nothing more than the oversized t-shirt Divine had given me.

The fabric grazed my thighs, making me keenly aware of my exposed state. Wow, I had to stop making a habit out of that. *Pants first, Nyssa.*

"It's a good look," Danika commented as she trotted into the room, my phone in her mouth. *"Shows off your legs."*

Could you not? I hissed back as my cheeks heated. Why in the hells had no one said anything?

Danika dropped the phone at my feet, her expression unamused. *"Your phone's been going off nonstop. Interrupted my nap,"* she grumbled.

I bent down awkwardly to retrieve it, conscious of the hemline that only just kept my modesty intact. The screen lit up with several missed calls from Indra and a text message urging me to call her back ASAP.

Dread settled heavy in my stomach. After the chaos of last night, I'd almost forgotten my original mission—to locate Edrik and the artifact. But now, with Indra's urgent messages, everything came flooding back, and my skin prickled with unease.

"One last question for you," I said, fixing my gaze on Kaelan. "Care to explain why your Order squad-mate is hunting you for murder?"

Beylin made a strangled noise of annoyance. I probably should've mentioned that earlier.

"Nathaniel." Kaelan scowled. "I don't know how they turned him, but he is hunting me for Aegis. I don't know what murders they are trying to pin on me."

"Then why were you at the crime scene yesterday?" I pressed, my voice edged with suspicion. "That was you out on that balcony, wasn't it? And then Nathaniel dove out the window after you."

"I followed you there, but when I sensed that attack and then Nathaniel's presence, I had to get him away from you."

Before I could demand more answers, my phone buzzed in my hand, Indra's name flashing on the screen.

"I need to take this," I mumbled, turning away as I answered the call. "Indra?" I said, bracing myself.

"There's been another murder."

Chapter Twenty-Two

A buzzing seemed to rise in my mind, drowning out all my thoughts. My breath came too fast as memories from yesterday—the nightbane—seeped out of the dark box where I'd locked it away.

"Nyssa?" Indra's concerned voice pulled me back from the shadows, and I realized she'd been talking.

"Sorry, what did you say?" I asked, trying to focus.

"The captain is asking if you'll come. We found . . . traces of blood that are Edrik's."

The air rushed from my lung. "Is he—" No, how? I'd seen him last night.

"The victim wasn't Edrik, but his blood being found here links him to these murders. This is all against protocol, and we wouldn't ask you without good reason, but we keep hitting dead ends and . . ."

I wanted to say no. I didn't even want to leave this building, afraid my friend would read the fear in my eyes. That she'd know what happened, that I hadn't trusted her, and see how afraid I was. But they needed my help.

What if I could see something they hadn't? What if this helped me find Edrik? I had to try, even though it terrified me.

"Of course," I said, my voice sounding weak even to my own ears.

"Thank you." Her voice was strained, with a slight hint of desperation. How bad were things if she sounded that way?

Indra's words hung in the air, the weight of them pressing down on me as I hung up. I knew I needed to go—there was no question about that—but I couldn't shake the feeling of unease at the thought of leaving Kaelan and Beylin.

After everything that had happened, the idea of stepping out of this room, away from the safety of their presence, left me in a pit of uncertainty.

"I need to go," I said, my voice wavering as I looked between them. "But . . . I'm not sure if I should leave you here."

Kaelan immediately straightened, the tension in his body sharpening. "I'm coming with you."

Beylin stepped forward, placing a firm hand on the nephilim's shoulder before he stood. "You need to rest, Kaelan," he said, his tone leaving no room for argument. "You've been through enough, and pushing yourself further won't do anyone any good. Especially with Aegis on the hunt for you."

Kaelan's jaw tightened as he glanced at me, unwilling to back down. "But she could be in danger—"

"I'll be with the enforcers," I interrupted, trying to ease his worry. "They'll keep me safe. And you need time to rest and recover. You can't protect me if you're injured."

"Oof, that was a low blow. Good one." Danika snickered.

Not helping, I hissed back.

Beylin nodded in agreement, though his gaze remained on Kaelan. "I didn't waste half my night healing you for you to run off before it's finished. Besides, I'd like to run some tests. We need to figure out what's going on with those mind spells—what they've done to you."

Kaelan's wariness was palpable, his eyes narrowing as he glanced between the two of us. "Tests?" he repeated, clearly not thrilled with the idea.

Beylin gave him a reassuring look. "Unlocking your memories could be crucial. If we can figure out what Aegis did to you, we can prevent another episode where you're knocked unconscious."

Okay, that one was the low blow. Hitting a nephilim where it would hurt the most, their ego. "And maybe even unlock the memories they took," I added.

Kaelan hesitated, his gaze flickering between us before he nodded, though there was still tension in his posture. "Fine. But be careful. Aegis is very dangerous."

"I know," I said, flashing him a reassuring smile before Beylin and I left. Despite myself, I glanced back, and hoped Kaelan would recover quickly.

"Don't worry, Divine and I will be able to manage him. Go do what you need to do," he said. Guilt gnawed at me as I took in the dark rings under his eyes, the fatigue weighing down his shoulders.

I took a deep breath, unsure of what I was about to get myself into. "Thank you. I owe you for this, for all you've done for me." I said the words as a promise. I would find a way to repay him, even though he just waved it off.

Why did he do this? The small question popped into my mind, and I couldn't help but wonder once again who my boss was—or had once been.

"Just seems part of my job these days," Beylin grumbled.

I slipped out the back door and found the unmarked car waiting for me. An enforcer, who I recognized as one of the enhanced officers, stood against the car with their arms crossed. She offered me a half-smile and opened the door for me. The backseat door.

The warded glass between the front and back was unsettling, but Danika jumped in next to me without a moment of hesitation.

"Never been in the back of a cop car?" the enforcer said, amusement sparkling in her eyes as they met mine in the rearview mirror.

"No."

She chuckled. "We'll be there soon."

I buckled up as the car took off at an alarming speed. My arm wrapped around Danika, hoping to anchor her, but in truth she was a solid and steady presence beside me. These days she seemed like the only thing keeping back the shadows that haunted my mind.

"You have a knack for getting yourself into interesting situations," she said. I could hear the half-smile in her voice.

You know me—wouldn't want things to get boring for you, I replied.

She chuckled and I clung to that sound, to anything that would keep my mind off the nightbane.

What do you think about Kaelan? I asked, my voice hesitant.

She was silent for a moment. *"His mind is quite a tangle. He's been through a lot. There are only small glimmers of the nephilim we first met. But perhaps you'll get some answers."*

I scoffed. Now wasn't the time for my petty questions or my need to know why he'd never called. It didn't ease the sting, but there were more pressing matters, and my concerns were at the bottom of the list.

"As much as I wanted to scorn him for how much he hurt you, I'm thankful that he was there last night."

I could hear the words she left unsaid, the ones that had been lurking in the back of my mind. If Kaelan hadn't been there last night, we might not have made it out alive.

My weaknesses had been used against me, and I'd been foolish to think I could achieve anything by myself. I'd charged headlong into unknown dangers and put both of our lives at risk.

If Kaelan hadn't been there to save me, we might not even be having this conversation.

No wonder he believed I needed a sworn protector. I wasn't made for the front lines—I didn't know why I couldn't get that through my thick skull. I belonged in the background, crafting potions for those strong enough to fight, offering support and healing when necessary.

The truth was, my fear almost drowned me. I knew it, Danika knew it, and I was sure everyone else did too. So why couldn't I just accept my place?

The car came to a halt, snapping me out of my thoughts. With a quick thanks to the officer, we slipped out of the vehicle. Yellow tape fluttered in the wind, and the thoughts I'd been avoiding swelled around me, dark and heavy.

My mind drifted back to a few months ago, when I'd returned to the place where my magic had torn the veil. I'd been grilled by the UMC for it. Or when I'd been arrested by the Inquisitors for using wild magic.

It seemed that law enforcement and I just didn't get along, and a tinge of fear skittered down my spine. Was there another reason they'd asked me to come? I couldn't help but wonder when the enforcers might turn on me.

Even reminding myself that I was no longer a suspect in Edrik's disappearance did little to soothe my anxiety. The world had a way of twisting the truth, making it seem like the blame would always circle back to me.

As I waited for Indra, I felt a mental nudge from Danika. I gave her a sad smile, sensing her silent reprimand.

"Yeah, I know," I muttered to Danika. "I'm going full 'the world is against me' again, aren't I?"

It was just another reason why I wasn't cut out for this kind of life. I doubted Indra or Rynac blamed themselves for what they faced in their line of duty. The moon-blessed probably didn't wallow in self-pity, especially not the nephilim. I was sure that even in their own minds, they believed they could never do wrong.

Indra greeted me with a tight smile and waved us over. We ducked under the tape, careful to stay out of the way as the last of the investigation team packed up.

A quick glance behind revealed Danika had slipped into the place where she was no longer visible to the eye. I could still sense her magic, but my gaze seemed to skitter over where my bond ended.

Captain Everson detached himself from a group of officers and approached us with a determined stride. There was tension in his movements, an unspoken weight that seemed to press down on his shoulders. It was clear that these murders were taking a toll on him.

He inclined his head towards me, a silent thank you, before motioning for Indra to remain outside. He led me into an empty garage, and bright lights assaulted my eyes. I blinked to clear my vision and noticed the large floodlights that illuminated the entire area, banishing all the shadows.

The captain muttered a quiet curse, then gently guided me out of the way of the door. The medical officers walked by with a gurney, I caught only the briefest glimpse of the long black bag on top.

My mind was too slow to process what I was seeing until a small voice whispered the word, *body*. That bag contained a body. It looked so small—how could one person fit in there?

"I apologize." The captain's voice brought me back to the world around me. "I thought they'd already taken it out."

I dipped my chin in the barest of nods, a tiny part of my mind appreciating that he tried to shield me from it. *It*. But it wasn't an "it," but a person. Who were they? Did they have loved ones waiting for them at home? Or friends that would miss them?

Not helpful, I snapped at myself. Those questions would get me nowhere. I was here for a reason—if I could help the MEA then I could help get justice for those that had been killed.

I surveyed the area from where we stood, off to the side, as the last of the investigation team cleared their supplies.

Boxes, a few ladders, and a whole bunch of junk were pushed against the far wall leaving the concrete floor exposed. The massive spell array covered every inch.

I kept back, looking at it from a distance at first, assessing. My eyes skipped over that too-dark patch near the center. There was great care put into the creation of this spell array. Here I could see that it had been drawn with attention to detail.

This was the kind of dedication and precision I expected to see in final exams. Where every line, every corner, had to be just perfect. Meticulous. Well-planned.

Then again, if you were going to sacrifice someone in a spell array, it wasn't something done on the spur of the moment.

"What can you tell me?" the captain asked.

"Just from a glance?" I tried not to fidget.

He nodded. "Sometimes trained eyes miss details. What does it tell you?"

I paused, studying the array. "They were meticulous with the drawing of each rune," I began, tracing the lines with my eyes. "That shows great care. But there are parts where they seem to have rushed.

"The two circles are near perfect, and the star connecting them. Though these sections that would've been drawn after are free-hand—you can see these points here where the line wobbles. It's still a straight line, but that kind of curve can weaken the structure. Not enough to break it, but it could lose some integrity.

"And this circle over here—see how the two points where they started and ended don't quite meet? There would have been some spillover with the magic."

"So you believe they were in a rush?" Captain Everson asked, his brow furrowing.

"Perhaps," I replied. "Or they got a bit careless, but with the crucial elements—the runes—they took their time."

I glanced at Danika, waiting to see if there was anything I had missed, but she remained silent.

"Indra mentioned blood that was identified as Edrik's," I said, unable to drag my eyes from the dark stain within the array.

"Over here," Captain Everson said, gesturing toward a small splatter outside the array at one of the points. "The investigators believe he was part of the ritual and offered blood to fuel it."

Why would they need blood if they already had a victim inside?

"Exactly," Danika said, sniffing at the stain. While blood could be a component, it didn't make sense that there were two sources. But then again, I wasn't an expert in ritualistic killings—that was a sentence I'd never thought I'd say in my life.

"Are the victims linked to Edrik at all? Or any other connections?"

"Not that we can find," he replied, voice weary. "So far they are all different races, ages, backgrounds. We can't find anything in common."

"Do you know when this ritual took place?"

The captain let out a heavy sigh, rubbing a hand over the stubble on his jaw, his eyes distant. "The preliminary report from the medical examiner suggests the victim died sometime near midnight."

Midnight—the word felt like a stone in my stomach. Midnight was close to when I'd seen the vision of Edrik, but he'd been with those four figures.

But now, with his blood here, was there something I was missing?

"I have good reason to believe that Edrik was in another part of the city around the time this killing took place," I said. "That he is being held by a hostile group. I do not believe he was present, but that his blood was placed here." It was a hunch, but things just were not adding up.

The captain studied me, likely trying to decide how much he wanted-ed to know. "You were able to use the opal?" he asked. I nodded. "Then it might be a possibility that those who took him are connected with these killings. They might've planted his blood to throw us off from thinking that he is a victim."

"The drawing that was also in the safe. I've learned it's the insignia of a group called Aegis."

The captain's face grew impossibly hard, and I backed up a step. "I'm aware of them. If Edrik left it for you to find, then he knew who was coming for him. Though his link to them is still uncertain, if it is Aegis operating within my city, then we need to be far more cautious. I hope whoever revealed the information about Aegis also expressed how much of a danger they pose."

I nodded. Even though Beylin had explained and I'd seen Kaelan's injuries, there was something about the captain reacting to Aegis that terrified me.

"What can you tell me about the runes? From what I understand, you use spell arrays in alchemy."

"I do," I said in a rush, thankful to be changing the subject. "But I doubt I use similar ones to this kind of spell. Runes are a whole other language. There are hundreds of them."

Even so, I walked around the spell array, taking in each rune and analyzing it. My eyes scanned over the different runes—some easy to recognize, others only slightly familiar, and some completely foreign.

Their style was unlike any runes I knew, as if they were written in a different language. But there was one that brought me up short. It shifted under the bright lights, but when I stood over it, I recognized its far too familiar shape.

"What is it?" the captain asked, noticing my reaction.

I stared down at the rune, my heart pounding harder with each second I looked at it. "It's demonic," I sputtered.

Chapter Twenty-Three

"How can you tell?" Captain Everson asked.

"Runes from different races can be very similar," I said. "Even those used by people from Terrarum resemble the ones we use in Trutina. Whether it's because they've morphed after hundreds of years of living here, or because runes are the language of the gods, the small differences are like accents.

"Same word, same intention, but spoken with a slightly different pronunciation. But there are some runes that do not cross over, that are only spoken by one god."

"Spoken by the gods?"

I blinked, tearing my eyes away from the rune to the captain's skeptical face. I knew humans had an aversion to magic, but I still thought they would understand some of the basics. "Runes are the language of the gods. Our mortal forms are unable to speak their language unless it's written this way. Some words are only uttered by a specific god, though for the majority of them, it's only in the infernal language that they are spoken aloud."

Understanding dawned in his eyes, realizing why only the broken gods would use words with such malicious intent.

"Though I don't know what this particular one means. There is a harshness to demonic runes—in their design and the way they are drawn—that makes them stand out against the others."

I'd heard the demonic language before. Even just the thought sent a shudder down my spine. The guttural harshness of the infernal tongue was not a pleasant thing to hear.

For a moment, my mind slipped back to a memory that replayed in my thoughts over the past few months—the unknown angelic words that had sung through my mind.

The harsh cold that bit against my skin as I stood on the rooftop with Kaelan. That I knew these might be my last moments before I gave myself over to Carmen, hoping to save my friends.

The skin on my chest tingled at the memory. The sound of the beautiful yet haunting words that sounded more like a song as they fell from his lips. I didn't know nephilim were able to speak the language of the angels, didn't know if I'd ever hear it again, and my heart mourned that thought.

Two languages from the same realm, yet polar opposites.

"So you believe the person who drew these runes was an erebian?"

"No," I hissed out. "Demonic runes can be wielded by those willing to face the consequences of their actions. The dark witch used them on several occasions to summon demonspawn—I would not brand one race just because of their origins." Too easily I knew the blame would fall onto the erebians.

The captain nodded, and I let out a silent breath, relieved that I hadn't made things worse with my careless words.

I resumed my pacing, pointing out the runes I recognized and explaining their possible intent, while he noted everything I said.

Why was a captain here with me? Surely there was a better use of his time.

"As I said earlier," he said, answering the question he must've seen on my face. "All this isn't exactly part of protocol. I'll add these notes as preliminary findings, while images will be sent to our rune master.

With only a handful in the entire city, and with all the killings, you can imagine how bogged down they are. I was hoping your insight might give us a bit of an edge, something to go on before they strike again."

More than ready to leave, I eyed the array one last time. "Why is the blood in the center?" Danika tilted her head and stepped closer.

"That is where the body was," the captain said.

"Not in this circle?" I pointed to what should be the sacrifice circle. Whatever power was within it would help to fuel the array.

Captain Everson shook his head. "They lay lengthwise." Meaning that the victim hadn't been standing in the sacrifice circle and fell when they died.

"Did the other murders look like this? How do you know they are linked?"

"We have considered a copy-cat killer," Captain Everson said, the lines around his face tightening. "But for now, we have been able to keep information about these murders from the news outlets, not that we will be able to for much longer.

"The rune master studying the arrays believes they were all made by the same person, though they haven't been able to decipher what the array does exactly."

There was something about the body placement that nagged at the back of my mind.

"Why was the body there? If they were lying in the center, how would they be connected to the array?" I crouched down on the edge of the array, scanning for another clue, when my gaze fixed on the sacrifice circle.

Trapped.

The edges of my vision blurred. I couldn't look away and struggled to breathe. My body refused to move.

Prove yourself to me, Nyssa. Carmen's voice swirled around me. A hulking demonspawn stalked towards me, the ground shuddering beneath me, yet I was frozen, staring up at it.

Saliva dripped from its grotesque jaw, and my arm throbbed, blood dripping from a wound.

I couldn't get away. Trapped. A hand grabbed my arm, and I flinched away.

"Nyssa." The voice was hard, but it was Captain Everson's worried face that appeared in front of me. "What in all the heavens was that?"

Danika curled around me, and I wrapped my shaking arms around her. "I . . . don't know. A flash of something. It must be from the residual magic."

"Let's get you some fresh air," the captain said, helping me stand. His phone buzzed as we stepped back out into the daylight, and I had never been more thankful to see the sun. "I have to deal with this, but I'll have Enforcer Terral escort you home. And thank you again."

I could only nod, not trusting my voice. I tilted my head back, letting my eyes fall closed as I used the heat of the sun to fight off the chill that had settled in my bones.

"Ready to go?" Indra said. Concern pinched her face as she took me in. "Did everything go well?"

"I hope my insight was helpful," I said with a weak smile. We walked back towards the street in silence, but I could sense her assessing me, the weight of all the questions she wanted to ask hanging in the air. I knew I wouldn't be able to evade them for much longer.

"Thank you for what you did," Indra said as we ducked under the yellow tape. "This isn't your job, and I know seeing all that can't be easy for you. I know that you won't talk about this, but when you are ready, I'll be here."

I squeezed her hand, unable to say anything, fearing what might tumble out of my mouth—words I wasn't ready to say. Indra headed over to another uniformed enforcer, signing the papers they handed her.

"Who is that?" the other enforcer asked, her smirk widening as she gestured with a tilt of her chin.

We both turned to see Captain Everson striding towards us with another person at his side. A creeping sensation prickled the back of my neck.

The man beside him moved with the controlled grace of someone used to commanding a room, his suit crisp, his posture perfect. He looked to be in his late forties, with a trimmed beard that framed a stern mouth.

Strands of gray wove through his dark hair, adding to the aura of authority surrounding him. It wasn't his appearance that unsettled me; it was his eyes. Cold and calculating, they held a darkness that spoke of secrets and shadows.

Magic skittered over my skin, like a thousand invisible fingers trying to burrow underneath. The taste of power, sharp and bitter, settled on my tongue. My blood turned to ice.

"We need to go," I hissed at Indra, trying to keep my expression neutral even as I fought the urge to bolt. "Now," I added, sharper, desperate. She didn't hesitate—her hand found the small of my back, and we started walking, each step faster than the last.

"What is it?" she asked, her tone calm even as she matched my pace.

Panic clawed at my throat, but I choked out the words, "Don't stop until we get to the car."

Indra watched me out of the corner of her eye, her lips pressed into a thin line, but she didn't question me.

Don't think. Don't think. I chanted the words. If I thought about my fear, he'd use it against me. I'd be trapped in another—

DON'T THINK!

I dove into the passenger seat and slammed the door the moment Danika was through. The engine roared to life as I put my head on my knees and wrapped my arms around myself.

"It's him," I whispered.

"Are you sure?"

"Couldn't you feel his magic?"

"Who?" Indra demanded, panic tinging her words. "Who was that?"

"You never saw the face of the person from your nightbane—"

"Not *from* my nightbane. He *is* the nightbane."

Chapter Twenty-Four

"Will you tell me what the hell is going on?" Indra snapped, her knuckles white as she gripped the steering wheel.

"I encountered him last night, when I was tracking Edrik. He has the ability to conjure magical nightmares called nightbanes, and should be considered very dangerous."

More words wanted to spill from my lips, but I refused to let them out. She didn't need to know the rest. It would only entangle her further with the danger around me.

"I need to go to the shifters." So much had happened in the last few days, and so much had gone wrong. But I needed to update them and hoped they could offer some insight.

"You went out alone last night?" Indra said, her gaze flicking between me and the road. "Why didn't you call Rynac or me? You could've been in danger."

"I'm fine. Nothing happened."

"Then how do you know he can create these nightbanes?" she challenged.

"I can manage on my own."

"Can you? Because when you came out of the crime scene with the captain, you were as pale as death." She hissed out a breath and all the heat drained from her voice when she said, "You can talk to me, you know?"

The silence dragged on, and I fixed my gaze on the road. The last thing I needed to do was talk, especially to Indra, to wrap her up in my problems again. Utter relief washed over me when Indra pulled to a stop in front of the shifters' den.

"You can trust us," she said. "We will always be there for you. We will stand by your side when you need us."

I swallowed hard, my insides twisting with the anguish in her voice. Reaching for the door handle, I hesitated. "I know. And that's why you were taken prisoner by Carmen and almost killed because of it." Anger laced my words, searing my throat.

Silence followed me as I slipped out of the car and headed for the entrance, refusing to look back. I cursed myself; I should've stayed quiet.

A young shifter greeted me at the door and escorted me to Nan, who took one look at me and ushered me into her private rooms without a word.

I settled on the couch, the teacup with a soothing brew trembled in my grip as I sipped at it absently. I squeezed my eyes shut, trying to still the tempest of thoughts rampaging through my head, but then the words started to fall from my lips. About the encounter at the magical site and the vision, then the same person in Edrik's shop, and when they'd used the nightbane against me when I searched for Edrik.

"You never saw their face, but believe they are the same person," Nan said.

"Faces blur together—magical signatures are much easier to tell apart. And the feel of his magic is hard to forget."

"This is most worrying." Her expression was grim, her usual calm replaced by concern. "Like Danika said, we also have records about those with the power to dreamwalking, where the magic user can enter others' subconscious minds. Though that is not an ability that our pack has ever possessed."

"So they are a shifter?"

"Most likely. Lunar magic has strong ties to both dream and nightmare. The ability to conjure nightbanes is a darker form of dreamwalking, tapping into the fears within the subconscious and bringing them to life. I think you already realize how dangerous these people are."

I shuddered. My mind was good enough creating my own nightmares, I didn't need any help there.

Tell her, a voice urged. What made me hesitate when she was aware of half of it?

But it wasn't that simple. I wanted to prove that I was capable enough to deal with this, to show that after all the dark witch had done to me that I remained strong. I'd been holding it all in for so long and my nightmares had only grown.

What if keeping it in was like letting it fester inside me? My attempt to convince the world I was fine, only making things worse. And all of this was so much larger than me now.

This wasn't just a hunt for a lunar artifact Selene wanted me to find—people were being killed, Edrik had been captured, and demonic runes were popping up all over the city. This was bigger than me, and no one person could solve all of it. We needed to work together. Only if we combined our strengths would we be able to take on this enemy.

Danika, a solid presence beside me, met my gaze in silent encouragement. I looked up, my thoughts still churning as I hunted for the right words.

"There's something else." My mouth opened and closed a few times as I hunted for the right words to admit my failure. Nan sat, sipping her tea, allowing me the time to gather myself. "I used the circlet when I tried to track down Edrik, but that person . . ." I shook my head, trying to fight off the memories. "He tried to steal the circlet, and it threw us into a nightbane. I lost. I was overwhelmed and he was able to take it. The only reason I escaped unharmed was because a nephilim I knew appeared and helped me get away. Kaelan, the nephilim, claims he was held by Aegis. They . . . dug through his mind and damaged him."

Nan's expression darkened, her mouth turned down in a grim frown. "Aegis is well known for conveting powerful artifacts in their determination to protect the realm. They target shifter packs, trying to convert the young and powerful to their fanatical cause.

"Once you join, there is no leaving. While they claim to want to protect those born of this realm, they will cut down anyone who stands in their way. From what you've told me, it is highly likely this dreamwalker is affiliated with Aegis."

The words hit me like a physical blow, stealing the breath from me. After seeing firsthand what Aegis would do in pursuit of their goal—the way they shattered the mind of a powerful warrior—I never stood a chance. I'd been so helpless against his nightbane, and now Edrik was going through that.

My mind snagged. The masks. "It's all connected." I forced the words out, failing to keep the panic from my voice. "He wore a mask that covered his whole face, but I also saw others wearing it, when they held Edrik."

"It wouldn't be the first time they have caused great harm to secure a lunar artifact. Though I never expected they would act this quickly, or how they were even aware of it awakening."

"But the killings started before the full moon ceremony," I said.

"Then something else must've brought them here, or they are not connected," Nan said, though by the set of her mouth she didn't believe that. "Did the nephilim know what they wanted?"

"No," I replied, the frustration gnawing at me. "His memories are gone besides the last few days." My gaze lifted to Nan but dropped to her hands, unable to look her in the eye. "I'm sorry for losing the circlet."

"While it is worrying that this person now has it, I know that it was hardly your fault. I'm more thankful that you are unharmed." Nan was thoughtful for a moment. "Do you think you can cast the spell to locate Edrik again?"

"Maybe," I shrugged, internally cringing. The thought of trying that spell again, especially after what I'd seen? "They sensed what I was doing. They likely have wards up against it. I still have the opal, but without the circlet—"

"Opal? May I see it?" Nan interjected.

I pulled it out of my bag and passed it over, though the surface no longer shimmered with most of the stored energy spent.

"Oh no," Nan said, already marching for the door before I could even stand up. I raced after her as she wove through the hallways, the urgency of her steps filling me with dread.

We spilled into an extensive library and all the texts filling the rows of shelves overwhelmed me. Not because of the number but the sheer amount of lunar energies that poured from them. I staggered, trying to steady myself under the deluge of power.

Nan pulled out an ancient-looking tome, the blue and gold cover creaking as she opened it and flipped through the yellowing pages. Her hands paused, and she turned the book to face me.

There was a drawing of a small box, the detailed lines of the design creating whirls like the starry sky. Though the sketch was dull, its hard black lines unable to capture the way it was alive with color, there was no doubt it was the artifact I'd seen.

"That's it." The breath rushed out of me. "That's what I saw in my vision."

Nan cursed, setting the book down on the table. "They're after the forge—I should've guessed. Aegis hunts the most powerful artifacts, and this one is up there. Though people believed it was only a myth, they say the forge can condense lunar energies and create celestial opals."

"Create them?" I sputtered. "Everyone would want to get their hands on that, the amount of money they could make from selling the opals."

"While there is the monetary aspect, Aegis stockpiles powerful items for the war they believe is inevitable. Being able to make an endless supply of opals would mean their lunar users would be even more powerful."

"But how are the forge and the ritualistic murders linked together, especially if I'm right about the runes being demonic in nature?"

Nan's mouth turned into a flat line. "Aegis despises those from Terrarum. They've a particular hatred of the demons. While I'd assume their hatred would stop them from using demonic runes, we can't rule it out. They might just be desperate enough. We need to study those runes to find out what they are up to. It might be the only clue we get."

"I'll need to contact . . . the MEA," I said. I cursed myself for how my conversation with Indra had ended. But the captain needed to know that male he'd been talking to was part of Aegis.

All of this was somehow related, and I had to get to the bottom of it if I was going to find the forge. I snapped a photo of the illustration of the forge, hoping Kaelan might recognize it.

"I'll have our archivist pull everything we have on demonic runes," Nan said. "And any memory spells we have so that we can help your friend. But I have to warn you, tampering with the mind is a dangerous thing and not to be taken lightly, or you might do more harm than good."

"Thank you. I need to get back to Divine." I hoped Beylin had been able to handle Kaelan. As I rushed out into the courtyard, someone called my name.

Jade hurried towards me, with Ruby not too far behind. "Where have you been?" she demanded, her usually cheerful face etched with hurt. "We were meant to brew last night, but you never came home."

"Oh." I cursed myself, with everything going on I'd forgotten. "My appointment ran late." The excuse sounded weak, but it wasn't like I could tell a young girl about Aegis and murders.

Jade crossed her arms. "But we will fall behind on the next order."

My gaze lifted to Ruby, imploring her to understand what I couldn't say.

"Come on, Jade, Nyssa is busy, she has other obligations right now." Ruby ushered her sister away before I could reply.

Her words stung, even though they were true. Jade's disappointment clawed at me and I felt like I was being torn in two, my life pulling me in opposing directions.

The threat of Aegis and the hunt for the forge warred with the life I was trying to create for myself. My desire to open my alchemy shop still burned deep in my soul, but how could I focus on that when there was so much at stake?

I hated that once again my life was going off the rails and there was nothing I could do about it. But if I stepped back, rejecting the path Selene had set before me, would I be able to live with myself if Aegis got what they wanted?

CHAPTER TWENTY-FIVE

It took the whole car trip back to Divine Coffee to work up the nerve to call Indra. As I pushed through the front doors, I half expected her to not even answer, but I needed to talk to the captain.

"Enforcer Terral," Indra answered, her voice stern. Okay, I deserved that. I raced up the stairs, into an empty hallway.

"I'm sorry for yelling at you," I said in a rush, fearing she would hang up on me. "It's just . . . there is a lot going on. I know it's not a good enough excuse, but I'm stressed and you didn't deserve for me to take it out on you."

More silence, and then a long sigh. "I understand where you were coming from," she somewhat begrudgingly admitted. "Do you really think it was your fault that we were put in danger?"

"I do because it's true. Being around me, what I am, puts you in danger."

"And my job doesn't?"

"It's different—"

"No, it isn't. It's my choice who I'm friends with and what job I do," she said.

I squeezed my eyes shut, trying to find the words. It *was* different. But how did I explain it? I refused to let anyone be put in danger for being my friend. What right did I have to ask that of anyone?

"What was your deal with that guy?" Indra asked.

"That's the other reason I'm calling. I need to talk to your captain, but only if that guy is gone."

"Hold on," Indra said. I could hear muffled conversation through the phone as I paced back and forth.

"Nyssa," Captain Everson said over the phone. "Indra says you're calling about the UMC liaison I was talking to."

My stomach sank. "I believe he is an Aegis agent. I encountered him last night I was trying to locate Edrik. He is very dangerous and has the ability to conjure nightbanes, a magical kind of nightmare." I held my breath as the silence stretched.

"I'll monitor the situation." There was an underlying tension in his voice, as if he didn't want to say anything else aloud. "Thank you again for the information."

The captain hung up. I let out a sigh and slumped against the wall. A UMC liaison. Why was he really there? To ensure the MEA hadn't found any credible leads? I shoved upright, remembering why I had been rushing back. Kaelan owed me answers.

I stormed down the hall, but all my determination sputtered out when I entered the examination room. I stopped dead. Kaelan lay on the table, a spell array beneath his head, the bruises stark on his skin.

"He woke up an hour ago," Beylin said as he came up behind me. "Agreed to let me use some arrays to find a diagnosis, though I gave him a brew to sedate him, so I didn't trigger any traps. That should've worn off, but I let him rest to aid in his recovery."

"I wonder the last time he got enough sleep." That thought panged in my chest.

Just how long had Kaelan been running on dregs? We had no idea how long Aegis held him. If he'd been surviving on his own for the last four days, I doubted he would've felt safe enough to sleep after what he'd been through.

He'd been out there, in a city he didn't know, with no idea who he was, who he could trust, with no way to contact anyone for help. To be so utterly alone. My throat tightened. Though I took some comfort in the fact he was at ease enough to rest here.

What am I going to do with him? It wasn't until Beylin grunted that I realized I said it aloud. Heat scorched my cheeks.

"We will figure something out," he said, patting my arm.

"Have your spells told you anything?" I said, hoping to change the topic.

"Not enough." Beylin let out a heavy sigh, his shoulders drooping.

"Do you need to rest? I can stay and watch him." Beylin was about to protest, so I added, "And we need to contact the Order. I'm sure they will know what to do with him."

The dwarf grunted at that, his gaze going distant. "I've already tried to reach my contact but haven't heard back. Something about this isn't right. If he was here on Order business and went missing, they should be trying to track him. If it wasn't linked to the Order, then wouldn't they have noticed his absence and started searching?"

"And Nathaniel is here, possibly Astrid," I said. "So the Order should know."

"As I said, it doesn't seem right." Beylin let out a heavy sigh. "I did some gentle probing, but the memories that are damaged don't make sense. The last specific date he can remember was almost half a year ago. If the information Aegis wanted was within that time frame, then it should be fragmented; instead, it's all gone.

"Then there is the issue with long-term memory—he didn't re-member his name, but knew where he was born. Could recall specific milestones in his life, but anything to do with formal training was spotty at best."

I winced at the extend of the damage. Yet he still seemed like the same nephilim I knew.

"Until my full diagnostics are back, I see two options," Beylin continued. "One, Aegis tore into his mind to find what they wanted and badly damaged it. Or two, the information they wanted was already gone, and they damaged his mind trying to recover it."

"Neither sound good. But thank you for helping."

"Of course." Beylin patted my arm. "Call me if anything changes."

The lights in the medical examination room were dimmed, but offered enough light for me to see as I sat down on the chair beside Kaelan.

His chest rose and fell in a smooth rhythm, his wings beneath him rustling every now and again. Compared to yesterday, he appeared far more peaceful despite the concern that was forever etched on his face.

Now wearing a dark t-shirt and jeans, he almost looked like your average nephilim. Well, as average as he could be when nephilim looked more like an ancient marble statue crafted by an expert artisan.

Besides the few visible injuries, I never would've guessed what he'd been through. Or how exhausted he must be. Guilt welled up at my earlier anger, and despite the driving need to get to the bottom of all of this, I pushed it down. He needed rest.

Being laid out on a metal slab couldn't be comfortable or warm, so I stood, ready to find a blanket, when something grabbed my wrist and I yelped.

"You're safe," Kaelan said, a heavy breath rushing out of him. "I thought I sensed you panicking, but I couldn't wake myself up."

"I'm fine," I said, patting his hand. How had he sensed that? At least he didn't comment on my yelp. "I just had a brush with the nightbane user you helped me escape from."

"What?" Kaelan lurched up as if bracing for a fight. "Where is he? What happened?"

I held my hands up in a vain effort to placate him. "As I was leaving the crime scene, I ran into him. I recognized the feel of his magic."

"Did he recognize you?"

"No, he didn't see me."

"You don't understand. That was an Aegis agent. The one that loved digging through my mind." Kaelan winced, pressing a hand against his head.

"Lie down." My voice wobbled, my hands shaking as I gripped Kaelan to steady him.

That guy's nightbanes were bad enough, but a shudder went through me knowing that he could also dig through my mind.

"We already guessed he was with Aegis," I said, "though he was posing as someone from the UMC investigating the murders. We also think we know what they are after." I pulled out my phone to show Kaelan the picture of the forge.

He frowned. "I don't know what that is."

"It's an artifact known as the forge, but it's believed to create celestial opals. While it has been missing for so long that it became a myth, I think it's here somewhere and you know where it is."

"Why?"

"Because you and your team were in Arkirith before you helped me out with the dark witch. This has to be the reason you were here and why Aegis captured you and your team."

Kaelan just shook his head. "But I don't remember any of it."

"Is there a chance, if you knew about something important, the Order might seal that memory away?" I asked.

He was silent for a long time, his brows furrowed. "Yes," he said slowly. "I think that has happened before."

My heart squeezed. I'd been right, they had forgotten me. Had they argued for the right to remember me, or were they not given a choice? Either way, it still stung. Even if it had been to keep the information out of Aegis' hands, I'd just been collateral damage.

I frowned, taking a step back from my own thoughts. What did it matter if they forgot me? Sure, it hurt, but the reasons behind taking those memories were far bigger than me.

It wasn't out of spite, but to protect a greater cause. My pain was nothing compared to what Kaelan had endured, and I knew he wouldn't have made his decision lightly. If the choice had been mine, to give up my memories of the nephilim in order to protect a secret from Aegis, I would've agreed in a heartbeat.

There were bigger battles to face, harder choices waiting on the horizon. All I could do was hope that when the moment came, I'd make the right decision.

Beylin cleared his throat, and I found him standing in the doorway. His expression was serious, his usual easy demeanor replaced by a focused intensity that made my stomach tighten.

"If the Order is known to take memories, then that lines up with what my reports are showing," Beylin began, his voice grim. "It does appear a spell of some kind was used to wipe a portion of memories, but the invasive magic of Aegis has left deep scars. Whatever they did to try to break the spell caused a fracture."

I frowned, the unease growing in the pit of my stomach. "What do you mean by a 'fracture'?" Magic effecting the mind was always a dangerous thing and wasn't a strength of witches, but during my training with the healers I knew enough about the damage it could cause. While a broken bone could be set back in place and heal, if the mind was broken, there was very little that could be done.

Beylin glanced at Kaelan before turning back to me, his expression solemn. "In this context it refers to a split or crack in the memories that goes beyond the ones that were removed. The traces of magic are difficult to distinguish, but I believe that a conflict between the original caster's intent and what Aegis did created this. The initial spell that took his memories was precise, but invasive. Though the mind is resilient and can sometimes heal from such wounds."

Kaelan's grip tightened on my hand. "You think it's the force Aegis used? That they didn't take care when they were digging around in my head?"

"Your mind is trying to repair itself, but with the added damage, it's struggling. That's why these fractures are so dangerous."

A heavy silence settled over us, the weight of uncertainty pressing down on me. "And these fractures . . . could they get worse?" I asked, my blood turning cold even before he answered.

Beylin nodded, his expression troubled. "Yes, they could. They can lead to memory loss, confusion, and even deeper psychological issues if not treated carefully. And because the damage is so severe, there's a risk that they could worsen over time, especially if the mind is under stress.

"I don't believe this was a trap for anyone who tampered with the spell, rather it's that Aegis didn't care about the state of the mind once they were done."

"What can we do?" I asked, hoping but knowing the harsh reality.

Beylin hesitated before answering. "There are methods to reinforce the mind, to help it heal more effectively, but it's delicate work. We'd have to approach this with caution, and there's no guarantee that we can fully reverse the damage.

"The scars Aegis left behind are deep, and the mind's healing process is unpredictable." Beylin let out a heavy sigh, his shoulders sagging. "For now we need to avoid anything that might trigger the fracture."

"So no thinking? I can manage that," Kaelan said, his mouth tilted in a half smirk. One I might've believed if the tension rolling off him hadn't been so obvious.

"Don't try to recall any specific memories, and if you start to feel any pressure or pain, stop thinking about whatever you were recalling at the time."

I winced. Here I had just been blabbing about the forge and I could've triggered more damage. One wrong thought and who knew what would happen to his mind.

"Easier said than done," Kaelan grumbled. Though he nodded, doubt clouded his gaze, the fear that maybe this was something even we couldn't fix. But I refused to believe that. We had to find a way.

"Come on, let's get you to an actual bed." Beylin waved us to follow, the heavy silence surrounding us as we walked down the hallway.

Beylin ushered Kaelan into a neat bedroom. The nephilim's gaze darted to me, and for a moment the uncertainty and disorientation shone in his eyes. I couldn't even imagine what this must've been like for him. To not be certain about your own memories, to feel utterly alone in a city you don't remember, and now knowing his mind was a ticking bomb.

I flashed him a smile, hoping I appeared reassuring. "Don't worry, I'll be close by." Kaelan nodded, and I followed after Beylin once the door closed.

Only once we were in his office did Beylin turn to assess me. "I'm sorry I don't have better news, but it's likely the only person who will be able to fix this is the one who cast the original spell."

"And we have no clue who that is and can't ask Kaelan in case it triggers a fracture," I said.

"Exactly," he grumbled. "I'm hoping the Order was responsible for this. So we need to wait for them to get in touch."

That did not sound promising. I slumped down into a chair, raking my hands through my hair. "How did everything get so messy again?"

Beylin patted my shoulder. "You will need to stay close to him. That rune on you will help reassure him. His subconscious understands it."

My fingers trailed over my chest, though I couldn't feel any magic. "You know what it does?"

"Though it's angelic in nature, I recognize parts of it. It is a promise of protection, like a sworn duty, as he said. But if there is more to it, I can't say, just that this is like a sworn oath, but deeper. Only the caster would know the full meaning of it."

I shot Beylin a flat look. "And that is the one person who I can't ask or I might harm him."

"I know it's not what you want to hear—"

I waved him off and hissed out a sigh. "It's fine. There are far bigger issues we need to deal with." One little angelic rune that offered me protection was right at the bottom of the list.

"How is your hunt for a shop location going?" he asked, all of a sudden. Did he have to remind me of another aspect of my life I was failing at? He nodded at the soul-crushing disappointment likely showing on my face and said, "Come on, then."

Chapter Twenty-Six

"That door's new, isn't it?" I said, frowning. Beylin had led me into Divine's cafe area, where a door was now wedged in between two of the large bookcases.

The window set in it only revealed inky darkness. Which should've been terrifying, yet the shadows didn't seem sinister. I paused at that odd thought: shadows just were, they didn't have intent behind them.

Beylin's face didn't give away anything as he nodded for me to go ahead. I strode towards it, far more curious than cautious. I clearly hadn't learned my lesson.

There was a faint snick as I turned the handle and pulled it open; the rich aroma I'd come to associate with Divine's magic spilled out around me. Even though the door was open, darkness obscured the inside, and I was not stepping into that.

"Can I've some light?" I asked Divine, and they obliged. Soft lights rolled over the new area and I stepped in, tugged forward by awe. Residual magic hummed against my skin, my tentative steps nothing but soft clicks across the polished hardwood floor.

The space, about half the size of the cafe, had shelves lining both walls, empty for now, but waiting to be stocked. A thick curtain blocked the large window at the front, but I knew if I pulled it back, the morning sun would stream in, bathing the room in its warm glow. Next to it was another door, this one led onto the street and was currently shuttered. Along the center sat several tables, gleaming with polish, perfect to catch the eye, while at the back was a long polished counter.

A wooden workbench drew my attention, its surface marred and weathered by the countless hours of work it had endured. Against the back wall stood a large, empty cabinet, perfect for storing ingredients.

The door at the rear stood ajar, revealing a glimpse of a cozy room beyond. The possibilities grew within me. This area, with its inviting emptiness and subtle charm, was the perfect space for my alchemy business. As the realization dawned on me, excitement and anticipation bubbled in my chest.

"I know you've a lot going on, but Divine couldn't wait anymore," Beylin said, a satisfied smile widening as he took in the amazement that was written across my face. "It seems that our esteemed building overheard you were trying to open an alchemy shop and feared you were leaving us. And without consulting me—" he shot a glare at the ceiling "—decided to create a new space."

"I love it, thank you," I said in a rush. *Did you know about this?* I asked Danika, who was trotting around, inspecting every inch of the store.

"Do you think all Divine and I do is gossip?"

No, there is probably some napping in there too. My fox laughed but didn't deny it. "Oh, can I bring Ruby and Jade here? They'll be so delighted." Divine's lights flickered in what I could only assume was excitement and approval.

"The space is yours to do what you will," Beylin said. "We can talk about rent and utilities another time."

Unable to contain my excitement, I typed out a quick message to the shifters, inviting them to Divine and said I had something to show them.

My fingers had hardly left the screen before a text from Rynac popped up, asking about a meeting to go over runes for the case. Even thoughts of that couldn't diminish the bubbling happiness as I tapped out a reply.

"It's amazing!" Jade said for the tenth time, as she continued to explore every nook and cranny Divine had created.

"We will have lots of work to do, to get everything set up," Ruby said, her gaze more calculating, but then a smile broke through. "But you finally have a shop front."

"We do." I squeezed her hand. "And I'm sorry about—"

Ruby shot a glance over her shoulder, but Jade was far too occupied with inspecting all the cupboards. "Nan asked for my help with researching the runes. She explained what's going on."

"Oh," I managed. "I'm sorry for not telling you."

"It's not that," Ruby said. "It just hurt that you seemed to forget about us."

"I'm sorry. That's the last thing I wanted, but everything kept crashing down around me and I got overwhelmed. I know it's not a good enough excuse. Both you and Jade have been a blessing. You've supported me more than I deserve. I hope you can both forgive me and know I'll do my best to be open and communicate with you."

Ruby shot me a lopsided grin. "I appreciate that. We don't want to lose you either. Being your friend and working on this project together has been a blast. It's the happiest I've seen Jade in a long time. You can't get rid of us that easily."

I huffed a laugh, so thankful I hadn't ruined everything. If I'd been doing this alone, I would be overwhelmed already. But knowing that I had these two there to help me, get things organized, and keep me on track, allowed me to not buckle under the weight of stress.

The door jingled open and a wide-eyed Indra and Rynac stepped inside. I grinned like a fool. I hoped this feeling never got old.

"Welcome to the alchemy shop!" Jade said, throwing her arms wide, but then she turned to me and added, "I think we need a better name."

I chuckled at that and stepped over to the siblings, giving them a quick tour. Not that there was much to see.

Their smiles matched my own when Indra said, "It's been a while since I've seen you smile. You seem . . ."

"Happy again," Rynac finished.

"Alchemy makes me happy," I said, looking over all the empty shelves just waiting to be filled.

Even though I'd a long way to go before the shop was ready to open—permits, stock, licenses—the reality of it was closer now, like I could almost touch it.

Alchemy was that steadfast part of my life that had always brought me solace and joy, and now it was as if that spark had reignited. Not to mention that having the store up and running when my family visited would be the best surprise.

Rynac wrapped me in a tight hug that startled a laugh out of me.

"What's this for?" I said, pulling back to look up at him.

"I've missed this Nyssa."

"We both have," Indra added, squeezing my hand. I wanted to apologize to her again, but the look in her eyes told me she understood, and she gave my hand a second squeeze. "But we need to get to work."

Right, the real reason they were here. Ruby shooed out a very reluctant Jade, but there was a hint of brightness in the shifters' eyes as the two of them left.

Only when the door closed did Indra pull out the photos and sketches, but I knew I had an apology to make first.

"I'm sorry," I blurted before I lost my courage. Warmth flooded through my bond with Danika as if she were offering me her strength. "I haven't been very open with either of you. It's so hard to talk about, to admit that I'm struggling with . . . what she did to you because you're my friends, what I went through—" The words cut off, like a demonspawn had wrapped its hand around my neck and squeezed.

It was like trying to breathe underwater; the pressure growing until my chest felt ready to burst, yet nothing came out. Worse, I feared when the words came out all I would get was looks of pity or confusion, so it was easier to just stay silent.

"I know you've been there for me," I tried again. "That you will support me but . . . whenever I try to speak, it's like the words get tangled and stuck, lodged in my throat with fear and shame."

The weight of their stares bore down on me, and I kept my gaze fixed on the table. All my words evaporated as I clenched my trembling hands tighter.

Indra reached over, her hands gripped mine and squeezed. "Thank you for saying something. You're not in this alone. We're always here for you. I'm sorry you've been suffering through this silently."

"It's because I feel like I have to," I said, my shoulders sagging. "Otherwise, I'll just be inflicting my burden on you, like I'm not strong enough to bear it alone."

Rynac wrapped me in a tight embrace, and I leaned into his warmth and steady strength. "We're your friends. We're always here to share burdens, to be someone to lean on, to listen, to offer our support in any way we can. It will get easier. Opening up and speaking about it is the first step. We're here whenever you are ready to talk."

Their soothing presence seeped into me, grounding me in the present. For a long moment, I basked in the certainty of it all. "I keep having flashes, nightmares, that I'm back down there," I said, my voice a whisper. Danika's unwavering faith pulsed through our bond as she offered me courage. "Trapped again. That I never got out. We never got out. All of it happening over and over. How do I fight back against that?"

Indra's grip tightened, concern creasing her features. "Healing isn't a straight path. There will be moments that drag you back," she said. "But that doesn't mean you're not moving forward."

"You survived," Rynac said, the words rumbling through his chest. "We survived. And we are all here now. That's what matters. The past can try to claw at your resolve, but it doesn't own you."

Tears stung at my eyes, and I blinked them back. "I'm scared that if I let you all in, you'll see how broken I really am," I whispered. The words slipped out before I could stop them.

Indra shook her head, her gaze unwavering. "Nyssa, we don't expect you to be perfect. We love you as you are—faults, scars, and all. None of us gets through this life untouched, and you don't have to be strong all the time."

"Just one step at a time," Rynac said, pulling back and wiping away a tear that spilled free. I nodded, not trusting my voice.

"And we will be beside you for each one," Danika added, a smile in her voice.

"Let's get to work," I said, pulling away and swiping at my eyes. "I won't be much help as a blubbering mess."

Indra snorted. She squeezed my hand until I met her gaze. Compassion and understanding shone in her eyes. A silent thank you for opening up.

She laid out the photos and sketches of the runes from all the crime scenes across the counter. Explaining the recent developments with professionalism and not as if I'd just spilled my heart to them. There hadn't been another killing, though it wasn't clear if the murderers were just waiting or if they were distracted with Edrik.

"From what the rune master has compiled, there are very few runes that are the same in the spell arrays," Rynac said. I scanned over the images and the notes attached to each, growing more confused with each one.

"I don't see an obvious link either," I said, lifting Danika up so she could take a look. "There has to be a key or link we are missing, because to me, these look like separate arrays to cast their own spell. I expected them to be copies, or at least very similar."

Rynac sighed. "The rune master said the same thing. There has to be a pattern, but we can't find one in the victims or locations either."

"Look at this one," Danika said. Her nose pointed at a sketch of a rune that looked like a random assortment of lines. The comment attached noted there were no matches to this rune in the MEA database. *"Compare it to the photo."*

The crime-scene photographer had been thorough, taking shots of the runes from various angles. When I compared the photo taken directly down to the sketch, I realized, "They look different." The top-down view had fewer lines. "This is a demonic rune. The last crime scene had one as well—they might be more hidden as they appear distorted from any other angle."

"Could the demonic runes be the link?" Indra asked.

"I don't know enough about how they work. But if we compare all the images to the sketches, we might at least be able to identify which are demonic first."

We sifted through all the runes, picking out the ones that might be demonic. Some were easier to spot than others, but it was like looking at different languages and trying to piece together which were from the same one.

By the time I had sketched out a copy of the possible runes to research, my eyes were gritty and dry. With one last hug, Indra and Rynac left to report to the captain.

I rubbed a weary hand over my face and collected my papers. Sleep tugged at me, but with these runes and now an alchemy shop just waiting to be filled, I didn't have time to rest.

Magic fizzled across my skin a moment before something tugged inside me. Frowning, I looked up to find a staircase at the back of the shop—one that I would have sworn hadn't been there before—with Kaelan coming down.

"What are you doing?" I scolded as I rushed over. Last thing I needed was more injuries if he fell down the stairs.

"I hate being cooped up."

I was about to protest, but something in his voice made me pause. While he did need rest, Aegis had imprisoned him for who knew how long. I couldn't blame him for not wanting to stay in the same place. "I'm about to head to my apartment. While I don't have a place for you to sleep, I do have a private garden terrace. It should be safe and you can rest there, but only if you promise to behave. No disappearing on me again."

The corner of his mouth quirked at that. "I wouldn't dream of it."

CHAPTER TWENTY-SEVEN

A yawn crept up on me, slow and unstoppable. I blinked my vision clear, attempting to locate the sentence I'd been reading.

The last few days had been very, very long. I'd managed to nap for a few hours, but it barely dented my exhaustion, and I was running on pick-me-up potions, coffee, and a healthy dose of spite. There was just too much to do and not enough hours in the day.

I'd hoped the cool night air out on the terrace would help keep me awake, but it didn't appear to be working.

While I knew figuring out what Aegis was up to was far more important, I missed my alchemy. And the pay. I refused to give up my shifts at Divine. Not only was this was peak tourist season, but I needed to cover rent.

Thankfully, Indra had secured a consulting contract for studying the runes, so at least I had enough income to stay afloat.

Another yawn overtook me, this one even deeper than the last, a creeping sensation that I couldn't resist.

"That's the fourth yawn in five minutes," Kaelan drawled.

"I didn't know we were counting." I glared up at the nephilim as he sprawled precariously on the roof above.

He'd been loitering around tonight, annoying me enough that I'd put him to work. Danika scouted the streets and connected with the other magical creatures within the city, gathering information to help pinpoint any movement by Aegis. I'd rather be out there with her, but my duties were research.

My primary focus was on runes and spell arrays, but I made time to look for information that could help Kaelan. Only the magic that altered the mind was far more complex and dangerous.

Even with all the resources at the guild and from the shifters, I found little with promise. I even resorted to hunting through *The Lunar Codex*, hoping for a miracle, but found nothing.

While there were a few potions to help calm the mind, which might aid Kaelan before he had a break, it wouldn't be enough to stop a fracture from triggering. I kept all of that to myself. Tonight was the first time he'd appeared to be in somewhat of a good mood, and I didn't want to take that from him.

Half-reclining on the roof, Kaelan worked through his stack of books, his long legs dangling over the edge as if gravity were nothing more than a mild suggestion.

My stomach twisted just looking at him, trying not to think about the sheer drop, but I guess that was the benefit of having wings.

If I hadn't known better, I would've believed he was relaxing with a good book. The moonlight filtering through the clouds softened the sharp angles of his features, casting shadows over the planes of his face and the slight smirk that curved on his lips.

"Did you fall asleep with your eyes open, or do you enjoy staring at me?"

I shook my head, more to wake myself up than to rise to the bait. "I need to make another coffee."

My body protested as I heaved myself up, especially my left leg, which had decided to fall asleep without the rest of me. Kaelan slid off his perch with ease, landing smoothly in front of me.

"Showoff," I muttered, trying to get around him.

"No more coffee," he said, blocking my path. "You need actual sleep and not to keep pushing yourself."

"Oh, and you're the expert on that Mr. I-escaped-Aegis-badly-injured-but-stalked-some-chick-for-days?" I narrowed my eyes, ready for a fight.

"Yes," he said, crossing his arms. "I was trying to survive; you, on the other hand, are trying to solve all these problems. But if they were easy, someone would've figured it out by now. You can't brute-force your way to a solution."

"So what am I meant to do, then?"

"Sleep."

"I don't want to sleep," I hissed back, my frustration and fear surging.

My lack of sleep made it harder to control my emotions. I knew the moment Kaelan noticed, saw beyond the words—that it wasn't just all this research, but a fear of sleeping.

He remained silent for far too long, but I refused to be the first to look away.

"Let's train," he said, and I bristled at the command in his tone. "I can sense your restless magic from a block away."

That seemed suspicious. I frowned, trying to guess what he was up to. "You're just trying to tire me out so that I'll sleep."

He grinned at that. "If you plan to go up against Aegis, you'll need to fight."

Without warning, he pulled two blades that I hadn't even noticed. I stumbled back a step and scrambled for my conduit, the thin wooden wand that helped to direct the flow of magic. Though if this had been an actual fight, he would've attacked before my slow reaction.

"Good, what else?"

I flicked my conduit, and with a snap, it extended into a thin stave as I fell into a defensive stance.

"What other spells do you have?" Kaelan asked, still holding the daggers in a loose grip.

I shook my head, holding my stance in case he was trying to distract me. "Besides the astral shield and my potions, I don't have anything to rely on. I mean, I've a low-level moonbeam, but as we're not up against demonspawn, so it won't be much help."

"That's it?"

My lip twitched with annoyance. "I've only had this magic for a few months."

"I thought you said the shifters were training you."

"They tried, but—" I pressed my lips together. This wasn't the conversation I wanted to have right now.

"Show me your shield then, what you can do," Kaelan demanded. I shot him an irritated look, but he crossed his arms and waited.

"Fine," I hissed.

Retracting my conduit, I settled into a relaxed stance and dipped into my magic. This would be easy. I could craft a shield, but my shoulders tightened as I pushed the energies out. An astral shield bloomed to life, shimmering in the moonlight. Though I made it smaller than usual, fearing my fire would flare.

"Can you alter it once it's cast?" he asked.

"I can, but for anything more powerful, I need to use a rune to contain my solar magic."

The words were out of my mouth before I could stop them. Why had I said that? I braced, waiting for him to ask the inevitable. How was I going to explain *that* to him? What would he think of me when I explained I couldn't even draw a rune without having flashbacks?

To my surprise, he just nodded. "Then show me what you can do without it."

Wordlessly, I complied, pushing the shield wider. Kaelan studied it, calling out different orders. Taller, smaller, closer, higher. I matched each of his commands even as sweat prickled over my skin. It'd been far too long since I'd given my magic a workout. "What about all around you?"

I stretched the energies, curving and shaping them until they formed a dome over me.

The ground slipped away beneath my feet and in a flash, I was back in that underground bunker. The click of claws on concrete echoed around me, magic saturating the air until it weighed against my skin, so potent and thick I thought I would suffocate. Trapped again. Helpless.

My fire magic flared, scorching my skin as I pushed more power into my shield. The golden spell array at my feet shimmered, hungry to consume me. I couldn't give in. I had to stop her.

Breathe. The command shuddered through my mind, and I sucked in a trembling breath.

"You are on the garden terrace of your apartment building." The words were so certain and I clung to them, breathing in and out.

The memories faded, and I blinked until the real world settled around me again. My shield was still intact, brighter than usual, and Kaelan watched me with a sharp intensity.

Pain throbbed in my left hand and I flinched at the fire surrounding it, licking the skin. My heart kicked up a notch, I released my shield then I blew out a long, slow breath, curling my fingers down and extinguishing the flames.

I winced as the pain grew, but as I inspected my hand, the flame had not marred the skin. A trickle of bright red blood cascaded down the back of my hand, my fingers trembling, but I could only stare.

Warm hands wrapped around mine, tilting them down and brushing over my skin.

"What do you see here?" Kaelan asked as he inspected my hand, but there was no blood, no damage. Words escaped me, and all I could do was breathe and remind myself where I was. His finger traced the line of the jagged scar. "How did you get this?"

"Demonspawn," I said, my voice tight. His finger began to trace a pattern over my skin that I couldn't help but follow.

"The scar bothers you." It wasn't a question, so I stayed silent. "Flesh can heal, skin mends, but too many wounds are deeper under the surface. Left to bleed unseen, they can do far more damage."

Far too tired to get into a philosophical debate I remained silent, yet I couldn't bring myself to pull my hand away.

"Was I there?" he asked, his voice too quiet.

"When it happened, yes, not after."

"Will you tell me what happened after?" he asked softly.

I wanted to say no. Why would I want to relive all of that again?

Maybe it was because I was so utterly exhausted, or that I was so tired of keeping all my fears inside . . . or that he still held my hand, but for the first time in a long time, I felt safe.

"I woke up not knowing where I was, what had happened, or if any of you had survived. Everything hurt and . . . I was terrified. The rune on my hand was the only way to control my solar magic, and with it damaged, I had nothing. No magic to protect me. All my potions gone. Alone, defenseless, and scared. Trapped in a spell array, in the sacrifice circle. No way to escape.

"It was going to consume the magic within me to open a portal, and I was helpless to stop it. She held my friends, used them to get me to do what she wanted."

I chewed on my lip, watching the mesmerizing movement of his finger. With a heavy sigh, I forced the words out.

"I would've done whatever she asked. Done anything in exchange for their lives." I winced at the admission and stepped away, Kaelan releasing my hand when I tugged.

"You believe that makes you weak?"

"If I'd been stronger—" I shook my head. "The scar reminds me of how badly I failed. Of the fear that I thought would drown me, that might still drown me. That I might have survived, but something broke within me that night and I don't think I can ever be the same again."

"There was a story they used to tell young nephilim warriors," Kaelan said, leading me over to a bench. "In our home realm, there was a group of humans who practiced a unique art form. When a piece of pottery broke, most people would throw it away, but this group would gather the broken pieces and put them back together.

"They didn't try to hide the cracks or pretend they weren't there. Instead, they used gold to mend the fragments, creating something new. They didn't shy away from the damage; they highlighted it, showing the world that just because something was broken didn't mean it couldn't be mended, that it couldn't still have use. It wouldn't be the same, but the damage would be filled with something else, creating a new piece.

"With every wound we took, we imagined bleeding gold, so that our scars, though visible, didn't signify damage or weakness but rather a transformation into something stronger. We didn't need to hide our scars or the broken parts of ourselves, because they weren't something to be ashamed of.

"So, even if you have scars or see yourself as damaged, it doesn't mean you're no longer whole. We just have to find a way to put ourselves back together again."

"But what is the gold that joins the broken pieces back together?" I asked. "I don't have golden blood to mend my shattered pieces."

Kaelan chuckled. "I don't think it's literal blood that repairs it. Some nephilim see themselves as the gold meant to bind the broken pieces of the world. But I believe the gold can come from many places. For me, it's about trying to bring the pieces back together, not holding on to the image of what we once were. We can move forward—but first, we have to admit that some of our pieces are broken."

I nodded, letting the words sink in. "So, we don't just hide our scars or pretend the damage didn't happen. We . . . fill it with something new. Something that makes us stronger."

Kaelan looked at me, a quiet intensity in his gaze. "Exactly. The world, the battles, even ourselves—they can shatter us in ways we don't see coming. But those breaks, those cracks . . . they're part of the story. They're how we grow. They make us into something we couldn't have been otherwise."

A thought crossed my mind. "But isn't there a risk? That we will break ourselves beyond repair, that we will never be whole?"

Kaelan's smile softened. "Sometimes it means we're more aware, more resilient. If we fill those fractures with gold—whether that's trust, hope, or just a simple willingness to try again—then those breaks become a part of us in a way that strengthens us. It is not always easy, and sometimes parts stay broken for a long time, until we discover the gold that will repair that piece."

I glanced down at my own hands, fingers that had felt fire and power, that had hurt and healed. "So, maybe it's not about becoming what we used to be, trying to be who we once were," I murmured, almost to myself, "but about seeing what we can become now."

Kaelan nodded, his voice warm. "We don't have to be the people we were before the damage—sometimes we can't go back. We just have to be willing to keep trying, to find our own way forward, even if we end up different from what we imagined."

There was a quiet moment between us, a kind of shared under-standing. I felt a weight lift, the smallest bit.

Maybe I didn't have all the pieces yet, and maybe the journey ahead would shatter me again, but I didn't have to pick up the fragments alone. I was just telling myself I did, that I would be stronger if I did it alone.

I'd even shut out Danika because . . . because I feared anyone seeing how broken I was. Feared they would think I was broken beyond repair, that I wasn't strong enough to put myself back together, and cast me aside.

And so I pushed them away before they could see that as a weakness. Told myself that I had to keep them at arm's length to keep them safe. But in truth, I was only making myself weaker, more vulnerable.

Chapter Twenty-Eight

The familiar scent of rich earth and moss greeted us as we descended into the shifters' den. But as Ruby and I entered the library, it mixed with the crisp scent of parchment and ink.

Nan hunched over a desk next to another shifter I recognized as her alchemy assistant. Papers and books filled the area, with a varied assortment of runes, as well as the photos of the arrays from the crime scenes the MEA had entrusted to us.

Nan waved us over, not even bothering with pleasantries. This couldn't be good.

A large map of the city, displaying a series of marked locations, lay before her, with a spell array below. The MEA may have mentioned the number of killings, but seeing them laid out before me like this was a blow to the chest. No wonder the MEA was desperate.

"I sent a group out yesterday to the last crime scene," Nan said, tapping the map. "They were to take readings to see if our devices could pick up any traces of the magic. It was a stab in the dark, but as we had little to work with, I thought it worth a shot."

"What did they find?" I asked, already knowing I wouldn't like it.

"There were still fluctuations of energy around it. Not enough to be noticed unless you were looking for it."

Residual energy was common around powerful spell arrays, but the way she'd called them fluctuations worried me.

"So I dispatched teams to all the locations to gather data. Every site had the same readings, the same levels, even what they believed was the first killing."

"The spell arrays are still active?" I asked. "I assumed the MEA would have the crime scenes turned over for cleaning."

Pulling out my phone, I called Indra. Another piece of the puzzle. But where did it fit? None of this felt right.

She answered on the third ring.

"Have the spell arrays been destroyed at the crime scenes?" I said in a rush.

A moment of silence passed before I heard the clack of keys. "Looks like all of them have, the last two were just released to be cleaned before being returned to the owners. The private crime-scene cleaning company listed them as complete."

While it might be all coincidence, my gut told me otherwise. "The shifters took readings from the locations. There are still energy fluctuations we believe are tied to the spell arrays." Either the arrays were still there and someone altered the records, or the arrays had been removed, meaning something else was anchoring the spell.

"I'll speak with the captain personally," she said, before hanging up. But the sharpness in her voice still echoed in my ears, and I knew she feared there were more traitors within their ranks.

When the dark witch had summoned her army of thralls, far too many of them had been within the ranks of the MEA and the UMC. They took an oath to protect and serve, yet they had sworn themselves to the witch, given her their loyalty in exchange for power.

"With the spells they cast still active," Nan said with a deep frown, "it means the magic will activate once again, or it's doing whatever it was intended to do."

"Neither being good."

"No, especially not since we found out what that hidden demonic rune is meant to do." Nan handed me the detailed page of notes. "It seems like some kind of converter. It takes the magic from within the array and transforms it into demonic energy. I didn't even know that was possible, and I've never heard of anything like it."

"What?" I pored over the notes. "From everything we're taught about energies, you can't just change one into another."

"It should not be possible, but I can find no explanation on how they are doing it."

"But what does it do with the transformed energy?" Ruby asked as she joined us.

I scanned over the map again. "It must be channeling somewhere, but not within the spell array. And that doesn't make any sense."

Nan leaned over the page, her brow furrowed in concentration. "If it's channeling the energy outside the array, there must be another focal point, something drawing the demonic energy to it. But where?" She traced a finger along the lines of the array, her eyes scanning for any clues.

If we could figure that out, we might be able to stop whatever this was before it got worse. Or figure out where they would strike next and stop them. The puzzle still gnawed at me.

Taking a few pages of dead paper, I traced out each of the demonic runes. The paper had been created to neutralize magic. This was the only safe way to draw a rune without fear of activating it.

I lay each rune over their location on the map. Something scratched at my mind and I tilted my head, trying to figure out why the pattern seemed familiar.

Tracing the lines with my finger, I tried to piece it together, but as I leaned closer, my heart pounded as a pattern I knew well began to emerge.

"The array isn't complete," I murmured. Everyone crowded around as I started connecting the runes, my fingers shaking slightly. "If we isolate just the demonic runes . . . they form their own spell array."

We scrambled to draw it out, laying parchment after parchment over the map until we revealed the massive spell array. It spread across the entire city, intricate and terrifying in its complexity.

"This . . . this isn't just about the murders." Nan's face went pale as she studied the array. "These three runes, it's targeting the veil itself."

My breath caught in my throat. "That's why they are transforming it into demonic energy. It's the only way to damage the veil."

Lunar magic created the veil and could therefore damage it, but very few with lunar energies would ever do so willingly. The only other magic that affected it was demonic, and though lunar magic was far more powerful, this slow, targeted channeling would eventually tear the veil.

Ruby's expression hardened, disbelief mingling with anger. "Why would they try to weaken the veil? That's what's holding the demons back. I thought Aegis was preparing to fight the demons, not help them."

Nan shook her head, her voice low and troubled. "If they're trying to unseal the protections around the forge, they likely need to weaken the veil first to disrupt the warding." Her gaze flicked up to meet mine, a storm of worry and determination swirling in her gaze.

Desperation clawed in my chest. I still had no idea where Edrik or the forge were, but the enemy was posed to attack at any moment.

Unless we could find a lead to follow, my only hope was attempting to locate Edrik again. To hit Aegis before they could complete the larger spell array.

Chapter Twenty-Nine

The dim light of the moon filtered through my bedroom window as I sat hunched over the new spell array to find Edrik.

The runes blurred before me, while the rest of my failed ideas lay scattered around me.

Exhausted after returning from the shifter den, I'd passed out, but my nightmares had sprung to life the moment I closed my eyes. And despite Danika's best attempts, the dreams were too strong.

She now lay curled up at the foot of my bed. The weight of her fatigue added to my own, but I didn't have the strength to block our connection. And in some ways, I deserved it. If these foolish nightmares didn't hound me, both of us would be fully rested.

Once the moon was high enough, I'd wake her and attempt the location ritual. My eyelids grew heavy, and with a frustrated sigh, I leaned my head against the wall. Only this time it was runes that danced through my mind, ever changing so that I could never quite grasp them.

A thud jerked me awake. Heart pounding as I snapped upright, the room swam back into focus. I blinked, disoriented, and caught sight of movement near the window.

My breath hitched when a half-illuminated figure stumbled inside, followed by a set of black wings.

"Kaelan?" I hissed, dread curling in my stomach as I shot to my feet.

Something was wrong. His usual grace was gone, replaced by a staggering, almost drunken gait. I rushed to him, my hand reaching out just as he stumbled again, colliding with my dresser.

The pile of books on top clattered to the ground. Blue light washed over us as Danika's fur glowed enough to reveal that he had a few minor cuts, but no major injuries.

"What happened?" I demanded, reaching for his arm and avoiding the small amount of blood.

His breathing was ragged and his skin clammy under my touch, but worse, his expression was slightly glazed.

My door burst open as Rynac and Voren barreled in, their faces drawn with worry. Rynac fell into a defensive position in front of Voren. With a baton in his grip, he was ready to strike, not seeming to care that he was only wearing boxers.

But it was Voren, with hands on hips, who recovered first. "Nyssa, why is there a *nephilim* in your room? You know we have standards here."

"I didn't invite him," I snapped back. "And he's injured, so if you don't mind . . ."

That was all Rynac needed. The grip on the weapon relaxed as he rushed to help me, realizing the wall was the only thing holding Kaelan upright. "What happened?" he demanded.

"I don't know. He just fell through my window."

"This looks like fun," Zola's light voice said from behind Voren as Rynac and I attempted to move Kaelan. "Where's my invite?"

Voren, without missing a beat, shot back, "Despite how it looks, it's not that kind of party tonight."

"Could everyone get out of my room?" I snapped, stumbling under Kaelan's weight as we coaxed him forward.

Voren and Zola retreated as we lumbered out into the living room.

"Just lay him on the ground." There wasn't anywhere else, as Kaelan kept flaring his wings and knocking down more things as he passed. That and I didn't want to scrub nephilim blood out of the carpet.

"Oh, it's *him*," Zola muttered.

"I know, thought she had better taste," Voren said.

I ignored them as I looked over Kaelan, but didn't find any new injuries. Under Danika's light, I hadn't noticed how pale he was or the sweat beading on his forehead.

He was barely conscious, his head lolling to the side. Then it hit me—the strange way he'd been moving, the sluggishness in his limbs. This wasn't just an injury.

Danika sniffed at the wounds. *"Mylock. He's been poisoned."*

"Mylock," I repeated, my mind scrambling for what I recalled about it. My heart stuttered. "They tried to subdue him."

The raw form of the mylock leaf targeted the nervous system, inducing a state of lethargy and impairing motor functions. The fact that Kaelan didn't seem to be able to talk worried me. I didn't know how he'd managed to make it up to my window at all without plummeting down.

"I don't know how to reverse it." My words were barely louder than a whisper. I could brew a general poison reversal, but there was no guarantee that would work, and I'd need time to make it.

"I should be able to slow it," Zola said, already rushing over to her garden on the balcony. "Voren, boil some water."

"Let's treat these wounds," Rynac said, his voice snapping me out of my daze. I managed a nod and ran to gather supplies. Just where had Kaelan been? There could be little doubt that he'd run into Aegis—who else would poison him to incapacitate?

We worked in silence, but the tension in the air grew heavier with each passing minute and all I could do was prepare for when it snapped.

Once the wounds were tended to, I sat back, wringing my hands, wishing I had something else to do. His pulse was steady. At least it would be for the majority of races, though I didn't know if that included nephilim.

What felt like an eternity later, Zola knelt down next to Kaelan. The pungent scent of bog moss hit me, and I wrinkled my nose as she propped Kaelan up enough to drink it. Once again, I had dumped my friends right in the middle of my mess, whether they liked it or not.

Zola moved her hands over Kaelan, and my skin prickled. The sensation was warm, like sunlight filtering through leaves, the subtle scent of rich earth wrapping around me as the faint sound of rustling leaves tickled my awareness.

The dryad sat back with a heavy sigh, her green skin duller than it had been after expending her magic. "That's all I can do, but it should slow it before it affects anything vital. His body will have to process the rest."

Goddess, it hit me all at once. Mylock targeted the nervous system, but enough of it would start to affect his lungs. I compiled a list in my head of what I needed to do; brushing up on poison reversals and antidotes, what to keep on hand, and how long it would take to prepare such items. Then I realized no one was talking, all waiting for me to speak.

"Thank you, Zola." I flopped back, resting my head against the wall, and stared at the ceiling. Where did I even start? Apologizing for being a terrible friend and roommate?

"I hope he had a good excuse when he showed back up," Zola said. Her arms were crossed as she gave me an "I expected better from you" look, but there was no resentment or anger.

I huffed a weak laugh. "He doesn't even remember me." This was a conversation I'd been avoiding, wanting to keep my friendship with them apart from my moon-blessed duty.

It'd been my hope that if I kept the two separated, I could keep them from getting entangled. That was until it came crashing through my window.

Rynac stood up, pulling Voren with him, before turning to offer me a hand. At some point he'd thrown on a shirt, but besides the nephilim passed out on the ground, we looked like we were having a slumber party.

"How about instead of sitting around the unconscious body, we sit on the couch and you can bring us up to speed on our guest?"

He waggled his fingers when I hesitated. There was no judgment in his expression, just the strong and steady presence he always had. Rynac hauled me to my feet, and we settled down on the couches.

"So Nyssa," Voren said, eyeing me up. "Why was a poisoned nephilim climbing in your window and will it be a regular occurrence?"

"I hope not," Zola called from the kitchen as she filled up the kettle again. "If management finds out, they will think we are trying to sneak guests in."

I sat down next to Danika, who'd already decided the excitement was over, and curled up in the corner of the couch.

"Let's start from the beginning, then," I said, my voice dripping with sarcasm. After trying to keep all of this to myself, it felt like I was telling every single soul I knew just how much of a mess my life was.

"Well," Rynac said, when I finally finished explaining everything. His gaze was fixed on the ground, but I could see the thoughts churning. I clenched my sweaty palms in my lap, bracing for . . . I wasn't really sure what. Anger? Rejection? Annoyance?

"What an absolute clusterfuck," Voren muttered.

"You're telling me," I said.

Kaelan, who had been doing a great job being just part of the scenery, lurched upright. Stumbling to his feet, he reached for his weapons, ones that Rynac had the forethought to remove. His wild gaze darted around the room before narrowing in on Voren. *Can't take nephilim anywhere.*

"Kaelan," I snapped. "Sit down and for just five minutes, could you pretend you are a normal, well-adjusted person? I think that's the least you could do after you crashed through my window, uninvited, and we helped to deal with that poison in your system."

Kaelan's usual confident demeanor faltered, and his wings drooped a few inches as he pressed his lips together.

Without another word, he moved to the nearest chair and sat stiffly. Arms crossed over his chest and his wings folded tight, he looked for all the world like a child forced into timeout. His eyes flicked up to meet mine, an apology written across his face.

"Now, care to fill us in on what happened to you?" I asked, holding onto my last threads of patience. He eyed the others with suspicion. "These are my friends. You've met most of them before. But they know what's going on and I trust them all."

"How long was I out?" Kaelan asked, looking at a point somewhere above my head.

"Maybe half an hour," I said. He nodded, and I feared he wasn't going to tell us anything, as a war waged behind his eyes.

"I had a run-in with Nathaniel. It appears he is trying to recapture me for Aegis, but he can't beat me one on one, which is why I assume he resorted to poisons."

"Does Aegis regularly employ poisons? If so, I'll need to start preparing ways to counteract them."

"That's a good idea, especially after tonight's encounter," he said. "I had a few flashes of memory that I believe were when they first captured us."

I sat up straighter at that, but he waved off my concern.

"No fractures, as I doubt our capture was part of the targeted memory. But they were trying to subdue rather than kill, which means they still want something else from me. Though that's not important right now."

I wanted to argue that point, but the concern etching his features made me hold my tongue.

"The important part is that I traced them back to their hideout, the same one they held me at." The room was silent as we all absorbed that fun fact.

"Are you sure it's not a trap?" Rynac asked. "After your escape, I would assume they would relocate, as you could compromise the location."

"Except they knew he had no memories," I said. "No way of contacting the Order, and likely assumed he had no contacts within the city."

"Finding a new location would not be easy, and I also think they stayed, hoping that I would come back to free the others. Like I said, they have been trying to recapture me and they would risk being compromised on the chance that I might return. Only I didn't even remember how I got out of there. I'd just run." He muttered the last part to himself, and my heart squeezed with how defeated he looked.

"You were meant to be lying low. Why did you go out?" I asked.

Kaelan's shoulders hunched over. "I couldn't sit around, not while people are in danger. But now that I know where they are, I can strike back. And they won't be expecting it right now, not if they think the poison is still in my system."

"That's far too risky," Rynac interjected. "You don't even know if the people you are looking for are being held there."

"No," Kaelan said. "But if I can get Nyssa close enough, she might be able to sense them. Then I can go in to free them." His eyes lifted to me, hope and desperation swirling behind them.

He didn't need to say a word, but I knew this was all driven by the guilt of leaving the others behind, even if Nathaniel was hunting him. Why else would he risk himself to give us a chance to find Edrik?

"I'll go," I said. "We need to act before Aegis has a chance to create their next spell array and make their larger spell even more powerful." Danika's support brushed against my awareness. Before Rynac could protest, I added, "Kaelan and I will keep out of sight and stay hidden until I can confirm they are there. We won't make a move until I'm certain."

"I'm not letting you go down there," Kaelan interjected, and Rynac nodded in agreement.

Great, just what I need, them to gang up on me.

"I only need you to confirm they are there, then I'll get them out."

"You against how many of them?" I shot back.

"I'm coming too," Rynac said.

Voren sighed. "Count me in. Someone needs to be the voice of reason."

"If you are our voice of reason," I said, "then we are in serious trouble."

CHAPTER THIRTY

Dressed in black, with my sturdy boots, potion belt, and a bag full of even more potions and healing supplies, I was ready to strike back against Aegis. Also, I was terrified. Thankfully, due to the wards, my shaking hands didn't make all my potions rattle.

We crept through a dark alley, Kaelan in the lead, Voren and Danika close to my side, and Rynac watching our backs. He'd called Indra on the way, knowing neither his sister nor their captain would approve of this foray into espionage.

The captain agreed to pull back any units in the area and put more on standby if things went south. The MEA had no idea what was really happening—Rynac had shared only what was necessary to keep them in the dark. Plausible deniability, or something. While I didn't want to get the enforcers tangled up with Aegis, they were the best equipped to fight them.

The city had a different feel tonight, as if it held its breath, waiting for something to happen. The streets were empty, abandoned by anyone with good sense, and we stayed close to the walls, avoiding the few pools of light from the occasional streetlamp.

With nothing to hear but the muted sound of our feet, it was impossible to keep my mind from wandering, fearing what lay ahead.

I replayed our plan—though it was more a concept of a plan. Neither Indra nor Rynac had been thrilled with it, but both acknowledged time was against us, and involving law enforcement was too risky.

If things went according to plan, once we were close enough, I'd try to connect with Edrik and pinpoint his location. Kaelan would move into position while Danika and Rynac created a diversion to draw Aegis out. Voren and I would hang back, ready to step in if things went sideways.

Kaelan prowled through the streets, his form blending into the darkness. Here he was in his element, doing what he was trained to do.

Voren was quieter than I expected, his gaze sweeping the shadows. And the way he moved, the fluidity . . . I'd only known him as a barista, the easy-going guy with a ready smile, but now I saw how much he'd kept hidden from us.

The air felt colder as we neared the supposed hideout. Kaelan slowed, motioning for us to stop. We crouched in the shadows, a small cluster of figures blending into the night.

Ahead, the office building loomed, a dark silhouette against the sky. It looked unassuming, almost forgotten, but we knew better. Aegis had a talent for making dangerous places seem ordinary.

Kaelan gave me a small nod, and I settled myself. I wove a thread of magic towards Danika, strengthening our connection. In theory, this plan might work, but the truth was I had no idea how the moon-blessed connection worked or how far I could reach. But hopefully, Danika would help to boost the distance I could cover with my magic.

The familiar hum of energy buzzed beneath my skin as I reached out, searching for Edrik in the void.

A frown tugged at my lips as I tried again, but the connection remained distant, too weak to hold. "I don't feel them," I whispered, frustration building. "I need to get closer."

Rynac glanced at the building. "We'll move in. There's more cover closer to their walls."

We advanced, slipping from shadow to shadow, as close as Kaelan dared to take us. This time, when I reached out with my moon-blessed mark, I felt something—a faint presence, barely there.

I wove more magic into the connection, pushing harder when my awareness brushed against his mind. Edrik. My power recognizing his signature from our last encounter.

"He's down there," I whispered. Relief welled in my chest, but the night was far from over.

Everyone nodded, and we broke into our assigned teams. Kaelan took off, his wings unfurling as he rose into the sky. Rynac and Danika slipped into the shadows, their forms disappearing around the building's side. Voren and I remained a little further back, keeping an eye on the entrance.

I reached out again with my moon-blessed mark, seeking confirmation that Edrik was okay. But instead of him, I connected with someone else.

Nathaniel.

A sharp jolt ran through me as his presence flooded my senses—unexpected, intense. Before I could make sense of it, Voren's hand gripped my arm, yanking me out of my thoughts.

"We've got to move!" Voren hissed. Panic surged through me as I realized what had happened.

They'd spotted us.

We broke into a run, darting down the alley, but the sound of footsteps echoed behind us. Too many footsteps. We turned a corner, only to find our path blocked.

Fear jolted through me as I spotted the glint of unsheathed blades, but the shadows shifted and I realized it was Kaelan.

"Keep going," he hissed, waving us past. "I'll lead Aegis away, buy you time to escape." Before I could even protest, he launched himself into the air.

Aegis is here, I called out to Danika as Voren grabbed my hand, not hesitating to pull me along with him.

He had better survival instincts than me. I stumbled after him, unable to stop myself from looking back over my shoulder, scanning the skies for a glimpse of Kaelan. My insides twisted in knots at the thought of letting him take Aegis on alone. At sacrificing himself, to give us a chance.

"I'm on my way," Danika said, and I sensed her sprinting toward me. Voren came to a skidding halt and cursed as I slammed into him. Dead end. A shiver of magic raked down my spine. They were here.

Voren jerked back, and I shoved him through the closest door into the inky darkness of a room. I closed the door with only the faintest click of the lock. Back pressed against the wood, I let out a whisper of a breath. We just had to wait it out until the others got here.

A force slammed into my back and I lurched forward. Voren's arms wrapped around me, keeping me upright. The door cracked, and I whirled, pushing Voren behind me as one final blow shattered it.

I stumbled backward, arms thrown out as if that would protect Voren, but we both crashed to the ground. Before I could stand, bright lights cut through the gloom, freezing me in place.

My chest heaved as I squinted against the light. Pooling magic into my hands, I waited. To use my magic to do harm was a last resort, and my basic self defense moves against trained professionals like Aegis would be laughable.

I wracked my brain, mentally itemizing the potions within my bag, but there were too many of them. Four figures rushed into the room, all dressed in black tactical uniforms, guns with flashlights attached, trained on us.

A shield. That was all I had. Any movement would make them shoot. A faint tingle of magic seemed to cover the enemy, and I feared that their gear was all magically enhanced. Would my shield stand up against their bullets if they held magic?

"What did you find?" a male voice rang out. The figures parted until a larger form blocked the doorway. The pair of white wings at his back turned my stomach to lead. "What is this?" Nathaniel glowered, and his gaze fixed on me. For a breath, I thought recognition flashed in his gaze.

"His accomplices," one figure answered. While the shadows hid their faces, I could make out parts of their features. They didn't have the same full masks covering them.

Nathaniel's gaze swept over us again. "Unlikely. He wouldn't involve a witch or a child."

Child?

"What were you doing here?" he demanded, stepping closer. His wings shifted, partially blocking the flashlights that had been blinding me. But as I stared up at him, I didn't know what he wanted me to say. Which Nathaniel was I talking to?

"We were just walking by. I heard a fight break out. We were just trying to hide."

"Let them go," Nathaniel said, waving dismissively at us. "We are wasting our time. Renatus is our target."

"How can you be so sure?" one of them snapped, stopping Nathaniel in his path. "Why don't we just kill them?"

"We have a sighting, heading northbound," someone outside the room called.

"I don't kill civilians." Nathaniel's words were a dangerous growl. "Leave them. Let's move." The soldiers rushed out of the room until only two remained. I whispered a silent prayer to the Goddess that the one who wanted to kill us had gone.

"What do you want to do with them?" the male soldier asked.

"Please," a small voice pleaded. Ice coursed through me at the child's voice. Where had they come from? "Don't hurt Mama."

A tiny hand gripped my shoulder. Wide-eyed, I turned to find a young boy hidden behind me. His bright coral hair fell in a sleek wave to his ears, and bright green eyes fixed on me, filled with such fear and desperation that my mind went blank.

What in all the heavens and hells?

"I'm not harming a child," he said, lowering his gun.

"We have our orders," the female said, raising the gun to train it on me.

"And we have our directive," he snapped back. "I won't harm one of my own, especially not an innocent child."

Voren can glamor?

The realization clanged through my head. Rumors of the erebians ability to glamor did not do it justice. Even though I knew I was looking at Voren, I still only saw the child.

The illusion was so real, so tangible. There was a general distrust and stigma around erebians and their abilities, likely the reason Voren had never mentioned it.

"Up," the female barked. "I'm taking them down to Holding. Go catch up with the squad." Gathering my magic, I knew I would only have one chance at this, but two against me were still odds I didn't like. But the child squeezed my arm, and I saw the smallest shake of their head out of the corner of my eye.

"It gets us inside," Voren whispered, in that unsettling childlike voice.

With my hands raised, I got to my feet. The female narrowed her gaze, then motioned towards the door with her gun. I took Voren's hand and complied.

He was right, this way we could walk straight into their secure building without raising any alarms. Well, any more alarms. Though the armed escort complicated matters.

Danika. I sent the thought out, pushing through the haze of fear and nerves to connect with my familiar. Her concern washed through me. *We have a way inside, but Nathaniel is coming. Keep Aegis busy and away from the base for as long as you can.*

There was a brief pause, and I could almost feel Danika's burning need to find me, but we both knew she would help more out here. *"Understood. Be careful, Nyssa."*

Chapter Thirty-One

We walked through the maze of alleys for an eternity as I strained to hear any sound of fighting over the pounding of my heart.

I fought every instinct within me, doing my best to draw as little attention to myself or the bag full of potions on my shoulder. If she looked in there . . . well, game over.

"Stop," the soldier snapped, before swiping their card through a reader next to the door.

It clicked open, and she pressed her gun into my back until I stepped inside. The soldier ushered Voren and me through narrow corridors. She didn't say a word, just motioned with her weapon for us to move forward.

The sterile concrete hallways stretched in an endless maze, offering no clues about what lay beyond or what purpose this place served. The cold, gray walls seemed to swallow any hint of life or history, leaving only silence in their wake.

I resisted tapping into my moon-blessed mark again to search for Edrik in case the soldier sensed it.

Still, every instinct screamed at me to escape. But we couldn't—not yet. My pulse thundered in my ears, but I kept my face calm. It was all part of the plan, or so I tried to remind myself.

Finally, the guard led us to a set of heavy metal doors and edged around us to reach them. She glanced back at us, her eyes cold and calculating.

A part of me wondered if she suspected anything, but she motioned us forward again. The door creaked open, revealing a small, barren holding cell beyond it.

Voren squeezed my hand, a silent warning before the woman moved to shove us in. We darted to opposite sides. The soldier faltered, her weapon swinging toward me.

In the blink of an eye, Voren dropped the glamor, lunging for her gun. She jerked back, the gun twisting in her grip.

Before I could second guess myself, I summoned a small shield and rammed it into her. She slammed into the wall, her head cracking against it with a sickening thud, and she crumpled to the ground, unconscious before she even knew what hit her.

I stood there for a moment, breathing heavily, adrenaline surging through my veins as I took in what I'd just done. Without batting an eye, Voren checked her pulse, then dragged her limp body into the cell and shut the door. All while I just stared.

"Piece of cake," Voren said with far too much bravado, then noticed my stricken expression. "She's still alive."

"Why do I feel like that's not your first time hiding a body?" I asked, half joking, half highly concerned.

Voren flashed me a wicked smile. My hands trembled, realizing I'd just harmed someone. But if I hadn't—

I shook off that train of thought. Time was against us. I could berate myself later.

My gaze scanned the corridor; both ways looked the same. I teased out a thread of magic and channeled it into my mark, weak enough that hopefully this time I wouldn't alert Nathaniel. A faint pull led me deeper into Aegis's lair.

"This way, I guess," I said, and we started off. I pulled out two vials and passed them to Voren. "The smoke-bomb potion will give us cover, and the flash potion . . . well, let's just say turn your back and close your eyes." They were the same as the enforcers carried, and it was better if he knew what to expect.

The corridor was empty, but I paused at each door, listening and reaching out for any drop of magic. So far, they were all silent. Somehow, that was more unsettling.

"Which way?" he asked as we paused when the corridor split in two different directions. "I don't think they will have signs saying which way the exit is, which is completely against code."

I quieted my mind and connected with the magic swirling with agitation in my chest. There was a small tug to my right.

With nothing else to go on I followed the pull and headed down the hall. "I didn't know you could glamor," I added in a hushed voice. This wasn't the time, but if he had magic, it could come in handy right now. "It was amazing."

"You . . ." Voren began, ". . . you won't tell Rynac, will you?"

I paused. I didn't want to lie to my best friend, but . . . "It's not my place to tell him." I turned back to Voren and held his gaze, the tightness around his mouth and the pain in his eyes squeezing at my heart. "Be honest with him—he'll be more receptive than you think."

Voren fiddled with his shirt collar, but gave me a small nod. "Thanks for not freaking out."

"Freaking out?" I huffed. "We work in a sentient coffee shop that is tries to play matchmaker, with grumpy ovens and a dwarf, not to mention that I'm a witch with lunar magic and you're dating an enhanced. Nothing about our lives is normal. I'd be more freaked out if things were normal."

I jerked to a stop as the faint connection pulled me backward toward another unmarked door. Letting my eyes fall shut, I pushed more energy into my moon-blessed mark, holding the image of Edrik's mark in my mind.

Pain, agony, guilt. The emotions slammed into me, threatening to drown me, and I gasped as I released the connection.

"He's in there," I whispered.

I could sense him on the other side of the door. With my heart in my throat as I pressed a shaking hand against the handle. Magic thrummed beneath it, a powerful ward to prevent those on the other side from leaving, but not from my side.

The runes lit up with a small push of magic, just like a lock and key. I pulled power from the rune that linked all the others, and the ward faded.

My hand wrapped around the doorknob. Locked. I hunted through my bag and pulled out the potion I needed.

The moment I uncorked the vial, a sharp, acrid scent hit me—like burning metal mixed with sulfur and something bitter. Holding my breath, I poured the corrosive potion over the door handle.

The liquid was a sickly green, thick and viscous, almost oily as it oozed down the metal. It hissed and bubbled, the metal warping and pitting as the liquid dripped, leaving behind a hole where the handle had been.

"That's terrifying," Voren said, his expression halfway between amazed and horrified.

I shrugged, trying not to remember that night months ago when I'd needed it. My fingernails dug into the edge of the door, well away from the splatter of dissolved metal, and pried it open.

Darkness clung to the room—only the shards of light broken by my body revealed what was within, and I didn't dare move.

The straps across his chest were the only thing keeping Edrik in place. Dark circles smudged under his eyes, while his skin was now ashen and sallow. If I hadn't sensed him through the mark, I wouldn't have recognized him.

"Edrik." His name fell from my lips, breaking whatever held me in place, and I rushed forward. My shaking hands fumbled with straps, trying to free him. His eyes flickered open but remained unfocused. Edrik's lips, cracked and dry, moved as he muttered something incoherent, too weak to form real words.

Voren pushed my useless hands out of the way and took over. He was in no state to leave under his own volition—one of us would have to carry him, which would slow us down far too much.

"Nyssa." Voren's hissed whisper snapped me back to reality, and I realized I'd just been staring.

Right, potions. I wanted to smack myself for freezing. I was better than this. He didn't appear to have any external wounds, and I was thankful for that as the memory of Kaelan's battered body flashed through my mind.

"Edrik," I said, hoping he didn't notice my voice shaking as I tried to sound soothing. "Can you hear me?"

He mumbled another string of nonsense, and I cursed. It was not safe or ideal to force someone to drink a potion, even one that would heal them, as they could choke on the fluid.

If I could only get him to drink one potion, I had to make it count. My fingers trailed over my choices until they settled on one. I plucked out the pick-me-up potion. He required healing, but right now I just needed him to have the energy to move his legs and keep upright.

"Edrik, it's Nyssa," I tried again.

I pressed my fingers against his arm, the faint knot of magic in his moon-blessed mark pulsing underneath. They had drained him of magic, probably to keep him weakened. At least this part I could manage.

Pulling out a thread of my power, I pushed it into his mark and it devoured it. While I didn't know how powerful Edrik was, or the depth of his reserves, I fed him enough of my own power until his eyes fluttered open. I couldn't afford to drain my own reserves, as I'd likely need every drop to shield us as we escaped.

Though still glazed, his eyes focused on me, his brow furrowing as if he wasn't sure if I was real or not. Edrik blinked a few times before he looked down at his moon-blessed mark, still glowing with a faint white light.

"It is you," Edrik slurred.

"We're here to get you out," I said, hoping I sounded reassuring and not terrified. "I've a potion that will give you a boost in energy. We need to get out of here before Aegis returns."

He hesitated for a moment before he took the vial. A thin wisp of his power brushed against the potion, likely testing the magic within, before he downed the contents.

"We will have you out of here in no time," I said, taking the empty vial and tucking it away before offering him a second. "This one is for vitality and should help—" I didn't even get to finish before he drank that one down too.

It only took a few heartbeats before his gaze sharpened and Edrik appeared to come into himself again.

"They know," Edrik croaked, his eyes boring into me. "I'm sorry. They know how to get the forge."

CHAPTER THIRTY-TWO

"It's fine, let's just get out of here," I said, not allowing myself a moment to process what it all meant. All that mattered right now was escaping here with our lives. "We can figure it out later."

"No, they know everything," Edrik said, his voice stronger as he seized my hand. His gaze frantic, he gripped me with all the strength he had. "I failed. Broke my sworn duty to Selene. I deserve this."

"No one deserves this," Voren said, working at the straps around Edrik's ankles.

He shook his head, letting my hand go when I pulled away. "But I do. I betrayed the Goddess. I couldn't resist the nightbanes, not when he had the circlet."

The breath rushed out of me. The circlet. And I'd handed it to them on a platter. I shoved my swelling emotions back down. Getting out of here was all that mattered.

"No one could have withstood what they put you through. We need to move. Now—those potions will wear off soon, and every second that ticks by is a chance they'll discover us."

Edrik hauled himself to his feet and wobbled. Voren gripped his arm to keep him steady and then nodded to me.

Right, I needed to find us a way out of here. Heading back out, I scanned the corridor, but it was as blank and empty as all the others we had passed.

I turned back the direction we had come, hoping to leave the same way. The potions must've kicked it as Edrik pushed forward now, not needing Voren's support.

"They know where the forge is," Edrik hissed. "It was my one duty to keep that knowledge safe. The Goddess should've burned my mark and stripped me of my second chance."

I flinched. Could the Goddess do that? "Why would she do such a thing?"

"Selene experienced betrayal before; she will not make the same mistake again."

"Yet you're still here," Voren said. "Perhaps there is still a chance to set things right."

Edrik eyed him for a long moment, but his eyes brightened as if a spark of hope had reignited. Voren's words stirred something within me, too. No one was perfect. We all made mistakes. And we still had a chance to fix things, and we had to keep fighting until that last hope was gone.

"We will set things right," I said, more to myself than the others. When we reached another intersection, I hesitated. We were completely lost.

"*Nyssa!*" Danika's voice burst into my head with urgency. "*Aegis units are returning.*"

I swore. "They're coming." How the hell did we escape this endless maze?

My gut told me to go right, and with nothing better to go on, we took off at a sprint. I rushed past an open door that led to a larger room, where something caught my eye.

I froze, skidding to a halt, barely catching myself against the doorframe. A solitary flickering light illuminated the empty room, casting

long, eerie shadows across the concrete floor. But it was the far end of
the room that I stared at.

A row of iron-barred cells lined the wall, their heavy doors bolted
shut. The air was thick with the scent of metal and damp stone, a
stagnant, oppressive atmosphere that made my skin crawl.

Through the bars, I spotted her—Astrid.

I knew it in a heartbeat. She was sitting in the center of the cell, perfectly still. Her midnight-blue hair hung limp around her shoulders,
and her wings—normally so vibrant—looked dull as they drooped
behind her, like the color was fading from them. Her skin was pale,
almost gray, but she didn't appear injured. Just . . . empty.

"Astrid!" I called out, my voice cracking. She didn't stir, didn't even
glance up. She seemed unable to hear me, as if trapped in some distant
place, unreachable. Panic surged through me. I had to free her.

But the moment my fingers brushed the doorway, magic flared to
life. A sizzling barrier sprang up, glowing with harsh light, and pain
shot through my hand.

I yanked it back with a cry, cradling my fingers to my chest. Unlike
Edrik's cell, this doorway was complicated and powerful; I hadn't even
sensed it. The magic that pulsed here felt twisted, darker, almost alive
in its malevolence.

"Astrid!" I tried again, desperation clogging my throat. She didn't
move. She was so close, but unreachable.

Behind me, shouts echoed through the corridors—Aegis soldiers,
closing in fast. I whipped around, hearing the heavy boots of the
advancing troops.

Voren grabbed my arm, his grip gentle but firm, pulling me back.
"We have to go, Nyssa!"

"No!" I struggled against him, my eyes locked on Astrid's unmoving form. "I can't leave her!"

"We don't have time!" Voren's voice was tense, filled with urgency. "I'm sorry."

A sharp whistle cut through the air, and before we could react, something slammed into the wall beside us with a deafening crack.

The impact sent a cloud of dust and debris exploding outward, showering us in grit and rubble.

My instinct kicked in, and I threw up my arm, summoning a shield as more bullets tore through the air. They were not regular bullets.

"This way." Edrik sprinted ahead, weaving through the concrete corridors.

"Just run!" Voren yelled, yanking my arm, and this time I didn't resist.

We sped after Edrik and stumbled up a set of stairs. I tried to stay close behind, my breath ragged, each step pounding in time with my heart. It was hard to maintain my shield and keep my legs moving as terror sunk its claws into my mind.

I flinched with every bullet that slammed into the shield, fearing the next one would be the one to shatter the spell.

The sharp and relentless echo of boots on concrete closed in around us, mixing with the sizzle of magic as my shield took another hit. I could feel it weakening with each one, but I couldn't let it fall.

Voren's tight grip on my arm was the only thing keeping me upright, and I fumbled through my potions again, looking for something to slow them down.

Would a vial be able to pass through my shield? Not likely, and as I hadn't tested it, I didn't need to discover it the hard way. Leaning into Voren's grip, I pulled in the edges of my shield so that it curved in around us.

I grabbed two vials, one my smoke bomb with irritants and the other an ooze that would stick to anything it touched. "Take the white one," I panted. "Hurl it at the wall at your side when we turn so you don't clip my shield."

Voren didn't even hesitate. We skidded around the corner where Edrik had vanished, Voren tossing his potion, and I dropped the ooze behind us.

The vials were sturdy, and being dropped wouldn't shatter them, but slamming into concrete or—the sharp crunch of glass was followed by a curse—being crushed underfoot would.

I chanced a look over my shoulder. One agent struggled to free his boot now attached to the ground, but the rest were closing in. Right, the masks. They were likely warded to protect them from both magical and mundane attacks.

A string of curses fell from my lips. Now was not the time for planning attacks. "Everything on your side is offensive," I hissed, not wanting to accidentally throw potions that might heal our enemy. "Just throw them. All of them."

Voren didn't need to be told twice. He released his grip on me and grabbed a handful of vials, hurling them at the wall one after the other.

I did the same, dropping some by my feet while tossing others. I tried not to cry at how many hours of brewing this stock had taken to create, or how much money it cost in reagents to replenish. If we got out with our lives, it'd be worth it.

Voren tossed three at the same time, the shattering glass followed by a sharp pop, then a rush of fire as the potions ignited. For a moment, the heat washed over us, pushing back the cold bite of fear.

Shit. None of these potions were lethal in themselves, but whatever he'd thrown had mixed into something volatile. Curses and cries of pain rose from behind, echoing off the walls.

"What do you have in here?" Voren shouted, looking behind us. "Remind me never to get on your bad side."

I glanced over my shoulder and saw shadows moving fast—too fast. The explosion had slowed them down, but not enough.

"Keep moving!" Edrik's voice cut through the chaos, and I turned back to see him skid to a stop and haul open a door, revealing a narrow stairwell. The concrete steps rose, leading upward, back to the surface. *Just a bit more,* I hissed to myself and I sprinted towards the door.

My chest ached with each burning breath, and my legs already quivered at the thought of all those stairs, but there was no time to hesitate. Worry pulsed through my connection to Danika, strong enough for me to sense it under my own frantic panic.

Almost out, I thought to Danika. *Coming up some stairs.*

"I sense you." Her words were more strained than usual. *"I'll gather the others and clear the path."*

Hot, white pain sliced through my arm and I gasped, stumbling forward, clutching the arm to my chest as my eyes watered with the searing agony. My shield shattered as I lost focus.

In the blink of an eye, Voren wrapped an arm around me, keeping me upright and hauling me into the protection of the stairwell. "What is it?"

I stared down at my arm, expecting to see blood, torn flesh—anything to explain the agony. But there was nothing. No wound, no burn. Just smooth, unbroken skin. Then the pain was gone, as if I'd imagined it.

"Go!" I shouted, pushing Voren up the stairs and following behind.

The tight turns would help to shield us from Aegis unless they came from the top.

Danika? I pushed the thought out, reaching for our connection, but sensed nothing. Panic clawed through my mind as I scrambled up each flight. The screaming in my head was almost as loud as the screams of my calves.

Edrik was already halfway up, his long strides taking two steps at a time. I followed, summoning a new shield. It flickered, but I gritted my teeth and held on.

All that mattered was getting us up, out, preferably alive. The stairs seemed endless, each step harder than the last; the walls closed in, the space around us growing narrower, suffocating.

Then a rush of fresh night air swirled to greet me as I staggered. Edrik held the heavy metal door open as Voren wrapped an arm around me and hauled me up the last few steps.

The door slammed shut behind us and I swayed. Edrik muttered under his breath. Magic seeped into the door as he braced himself against it.

I stumbled forward, gulping in the cool air, and let the shield drop when I took in the empty streets. The sounds of the city wrapped around us, only broken by our gasps for air.

But where were the others? Should we look for them or try to make it to somewhere safe? And why the hell hadn't we made a plan for that?

A yip cut through the air and I whirled, bracing myself, but Rynac charged around the corner of the building with Danika cradled in his arms.

I sagged with relief until they were close enough that I could make out the blood on both of them. Rynac favored his left side. Various cuts peppered his arms, and there was one across his neck that made my heart stop.

"Thank the gods," Rynac panted, coming to a stop. I reached for Danika, but Rynac pulled back. "Her leg's badly injured. I don't want to aggravate it more."

I nodded, my chest knotting with fear as I brushed my hand against her head, sending in a trickle of power. "Where's Kaelan?"

"He led the ones still on us further away."

Something banged against the door we had just come through and I jumped.

"My spell will only hold for so long," Edrik warned.

Right, we were not out of the thick of it yet. The streets stretched out before us, a maze of shadowed alleys and dim streetlights.

"Follow me," Rynac commanded.

The city was eerily quiet, the usual buzz of life muted at this hour. Our footsteps echoed off the empty streets that seemed endless, but finally we started to spot people going about their evenings and slowed.

Time blurred as fatigue gnawed at me, the last of my adrenaline fading when Rynac brought us to a stop. No one protested as we piled into an unmarked MEA vehicle.

But as it drove us away, I couldn't help scanning the sky for signs of Kaelan, and prayed he'd find his way back to us.

Chapter Thirty-Three

Indra and Beylin ushered us upstairs at Divine. My body complied, but my mind was detached from the world. We'd failed.

Aegis had stopped the killings, stopped creating more arrays, because they had got what they needed. How to get to the forge. All of this, and we arrived too late.

My bed called to me, but first I needed to see to Danika's injury. I set her out on a blanket, doing what I could as Beylin tended to Edrik first.

Indra patched up her brother while Voren fretted. No one spoke beyond the necessary, the others realizing all we had was bad news.

I'm sorry, I whispered to Danika, trying to ease her pain. Beylin came to check her over.

"It's not broken," Beylin said as he probed and prodded. "But we will need to rest the leg."

A door clattered open down the hall and we all spun towards it as Kaelan appeared, looking worse for wear. Blood trickled down his face from a cut above his eye, and a deep wound marred his bicep, but nothing life threatening.

He took in the room with a critical eye, as if inspecting all of us for injuries, before coming to sit on the open bench next to Danika.

Gathering up more supplies, I set them next to Beylin as he examined the nephilim.

"This is becoming a habit," the dwarf grumbled, and Kaelan huffed.

"Injuries are just part of the job." Kaelan reached out and ran a careful hand over Danika. "Though this one ensured they are not as severe as they could be."

Danika opened her eyes and stared up at Kaelan, some silent communication passing between them.

"Now that everyone is here, will you tell us what happened?" Indra asked. I winced, but given the look in her eyes, she was bracing for a blow.

"Aegis knows where the forge is and how to retrieve it," Edrik said, his voice void of emotion. "The Jackal, as they call him, is a skilled wielder of nightbane, and at first I was able to resist. But once he obtained the circlet, it was impossible not to reveal exactly what he wanted to know."

My breath caught. *The Jackal.* His name shuddered down my spine. My stomach twisted, nausea rising as memories of our encounters clawed at the edges of my mind—his unsettling gaze, the way he seemed to know every fear I tried to bury, the burrowing sensation of his magic.

"How can you be sure he has that information?" Indra asked.

"You feel it—the sharp talons clawing into your mind, dragging you down into a nightbane crafted from your own worst fears. Then they pull you out, scraping through your memories, searching for what they want. You feel every second of it. Relive every moment."

That is what Kaelan went through, a voice whispered and my heart squeezed. They did that to him—possibly for weeks—enough to fracture his memories and almost shatter it. Like being broken from the inside out.

"Do you still remember exactly what you told them?" Kaelan asked, a fierce intensity in his gaze.

"Yes," Edrik said, squirming under the nephilim's full attention.

"Then there's still a chance," I said, the words rushing out of me like a sigh. "If we act right away, we might be able to catch up."

"They likely didn't expect your escape," Kaelan explained. "So they didn't see a risk in allowing you to retain your memories. But now that you are gone, they will know we're coming. So tell us everything."

Edrik hesitated, looking over everyone in the room, and I realized they were all strangers to him.

After a quick introduction to my friends, I said, "Though Kaelan is the only one from the Order, I trust everyone here with this information."

"Underneath the city is the first headquarters of the Lunar Order," Edrik began. "It's heavily fortified, and even after all these years, the traps are still functioning.

"My task was to watch over it to ensure that no one stumbled upon it or broke into its vaults. Though I understand the tunnels, they are ever changing and there is no knowing which traps we will face. But for each, there is a way to deactivate them."

"How did anyone get in and out of this place when it was in use?" Rynac asked.

"From the research I've done, the traps can be turned off in times of peace and were used for training. But in their current lockdown setting, the traps are quite deadly. I've spent years studying them and still come across new ones each time." Edrik paused, realizing the rest of us didn't find that as fascinating as he did.

He cleared his throat and pressed on. "It is believed to hold many ancient artifacts that have fallen into obscurity, but most believed they were better left under safeguards. The forge was one of the artifacts known to be sealed under the city.

"I was also tasked with researching what it did and how one might open the seal if it was needed. Though I never fully uncovered how to unlock it, I fear Aegis have their own means. I'm willing to lead you down there, but we can't enter until the moon is out to unseal an entrance."

"Do you have any idea what they want with this artifact, what they're planning?" Beylin asked.

Edrik shook his head. "They might want it for the celestial opals it produces, but there is a possibility they want the power fueling the forge. If they could shatter the protections binding the artifact, they could absorb what's inside." He rubbed his face, the exhaustion appearing to weigh his whole body down. "This realm hasn't seen a magic user with that kind of power since the Great War."

"We'll need to make a plan," Kaelan said. "As much as I'd like to understand what happened under there, we need to strike hard and fast if we are going to reach the artifact first."

A heavy stone sank in my stomach; with everything going on, I hadn't said a word. "I saw Astrid. She was being held in a cell, but she was unconscious and I couldn't get her out."

My throat closed up at the thought of what I had done. Tension rippled through Beylin. The two were friends—though I didn't know the details, it was clear they cared about each other.

"We didn't have time to try," Voren added. "Aegis soldiers were right on our heels. If we'd stayed, they would've captured us."

Kaelan's expression darkened, but he made no move to interrupt and Voren explained the rest. For over an hour, we began to form our plan. Edrik explained the tunnels and traps we'd encounter, while

Kaelan went over what to expect from Aegis, before Beylin ordered us all to rest.

Edrik reached out to his Order contact, but there was no telling when they might respond. He had two emergency devices that would alert the Order to trouble, but one was at his shop and the other at his apartment. Both locations were almost certainly being watched by Aegis, lying in wait for any sign of Edrik.

Indra excused herself to make some calls, to find trusted enforcers who could locate the items. If we could get the Lunar Order involved, we'd have a fighting chance when it came time to face Aegis. It was a slim hope, but right now, it was all we had.

Danika slept through most of it, and I decided not to move her, fearing I'd hurt her leg.

The others had begun to filter out when Edrik waved me over. "I wanted to talk to you about the circlet. I uncovered some information about it that I hoped to share that night, only . . ."

"Aegis captured you. I tried to locate you using the opal; unfortunately, the Jackal sensed my spell. That's when I lost the circlet."

Edrik squeezed my arm. "I'm just thankful you survived that encounter. When I saw him with it . . . I feared I'd thrown you into his path." He shook his head. "Though there isn't much, the relic is called the Circlet of Duality and has strong connections to both dream and nightmare. They crafted it to aid in dreamwalking, though, as I experienced, it also enhances a person's ability to create nightbanes."

My heart sank, and a cold dread settled in my chest at the truth of it all. The Circlet of Duality wasn't just a tool; it was a weapon that could bring our own fears to life. If I were to go up against Aegis and retrieve the forge, I'd have to face the nightbane again.

"Then we will need to be prepared," Kaelan said, coming up beside me. The warmth of his body seemed to wrap around me, but it couldn't do anything to ward off the bone-deep cold. "They will use all their powers against us when we strike, but together we have a chance."

Edrik excused himself and hurried from the room, as if he couldn't escape the nephilim's looming presence fast enough.

I turned, heading for the kitchenette to make a coffee, but stumbled to a halt when a wing blocked my path.

"No coffee, you need to rest," Kaelan said, crossing his arms as if daring me to say he was wrong. I crossed my arms too and glared back. He huffed, his expression softening. "Are you alright after earlier?"

"Fine, I wasn't injured. How's the arm?" A bandage covered the injury, but it still looked painful.

"I've been through worse."

I snorted, earning a somewhat amused and perplexed look. "You've said that before." But my smile faded as the realization settled in.

"I hope I don't make it a common occurrence to get injured in front of you. But when I asked if you're okay, I meant about what happened when you were retrieving Edrik. Seeing Astrid."

"No, I'm not. I feel horrible that I didn't do more to free her."

"We will free her, but we need to find the right moment. And judging by what Voren said, you didn't have much of a choice. They would've captured you if you'd tried."

"Doesn't seem like much of a consolation." *I just left her there, to suffer at their hands.*

"It is for me. Otherwise, I would've had to come down there and get you."

I looked up at that, at the intensity of those words. "You and what army? And nephilim arrogance doesn't count," I said, quirking a brow. His words were so absurd. Why did he say such things?

Kaelan caught me under my chin, tilting my head until I met his gaze. "I would storm any stronghold to keep you from their grip." My breath caught and I could only stare, then he flashed me a lopsided grin, one that made my heart flutter. "And Danika would've come too."

"Stop being ridiculous," I said, shooing his hand away and heading towards my room. Kaelan's chuckle dogged my steps.

"Sleep well, Nyssa."

My attempt to sleep lasted about an hour, then I was far too restless. Each minute that slipped by added more weight to my shoulders, a countdown toward tonight's mission.

Every hour that passed coiled tighter around me, dragging me down until it threatened to drown me. The odds against us loomed larger with each breath, an unshakable presence at my back that seemed to grow heavier and darker, pressing closer.

Rest was impossible with each tick of the clock moving us toward danger. There was no telling what Aegis would do if they got their hands on the forge. But if it endangered Selene and our realm, then we had to stop them.

The sun blazed through the window of the alchemy shop as if to taunt me that I wasn't allowed even a single evening to brew more potions. Nothing to bolster us for what lay ahead.

Too much frantic energy zipped through me with no outlet as I sorted through every single potion I had on hand. Not enough. Not to go up against the odds we faced, not to take on Aegis, who already had a head start. I divided up the potions that I would split with the others and packed everything else in my bag.

One last step. Through my connection with Danika, I knew she was still sleeping, and I let out a long breath.

My fingers trembled as I opened the ink vial, my palms already sweating. I could do this. Had to do this. Going down there into the unknown without being able to use the full extent of my magic wasn't possible. Not if I wanted to succeed. Not if I wanted to keep everyone alive.

Clenching my jaw, I dipped my brush into the ink. It hovered just above the skin, but I couldn't move. *Do it,* I ordered myself. The stench of sulfur surrounded me as a drop of ink splattered my hand. Hot, putrid breath washed over my neck, and I sensed the presence behind me, looming, waiting.

The brush snapped in my grip and I jerked back, the sound far too close to bones breaking.

"You don't have to put yourself through that," Kaelan said behind me, and I whirled. He watched me from the base of the stairs, dressed in black with two daggers belted on his hip. "We will manage either way."

"How long have you been there?" I demanded.

He didn't answer, instead cautiously moving closer. "It's almost time to go."

"Which is why," I ground out, turning back to the ink vial, "I need to do this now."

"You can't force yourself to heal. It takes time. But tonight won't wait. Trust in the rest of us, trust in what you have at your disposal."

"But I need to fix this. I have to get over it, eventually. I worked so hard to fix my magic, I can't let this stand in the way. Without the runed band to contain my solar magic, I'll be severely limited. And especially tonight, I need the magic to keep us safe."

"I'll keep you safe."

"But you won't always be here," I snapped. Kaelan flinched like I'd slapped him. "You'll be going back to the Order and I'll have to learn to get over this."

"I don't have to," he said, staring out the window.

"What?"

"I could stay here, if that's what you wanted."

For a long moment, I could only stared at him.

Why in all the realms would he even offer that, just because I was struggling to deal with what had happened to me? Uproot his life, live with a fractured mind, because of me.

"No, you have to go back to the Order. They are likely the only ones who will be able to help mend your fractures, not to mention that it is your sworn duty."

Kaelan let out a slow breath, but didn't deny that it was true. "It's also my sworn duty to protect you."

"Which you don't even remember, because they sealed your memories. So how can we know for sure?"

"Sealing memories is not a common practice," Kaelan said with conviction. "It's a last resort. That I remember."

I wanted to throttle him. How could he act so casually about all of this? "You can't blindly trust this," I said, jabbing at the rune on my chest. "Making life changing choices on a feeling when you don't remember the details. Not to mention you swore yourself to Selene long before you met me."

His fingers traced over the design on the hilt of the dagger. "Then why don't you come with me? Join the Order."

Silence hung heavy around us as my mind tried to process.

I wanted to say no. That it wasn't the life I wanted, that I was barely surviving Aegis, that I almost didn't survive Carmen. But when

Kaelan and Astrid had never returned my messages, it had felt like the Order was rejecting me.

At first I thought it was just the rejection that bothered me, but the more I thought about it, the more I realized that maybe I did want to be a part of that.

But here I had my life. My friends. My alchemy shop. My work. I didn't want to give that up. For the first time in my life, I'd been happy and looking forward to what the next day would bring.

That was until Carmen came and ruined it all. The thought of giving all of that up . . . I couldn't do it. I liked my life. Wanted to work hard and get it back on track.

Yet . . .

There was that part of me that was tugged towards what the Lunar Order could do for me. Being a part of something bigger, part of a community that understood me. And I had friends there, too. If we could survive all of this.

"You will be safe there," Kaelan added. "We can help train and strengthen you. Work through this together. And then you will have a team who has your back."

"I . . . don't know." And that was the truth. "I don't know if that is the life for me." I held his gaze. "But I'll consider it."

Kaelan flashed me a half-smile. "I'll take that for now."

Chapter Thirty-Four

The air hung thick with anticipation, the cool night breeze doing little to soothe the weight in my chest. We hid in the shadows of the nearby building, but the tunnel Edrik was leading us to was hidden within the park.

The thick canopy of trees swayed as silent witnesses as we waited for the moon to rise and open the way below. Every moment stretched too long, tension crackling between us.

Indra leaned against the opposite wall, her gun resting on her hip, which was the only outward sign of her prowess. Though it was probably better her true weapon wasn't on display—the sword she could summon would draw far too much attention.

She looked calm, as if it was just another night, rather than about to descend into a labyrinth filled with traps and likely swarming with Aegis. Then again, I'm sure being an enforcer had put her in many situations like this.

Rynac stood at her back watching the other direction, his fingers tapping over his supplies, as if going through a mental checklist.

Kaelan lurked above us, his form barely visible in the darkness. He'd been far too quiet while we had been preparing earlier, and for the entire ride here. His silence weighed on me more than it should, but his presence was a steady force, a strange comfort.

Edrik, the only one without a weapon, remained close to me. He'd refused anything offered, claiming he was no good with them. His priority would be guiding us through the tunnels and disarming the traps we would come up against. Tension rippled off him as his gaze flicked upward toward the sky every few minutes.

Danika's steady presence pulsed as if trying to reassure me, even though her injured leg still caused her discomfort.

If it had been my choice, I would have made her stay behind, though I kept those thoughts sealed away, not wanting her to hear them. She was a stubborn bonded, and despite wanting her by my side, I worried more about her being harmed again.

My own hands refused to be still, trailing over the potions on my belt—half offensive, half for healing—memorizing their locations.

The potions within my bag jingled softly as I shifted my weight from one foot to the other, trying to shake off the anxiety crawling up my spine. Even with every potion I had on hand, I knew I was woefully underprepared.

Time was against us—with no chance to brew one that could help shield us against nightbanes, Beylin had prepared a tea to aid in fortifying our minds. The sour taste still lingered on my tongue, but I'd take that if it gave us a chance against the Jackal.

Edrik had explained there were several entrances, but when they sealed, only moonlight and magic could unlock them. I don't know if it was a relief that there was no sign of Aegis at this entrance, or if that meant they were already below.

It would be a race to beat Aegis to the forge; that is, if they didn't learn of our presence and decide to deal with us first. We had no estimate on their numbers, but the information we had indicated there was a mix of high-ranking members forming the strike team, including the Jackal. And then low-ranked ones who were there for numbers, like the soldier who'd captured Voren and I.

My hands itched to check my supplies again, though I resisted. Now wasn't the time to let doubt creep in.

I glanced up, squinting through the dark. The moon was taking its time, teasing us with the faintest glow on the horizon. Any minute now, its light would fall on the entrance. But until then, we waited, the stillness between us punctuated only by the distant sounds of the city.

On silent wings, Kaelan dropped in front of us, all the signal we needed to know it was time. We moved in silence, shadows among shadows.

Every step felt too loud, despite the muffled footfalls, as Edrik led us onto the overgrown path leading into the park. The dense foliage closed in around us, thick with the scent of damp earth and moss. Trees loomed like sentinels, their twisted branches clawing at the night sky, hiding the moon's glow.

My senses were on high alert, every creak of wood and rustle of leaves setting my nerves alight. Edrik guided our way while Kaelan stalked beside him, his wings pulled in tight and his hands never far from his weapons.

It was easy to imagine him with Nathaniel and Astrid flanking him as they hunted for their enemy.

At first I thought the park had long been abandoned, left to nature's relentless reclaiming. The overgrowth tangled around our legs and thick roots weaved across our path; I couldn't help feeling like these trees had always been here, and it was the city that grew up around them.

We moved deeper into the park, Edrik leading us into dense underbrush. I could sense it before I saw it—something subtle but potent, a hidden current of magic pulsing beneath the surface.

Edrik stopped, crouching low to push aside the thick leaves. "It's here," he murmured. He knelt in front of a patch of ground that, to anyone else, would look like nothing more than dirt and roots.

But as the moon broke through the trees, its pale light filtering down in thin beams, I saw it—the faint outline of a symbol etched into the earth.

I crouched beside him, watching as his fingers brushed the ground. His eyes narrowed in concentration, and his magic shivered through the air and channeled into the ground.

The symbol began to glow faintly, more lines appearing, weaving through the underbrush and spreading outward.

Edrik squeezed his eyes closed, his breathing becoming more ragged. Just how much magic did it need?

Before I could offer to aid him, Danika settled beside him, her front paws pressed into the glowing runes, and bowed her head. A heartbeat later, the ground beneath us trembled, a slight shiver at first, before it started to shift.

More symbols appeared, lighting up in the moon's soft glow. It was as if the earth itself was waking up, recognizing the touch of lunar magic.

Their power intertwined with the symbols, guiding them to reveal the hidden entrance. The ground groaned, sliding away with a grinding noise, roots pulling apart as an opening appeared beneath us.

I winced at the sound, praying to the Goddess that Aegis wasn't lurking around.

A dark tunnel yawned below, the air inside heavy with the scent of damp stone and ancient secrets. I swallowed hard, the weight of what lay ahead settling in my chest. Edrik looked up at me, a flicker of determination in his eyes. We'd found the entrance. Now came the hard part.

After a nod from Edrik, Kaelan descended first into the thick darkness before Edrik, Danika, and I followed.

I inched down into the hole, the stone sturdy beneath my feet, but it was the utter darkness that terrified me. A hand reached out and guided me down a few steps, and I wondered how Kaelan could even see. Maybe a perk of lunar magic I had not learned.

I clenched my teeth, the weight of the unknown pressing down on me. The tunnel stretched into darkness, its depths unfathomable.

Indra and Rynac dropped down with soft thuds, landing with practiced ease. I couldn't stop myself from glancing up, desperate for one last glimpse of the world above—the moonlight filtering through the trees, the fresh night air, the stars twinkling beyond the canopy. It felt like a lifeline, something to tether me to reality.

But then, with a low, grinding rumble, the ground began to shift again. The dense foliage crept back into place, and the earth sealed itself off, closing the entrance behind us. The last sliver of moonlight flickered and vanished, leaving only the suffocating dark.

A shudder crept down my spine even though I knew this had been the plan. The scar on my left hand itched, the skin still bare. A faint cracking made my skin crawl, even as the mundane glow sticks' light bloomed in the darkness.

The narrow stairway, hewn from the very earth, spiraled endlessly downward, the cold stone walls pressing in from all sides. Kaelan tossed one of the glow sticks into the open middle, and it fell down and down until I couldn't make out its light anymore.

Lovely. Did I mention I hated being underground?

I could almost sense the weight of the earth above pressing down, suffocating me. It was an innate fear all witches had of being cut off from their power source. I longed for the open sky, the light of the sun and moon. But we had no choice; we had to find the forge before Aegis.

With a quick shake, my glow vial began to emit a soft green light that spilled over the damp walls. Without hesitation, Edrik took the lead, guiding us down the stairs. The sound of our footsteps and the occasional drip of water echoed around us, breaking the tense silence.

"Stay close," Kaelan warned, his voice steady but taut. Like I needed the reminder. I would have made us all hold hands like we were toddlers if I had my way. The thought of getting split up or lost . . . I shuddered.

As we descended further, the air grew colder and more stale, until the stairs ended and led into a tunnel. Danika yipped softly, bringing all of us to a sudden halt, and only then did I notice the faint shimmer across the path ahead.

Before she could even tell me what was wrong, Kaelan muttered, "Lunar wards." I cursed myself for being caught unaware—I'd been so focused on each step on the slick stone I hadn't even sensed the shifting power.

Edrik stepped forward, examining the shimmer with a practiced eye. His fingers brushed over the walls and floor just before the first ward, searching for something.

"Ah," was all he said before a glow appeared under his finger and the silver ward disappeared. Only now it was gone did I notice the difference; I'd thought that prickling sensation was dread from being underneath so much earth.

"They will get a bit trickier than that," Edrik said. "So stick close and stay on guard."

We kept to the middle of the tunnel in a loose formation. The passage measured about twelve feet wide and nine feet high, and though I kept reminding myself it was larger than my bedroom, my mind insisted the space was shrinking.

Kaelan held up a hand to stop. Edrik inspected the ground, but from here it only looked like more solid stone.

"Cover your lights," Edrik said. Dread prickled over my skin at the thought of being trapped underground with no light, but I tucked my vial away.

Pitch black swarmed around me. I squinted at a pinprick of light, then another, like the stars winking into existence in the midnight sky. The small dots of light soon covered the floor and the walls on either side.

"What is that?" Indra asked.

The breath rushed out of me as I inspected the ones closest to us. I noticed a rune carved into each stone, but only the glow made them easy to spot. Worse, there were many I didn't recognize.

Edrik motioned for us to take a step back and pulled off a shoe. I frowned as he tossed it ahead. Spears shot out from the wall, impaling the shoe midair. I jerked backwards right into Rynac, who was a solid presence behind me.

"Effective," he muttered. The spears retracted back into the wall until there was no sign that they had even been there. "Though a bit more deadly than the type of training I'm used to."

Edrik, retrieving his impaled shoe, appeared to be the only one not apprehensive about the spiky corridor of death. "I assume they blunted the spears, and this was to test knowledge of runes. It'll be slow, but I'll make my way across—there is a rune at the end to deactivate the trap."

I swallowed hard. Each rune offered enough space to stand on, but picking the way across would take time we didn't have. But what choice was there?

"What does the rune look like?" Kaelan asked, eyeing the walls. Edrik held out his palm and drew the rune, which looked like the witch rune for 'stop.' At least that one was self-explanatory. "And do the spears only trigger when the wrong rune is pressed?"

"I believe so," Edrik said. "Though you can't try to step on the empty area around the runes, the ground is all linked back to the closest one."

Kaelan stepped up to the first line of runes without touching them and stuck his hand out into the air. I flinched, waiting for the spears, but nothing happened. He even waved his arm all around, but again, no traps activated.

"Right," Kaelan said, walking back down the way we had come from. He stopped about ten paces back, shaking out his wings and testing the space.

"Wait!" I shouted, realizing his plan, but he was already running.

We all pressed against the walls as he rushed by, a force of wind buffeting me back as Kaelan flapped his wings and leaped into the air.

His wings beat again in one tight flap, the feather tips just a breath away from the walls. He tucked himself in and rolled as he landed on the opposite side, and was on his feet before my mind even processed what had happened.

"For fuck's sake!" I yelled, my anger catching back up with me. "A little warning next time."

Kaelan just shrugged as he pressed the rune to deactivate the trap. Edrik checked it once more with his destroyed shoe, before we all hurried across.

"It worked, didn't it?" Kaelan said with a smug grin. I glared at him, even though it had saved us a lot of time.

Bloody angel-born.

Chapter Thirty-Five

The shadows clung to the stone walls, deep enough that our weak lights couldn't pierce it. The weight of the ancient magic pressed in on me, making the hairs on the back of my neck stand on end.

We came to an abrupt halt when the tunnel split, branching off in three different directions. Right, left, or forward. Each looked the same.

"Huh," was all Edrik said. "I've never encountered this—"

A bright flash followed by a sharp crack cut through the air. A force knocked me sideways. Someone screamed. I caught myself, bracing for whatever trap we had stumbled into.

Shouts and the sizzle of magic bounced off the tight walls. Blue light flared as Danika's fur crackled with power, and she surged forward.

Dark figures poured from the tunnel on the right, their faces obscured, but I spotted one with a dark mask. Aegis.

I backpedaled, reaching for my potions, until I collided with a wall. Everything was happening too fast.

Kaelan charged in, pushing one agent back as Danika lunged at another. Edrik was on the ground, clutching his shoulder. Rynac sprinted toward him, Indra close behind, to cover his retreat.

Edrik gasped, pain etched into his features, as Rynac dragged him toward a tunnel opening.

I hurled a potion at an agent trying to break away, but missed as the enemy jerked back. That was all the opening Indra needed.

Her sharp eyes stayed fixed on the enemy, her gunfire echoing like a heartbeat in the tunnel. I flinched at each shot. She took down another enemy, buying us a breath of space, but it wasn't enough.

Everything turned into a blur—too many bodies, too many voices, not enough space. Fear clung to my bones, weighing my body down until each movement became an effort.

Magic pooled in my palm, fire flickered in my chest, while my fingers hovered over my potions. Keeping low, I shifted along the edge of the area, hunting for the moment to strike. The stone walls seemed to press closer, each sound reverberating and magnifying the chaos.

Sparks lit up the narrow space when steel clashed. The air thrummed with magic as four agents descended on Kaelan, driving him back. He stumbled, his boots skidding on loose stones.

My heart stuttered, but it was the opening I needed. One after the other, I hurled the stinging nettle potions, glass shattering as they smashed into stone and armor, showering Aegis with the concoction.

An agent screamed, clutching their face, but three others pressed forward. Danika's fur crackled again, her growl cutting through the din as she barreled into another assailant, who let out a strangled cry as she latched onto their arm.

Another agent hurtled towards Indra, the hulking form not even flinching as bullets slammed into his armor. Rynac lifted the injured Edrik, retreating further into the tunnel on my left.

With all the strength I had, I hurled my ooze vial at the enemy's feet. The black liquid splattered over one of his boots; it stretched as he lifted his leg and then snapped. What in all the hells was he?

I lifted a second vial when a warning pulsed through my connection with Danika. Rough fingers closed around my wrist like iron and twisted. I gasped, dropping my vial, panic surging in my chest as I tried to jerk my arm free.

The figure loomed over me, their features shrouded in darkness as their grip tightened, and I stumbled back, the cold, damp stone biting into my skin. I kicked out, striking their knees, but it was like they were made of steel.

"Nyssa!" Kaelan's sharp voice cut through the chaos.

My heart thundered, each beat echoing like a drum in my ears as I reached for my magic, desperation clawing at me. Danika leaped from the shadows, as I was driven back another step, deeper into a different tunnel, cutting me off from the others.

Magic crackled through the air as her teeth sunk into his calf. He flinched, his grip loosening enough that I could wrench myself free.

I scrambled away. His boot lashed out, striking Danika with brutal force. I screamed as phantom pain slammed into my chest, leaving me breathless.

The enemy drew a blade that glinted, silver and menacing, as it screeched free of its sheath. He advanced faster than I could track. I reached for my power, and a small shield flared to life just in time to deflect the first strike.

The blade clanged against it, the impact vibrating up my arms. He pressed forward, relentless, each blow driving me back a step. Away from the others. Away from help.

I focused all my energy on holding the shield, reinforcing it as best I could while his attacks came faster, each strike chipping away at my resolve.

The enemy staggered and cried out as a blade drove into his shoulder. Kaelan descended on him.

The agent whipped around, trying to throw Kaelan off, but the nephilim darted underneath his arm until he stood between me and the enemy.

Kaelan shifted his stance, his blades lifted for the next attack as he pressed me back. The Aegis agent launched himself forward with a snarl. A hidden mechanism clicked.

A sharp, whirring sound filled the space, followed by beams of light that cut across the tunnel.

Pain seared through my arm, my shield shattering as I lost concentration, and I flinched back.

Kaelan wrapped himself around me, holding me in place. The air shimmered with scorching heat as more beams sprung to life.

"Don't move." The command in Kaelan's voice froze me in place.

I blinked against the sudden brightness to find a crisscross of beams surrounding us, some only a hand's breadth away.

Kaelan stood perfectly still, his wings tucked in as tight as they could, as he took in every inch of the hallway. With small, careful movements, he pulled me in closer as if he thought his body could shield me.

The smell of burnt hair clogged my nose. "What happened to the Aegis agent?" I shifted, trying to see around him, fearing Aegis would attack while we were trapped, but Kaelan held me tighter.

"Don't look."

My mind went blank, trying very hard *not* to think about what was behind him. "What do we do?" I whispered.

"It's a maze of types," Kaelan said, sounding far too calm. "We just need to work our way out."

Danika? I called out, hunting for that connection between us, but there was nothing but silence. "I can't reach Danika." Panic wrapped its fingers around my throat and squeezed.

"Just like the other traps, there has to be a way to turn this off," Kaelan said. "It's fine, just breathe."

A shaking breath wheezed out of me, and I told myself to calm down. I had potions. I had my magic. But the silence was the worst.

I couldn't hear anything over the hum of magic. Were the others still fighting or . . . I pushed the thought away. All I needed was to create a shield and walk out. Letting out a slow breath, I called to my magic.

The astral shield shimmered and then shattered as it touched a beam. I reeled back, pain slicing through my head. Kaelan hissed, and a few black feathers drifted to the ground.

"It's alright. If you're careful," Kaelan said in a low, calm tone, "I think you can crawl to the other side and find the rune."

Inch by inch, I turned myself around in Kaelan's grip until I faced the maze of beams that barred our way.

Shit. Unbuckling my potion belt, I attached it to my bag. Kaelan grabbed onto the strap as I lowered myself down.

The cold stones bit into my palms, every muscle tense with the awareness that one misstep could mean disaster.

I sank lower, taking in the tight, unforgiving space. A bitter laugh threatened to escape as I measured the gap—barely enough for my body, with only a few inches to spare on either side.

Crawling through this would mean pressing myself flat against the icy stone, every move precise, each breath controlled. The urge to laugh morphed into a rising need to cry, but I forced it down and pushed forward.

As I slid onto my chest, flattening myself to maneuver under the first beam, the stone's chill seeped through my clothes. A faint hum of energy buzzed just above my head, close enough that I could feel its heat prickling against my skin.

Bit by bit, I dragged myself forward, nails clawing into the ground for purchase as my knees scraped over the stone.

The path ahead was a jagged puzzle, beams crisscrossing at odd angles. I shifted to my side, sliding an arm ahead and pulling myself along, every muscle straining with the effort. The room seemed to close in, each breath shrinking the space.

A sudden clatter from the distance sent a jolt through me. I froze, heart pounding as the noise reverberated through the tunnel.

"Keep going," Kaelan urged. "Find the rune."

I swallowed the lump in my throat and pressed on, a cold sweat beading on my brow, each movement slow and deliberate.

The last beam was just ahead, a thin line of light cutting through the dark, and there, hovering in the darkness, was the faint glow of the rune.

I held my breath, flattening myself even more as I edged past the final beam.

The acrid smell of burnt hair wafted around me as my shoulders passed through the gap.

A sharp pain lanced through my side as one beam grazed my skin. I bit back a gasp, fighting the pain as my eyes watered.

Almost out, I shifted forward. The stone under my hand lowered a fraction and something clicked. Panic pounded through me, adrenaline spiking as the beams started moving.

I scrambled forward, hissing every curse I knew as new cuts opened up on my skin. I pushed through the searing pain, dragging myself the last few feet.

"Come on," I muttered through gritted teeth, my fingers trembling as they stretched toward the rune.

My vision tunneled, the rune the only thing in focus as I willed myself to reach it. With a final surge of strength, I pressed my palm against the glowing rune, shoving energy into it.

The stone pulsed beneath my hand, sending a ripple of energy through the hallway. The beams vanished, stealing all the light, and I collapsed on the ground, every muscle in my body trembling.

And then Kaelan appeared, the soft glow from his light spilling over us as he lifted me to my feet. His hands examined me as his cool magic brushed over my wounds.

I clutched his arm, wanting to ask if he was hurt, but I could only gasp for breath. The pain subsided, but my arms trembled.

"It's just the adrenaline," Kaelan murmured, and wrapped me in a tight embrace. I clung to his warmth, my breathing still uneven, each inhale a struggle against the lingering tension.

"We need to find the others," I said, reluctant to leave his warmth. "Danika—"

"I'm here," she said, her voice strained. I almost crumpled to the ground as relief crashed into me.

Reluctantly, I pulled away, my steps still shaky as I followed close to Kaelan, letting him shield me from the body of the dead agent.

Activating a new glow vial, I lifted it to fight back the shadows as we headed back down the corridor we came from. My heart leapt into my throat when I spotted Danika limping towards us, and I crashed to my knees.

"I'm . . . okay," she murmured, though her voice lacked its usual strength.

Kaelan set my bag down, and I pulled out the special potion I'd crafted just for Danika. She lifted her head, allowing me to pour the healing brew into her mouth. Slinging my bag over one shoulder, I lifted her with great care and cradled her in my arms.

We pressed forward, and I strained to hear anything from the tunnel ahead.

The metallic stench of blood hit me first. Kaelan gripped my free hand, helping me to step over the prone body and into the area we had first encountered Aegis. I tried to avert my gaze from the unmoving bodies strewn across the ground.

My chest squeezed, but Kaelan's grip kept me moving. His free hand hovered over his dagger, as if expecting one of the dead to lunge at us.

I peered down the corridor I'd seen the others disappear into, but only darkness lay ahead. Kaelan guided me behind him as we crept down the tunnel and around a bend.

A figure darted out. Kaelan tensed, and then his wings drooped.

"Thank the gods," Indra hissed as she waved us to follow.

Just beyond her, a battered-looking Edrik sat propped against the wall, a bloody bandage wrapped around his shoulder, with Rynac crouched on the other side.

"Is everyone alright?" I asked as relief washed over me.

Rynac nodded, though there was strain around his eyes.

"We're almost there," Edrik said, pointing further down the tunnel.

"Do you need another healing potion?" I asked. His face was far too pale, even under the weak light.

"I'll be fine for now—we must move. I can sense great power."

Rynac lifted Edrik to his feet, while Kaelan took the lead, advancing with silent precision. Indra followed close behind, gun raised, guarding our rear.

A bright light glimmered at the end of the tunnel, causing us to slow our pace, but the open room ahead lay empty.

As we cautiously emerged from the tunnel, the polished floor, smooth beneath my feet, reflected the light from my vial. The splash of color was startling after the dull stone of the tunnels.

The chamber opened up before us, its ceiling soaring high, lost in shadow. Intricate carvings adorned the stone, depicting designs that mirrored the night sky, with constellations sprawling across the walls. The carvings depicted the moon and stars, their celestial patterns winding through the stone in shimmering silver and luminescent white. Some designs glinted as if sprinkled with stardust, creating a mesmerizing effect.

But I sensed it now, the steady pulse of magic washing over us, a subtle vibration in the air that tingled against my skin.

I followed close behind Kaelan as we approached the narrow archway that connected to a hallway curving out of sight. As we crept closer, light spilled from the doorway ahead, illuminating the edges of the arch, and a flicker of movement made us freeze.

Aegis had already breached the wards. We were too late.

CHAPTER THIRTY-SIX

Muted voices echoed off the walls, and I gestured for Indra to stay back as Kaelan and I pressed ourselves into the shadows. The next room was grander, illuminated by the myriad of lights Aegis had brought.

The beauty of the space struck me. A full moon glowed at the center of the ceiling, cradled by Selene, whose flowing hair stretched across the sky, transforming into shimmering stars.

But the far wall lay in ruins, bricks and dust strewn across the floor and tracked across the circular designs that rippled out like the phases of the moon. The shadowy figures of Aegis filled the room. Did they know we were coming?

At the center, a lone agent hunched over a stone pedestal pulsing with silver light—the forge. Even from this distance, I could sense the heavy wards still protecting it.

A chill crept down my spine as recognition hit me. It was the Jackal, his dark presence unmistakable.

His magic brushed against my awareness and I shuddered, pushing it away as it tried to burrow in. His twisted energy was everywhere, saturating the air as it waited to devour any lunar magic it touched.

My heart raced as I realized the true danger; he was trying to break the forge. I exchanged a panicked glance with Kaelan—did he sense it too?

We rushed back through the archway, the air thick with impending dread. When we reached the others, Edrik looked up, worry etched on his face.

"The Jackal has already started the ritual, hasn't he?" he said, breathless.

"What is it? How do we stop it?" I said in a rush, as panic constricted my throat.

"He's trying to take control of the forge—to command its power. But he will have to break the protection wards placed directly on the forge."

My stomach dropped. We had to stop him, but time was slipping away.

Rynac waved us toward a different door, which led to a small, dark chamber. I could only hope Aegis wouldn't venture this way. The room was cold, the only sound our hurried breathing as we huddled together.

Edrik leaned against the wall, still pale from his earlier injury, while Indra's eyes darted to the entrance, gun ready. Kaelan took charge, speaking in a low voice. "We need to hit them hard and fast. Overwhelm their defense and steal the forge before they know what hit them."

"There are too many," I hissed.

"This isn't about beating them," Kaelan said. "We will distract them, draw the Jackal away to give you an opening to get the forge. Then you run."

I shook my head. That was a terrible plan. A plan that might get them all killed.

"It's all we have." Conviction shone in Kaelan's gaze as if he had complete faith in me.

Rynac nodded, stepping forward with a serious look. "I'll scout for possible exits in case things go sideways." He disappeared into the shadows without another word, his movements silent and practiced.

The weight of the plan settled over me, pressing into my chest. The others began whispering strategies, and I slipped away to a corner where darkness cloaked me.

I slumped to the ground, my fingers fumbling to open my bag. I needed the runed band. If I was going up against the Jackal . . . I swallowed hard.

The silence wrapped around me, broken only by that faint, cruel laughter. The glass vial of ink clinked on the floor as I clutched the brush, my knuckles white. I clenched my jaw, dipping in the brush.

It was just one rune. How many runes had I drawn in my life? One more, that was all, just one. The ink was cold, thick, as I painted the first line. My heart hitched as I managed the next, blinking, the black ink turning red as I dragged the brush across my hand.

The room tilted, blood dripping down my arm as I connected another line. My breath came in shallow, erratic gasps and I swayed. My name echoed in my head, but I couldn't tear my gaze away.

"They're coming," someone shouted, but I couldn't move. Dread swept over me, pulling me under like a riptide.

Voices around me merged into a muffled buzz, words indistinct and meaningless. My body refused to respond, frozen in place as Carmen's voice echoed through my mind. *"A lunar witch worthy of wielding her powers,"* she sneered. *"How wrong I was."*

My vision blurred at the edges, the shadows twisting into a mass of demonspawn lining the walls. A cold sweat coated my skin, gold runes glittering on the floor next to me.

The walls seemed to close in, pressing on me until I could no longer tell if the pressure came from outside or from the chaotic storm within me.

The stench of sulfur and blood clogged my nose and the echo of footsteps—heavy, deliberate—resounded in my ears. A clawed hand gripped my throat and squeezed, pain slicing through my arm.

"You do not deserve your power."

I tried to move, to command my limbs to action, but fear rooted me to the spot, paralyzing me from the inside out. Rynac and Indra, bound and gagged.

My fault.

The air seemed to grow thick and heavy, pressing against my lungs until every breath became a battle. A vice wrapped around my chest and squeezed tighter with each second.

"You failed. Again. And again. Just give up."

"Nyssa," a different voice called, but it was so far away. *"We need you."* My chest burned. Fury. Desperation. Agony. Each emotion slammed into me, molten fire coursing through my veins.

I blinked, trying to clear my vision. The echo of Carmen's voice faded, drowned out by shouts and chaos.

A surge of power crackled nearby, followed by a bright flash that painted the scene in harsh light. My heart pounded. Where was I?

Streaks of silver and blue magic cut through the air, my sluggish brain trying to piece together what was happening. I was in a different room, my bag gone. Danika and Kaelan locked in a vicious struggle—against Nathaniel.

Goddess, they've found us. Where are the others?

Nathaniel was ruthless, his face a mask of grim determination. I groaned, struggling to my knees.

The clang of metal against metal sent a shiver up my spine, and my breath caught as I watched them battle. Nathaniel's sword arced through the air, driving Kaelan back. He was relentless, strike after strike. He shifted his weight and brought his sword down in a sharp, ruthless arc.

Kaelan moved to block, but the strike came fast, slipping past his guard and sliced across his forearm, gold dripping from the wound. Nathaniel didn't slow. No, he looked ready to kill.

I called to my magic, but it guttered in my chest, leaving me with only a whisper of power.

Without thinking, I pushed it into the moon-blessed mark and reached. The world seemed to pause. My power brushing against him, sensing the desperation and guilt beating in his chest. And then I wrenched it in one brutal twist.

Nathaniel let out a strangled cry, his sword clattering to the ground as he crashed to his knees, clutching his chest. Kaelan didn't waste a second. He stepped forward, knocking Nathaniel's fallen sword away with a swift kick. Kaelan pressed his dagger to Nathaniel's throat in an instant, steady and unyielding.

The room pulsed with tension, the sound of ragged breathing the only thing breaking through the silence.

Nathaniel's eyes flicked up to mine, wide and stricken, pain and something raw swirling in their depths. His fingers trembled as he clutched his chest, his breaths coming in shallow gasps. He winced, a grimace twisting his features.

"I had to do what they said," Nathaniel said through gritted teeth. "For Astrid. I was just trying to protect her."

"Kaelan's life for hers?" I demanded, my throat raw.

He nodded, his gaze flickering to Kaelan. "He can withstand them."

Danika padded over to me, her eyes uncertain.

What happened?

"Aegis found us. I couldn't get through to you." Her voice wobbled, and she hesitated. *"They took the others. Kaelan grabbed you, but then Nathaniel trapped us in this room."*

I'd failed. So utterly and completely failed.

I pulled my knees up, wrapping my arms around them, seeking some illusion of safety, some barrier between me and the world that now seemed to collapse around me.

My fingers dug into my sleeves, shaking as I buried my face, blocking out everything but the crushing truth of my failure. I was supposed to be the one to stop this, to stand between Aegis and their victory. The one moment everyone had needed me, I'd faltered.

The silence deepened, a suffocating blanket, broken only by the sound of my ragged breathing. Each breath was a struggle, shallow and sharp, drowning out reason, hope—everything but the relentless echo of defeat.

"It's coming," Nathaniel hissed. "The nightbane."

In the back of my mind I could sense it, creeping closer like a living shadow, a cold, suffocating force that leached all the light from the world.

An ancient power—cold, impersonal, and vast. It carried the scent of night air, metallic and sharp, with a bitterness that coated my tongue. I pulled Danika into my lap, wrapping my arms around her as if that could shield her.

A chill skittered down my spine. Every hair on my body stood on end as the power wrapped around me, slick and oppressive, but I didn't fight it as it washed over me.

The dark shadows rose like a viscous liquid until they surrounded me, trying to pull me under into a suffocating darkness.

CHAPTER THIRTY-SEVEN

S ilence.

Nathaniel and Kaelan stood immobile, their eyes closed, their faces drawn tight with unspoken fears. But there was no nightbane for me.

None of my deepest fears manifested, because I was living them.

A sound whispered through the suffocating quiet, delicate and haunting. Faint at first, like the chime of silver bells caught on a breeze, yet otherworldly.

My breath hitched; the eerie melody pierced the stagnant darkness and curled into my chest. Familiar.

It hummed with an ancient resonance, low and melodic, vibrating through my core and aligning with something buried deep within me.

The sound was pure, clear as starlight, with an undertone that thrummed like the gentle pulse of waves against a shore. Each note seemed to call to me, as if the cool glow of moonlight was spreading over my skin, soothing and invigorating at once.

It wrapped around me, soft as velvet, pressing against the heavy ache in my limbs and easing the tightness in my chest. The music grew, its song weaving through the cracks in my fear.

Blocking out the oppressive darkness that coiled around the others, I closed my eyes and opened my heart to the music of my soul.

I gasped for breath, swaying as my mind spun. I blinked away the darkness, and found I stood in ankle-deep water at the edge of a lake. Snow coated the trees around me, their branches heavy with white.

The thick clouds above parted and the haunting full moon loomed above, casting an eerie glow over the lake. Its light reflected in the still water, creating a mirror image that made the surface seem deeper, almost bottomless.

The tranquility of this place stood in stark contrast to the chaos I had just endured, leaving me breathless and disoriented.

Silence pressed in around me, almost deafening. My mind screamed and an unsettling realization crept over me. This was exactly like the night I drowned. The same biting cold, the same snow-covered trees, and the same luminous moon.

I lifted my shaking hands, as if I could tear this nightmare apart, knowing what was to come. How many times had I dreamed of this place? How many nightmares had I endured over the years?

And yet, this time, it was different. I knew I was awake. My body was back in Arkirith. Yet, this place felt far too real.

My eyes caught on my hands—smaller—and then looked down at my body, wearing the same clothes I had been wearing that night. The fabric was damp and clung to my skin as if—

No, don't think about it. That thing has a hold of your mind, pulling your memories from you.

But if that was true, why wasn't I ten feet under the water? I glanced to either side, but my two friends weren't there.

The lake stretched out before me, its surface eerily calm, reflecting the moonlight like a sheet of glass. The branches of snow-coated trees loomed overhead, casting long shadows. It was only me, alone, with the oppressive silence pressing in.

"You are not alone." A voice like the soft evening breeze slipped through my mind. I should have been terrified, but instead, it felt oddly familiar.

Then, before me, a figure of silvery moonlight appeared. She stood effortlessly, as if floating above the water.

Deep and mesmerizing, her dark eyes sparkled like distant stars, their depths revealing ancient wisdom and unspoken secrets. Ethereal silver waves cascaded down her back, moving with a life of their own, catching the moonlight and turning it into a halo around her head.

Her features were a perfect blend of grace and otherworldly beauty—high cheekbones, a delicate, almost translucent complexion, and lips that hinted at a gentle, knowing smile.

The aura around her was both serene and commanding, a presence that seemed to defy the bounds of the mortal realm. She wore a flowing gown of woven moonlight, shifting with each movement. This was a being untouched by the constraints of our realm.

My brain screamed that I should be terrified. The being stood near eight feet tall with a presence that seemed to saturate the area, and I knew that in a thought could bend the world to her will.

She seemed to smile as if she could read every single one of my thoughts. Her eyes held a knowing glimmer, and her smile was both reassuring and enigmatic.

She dipped her chin, a subtle gesture that seemed to encourage me to speak, her presence radiating a gentle, inviting warmth.

"Selene." It wasn't a question; it was a declaration that resonated deep within my heart and soul, a truth felt in the way her magic danced through my veins. "What is this? How are you here?"

She gave me a sad smile. "This is just a memory, the moment you met me. Through that, a connection between us opened. As the centuries drag by, it becomes harder to speak to our children. My power is diminished, but I twisted the nightbane power with the lunar energies of the forge to give us as much time as I could."

"Why am I here?" I asked, still fearing this might be a nightbane.

This particular night had haunted my sleep for many years, not that I had ever seen the Goddess. This was the moment where I had died and the Goddess offered me a second chance at life.

Too many thoughts swirled through my mind. I gritted my teeth as pain sliced through my head, struggling to make sense of it all.

"My time is limited here," she said. "But I'll offer you what I can. The power of the forge cannot fall to the enemy. My other two chosen, the enemy has trapped them in their first deaths. They will not be able to break free on their own. You must help them. Only with their strength can you protect the forge."

"Kaelan and Nathaniel?" I asked, my voice tinged with worry.

Selene stepped closer, lifting her silvery hand to cup my cheek. The warmth of her touch flushed through my body, and I wanted to lean into it.

Hope, gratitude, unwavering love, strength, and comfort—these emotions seeped into my skin, as if they were the very aura that surrounded my Goddess.

"I don't remember you talking to me," I stammered, "the deal I made. I remember the vision . . ." The memory of the scorching fire, which had threatened to melt my skin, lingered in the back of my mind. "And then I was under the water."

"I know, my child. I had to seal the memories away from you. There were truths I needed to tell you that you weren't ready to handle—information that no thirteen-year-old should bear. But you opened the connection between us, and I didn't know if I would ever get another chance to speak to you. To the last of the lunar witches. One of my cherished children."

I swallowed hard, grappling with the weight of her words. I'd forgotten what she said that night.

That I was the last lunar witch. That I was loved.

Each revelation hit me like a physical blow. Selene closed her eyes, her expression one of deep concentration and sorrow, as if drawing on the last reserves of her strength to communicate her message.

"My power is dwindling," she said, her voice carrying a weary undertone. "Spread too thin as I try to shield this realm from the enemy lurking within Terrarum." Her gaze held a desperate intensity, her silvery aura flickering like a dying flame. "You have the power to make a difference, to strike at the enemy that seeks to consume our lands."

Her words carried urgency and a plea for hope, echoing with the weight of countless battles and the fragility of her remaining strength.

"I offer the choice to you again. Will you accept the lunar magic within you and stand at my side to protect our realm?"

"Yes." The word fell from my lips in an instant.

Selene's smile radiated warmth and approval. "No hesitation once again. I knew you would choose well." Her chuckle was like the whisper of silk, a gentle, melodic ripple through the night air, soothing and reassuring. "This is a path you must walk yourself. Just know that you are making the right choices. I have faith that you will continue to carry out your moon-blessed duty."

"Thank you." My voice tinged with awe and uncertainty, as the realization of the weight I carried sunk in.

The moonlight around Selene seemed to shimmer brighter, casting a celestial glow that underscored the gravity of her words.

A deep sadness filled Selene's gaze, the breeze around us swelling with a mournful sound, as if echoing her sorrow.

"While I might be a goddess, I am still bound by many rules," she said softly. "I can only offer my blessing to those outside my children before the moment of their death. Not all of them accept the offer, and not all who do have the strength to live on again. Many of those who do accept my blessing still bear deep wounds that need to be healed.

"Your blessing is different," Selene continued. "You already had a connection to the lunar energies, but unlike the others, you retained some of your solar powers from your other bloodline. You were given the choice of which power you wished to embrace.

"I am sorry for the pain it caused you. My twin is not known for relinquishing what she believes is hers; she is not one to be outshone."

"And what about the other vision?" I asked, my voice urgent, needing to know more about it.

A darkness grew in the Goddess's gaze, as deep as the void between the stars, and I almost wanted to shrink away. "You asked, and I revealed it."

She closed her eyes for a long moment, and when they opened, they were bright and clear again.

"Not everything I show can be what those who ask want. But know that I reveal what needs to be seen, to help you understand."

I opened my mouth to ask more, but Selene leaned forward and planted a soft kiss on my forehead, like a mother to her daughter.

"I know you have more questions, but now is not the time. Trust in my wisdom."

"Then what do I need to know now?" I asked.

"Surround yourself with those you trust—those who will offer you their strength and stand by your side when you most need them. Trust in my blessing. Train your powers. You have a long way to go before you are ready for what is to come. But tonight is the first step and the first true test."

Determination swelled within me. "What must I do?"

Chapter Thirty-Eight

"At the bottom of this lake is a shard of my power," Selene said. "Reach it, and it will free you from this memory."

A shiver ran through me at her words. The lake stretched out before me, its surface reflecting the cold, eerie light of the full moon.

Apprehension washed over me at the thought of diving into its depths. Although the water appeared peaceful, I was aware of potential dangers hidden beneath its placid surface.

The idea of plunging into the dark, frigid water stirred a primal fear within me, a dread of the unknown that lurked below.

Despite the fear gripping me, I knew I had no choice but to face it. Each breath felt heavier as I prepared myself, the weight of the task ahead pressing down on me.

The lake's cold allure seemed to mock my hesitation, and I could almost feel the pull of the darkness beneath, challenging me to confront it.

"You cannot allow my power to fall into the wrong hands," Selene said, bringing my attention back to her. "They chip away at me, but I will hold on for as long as I can."

"The forge?"

"It contains a great power, one that this world has not seen for hundreds of years. You cannot let the enemy take it. Destroy it if you must."

"But won't that hurt you?" All lunar energies once belonged to the Goddess; the power she offered us was just a drop from her wellspring. When a magic user dies, their energies return to the source, but if corrupted, they would never return to the Goddess, making her weaker.

"Better than falling into the enemy's hands."

I took a deep, steadying breath, trying to brace myself for what I needed to do. I could almost feel the pressure of the water around me, as if it were already pressing against my body.

"Our time is gone," Selene said, her voice carrying the weight of her pain.

Sorrow shone in her gaze, and she wrapped her hands around mine. Sensations crashed into me, overwhelming my awareness. The strength of her power, the steadiness of her touch, and the peace of her aura.

"You are not alone, Nyssa. You have never been alone in this. But you have to open yourself and let them in."

And then she was gone. I could still feel the lingering echo of her magic, a warmth that had swelled around me. But now, I was alone once more, standing at the edge of the lake.

I swallowed hard, trying to will my legs to move from where they felt rooted to the ground.

Fear and panic swirled within my chest at the thought of what I needed to do—walking back into this lake that had claimed my life.

The water's dark surface seemed to mock me, an ever-present reminder of the danger below. But it was the only way out.

Danika, Nathaniel, Kaelan. They were out there. Rynac, Indra, and Edrik. Waiting for me.

If what Selene had said was true, they needed my help to break free from the memories that held them captive. The weight of their plight pressed down on me, driving me forward despite my fear.

I tried to remind myself that this was just a memory, that I had survived it before and I would survive it again. I took another deep breath, bracing myself for the dive, the cold water, and the unknown dangers that awaited below.

And if you don't? a small voice seemed to whisper in the back of my mind, but I pushed it away. There was no other choice. The shard at the bottom of the lake was my only way out. I couldn't wait for someone else to save me.

I tried to steel my mind, focusing on the source of my fear. This one was straightforward; I didn't want to drown.

My fear was for my life, and it was entirely valid. But the deeper truth was what was I prepared to lose? Was I ready to risk my life? Or would I stay here and let the corruption take the forge—and my friends?

The stakes were clear; confront my fear or risk losing everything I cared about.

I stepped forward, my foot splashing into the water, ripples spreading out. Another step followed, pushing through the water toward the shimmering reflection of the full moon.

Each movement distorted the image on the lake's surface, but I pressed on, ignoring the freezing water as it reached my thighs and then my waist.

The ice-cold water stole my breath as I pushed off, my body forgetting how to work as I splashed to keep myself afloat. I swam toward the middle of the lake, the water sapping the strength from me with each passing second. I sucked in a deep lungful, praying it wouldn't be my last. Then, I dove under the water.

The cold of the sacred lake leached the heat from my body as I swam deeper, kicking with all my strength. My arms churned through the water, propelling me toward the bottom. Each stroke a battle against the encroaching gloom and the crushing pressure of the depths.

My lungs began to burn as the last of the moonlight disappeared, and I clawed through the darkness. For a moment, panic seized me; I hoped I was still swimming downward, though I couldn't be sure of my direction.

Magic. I chided myself for not thinking of it sooner. I reached deep into the well of lunar energies within me and let it shimmer over my skin. A flicker of light appeared ahead, a faint beacon in the overwhelming darkness.

It was barely more than a glimmer, but it drove me forward. I ignored the voice whispering that I wouldn't have enough air, that I wouldn't make it, that this time I would drown.

Using every ounce of my strength, I focused on the light and fought on. Driven by sheer willpower, I pushed myself harder as the darkness closed in.

And there, nestled at the bottom of the lake and surrounded by black sand, was the shard. One I had seen before, though I couldn't quite recall where.

Without hesitation, I wrapped my fingers around it. Before I could even shift to push off the lake's bottom and fight my way back to the surface, a surge of energy crackled across my hand.

The power coursed through me like an icy fire, burning every nerve in my body and threatening to make me scream out in pain.

Silvery light rippled off me, a raw energy that I couldn't contain. The intensity grew until it overwhelmed my senses, leaving me adrift in a sea of blinding light and searing force.

Seconds, minutes, hours—I lost track of time, surrounded by the oppressive darkness until I jolted back into myself. Even with my eyes open, the heavy weight of the dark still enveloped me. I tried to gasp for air, but my lungs filled with water.

I was still in the lake, still many feet below the surface, below the air that my lungs cried for. As I struggled, I noticed tiny bubbles escaping from my frantic movements.

A small part of my brain, still functioning amidst the chaos, urged me to follow those bubbles up.

With every ounce of strength I had left, I clawed upward, forcing my legs to kick with whatever energy remained in my body. My gaze locked onto the shimmering moon, visible above the water's surface.

I was almost there; I could make it. It was only then that I realized the darkness wasn't just from the lack of light. Spots of darkness danced across my vision, cutting off the small glimmer of the moon.

I'm going to drown.

The thought should have sent fear spiking through me, yet it was so matter-of-factly that I just knew it would be true. But I wasn't afraid.

I kicked one last time, reaching for the moon high above, knowing that she could not save me. The darkness encroached, consuming the last of my vision until only a tiny pinprick of light remained.

And then I saw her.

She appeared, shrouded in an ethereal glow, as if made of stardust and moonbeams.

The water rippled, splitting her reflection as her hands reached out to me—one gripping my wrist, the other wrapping around the back of my neck, lifting me upward.

That same power flowed through me, pulsed through my neck, branding my skin with its warmth. I almost smiled at the familiarity of that touch.

My lungs no longer burned, my limbs no longer ached. I surrendered to the darkness, comforted by her presence.

Chapter Thirty-Nine

I shuddered in a breath as I jerked back into my body, my eyes wide as I took in everything.

Danika? I asked, not wanting to move, fearing that I'd fallen into another nightbane.

"I'm here," she whispered, her voice strained. Danika's slight form huddled in my lap, but she blinked up at me, understanding glowing in those brilliant blue eyes. I knew she'd seen everything I had in that vision. That should've terrified me. And yet, there was a relief in knowing she knew the truth.

"Thank you for always being by my side."

"Always." She butted her head against mine and I wanted to stay here, in this moment.

A heavy sigh escaped me. There was work to do. I set Danika on her feet and hauled myself up.

It was unsettling, the unnatural stillness of the two nephilim. The shadows clung to them like living things, a dark shroud wrapped around their forms. Kaelan clenched his jaw, his eyes squeezed shut as if he was fighting some unseen battle.

Nathaniel stood like a rigid, haunting silhouette. His head bowed, strands of white hair falling over his closed eyes. His hands hung limp at his sides as anguish shadowed his features.

Trapped within their own darkness, unable to escape. The suffocating realization made my chest ache; how did I free them? I reached for Kaelan, but magic crackled around his body and I flinched back.

"That shield erupted around him when he fell into the nightbane," Danika said.

I probed it with my awareness, but couldn't find a way through; worse, it appeared to be Kaelan's own magic. I didn't want to free Nathaniel first, fearing he might turn against us, but Selene still had faith in him.

Cautiously, I extended my magic toward Nathaniel, not sensing anything sinister, and then it snagged, almost as if he was drawing my power into him. I reached out, my fingers grazing his arm, then I lurched forward.

The hot air swirled around me, humid and sticky, clinging to my skin. Beads of sweat formed and cascaded down my face, their salty taste coating my tongue.

I inched forward, squinting through the light fog that seemed to surround me. As it lifted, I found myself in a darkened room.

My eyes adjusted, and it took me a moment too long to realize what I was seeing. I stumbled backward at the tangle of limbs, the crumpled sheets, bright red hair.

I squeezed my eyes shut, not wanting to see Nathaniel in that position, trying to block out the sounds and moans coming from the pair. What in all the hells had I stumbled into? Nathaniel didn't seem like he needed saving.

But we needed to get out of here . . . was I meant to protect him from lust? But Selene's words echoed in my mind: they were trapped in the moment of their deaths.

I whirled back around, my breath catching as the dagger glinted in the light. The woman in Nathaniel's lap, still locked in the kiss, drew back her blade.

I called out a warning, but my body refused to move as the dagger plunged into his heart. It was the tiniest of sounds: that small intake of breath. Betrayal burned in his eyes.

And yet, he still reached for her. His fingers fumbled before they could touch her cheek, and she leaned down, whispering words into his ear that I couldn't hear. Pain rippled over his features, as if each word were another blade in his heart.

His anguish squeezed my chest until I thought it would burst, and then a hot fury rose within me, burning through whatever had tethered me in place.

I lunged, shoving the woman away, and she evaporated into nothing as her haunting laugh cut through the air.

"Nathaniel?" I croaked, pressing my hands around the wound, but there was too much blood.

I knew it was a killing blow, knew there was nothing I could do to repair it. Yet the pain of his death was nothing compared to the anguish on his face.

He looked down at the dagger and then slowly lifted to meet my gaze. There was such a bleakness behind that one look. Resignation. Hurt. A sadness so deep that I didn't think I could ever understand.

"It'll be alright," I said, despite knowing it was anything but. "I'm here. You're not alone."

Power swelled within my chest, pooling into my palms unbidden. As if my body had a mind of its own, I could only watch as I pulled the dagger from his chest and replaced it with my hands.

The raw power within me seeped into his chest, staunching the blood enough to buy him a few moments, but it would not save him.

Fear and anxiety clutched my throat, yet when I spoke next, my voice was steady and smooth. "You will have a second chance at life if you want it. A chance to reach your full potential, to make amends for your mistakes, to serve the Goddess."

The words spilled from my mouth, yet they were not mine. I was just a conduit, a puppet trapped in this infernal memory.

"Selene is the Goddess of the Night, the Goddess of Healing, of Protection, of Unwavering Strength. She offers you a chance to heal, a chance to serve, and a chance live again. She has seen your bravery, your skill, and your determination. But she has also seen the other side of you—the pain and anguish, the guilt and gluttony.

"She watched them use you like a puppet, and you willingly danced to their tune. Now, she offers you a chance at freedom, a chance for redemption. But she will not bind the unwilling. All she asks for is your devotion and dedication, that you trust in your heart to make the right choice this time around."

Nathaniel coughed, a trickle of golden blood spilling from his lips as he blinked, trying to keep his eyes open.

"Selene and her moon-blessed stand united, bound by loyalty and honor. With them, you will find a deeper purpose and a true family, one that supports and uplifts.

"The path will not be easy. If this is the death you have longed for, then you may take it. But she has seen more in your future if you wish to walk that path. She believes in you."

Nathaniel's eyes slid closed, but it didn't take long for them to reopen, filled with a determination I had never seen before in him. He didn't say a word, but met my gaze and then dipped his head.

That was all it took for the power within me to surge, coursing through his body and filling the spaces where his god-blessed magic had once been.

It burned away most of what had been, filling him anew with that silvery, subtle power I knew so well. He didn't scream, even though I knew agony coursed through his body as the will of the Goddess breathed life back into his dying form.

The power stopped, but I could feel it thrumming beneath my hands, echoing with my own magic. I knew that if I lifted my hand, I would see his moon-blessed mark. A weight suddenly lifted from my body, and I was once again in control.

"I need your help," I said, my voice barely louder than a whisper. "I cannot face this next battle alone. Will you offer me your strength, Nathaniel?"

His gaze sharpened as he took in my features, and I knew he was seeing me for who I was and not just a figment of this prison.

"They are trying to steal Selene's power. We can't let that happen. I need you to stand with me."

His hands wrapped around mine with a fierce strength I hadn't expected. I gasped as if I'd just emerged from an icy cold river, and at once we were in the waking world. Nathaniel's hands still held mine against his chest.

For one moment I stared into his eyes, the same strength and vulnerability behind them before he squeezed his eyes closed, turning his head and letting go as if my touch burned.

I swayed for a moment, my brain figuring out which way was up, and trying to pretend I hadn't just witnessed one of Nathaniel's darkest memories. I turned away. There would be time to apologize later, to fix whatever mess I had created.

"One down," I hissed, my head still swimming. I knew time was running out. "One to go."

CHAPTER FORTY

K aelan still looked the same, eyes closed, his features taut, and I swallowed hard as I tried to steel myself for what was to come.

Nathaniel might be an ass, but witnessing his first death had made me reconsider my perspective of him. Though I doubted he wanted that—he'd prefer never to have to look at me again, knowing the secret I now held against him.

Not that I would ever utter a word, but after what I had seen, his distrust of females—witches—became obvious.

Would he hate me now, too? Would this destroy whatever tentative friendship there had been between us? I didn't have any right to witness that moment, not to mention that I was forcing them to share it with me without their consent.

I hated that, and yet I had to go in there. There was no other way to free Kaelan. I didn't have any right, and yet I wouldn't leave him trapped in there. No matter what it cost.

I took a step closer, and Nathaniel gripped my arm. "Are you sure about this?" he asked.

"What choice do I have? We have to free him. Selene said I would need both of you to be able to save the forge."

Nathaniel was silent for too long, and I pulled my arm away. "He's not going to like it."

"So it's better to let him suffer? Should I have left you in there?" I said, anger rising within me. I couldn't leave him, not because I couldn't do this without him, but because I knew he was suffering.

"None of the moon-blessed like talking about their first death." His eyes seemed to glaze over at that, as if realizing that I had witnessed his own, and thinking of the ramifications that would come with that. "But with him," Nathaniel said, with a nod at Kaelan, "he doesn't talk about his life before the Lunar Order at all. Never talks about his past."

"So, what do you want me to do?" I bit out each word. "Selene said neither of you could escape without help."

He was wasting my time, and he didn't need to know any of this, because it wouldn't change the fact that I was going in there. And if he hated me after . . . I couldn't finish that thought.

"Sacrifices have to be made," was all I said as I took a step toward Kaelan. And if that meant giving up whatever might be between us, so be it.

Nathaniel let out a resigned sigh. "I'll place a seal on the door in case Aegis sensed you breaking me out of the nightbane and comes looking. Do what you have to."

The magic crackled when I stepped closer, surging in the air around Kaelan, somehow more fierce than before. But I pressed forward, pain prickling across my skin, and Kaelan winced in response.

Heat rippled through the rune on my chest and pulsed through my moon-blessed mark. If I kept moving, would the pain of his defensive magic be enough to snap him out? Better that than to delve into memories that he didn't wish to share.

I pushed forward again, but rather than painful magic slicing across my skin, it was as if there was a force field pushing me back. I swore, having to cast that plan of attack away. Of course, there wouldn't be an easy option.

The barrier shimmered with a harsh, unyielding light, keeping me out. He was still protecting me, despite the fact that he was hurting. I took a deep breath, centering myself, and tried to think of another way through.

"Kaelan, let me in," I called out, unsure if he would hear me. "I need to help you."

I had to find a way through. Desperation pulsed through me. I willed my power into the protection rune, opening that connection between us, and hoped it would offer me a way through the barrier.

I closed my eyes, channeling my energy into the rune with as much force as I could muster. Power surged through my body, the protective magic answering my call. The rune flared, its light intertwining with the barrier's shimmer. It resisted at first, but the force of my will began to shift it.

Sweat beaded on my forehead as I pushed harder, merging my energy with the protective magic. The barrier started to flicker and waver, its brilliance dimming in response to the strength of my power. I could feel the resistance weakening, the space between us beginning to thin.

With a final, determined push, the barrier gave way just enough for me to slip through. I stumbled, my heart pounding as the raw intensity of his emotions and magic crashed into me.

Gritting my teeth, I closed the gap between us, my hand gripping his arm. Unlike with Nathaniel, I didn't fall in. I moved closer, placing both hands on his chest as if I could will myself inside his head.

"I'm trying to help," I whispered, pushing more magic into the rune. "Please." Danika's warm awareness brushed over me and wrapped around us.

And then I was falling. Again. Tumbling, head over heels, through darkness that swelled around me, shoving me back and forth. But unlike with Nathaniel, this darkness seemed never-ending, as if I were going to fall forever.

I clawed my fingers into the rune above my heart and willed it to take me to Kaelan. I crashed to the ground, yet somehow made no sound.

My stomach churned and my vision wavered. I rubbed the palms of my hands into my eyes, trying to clear my vision, but it made no difference. The world blurred around me—some parts sharp and clear and others just smudges of shadow.

The oppressive weight of the darkness pressed in from all sides. I strained to see through the haze, searching for any sign of Kaelan. The air was thick, almost suffocating, and each breath felt like a struggle.

"Kaelan!" I called out, my voice echoing in the void. "Where are you?"

The shadows shifted and twisted, making it hard to distinguish reality from illusion. I took a hesitant step forward, then another, feeling my way through the murk.

Voices snaked their way around me. With hands outstretched, I blindly crept towards the sound, trying not to think of whatever terrible vision I might see.

A million different scenarios played through my head of how I thought Kaelan might have died the first time. But when I came across the source of the voices, I knew something wasn't right.

All the figures that stood around me were blurry, their edges not quite there. I tried to move through them, searching for Kaelan, but he wasn't there.

I searched the faces, but they were undistinguished—just the general impression of a face, but no details. The only thing I knew was that they were all nephilim, their wings a mixture of whites, blacks, and mottled shades in between. Several had pure black wings like Kaelan, but none of them were him.

What is this?

At the front of the room, there was a cluster of three figures, all with black wings. I moved toward them.

One was a woman, another a child, and the third seemed so familiar. I tried to call out his name, but I no longer had a voice. My movements made no noise, and when I tried to reach out and touch the figure, my hand slipped through them like they were nothing but smoke and shadows.

How could I free him if I didn't even know where he was?

I focused harder, squeezing my eyes closed and channeling more power as if it could help me stabilize whatever hell I was in. A memory, a prison, a cage formed by that corruption with a mixture of memory and magic.

Too many voices shouted and called out, their words blurring together but I could only pick out a few. *Cursed. Dangerous. Murderer.*

I opened my eyes. Though the faces were still blurry, I could better understand their words and see their movements now.

The foul cries echoed all around me, and my gaze shifted to the back of that black-winged nephilim. Then I realized that the words they were hurling were not for him but for the young boy.

He could barely be older than eight years old. Two adults stood beside him, but were doing little to shield him. Pure terror shone in that small child's eyes.

My heart hammered. What happened to that child that had driven Kaelan to his first death?

"You did this," the woman beside the child screamed, such anguish and pain echoing in her voice as her nails dug into the boy's shoulders. "You're a murderer."

My blood turned to ice at the venom in her voice. I didn't know how I knew she was the mother of this child, but I felt it deep in my bones. How could a mother say that to her own flesh and blood?

Some of the other nephilim tried to pull her back, but she wouldn't relinquish her grip on the boy. The others began to fade to smokey figures as if they were nothing but an illusion until it was only the small boy and the woman.

Occasionally, there were still shouts from other people, but I could no longer see them. I took a few steps closer, trying to figure out what was going on. I could no longer see the nephilim I had assumed was Kaelan.

The boy's eyes, wide with fear, full of desperation, scanned the room in a silent plea for help.

No . . .

A cold, creeping terror sank into my bones. My chest seized as the air rushed out of me.

Kaelan—Goddess, no . . .

"Cursed," the woman spat. "Marked from the day you were born, but nobody would listen to me. And now look at what you've done."

I lurched forward, fighting against the dream that tried to hold me in place as the woman pulled out a dagger, pointing it at the child's neck.

Tears cascaded down the child's face as the watchers did nothing but stare. Fists clenched at their side, they lifted their chins and just stared.

Why would no one help the child? I willed someone to say something, to defend the innocent kid, but all the smoky shadows remained silent, watching.

I lurched forward another step, fighting the force that held me, desperate to reach the child.

"But I'm going to end this. You will not be a black stain upon our family anymore." Such hatred from her, and I could see each word landing on the child like a physical blow.

A scream tore from me the moment I saw the blade moving, my mind unable to comprehend what I was seeing, the utter atrocity of that act. Pure hatred burned in that woman's eyes.

A form lunged at her, but not fast enough. Magic exploded from me, shoving everyone else away, and I dove forward, my arms wrapping around the boy as he fell.

His scared little eyes stared up at me as I pressed a hand against his neck, but it didn't stem the golden blood that dribbled out between my fingers.

I couldn't find words. My mouth opened, but only a strangled cry came out.

He seemed so small, his eyes so wide and full of tears, hurt, and abounding sadness. What could I say to make any of this better?

I blinked away the tears that streamed down my face until I could see into his eyes again. He moved as if to reach for the wound, but I wrapped my hand around his and squeezed.

"I'm here," I said, even as my voice faltered. "I won't leave you." Wrapping my arm around him, I squeezed, willing the magic to flow through me again. "You're not alone."

More words spilled from my lips, whispering to the boy that shuddered beneath me.

But I didn't hear what I said, not as the grief tried to strangle me. The utter disbelief crashed into me. I pulled back the moment I felt that power well inside me again, trickling into the boy.

Hot, wet, angry tears poured down my cheeks, and I never felt so utterly useless. The small hand finally squeezed back as his body shook.

"I'm sorry," I whispered, my voice shaking. "I won't leave you. I'll keep you safe."

"Promise?" The boy's voice was nothing but a whisper.

"I promise."

Chapter Forty-One

The world around me lurched, and I left my stomach behind. Warmth still pressed against my hands.

Tears streamed down my cheeks as I tried to blink my vision clear and look up at Kaelan.

His green eyes seemed to burn into me, but I couldn't read the emotions rippling behind them. For the first time in a long while, there was clarity in his expression.

I didn't dare move, didn't know what to say. His pulse raced beneath my hand, still pressed against his neck, but blood no longer coated my fingers.

As my gaze flicked back up to his, realization passed between us. He understood I'd seen everything, that I knew the truth, that I saw all of him.

Then his gaze shuttered, and I feared his mind might fracture.

"I promise," I whispered again. I wanted to ask if he was all right. Feared the toll that reliving that experience had taken on his mind and soul, but the reality of where we were came crashing into me. This wasn't the time or the place.

Uncertainty flickered in his eyes; the air around us was too heavy. I released my hold on his neck, my hands trembling as I stepped away, too aware we were not alone. Swallowing hard, my eyes dropped to the ground as I turned around.

Nathaniel stood with his hands pressed against the door, chanting under his breath. His gaze lifted to mine and then to Kaelan.

I waited for him to make some quip about taking too long or my tear-soaked cheeks, but he simply nodded. The shadows still lingered in his eyes from everything he had lived through. For once, he seemed to know when to hold his tongue.

"My spell sealing the door will last a bit longer," Nathaniel said. "We can only hope they assume we are under the nightbane and don't come looking for us. What do we do now? It's suicide to go up against all the Aegis agents out there."

"Tell me what to expect out there," I said, "then you can leave."

"Leave?" Nathaniel bristled. "You asked me to stand with you, and that is what I'll do. But it's not going to be easy. Of the twelve agents out there, five are full initiates and are the strongest magic users.

"One is a female shifter skilled in barriers. We'll need to deal with her if you want to reach the forge. The remaining agents will all be armed with magically enhanced firearms. And then there's the Jackal. You know what he can do."

"What about the rest of our team that was captured?" Kaelan said. "Any idea where they might be?"

"My guess is nearby. They want all their strength concentrated here until they take control of the forge's power."

"And what about the ritual?" I asked.

Nathaniel frowned. "I don't know what it entails, only that it will require the Jackal's full concentration."

Which still left us with nine agents to deal with. "I need to get my potions back—we will need every advantage we can get." *Can you scout around, see if you can find where they are being held?*

"*On it.*"

Nathaniel deactivated his spell and opened the door enough to peer out. He signaled to follow, and the four of us padded down the dark corridor, but we didn't encounter a single agent.

Then again, if they knew the nightbane was active, they probably doubted we could escape. The Jackal's spell was like a steady hum in the back of my mind. He was only channeling the spell to hold us captive inside, which meant he didn't know we'd broken out. Though if he realized, he might cast the nightbane again, and I had no idea if we would be able to escape a second time.

Kaelan split off when we reached the familiar area as I followed Nathaniel to spy on Aegis. Nothing much had changed—the Jackal still stood in the middle with the forge.

The other agents formed two wide circles around him, spread throughout the room but each facing one of the three entrances. They were more alert, standing at the ready, a few with weapons in hand.

Nathaniel pointed out the shifter, her posture rigid as she stood near enough to the Jackal that she could create a barrier the moment trouble started.

The question was, what shape were her barriers and how large would they be?

Nathaniel and I crept away to a safe distance. Relief washed over me when Kaelan returned, my potion bag in hand. I whispered a silent prayer of thanks that they had missed it. Danika had already slipped away to scout for the rest of our team.

I pulled out every single potion and laid them out in front of me, sorting them into groups as a plan started to form. Any way I looked at this, it was going to be difficult.

"The moment we attack, the shifter will raise her barrier," Nathaniel said. "She can form a dome, and it will take a lot of power to break it. Leaving us to deal with the rest."

"Four apiece doesn't sound bad," Kaelan shrugged.

"Unless the Jackal can ensnare us in nightbane again."

"How are the Aegis agents not ensnared by it too?" I asked. "When I sensed the nightbane this time, it was like a wave of magic washing over the area, not a direct attack."

"It's the shifter," Danika said. *"She is already channeling a barrier, one that shields them from the nightbane."*

"But the Jackal is outside of it?"

"Yes." Danika paused, and I could sense her hesitation. *"I found the others. They are unharmed, but trapped in the nightbane. There is no way for you to reach them, except going through Aegis."*

I relayed what she'd told me to the nephilim. "The question is, can she cast two barriers at the same time?"

Nathaniel chewed on his lip, his eyes darting over the ground as if he could see all the possibilities play out. "Either she would have to drop the shielding from the nightbane to form a barrier around the Jackal that stops both magical and physical attacks. Or she must maintain the magical shield and form only a physical one over the Jackal."

"We will have to change the plan as we go," I said, rubbing a hand over my tired eyes. There were far too many variables to account for. "The main objective is reaching the forge. The longer the Jackal has it, the more powerful he will be."

I divided up my potions, explaining what each did to the nephilim. The start of my plan was easy: hit them hard and fast, creating enough of a distraction that I could reach the Jackal before the shifter made a barrier around him.

After that, there was no telling what would happen. I removed my potion belt and attached it to Danika so she could slip it to Indra and Rynac. I hoped to force the Jackal to drop the nightbane and free my friends from it.

The only thing left to do was ink my rune. Ink from the half-finished rune smeared the back of my hand, and I rubbed off the rest as best I could. My fingers trembled as I reached for the vial, but Kaelan took my hand in his.

Not wanting to face the pity, I whispered, "I need to ink the rune. I can't go in without my magic."

"You need the rune, yes," Kaelan said, "but *you* don't have to draw it."

I didn't, and yet it felt like a failure if I took the easy way out. "It's a solar rune." It would be far more powerful if drawn by my own hand. But the option between going in without the rune to control my solar magic or having a weaker version was an easy one to make.

Yet, didn't this just prove that I didn't have the strength to overcome this on my own?

"There is also a strength in knowing you need to ask for help," Danika said, her words wrapped in a warmth that seeped into my heart. *"Do you think your friends are weak when they ask for your help? Were the nephilim weak because they couldn't escape the nightbane without your aid?"*

No, I'm always happy when I can help them, that I can be of use. I sighed and admitted grudgingly, *And I should acknowledge it's likely the same if the roles are reversed.* A smile tugged at the corner of my mouth as Danika's smugness radiated through our bond.

Kaelan squeezed my hand until I met his gaze. It wasn't pity, but understanding. "Can you draw the rune on the ground to show us?"

My heart raced, but I nodded. I uncorked the vial. My fingers still trembled, but I dipped in my brush and traced the rune on the ground between us.

A wave of relief crashed into me as I finished the last line. Kaelan nodded to Nathaniel, who'd been silently watching us, and he took the brush and held out a hand.

"You wanted our strength and support," Kaelan said, taking my right hand again. I blew out a breath, hating that he was right, and gave my other hand to Nathaniel. The ink was cold as it brushed over my skin, and I forced all my attention on the warmth of Kaelan's grip.

"Done," Nathaniel said, releasing my hand, and for a long moment I could only blink down at the rune. Just a rune. No blood. No wound.

My solar energies stirred within my chest, waiting for me to call on them. I teased out a thin thread and pushed it into the rune.

A tiny flame flickered to life, dancing across my fingertips before I snuffed it out. The magic within me shivered with excitement, and I couldn't help but grin. I could wield my powers to their full extent again.

Clearing my throat, I muttered, "Thank you."

We stood up, gathering all of our supplies, which didn't seem nearly enough for what we were about to go up against.

"Let's do this."

CHAPTER FORTY-TWO

The silence was suffocating. Kaelan and I pressed our backs against the wall next to the archway, our gazes averted. He stood firm, but his body was tense like a coiled spring, ready to strike.

It took every ounce of restraint not to turn and look back at Aegis, ensuring they weren't about to descend on us.

Every second seemed like an eternity as we waited for Nathaniel to get into position.

The dim, shifting light cast jagged shadows over the stone walls as the pulse of magic thrummed through the air, more insistent than before.

A flash lit up the chamber, searing and blinding. Our signal to move. Startled cries rang out.

Kaelan and I hurled our smoke bombs. We dove inside as shouts and chaos erupted. The dense clouds billowed up, covering us. I kept low, scanning for threats.

Nathaniel launched himself into the air, drawing every eye as he rose above the smoke. And then split into five.

My steps faltered, struck by awe as five Nathaniels swooped down, even though I'd been expecting it. Curses and shouts rang out as Aegis tried to regroup.

Kaelan stayed close, a protective wall at my side as we raced toward the center of the room.

The smoke thinned, and I caught sight of the Jackal, the silver circlet on his brow gleaming, but he didn't look away from the forge. His hands pressed against the surface as his lips moved in hurried whispers.

An agent stumbled into our path, and Kaelan spun off to intercept, blades flashing as he engaged them. I didn't stop, my pulse thundering as I dove toward the Jackal, but a dark figure emerged from the smoke.

The shifter. She hissed a word that crackled with unfamiliar power. But I didn't hesitate. I whipped the small, viscous vial from my belt and hurled it. The ooze splattered across her masked face, and she reeled back with a shriek.

The Jackal lifted his head, full attention now on me. I barreled forward, pulling free my next potions. The circlet on his brow glimmered, the gem at the center black, radiating malice.

His hands flexed, shadowy tendrils writhing across them before he thrust them at me. Only steps away, icy fingers clawed at my mind, but I couldn't stop.

The darkness tugged at me, but I slammed my hand onto the forge. The glass shattered beneath my palm, slicing into my flesh as ooze spread across the white surface, binding me to it.

A sudden jolt surged through my body as the forge connected with my magic, its energy intertwining with mine in a rush so intense it took my breath away.

The nightbane clawing at my mind and the chamber shifted; the pulse of the artifact now matched the pounding of my heart.

Linked by the forge, I became a conduit and wrestled the power away and broke the Jackal's control. I sensed his presence, sharp and invasive, as if he were trying to reclaim dominance. But I wasn't done yet.

My fingers found the cork of the second potion, and with a practiced movement, I flicked it open and sucked in a deep breath. The liquid slipped through my fingers, and I poured power into my rune.

Flames burst to life, hot and angry, vaporizing the binding potion as I shoved it into the Jackal's face. Potent enough to overpower the mask's protections.

His power faltered as the potion locked it away, but with the power of the circlet, I knew it wouldn't last for long. Pressing both hands onto the forge, I poured myself into it.

A pulse of energy rippled out, filling the chamber with a luminous, silvery glow. Threads of my lunar power intertwined with the ancient magic; a deep, resonant hum shivered through the air.

Then I felt it—a pull, sudden and inescapable. The circlet. Its presence was no longer just on the Jackal's brow; it was here, woven into the heart of the forge's power.

The Jackal's energy twisted, grappling to reassert control. His awareness bore into me, burning with anger and desperation. But the forge bound us together.

The darkness rose up to swallow me, and I dragged him down into the depths too.

His dark power speared towards me and coiled around my consciousness, sharp and icy, and I gasped in a ragged breath.

It was like plunging into frigid water, the cold seeping into my very bones. His malice and his hunger threatened to consume me. It was a struggle not to recoil, to keep my mind open and inviting, and willingly enter into the abyss.

I took a deep breath, steeling myself against the terror clawing at my resolve, then let the tendrils weave through me, embracing the darkness they brought.

The shadows seeped into my being, filling every corner with their eerie presence.

The nightmare seized me with a cold, unrelenting grip. My heart pounded in my chest, each beat a desperate plea for escape.

Shadows whispered of my failures, my fears, my deepest insecurities. The world tilted. My surroundings dissolved, replaced by a suffocating blackness. Alone.

I squeezed my eyes closed as the world around me shifted again. The stench of sulfur stung at my nose, the metallic taste of blood coating my tongue, and my stomach churning as screams of agony rent the air.

I knew what I would see the moment I opened my eyes, and feared it all the same. My knees gave out, drowning in the realization that my weakness had done this.

Broken and bloodied bodies littered the ground. Unable to stop myself, I searched for faces I knew far too well. Rynac's lifeless eyes stared at me, his body bent in unnatural ways as if even in death he tried to protect his sister, her features still twisted with agony.

All my friends lay dead around me, their lifeless bodies a testament to my failure. The stench of blood and the sight of their still forms overwhelmed me, and I slumped down.

Carmen stepped from the shadows, her eyes blazing. "You did this," she said, her voice thick with pleasure.

Her eyes fluttered closed as she sucked in a long breath, as if savoring the scent of death. When her crimson eyes opened, they burned with glee as a savage smile grew on her lips.

The grim reality pressed down on me. And then I noticed my hands.

Black, twisted claws that still dripped with blood. My breath caught in my throat, a choked sob escaping me. The blood was fresh, warm, and unmistakably real.

I'd done this. Done it willingly.

"Nyssa . . ." Danika's faint voice echoed in my head and my gaze slipped past my hands.

Then I saw her. My little fox lay before me, her small body lifeless and cold. A fresh wound marred her delicate fur, and the sight of it broke something inside me.

My breath came in ragged gasps, the weight of it all crushing me.

"No." The word was a strangled whisper. I couldn't have done that. Never. But the realization hit me like a tidal wave, drowning me in a sea of guilt and despair. The darkness pressed in, a suffocating void that threatened to consume me.

"I knew you had the strength to grasp your true destiny," Carmen said, her voice soft. "To accept the full power within you. Your transformation is almost complete, Nyssa. You're everything I thought you were. I chose well."

Her words cut deeper than any blade. I stared at the carnage, the weight of her truth pressing down on me. I'd always feared this moment, feared that I was capable of such destruction. But now, confronted with the reality, a chilling conviction settled over me.

Carmen's smile widened, a triumphant gleam in her eyes. "Embrace it, Nyssa. Embrace the power. This is who you are. This is what you want."

I closed my eyes, trying to block everything out, but the images were seared into my mind.

Tears burned my eyes, and I curled into myself, trying to block out the relentless assault. Why had I ever thought I was worthy of my friends? I didn't deserve them, the friendship and love they offered me, the unwavering trust.

And Danika. A force gripped my heart and squeezed until I thought it would burst.

I was just so scared. So scared that I would lose it all, lose my friends, lose my familiar, my alchemy, my magic. Everything in this life that I fought so hard to build up.

Scared of Carmen hunting me down again, the demons, and all the other dangers that lurked in the world. I thought my fear was just trying to protect me, but in turn, it became my greatest weakness.

As Carmen stared at me, I saw in her eyes the conviction that I had made this choice. I'd wanted to be stronger. To protect my friends, my family, everything.

But I was so scared that I kept it inside me and believed the words Carmen had said—that I needed to be stronger. I wanted to do it for them, for all of them, and now I had destroyed it all with my own two hands. My fear had killed them.

Words echoed in my head, the faintest of memories. True friends are there even when the going gets tough. True friends are there to pick you up when you make mistakes, to support you even when you make the wrong choices.

I'd known that, or at least believed I did. Yet when I said it, I'd only meant that I would stand by them, never expecting the same from them.

"What would they think if they could see you now?" The venom dripped from Carmen's lips, and she reveled in my discomfort as I flinched at each word. But there was something else, something that scratched at the back of my mind as she spoke.

My gaze turned to Rynac and Indra. I forced myself to look at their faces, to stare into the eyes that no longer had that spark of life behind them.

If I could bring them back for just one moment to see what I had done, what would they say? Their mouths began to move, cursing my name, cursing everything I had done, that they hated me.

But I knew those voices were not them. Indra would have asked what she could have done to help me. Rynac would have said that he understood, that he still cared for me, and was sorry he didn't protect me.

And Danika?

Pain rippled as I reached along that shredded connection between us, the hole that ached in my chest.

But then I sensed that small bit of warmth, of understanding, of seeing me—all of me—mistakes and faults, and still accepting me for everything that I had done. That endless love. Unwavering. She only mourned that she could not follow me wherever I was going.

"What would they say?" Carmen hissed again, but this time, her voice vibrated with fury.

My gaze lifted to hers and I could start to see the cracks. The desperation. Her words were a challenge. A challenge for control. Something clicked into place.

Nightbane.

I was within the nightbane. This wasn't reality. The realization tried to slip away, but I fought its power. I needed to break its hold.

"Let's ask them," I ground out, fighting to hold on to the truth.

I stretched out along that bond that wound around my heart, pressed that small bit of magic that remained within me into the mark that burned on the back of my neck.

I opened myself, called to my friends, and let them in. Let them see me. See all of me.

The cracks. The shattered remains.

"I need your help," I whispered, knowing the moment they set foot in my nightbane, they would understand everything. Knowing and opening myself despite it. "I need your strength. Will you be the gold that fills the gaps?" For a moment, there was only silence.

The despair I'd been holding back began to pour through the cracks in my resolve. My clawed hands, still dripping with blood, shook as I held them out, reaching, waiting. Hoping.

Magic crackled across the palm of my right hand a moment before a soft head pressed into it, despite the blood and deadly claws.

The familiar sensation of Danika's touch sent a wave of comfort through me, and as her sapphire eyes met mine, her love flooded through our bond. Love. Even though at a single glance into those shining eyes, I knew, knew with every fiber of my being, that she understood everything that had been happening inside this nightbane. But she didn't shy away.

My throat constricted, hot tears trailing over my cheeks as I poured my own love through our bond, expressing what I could not articulate. Her presence was a soothing balm, the warmth of her fur grounding me, pulling me back from the brink of despair.

And then strong and steady fingers closed around my left hand, not hesitating to grip the blackened claw. The warmth of that touch spread through me, igniting a spark of hope in my heart, enough so that when he squeezed my hand, I complied and lifted my head.

Kaelan didn't flinch away from what he saw. The ground covered in bodies, their blood dripping down my talons, splattered over me.

Determination and acceptance shone in his gaze. Heat prickled over the protection rune and for a moment, I allowed myself to lean into the surety of the promise it held.

A firm grip settled on my other shoulder, solid and reassuring. And there Nathaniel stood, his defiant gaze fixed on my enemy, his touch an anchor, grounding me. The strength in his grip spoke volumes, a silent promise that he was with me, that he believed in me.

Their unwavering support wrapped around me and I basked in the strength they offered me, then one by one, the tendrils of the nightbane snapped.

The twisted claws dissolved, the blood on my hands drying and flaking away, replaced by the warmth of their touch. Their magic mingled with mine, a symphony of strength, unity, and friendship.

With them by my side, I was whole again. I was no longer alone in my struggle. Together, we could face anything.

A burst of silvery light erupted, searing through the nightbane, and the connection snapped.

The shadows of nightbane disintegrated, and I was once again standing in the chamber. Danika pressed against my leg, her power pouring into me.

The nephilim stood at my side, one hand gripping me and the other poised on their weapons, ready for whatever came next.

A weight settled on my brow, warmth radiating from it as its magic thrummed through me. I lifted my hand, fingers trailing over the circlet now resting there. It had chosen.

The nightbane's hold shattered, and the power was now mine to wield.

CHAPTER FORTY-THREE

T he Jackal staggered back, a strangled cry ripping from him as he clawed at his head, before crashing to the ground.

Nathaniel darted forward to secure him, binding his feet and hands. I blinked, taking in the damage around me.

A few bodies lay strewn around the room, the walls pocked and crumbling from the attack. But it was the Aegis shifter, her mask tossed on the ground beside her, who startled me. She held her hands up, a dome barrier shimmering in the air, shielding us.

"What happened?" I asked.

"After you glued yourself to the forge," Nathaniel began, and I glared at him, "and the Jackal ensnared you in a nightbane, he also pulled all the Aegis agents in with him."

"We linked our powers," the shifter snapped, shooting daggers at Nathaniel, "to aid in his attempt to gain the forge. When you two battled for the circlet, he tapped into our magic too. We saw glimpses of his nightbane, revealing him to be a traitor."

Before I could ask what that meant, Kaelan said, "Move the forge." I shifted it to the side, and beneath, carved into the pedestal, was a spell array, each rune demonic. This was the focus, where all the other spell arrays were channeling their power to corrupt the lunar magic within.

"He fights for that cursed cult, for the demons." The shifter spat the words at his prone form. "He represents everything we stand against, what we fight for. The power of the forge was meant to help us fight back against the demons, but he betrayed us, trying to corrupt the magic and strengthen the enemy. The other agents ran, knowing we had lost."

"And why did you stay?" I asked.

She scrunched her nose. "I may not like you, but I'll do what I have to if it means protecting my realm." Her jaw worked, as if it was a struggle to say the words. "The traitor tainted the forge with *their* power. Even if it means giving you that power, it's better than our enemy having it. So I stayed to protect you in case there were any more traitors among our ranks."

"They are all gone," Rynac called out. My knees almost buckled as he and Edrik limped into the room.

"Unless they're really stupid," Indra said. But it was the nephilim she supported that I couldn't look away from. Astrid's face was gaunt, but despite the dark rings under her eyes, she flashed a weak smile. Relief crashed into me. They were safe.

Nathaniel rushed over to Astrid, taking her from Indra. "They moved her here to ensure my compliance. Thank you for freeing her."

"I'll be going then," the shifter said, her shield dropping.

"Thank you for your aid," I said. The shifter hesitated before giving me a small nod, then disappeared down a corridor. I knew she was meant to be the enemy, but I hoped she stayed safe after what she did for me.

"Was that wise?" Kaelan asked.

"I think it's an even trade. Besides," I said, lifting the forge off the pedestal, "I've more pressing matters." Heat radiated from the artifact as I set it on the ground, the ooze already beginning to crack away.

"Do what you need to," Kaelan said, shifting to take up a defensive stance. I settled myself on the ground, Danika climbing into my lap.

Closing my eyes against all other distractions, I reached out with my awareness, sifting through the dense energies that swirled around the forge. Then, like a delicate strand of light, I sensed it—a presence, potent and steady.

Its power reached out to me and I opened myself to it. Our magic met, intertwining in a silent acknowledgment. The connection poured warmth into my veins, a song of unity, of a shared purpose stretching back to ancient oaths and moonlit nights.

Magic shivered through the circlet as if trying to encourage or warn me; I wasn't exactly sure.

I lowered my mental block and allowed the power of the circlet to flow into me. The world seemed to sharpen, colors more vibrant and shadows far deeper.

When I looked down at the forge, it glowed with an ethereal light. The power around it sparkled and shimmered in the air, like a diamond reflecting the colors of the rainbow.

But then I spotted the small pool of darkness that lingered within it. Just a pinprick at first, but the more I focused on it, the more I could feel the malevolent nature behind that tiny speck.

The magic seemed to whisper in my ear, crying out in warning. I reached for the foreign power, ignoring the whispers that told me to stop. I needed to know what I was facing.

The moment I touched the darkness, it was as if a storm raged inside: dark and turbulent, trying to consume and twist my magic.

A writhing mass of disorder, seething with malevolent intent. The sensation was dizzying, almost nauseating, as if the very fabric of reality warped around the corruption. The touch of chaos left me breathless, struggling to maintain my hold on my own power.

I reeled back, snatching back my magic before it could strip more away from me.

"Something's inside it," I hissed, barely able to hear my voice over the buzzing in my ears. "Something . . . terrible." I didn't know how to describe it.

"Do you think it's a part of the forge?" Danika asked.

"I don't know," I replied, shaking my head. "It feels like corruption, something that shouldn't be there. We need to be careful."

With renewed focus, I tightened my grip on my power, preparing for the next step. We were in this together, and no matter what darkness lay ahead, we would face it as one.

I quieted my mind again and listened. "No," I hissed. They'd planted that darkness within the forge. It felt as if it was trying to consume its power. The other Aegis agents had wanted to control the power for themselves—was this how they would do it, by twisting the lunar energies into something they could wield?

Every time I pushed my awareness towards that cluster of darkness, every instinct deep within me screamed at me to destroy it. Whatever they put in there . . . I shook my head. Pure evil didn't seem to come close to the malevolence I sensed.

There was no option left. I had to stop it.

The lunar magic pooled in my hands until a silvery glow surrounded them, and I reached towards the forge.

My magic skittered over the surface as if trying to find a hole in the shield surrounding the artifact. There. My power seeped into the cracks. I poured more in, wedging it into the tiny hairline fractures until they widened enough for me to slip my fingers through and touch the cool metal of the forge.

The faint bells and chimes that had been scratching at the back of my mind increased until they were almost a musical voice surrounding me.

My touch seemed to intensify the call, as if it sang my name, whispering words of encouragement in a language I did not know.

The power contained within brushed against my awareness, as if it were reaching for me, willing me to pick it up. I pushed my magic deeper, searching through the forge for the tethers that bound it to the spell array.

I shoved harder until I finally saw what looked like tiny black spider webs that wrapped around the power at its center.

One by one, I severed the threads, slowly freeing the power source. A strange power enveloped me, yet oddly familiar, like a memory from someone else. The forge's ancient power brushed against mine, intertwining for a moment.

Bells and chimes rang out a moment before the darkness surged, their soothing melody twisting into a cacophony of alarm.

The unsevered threads tightened like a noose around the power core. Once pure and vibrant, the energy flickered, tainted by dark corruption.

Every minute that passed, more of its power was corrupted. It was fighting back, but for how long? I dove back in, my hands trembling with urgency, trying to sever the threads before they could choke the life out of the forge.

The darkness pushed against me, icy and relentless, as I fought to free the trapped magic. I could feel its power being drained away, funneled into the spell array that seemed to pulse with dark satisfaction. The forge's energy, once a brilliant beacon, was now a dim and fading light, fighting desperately against the encroaching shadow.

And then, as if the corruption festering within it was a living thing, its gaze shifted to me.

A torrent of magic hit me with such force that I stumbled backward. I reeled not only from the sharp pain cutting through my mind, but the agony slicing through my body.

Blood coated my tongue as it shoved me back into my own mind.

Before I even had a chance to gather my magic once again, the darkness lashed out. Its attack was a cold, invasive force that seemed intent on overwhelming me.

The corruption's malevolent presence loomed, pressing in on all sides, making it hard to breathe, to think, to fight back.

YOU.

The word pounded in my head, coming from everywhere and nowhere. The chaos was unyielding, a maelstrom of jagged thoughts and violent energy tearing through my mind.

Danika! I screamed, but couldn't form words.

For a moment I sensed my bonded, but her magic flickered out like a dying star. Endless, swirling madness surrounded me, without center or calm.

Every time I tried to focus, the chaos dug deeper, ripping at my thoughts, unraveling my sense of self.

It was bitter and cruel, sharp as broken glass and just as unforgiving. Whispers echoed in the storm, voices that weren't mine, taunting me, telling me to give in, to let the chaos consume everything.

I clenched my teeth against the onslaught, but it was like holding back a tidal wave with nothing but willpower.

The forge's power was slipping through my fingers, and I could feel the corruption worming its way into the core of it, twisting it into something dark and corrupted.

Panic clawed at me. It wasn't enough—I couldn't stop it. The whispers laughed, mocking my struggle, growing louder as the storm raged on. My resolve wavered as the cold slithered deeper, coiling around the last shred of my control.

A voice broke through the chaos, not from the storm, but from somewhere deeper, somewhere untouched. *Find your strength,* it whispered, a gentle plea in the midst of the fury.

But how could I? I wasn't strong enough. The storm was too vast, too overwhelming, and I . . . I was just one person. It would break me just as it broke the forge.

The chaos stilled. Only for a heartbeat, I saw them. My friends.

I reached out to them with something deeper, something that flowed through the core of who I was. In my mind's eye, I reached out over the battle-scarred chamber, my presence brushing against those I held dear—Danika, Rynac, Indra, Nathaniel, Kaelan.

I didn't force them; I opened myself willingly, exposing my vulnerability, my need.

And one by one, they accepted.

Danika's steadfast loyalty, Indra's fierce determination, Rynac's unshakable faith, Nathaniel's battle-hardened strength, and Kaelan's unwavering resolve.

They stood with me, not just in body, but in spirit, their energies intertwining with mine, forming a shield against the chaos. The storm began to weaken, its grip loosening as our combined power pushed back.

Together, we severed the last thread of the corruption, the chaotic tendrils unraveling and disintegrating into nothingness. The forge's power pulsed beneath my hand, no longer dark, no longer corrupted. But something was wrong.

The magic whispered to me, its voice faint and strained. *Its form is damaged.*

In the space between thought and reality, I saw it—the box that held the forge's power was cracking, shattering under the weight of the battle. It couldn't hold it anymore.

There was only one choice left.

I closed my eyes, took a breath, and opened myself to the power. The moment I surrendered, it coursed into me, a tidal wave of raw, unbridled energy that swept through my body and soul.

It was overwhelming, immense—like standing at the center of a storm made of stars. The forge's essence mingled with my own, ancient and potent.

The power seared through my veins, not burning, but illuminating, coursing like molten silver. It washed away the bone-deep cold that had anchored itself in me, scattering the darkness in a burst of radiant light.

My muscles tensed, then relaxed as warmth spread, a soothing yet fierce presence. The torrent of power swept through every frayed edge of my being, bolstering and fortifying every inch.

Lunar magic pulsed in rhythmic waves, wrapping around me like an embrace, weaving into my essence. The magic began knitting me back together with silvery threads of light that shimmered and pulsed with life.

Each strand hummed with power, connecting me to something greater, binding me to the forge and its purpose.

The whispers of doubt, of fear and pain, fell silent. The purity of this energy silenced the voice of the storm that had taunted me.

Magic flooded my senses, sharpening my awareness until I could feel every pulse of energy around me, the ancient will of the forge, and the echo of countless lives it had touched.

It was as if I'd become part of something boundless, a vessel filled with light that transcended the here and now.

My heartbeat synced with its hum, steady and sure.

This was more than power; I was reforged.

As the last remnants of the corruption faded, I opened my eyes. Radiant power coursed through my veins, filling me to the brim, and I stood ready to face whatever came next.

Chapter Forty-Four

A deep breath shuddered past my lips, and the chamber seemed to expand with it.

Magic thrummed through me, around me, and for one glorious moment, I sensed it shiver through the entire complex. Awareness of all that it encompassed. All that lay within. And the tiny pinpricks of light returning home at last.

"The Lunar Order is here," I said. Kaelan and Nathaniel shared a look. I tilted my head, trying to decipher what I sensed. "As well as the enforcers."

"They're a bit late to the party," Rynac grunted.

"Now that the traps are deactivated, they will be faster."

Danika gave me a curious look, but I just shrugged, not having the words to explain.

That strange awareness faded, as the last of the forge's power slipped like a dream on waking.

The world around me seemed to shrink, drawing back into the limits of my own skin. The vast, echoing presence that had filled my mind vanished, leaving me with only the steady rhythm of my heartbeat, the familiar weight of my own body.

Rough stone beneath my boots. The slight chill in the air. The ache in my muscles.

Each sensation grounded me in the present moment. It was just me again, no lingering threads of moonlight, no sense of something greater humming through my veins.

Only my own breath and the solid stone beneath me, grounding me in the here and now.

"We will go meet the Order," Nathaniel said, helping Astrid to her feet while Kaelan hauled the Jackal upright and dragged him with them.

That would be a problem to face another time. The last remnants of my energy seeped away, leaving my body heavy and unresponsive.

"And I think I'll sit for a bit," I said. The last of the ooze cracked away as I pulled my hand free from what remained of the forge, just a husk now. The cuts from the shards of glass were only angry red lines.

People poured into the chamber like a tidal wave, including medics from the MEA rushing around to tend to all of us.

Captain Everson, his face stern as ever, approached, eyeing everything that went on around him.

"Is the threat dealt with?" he asked.

"I believe so," I said. He gave me a nod and went to bark orders somewhere else. "Guess I get to wait until tomorrow to be grilled."

I let the world wash over me, just taking everything in. People scurried around, and I watched until Indra and Rynac came over to help me up.

The enforcers wanted to document the remaining parts of the forge. It was those who wore UMC uniforms I examined; I could almost see the lunar magic churning inside them, but decided to stay silent if the Order didn't want to talk to me yet.

Controlled chaos was what it looked like. Indra and Rynac flitted in and out, gathering information, but no one bothered me.

"They captured most of the Aegis agents," Rynac said. "They all rushed out the same exit where the MEA was waiting. Though there are a few unaccounted for."

An odd feeling swelled within me, urging me to hurry. Telling the siblings I'd be back in a bit, I slipped away, Danika trotting beside me.

A subtle tug in my chest pulled me forward, insistent and unyielding. I followed it, weaving through the narrow, stone-lined corridors that stretched deeper underground.

My steps slowed as the sensation led into a dark archway, one I wouldn't have noticed if it wasn't for that tug. But as I stepped through the entrance, a shiver ran over me and I blinked against the sudden brightness.

Orbs of light hung in the air, illuminating the five figures within, and my heart stilled. Nathaniel, Kaelan, and Astrid were on their knees, eyes downcast, and hands behind their back as a male moved to handcuff them.

None of them resisted, but the sight of them sent a wave of anger surging through me.

Before I could stop myself, I rushed forward, demanding, "What the hell is going on here?"

Only the female standing in front reacted to me. "Can I help you?" she said, her voice eerily calm.

Her presence was unsettling, as if she occupied a space larger than her physical form. Long, dark waves of hair fell over her shoulders, framing her sharp but elegant features.

A predatory gleam of intelligence shone in her silver eyes.

"Yes, actually. Who are you?" I demanded, my voice trembling with barely contained fury. "And why are you arresting them?"

A small part of my brain screamed that I really shouldn't try to antagonize her, but I didn't care, not when they were treating my friends like this.

"She's with the Order," Nathaniel simply said.

"Yeah, I gathered that," I drawled. "But that doesn't excuse how they are treating you, let alone that Aegis held you captive, and no one came to rescue you."

"Sounds like you have a bone to pick with me?" she said, a dangerous spark igniting in her eyes.

Kaelan's head snapped up, eyes locking on mine, imploring me to back down. "You wanted me to go back."

"Not in handcuffs," I snapped. Why was I the only one outraged? Danika bristled, taking a defensive stance between my feet. *That makes two of us.*

"Are you going to erase their memories again?" I demanded.

"Ah," she said slowly, "this is the lunar witch." Her gaze shifted from me to Kaelan. "I should have known you'd find your way back to her, memories or not. Though not this quickly."

She acted with such familiarity and the nephilim didn't protest, but it was impossible to tell if that was their own free will or the influence of a spell. I'd just have to find out if she spoke the truth myself.

Gathering the last threads of my magic, I wove them into my moon-blessed mark and reached. In an instant, I sensed the nephilim and the other male. I pushed harder, my gaze fixed on the female.

For a fleeting moment, her pale skin seemed to glow brighter, then a crown of moons twinkled to life on her forehead. A genuine smile broke across her face and in the blink of an eye, she stood before me, grasping my hands between her own.

"It *is* you," she breathed, trying to take me in all at once. "It's wonderful to meet you. I'm Yirathax, but please call me Yira."

"Nyssa," I murmured, her presence overwhelming this close. "Are you going to tell me why you're imprisoning my friends now?"

"This is standard protocol. Aegis held them for some time—there's no telling if they implanted anything dangerous into their minds. It is for their safety as much as our own. And we need to repair the damage they did to Kaelan's mind." The last part came out as a growl, and I was thankful her anger wasn't directed at me.

"Why did it take you so long to come? We tried to contact the Order days ago."

"There have been some . . . internal disruptions. Something that will not happen again. But I do thank you for returning them to our custody."

Custody? "I'll testify if you need me to. To prove they're innocent."

"They are in little danger of being judged, but I would be more than happy to hear your story sometime. Though we do need to leave soon, perhaps we can set up a time to talk?"

"I'd like that," I said, but my gaze strayed over to Kaelan. "I've also been curious about the qualifications one needs to join the Order."

Yira blinked once and then a smile bloomed across her lips. "I was under the impression that didn't interest you?"

"Interests change."

Yira laughed, low and melodic. "That they do."

She flicked her fingers and a small business card appeared between them. One side had a full moon, the other simply said *Yirathax.*

"And to answer your previous question, no, I'll not be taking their memories. It's not an ability I use lightly, and I only use it with consent from all parties. However, since you wish to join the Order, it's not necessary."

"What?"

A warm smile spread over Yira's lips at my confusion. "Their memories were removed to keep the knowledge that there was a lunar witch a secret. These three didn't want to disrupt your life, as that was the path you chose."

"Oh," I muttered. "Well, it would've been nice if I'd been consulted." I glared at the nephilim. Kaelan's lips twitched.

"It would hardly be fair to berate them now. But I promise you can yell at them all you want after they recover." Yira held my gaze, awaiting my approval.

I nodded. "Until then."

"I'll be in touch." At a gesture from Yira, the nephilim stood and followed the male out of the room. Kaelan paused and looked back for the briefest of moments, then was gone.

"I'm looking forward to seeing you again, Nyssa," Yira said.

Her card warmed in my hand and despite the fatigue, the exhaustion weighing at my limbs, the world felt . . . right.

As if this was the path I'd been searching for my whole life. I clutched the small card, fearing it might disappear, or I'd wake up and realize it was only a dream.

This path before me, no matter where it led, was the direction I was meant to be going. I knew it deep within my bones. My heart and magic beat in sync, both of them aligning to whisper that, yes, *this* was my purpose.

"Oh," Yira said, pausing at the doorway. "Love the crown, by the way."

I blinked, my fingers lifting to my brow where the circlet still sat. I groaned, "Again?"

Danika snickered, but I was too tired to laugh at myself. Yira disappeared from sight and, in her absence, a heavy weight seemed to lift from my body.

With a weary sigh, I unceremoniously slumped to the ground. "I'm exhausted."

"Yes, I think it's nap time," Danika said, curling up in my lap. I thought about protesting, but I didn't have the energy to even shift, let alone stand.

"So, the Lunar Order. What do you think?"

She peered up at me with curious eyes. *"It will make for an interesting life."*

I let out a slow breath. How'd my life changed so drastically in a few months? "By interesting, do you mean dangerous and life threatening?"

"Your life is already like that half the time." She blinked up at me, poking her wet nose under my hand, and I grumbled in agreement. *"But as long as I'm by your side, that is all that matters."*

A smile spread as I scratched behind Danika's ears. "Whatever is to come, we will face it together."

Epilogue

One Week Later

I rushed down the street, caught between that awkward brisk walk and an almost jog. I was going to be late.

If I ran, I'd show up to my alchemy shop sweaty, and no one wants to take photos with someone with sweat marks on their top. Why didn't I know a spell for this?

Danika stayed silent as she trotted beside me. She had tried to get me to move faster, but I had spent too long making sure my outfit was perfect, my hair just right, and my makeup flawless.

As my eyes fixed on the familiar corner, I slowed. Showing up breathless wouldn't help either. Danika, now a few steps ahead, zipped around the corner, but my steps faltered.

All the fear and anxiety I had been ignoring hit me like a brick wall, and my stomach churned.

"Take a breath," Danika said. Was that a slight smile in her voice? I had told her about my fear—about twenty times in the past few hours—that no one would show up for the grand opening. Her response was always the same, *"So what? Would you close your shop?"*

She'd then remind me how silly I was being. Ruby and Jade had promised to be there, Indra and Rynac as well. Even Zola and Voren had left my apartment early to help set up.

If no one else showed up, that would be enough. So why was I still afraid I'd walk around the corner and see no one?

"*Nyssa.*" Danika's soft voice broke through my spiraling thoughts. "*Trust me and step around the corner.*"

I didn't let myself think. I just followed her words like a command, letting her strength and certainty give my noodle legs enough power to take those final steps.

One, two . . . *Hells, I can't do this.* I leaned forward ever so slightly, the curls of my hair falling in waves as I peeked around the corner.

Oh, Goddess. That was a lot of people.

"Can I run away now?" I said, straightening before anyone spotted me. Why were there so many people? Was there something going on at Divine that I didn't know about? Surely, they couldn't all be here for the opening of my shop.

"*Nyssa,*" Danika scolded.

"Fine." I took a deep breath, threw my shoulders back, raised my chin up, and channeled every ounce of confidence I could muster as I stepped around the corner.

People clustered around the entrance to the alchemy shop, which was now covered by a thick black curtain. Where had they gotten that from?

I recognized many faces—my friends, coworkers from the coffee shop, shifters, and a few others who had already purchased alchemy products from me. There were at least twenty people, more than I could have asked for.

Indra spotted me first, followed by Rynac. The siblings bustled over, linking their arms through mine, guiding me to the front of the store.

Neither said a word, but they didn't need to. The joy shining in their eyes was enough to bring a smile to my face. Rynac covered my hand, giving it a gentle squeeze, while Indra hugged my arm.

"And here she is," a bright voice called out. Jade. The young shifter was standing on a step-stool above the crowd.

For once, she seemed in her element, a bright smile lighting up her face. Ruby stood beside her, staring with a wondrous look as she beamed up at her sister.

"The alchemist you've all been waiting for," Jade said, waving me over. Rynac and Indra released me, and I took my place next to Ruby. "Thank you, everyone, for coming to celebrate the opening of Nyssa's alchemy shop. And today is not only the grand opening but also the official reveal of the shop's name."

I bit my lip, staring behind me, wondering what name they had come up with. It turned out I'm terrible at naming things.

Why did it feel so important, so terrifying, to name my shop? I'd even considered calling it "Alchemy Shop." But no, that was too stupid. In the end, Ruby and Jade had convinced me to let them choose a name, with the reassurance I could always change it later.

"Where did the curtain come from?" I whispered to Ruby as Jade continued talking to the crowd.

"That was all Divine," Ruby said. "They seemed very excited about this grand opening." There was a twinkle in her eye, one that made me unsure if I should be worried or not.

Danika, did they tell you? I asked, but my familiar remained knowingly quiet, her tail swishing with excitement. Oh, she knew. That little rascal had kept it from me.

"And with that," Jade said, pulling my attention back to the matter at hand, "it's time for the official unveiling. Nyssa, if you will do the honors."

The crowd shifted and moved to the side, revealing a fancy-looking gold cord hanging down. My throat tightened as I looked out at the crowd staring at me.

I'd asked Jade to give the speech, knowing I'd never be able to talk in front of so many people, but now all eyes were on me. I had to say something.

"Thank you . . ." I began, my voice shaky. I cleared my throat and tried again. "Thank you all for coming to celebrate the opening of my alchemy store." The silence stretched as everyone kept staring at me, but my mind had gone blank.

Pull the cord, Danika prompted.

Right. "Welcome to . . ." I yanked hard on the cord. The black curtain parted, revealing the large window filled with potions and reagents. Hand-painted above the store, in curling script, was a name that made me grin. "Divine Alchemy."

A cheer erupted from the crowd, and Jade rushed forward to open the door. People streamed into the shop, many offering congratulations or nods as they entered.

Once they were inside, I took a step back, staring up at the name of my shop as tears brimmed in my eyes. I'd done it. I'd done what I'd set out to do, the whole reason I had come to this city.

My shop, something that had been nothing but a dream, was finally here.

I swiped at the tears spilling down my cheeks, blinking to clear my vision just so I could see the name again.

"Do you like it?" Ruby asked, uncertain.

"I love it," I said, my voice catching. "It's just . . . hard to believe this is real. I never would have been able to do it without all of you."

Ruby pulled me into a hug, and I let myself take strength from her warmth.

"You deserve this, Nyssa," Danika said, twisting between our legs. *"All your hard work has paid off. Now, go inside and mingle."*

I let out a stuttering laugh, gave Danika a little scratch behind the ears, and let Ruby lead me toward the door. "Are you sure Divine is okay with the name?"

"They were more than pleased," Ruby said with a grin.

As I stepped inside my shop, filled with people, the rumble of voices, and the clink of glasses, I could have sworn Divine was glowing.

If they had a face, they'd be smiling. The welcoming warmth that wrapped around me was familiar, like the one I felt when I first entered Divine Coffee, but different. The scent of crushed herbs and flowers floated through the air.

Bundles of drying herbs hung from the ceiling, more for decoration than anything, but they gave the shop a cozy feeling.

For a long moment, I just stood there, taking in the sight. Ruby excused herself to help someone, but I stayed, soaking in the buzz of excitement. It was intoxicating.

"Congratulations, little sister," a familiar voice said behind me.

I turned to see my brother standing in the doorway with a massive grin on his face. Tobin's tailored clothes were a stark contrast to his bright red hair, which was tousled and wild as always. With his navy blazer thrown over his shoulder, a crisp white shirt with the sleeves rolled up, and dark jeans, he looked effortlessly chic. And I could only stare.

He'd actually come. I had sent a message to my family about the grand opening, but I didn't expect them to show up on such short notice. Tobin had been busy with his training in the Witch Guard, and I'd heard the "we'll try" promise a million times from my parents. I hadn't let myself get my hopes up.

"You're here?" I managed to blurt out, still staring at him as if I expected him to disappear.

"I wouldn't miss this for the world," Tobin said, stepping closer. "Now, can your brother get a hug, or am I just going to stand here? What kind of customer service are you running?"

A laugh startled out of me, and I rushed toward Tobin, throwing my arms around him. He squeezed me back, and my eyes prickled with tears. I'd forgotten how much I missed him, how much his presence meant to me.

"I knew you'd do it, Nyssa," he said, pulling back just enough to look down at me. "You're brilliant as always. It's wonderful to see how happy you are, that you've finally found a place to be yourself."

"You've only been here for a few minutes," I hissed, swiping at my tears, annoyed. Good thing I wore waterproof mascara.

"I know." His grin widened as joy danced in his eyes. "But I can already tell you've found where you belong."

"Stop, or you'll make me cry even more," I scolded, swatting at him, but I couldn't hide my smile.

"You should mingle with everyone. They're all waiting to talk to you," Tobin said, nodding behind me.

Sure enough, several people hovered nearby, not wanting to interrupt our moment.

"I'll be here when you're done. You're not getting rid of your big brother that easily." He wiped away the last traces of my tears and gave me a gentle push toward the waiting crowd.

I moved to greet the people who had come to support me, and I swear I was floating on air as I flitted between them.

My cheeks ached from smiling so much. I tried not to think too hard, fearing that this was all just a dream, that I'd wake up and it would all be gone.

Beylin greeted me with a warm smile and a hearty pat on the back, which sent me stumbling. Zola and Voren followed, pulling me into quick hugs before whispering about celebratory drinks later. They nudged me back toward the crowd, and I found myself meeting even more people—some familiar, some new. It amazed me that so many had come, not just to see the shop but to support me.

Ruby and Jade were busy rushing around, chatting with customers, and helping them pick out products and taking orders. We only shared fleeting moments, as there was much to do.

The stock on display was small—after all, I couldn't predict what people would want to buy—but it was wonderful to talk about alchemy, to help people find what they needed. I even set up a few custom orders for specific products.

I had no idea if my business would stay afloat, but for now, I tried to embrace the moment, soaking in the brilliance of opening my alchemy shop.

A strange warmth spread from my pocket, followed by a faint crackle of magic over my thigh. My heart paused. Excusing myself from the nymph I was speaking to, I headed to the back of the shop, my fingers trembling as I reached into my pocket. When I pulled out the lone business card, my heart skittered. I knew I hadn't put it there.

I stared at the card, the moon shimmering as if the image itself was alive. Magic tingled and thickened in the air. I didn't have time to process what was happening before Yira appeared right in front of me, as though she had always been there.

"Hello, Nyssa," she said in a low, commanding voice, a wide grin spreading across her face. Her sharp silver gaze held a weight of its own when it fell on me. Something deep within me responded, like a force I couldn't resist, as if the gravity in the room had shifted, centering entirely on her. "Congratulations on your alchemy shop."

"Thank you," I managed, struggling to remember how to breathe. Had her presence always been this overwhelming?

"I thought it was time we talked about your position with the Lunar Order," she continued. I could only nod, the words stuck in my throat. "You do still want to join, right?" Another nod. "Perfect."

Before I could even think to respond, she swept aside the curtain dividing the back room from the shop and strode out.

It was only then I realized how eerily quiet it had become. I rushed after her, my heart pounding, only to find the entire shop frozen—everyone still, as if caught in a moment of time, locked in place like statues.

Yira wove through the shop, taking it all in as if the people frozen all around her were perfectly normal. Her form appeared to flicker the longer I stared, and I dropped my gaze, something telling me I wasn't ready to witness her true form.

"Just lovely," Yira murmured as she strolled through the shop. She seemed more inclined to investigate than talk to me, but I was about to burst with all the questions bubbling within me.

"How are they doing?" I blurted. Yira half turned and raised an eyebrow. She knew exactly who I was talking about, but was going to make me spell it out. "Are the nephilim recovering?"

"They are, though it will take some time. They will be in isolation for a while." She noted my wince at that. "Why do you ask?"

"I was hoping to talk to them, that's all." I chewed on my lip, weighing how much to say. "We went through some tough situations, we all . . . saw aspects of each other in the nightbane that were very personal."

Yira stepped closer to me, her sheer presence overwhelming, as she cupped my cheek. "Wounds of the soul are never easy to heal." Her voice shifted, like the winds blowing on a winter solstice night, carrying a chill that spoke of both harsh truth and quiet understanding. "But if we surround ourselves with loved ones, their light can guide us from the darkness lurking within."

Then she stepped away, the weight of her being gone, and she continued on as if nothing had happened.

"There will be tests and trials to find out all of your strengths and where you will best fit." She paused, picking up a potion and holding it up to the light. "Your skill with alchemy will be a great asset."

I swallowed hard. What was I even meant to say to all that?

With a flourish, she swept back toward me. "Welcome to the Lunar Order, Nyssa. Your initiation is in four days."

And with that, she was gone in the blink of an eye, as if she'd never even been there.

Time began to flow again, but not a single person reacted, especially not me, as I could only stare wide-eyed at the space she had just occupied.

What in the realms had I gotten myself into this time?

***

What will happen when Nyssa joins the Lunar Order and will the sparks between her and Kaelan ignite? Find out in Book 3 <u>Sworn in Twilight</u>

SWORN IN TWILIGHT

Book 3 of The Lunar Order Chronicles

Chapter 1

Alchemy was an art of balance, control, and finesse. These days, it also involved dodging claws while a demonspawn tried to eat my face.

Sulfur and rot burned my nose as I slid beneath a half-toppled wall, my reinforced leather armor the only thing between me and shredded skin.

I scrambled up and hurled another potion. Glass shattered at the demonspawn's feet, ooze spilling out to trap it mid-lunge. Mirell didn't waste the opening. Her blades crossed in a silver blur, and both creatures dropped before I caught my breath.

Under the moonlight, her horns and short midnight hair gleamed. With a flourish, the erebian twisted and flashed me a grin—white teeth bright against dusty red skin—before lunging at two more demonspawn. Her movements were fluid, almost reckless, but undeniably effective. I could only huff at my teammate. Mirell always treated danger like a game and chaos like her favorite toy.

"You do surround yourself with the strangest people," Danika's voice brushed through my mind, smooth and cool as moonlight. A cobalt blur streaked by as my familiar wove between my legs before she launched herself at a demonspawn.

You're one to talk, I shot back, scanning for my next target.

A guttural screech split the air, echoing off the narrow walls of the alley.

"On your left, Nyssa!" Astrid called from the roof above.

I pivoted hard, boots skidding in the slick black ichor. One hand dropped to the leather straps of my potion belt, while the other tightened on my conduit—extended now into a thin stave.

A demonspawn crawled from the shadows, its body a twisted knot of sinew and bone. Wicked claws scraped against the ground, each talon at least two inches long—perfect for flaying flesh.

"Goddess, how many more?" I cursed.

Danika's tense energy seeped through our bond. *"Something's off about this."*

We'd come to investigate a weakened rune, but from the number of demonspawn pouring through, I already knew the damage was worse than the report had stated. The Order had created a network of runes to anchor the veil at its weakest points, and keep the demonspawn at bay. With this rune's power wavering, the veil thinned allowing these creatures to claw their way through.

But first, we needed to move before they pinned us down.

The moment I'd set foot in the alley, I'd known it had been the wrong choice, an uneasy sensation had slithered over me, but there was little time to scold myself now. Tonight, I was leading the team—the final test of my initiation into the Lunar Order.

The demonspawn slunk toward me, its black eyes shining in the moonlight, and filled with nothing but hunger and destruction. A shudder crept over my skin, but I shoved my unease away, trailing my fingers over my potions.

Adapt, get us out of here alive, and learn from your mistake, I told myself.

"You've got this," Danika said, already knowing what I was about to try. She'd sensed it through our bond, just as I could perceive she gnawed on the leg of a demonspawn without looking.

I swallowed hard. If I wanted to call this mission a success, I needed to showcase all of my abilities and prove how far I'd come.

I inhaled, letting the chaos settle inside me, then exhaled and unleashed my magic. Not the gentle pulse of lunar energy that always thrummed beneath my skin, but the molten fire I'd spent the last month honing for this exact moment.

The rune on my hand burned hot, fire curling and twisting around my wrist, almost alive in its lust to be wielded.

I am in control.

The demonspawn flicked out its tongue, tasting the magic thick in the air, then it snapped its teeth and lunged. I jerked my hand upward, and a burst of flames erupted from my fingers, searing its face. Not a kill strike, but effective enough to make it reconsider its life choices. It shrieked, a high-pitched scream that made me flinch, and scrambled backward before bolting away.

I staggered, heart hammering, eyes wide with disbelief. It had worked. My hands trembled as shock mingled with exhilaration, but a fierce pulse of triumph swelled in my chest.

After weeks of relentless practice, cold sweats, and long sessions with the Order therapist, I'd done it. I'd wielded my solar magic under pressure and stayed in command. The fire throbbed in my veins, alive and demanding—but it had obeyed me.

A grin spread across my face before a sharp tug on my awareness yanked me back to the situation. Right. I was in the middle of a fight, with Danika guarding my flank.

I spun around as a demonspawn swiped at her. My fox flattened herself against the ground, dodging its claws. Blue energy crackled over her fur, making her shimmer, but the demonspawn didn't even flinch as her power lashed out at him.

The putrid stench of singed flesh hit me like a wall, but my training took over. I swung my stave, fire spiraling along its length, and slammed it into the creature's sternum. It screeched as the heat and force sent it skidding across the alley—and it didn't get up again.

"*Showing off now, are we?*" Danika's teasing voice cut into my mind.

"That was . . . new," I mumbled, reining in my emotions before they overwhelmed me. "My solar magic doesn't like coming second."

Pride seeped through my bond with Danika, and I anchored myself to that sensation, letting it swell within me.

Danika and I regrouped and jogged to Mirell, who flicked ichor off her swords with an annoyed look. Astrid jumped down from her vantage point and, with one flap of her midnight-blue wings, landed next to me. This was just an average night for moon-blessed wardens like them.

"Good work," Astrid said with a wide grin. Both she and Nathaniel had worked hard to train me since my initiation into the Order, but we'd all known my solar magic would be the biggest hurdle. Relief, excitement, and overwhelm swirled in my stomach, but I tamped them down. I couldn't allow myself to become distracted or complacent. The night was far from over.

"We're three blocks from our target location," I called out, hoping I sounded like a decisive leader. "Let's keep moving before more show up."

We fell into our formation: Mirell in the lead, Danika and me in the middle, and Astrid guarding the flank. Each of us had a role. Whether fighting with blades, arrows, or potions, we had to work as one unit. And while I trusted them, I still needed to prove myself and show I was worthy of their trust.

I pressed my awareness outward, letting it sweep the narrow alley for anything hiding in the shadows. Overflowing trash bins and broken bottles littered the way, the kind of place demonspawn loved to haunt. Alleyways and I didn't have a great history—especially when demonspawn were involved.

Fieldwork would be part of my duties as a warden once I swore my oath to the Lunar Order. The streets of Arkirith had the occasional run-in with demonspawn, but since Aegis's attack targeting the veil, there had been a significant increase of the creatures.

I caught my reflection in the mirrored windows of a closed office building. My coral hair, tied back in a ponytail, contrasted nicely with the black leather. Danika giggled in my head, and I realized I was grinning like an idiot.

I'm not used to wearing this gear. And you have to admit, I look like a badass.

Danika laughed again, and I snorted at myself, though I did not stop smiling. The dark leathers fit like a second skin, etched with wards to turn blades and claws, dampen the bite of certain spells, and still let me move freely.

Every time I slid into this gear, a spark flared in my core. The leathers transformed me into the witch I wanted to be—sharp-edged and unshakable. One day, I'd be that witch, inside and out.

A shiver trickled down my spine. Something was off, but I couldn't quite place it.

"I sense it too," Danika whispered, her tail swishing with agitation.

Every step we ran in this direction, it only increased. My awareness recoiled as it brushed over something sharp, like nails on a chalkboard.

My pulse stumbled. The magic here was wrong—thin in some places, too dense in others, like a current that had lost its flow. The faint tang of iron and ozone clung to the back of my throat, sharp enough to make me gag.

"Something's not right." I squeezed my conduit as a cold sweat broke along my neck. Whatever lingered ahead wasn't just demon-spawn.

"We're almost there," Mirell replied, which was anything but reassuring.

We rounded the corner and came up short as soft chittering bounced off the brick walls. Goose bumps prickled over my skin, and I scanned the street. Rusted fire escapes zigzagged overhead, their shadows broken by the flicker of a dying streetlamp. But no matter which way I tilted my head, I couldn't pin down the source of the noise.

Something oily slithered across my awareness, and I hissed through clenched teeth, "Right side."

We shifted as one, readying ourselves for a fight.

Five demonspawn slipped out of the shadows in a pack, but what unsettled me was that there was far more intelligence behind their eyes. Three hunched low, their limbs knotted and uneven. The others loomed taller, their jaws stretched too wide, displaying their jagged teeth.

"Twenty feet past them on the left is our building," Mirell murmured.

Most of the windows were dark, but a few flickered with the light of TVs while the lower levels had heavy shutters sealing them. The clouds overhead parted, offering just enough moonlight to make out the fire escape attached to the seven-story building, and at the top, the rune in question lay.

Indecision gnawed at me—we could stand and fight, which would not only risk injury but might alert other demonspawn in the area to our presence, or retreat and find a different route.

And then I sensed them. On the edge of my awareness, like tiny drops of darkness, more demonspawn converged on us.

"Astrid, get to the stairs and lower the ladder for us," I said in a low voice, projecting more confidence than I felt. The others tensed, reading the tightness in my words. "On my mark, go left and run."

We didn't move, all poised to take off, but I let the enemy move closer.

"Now!" I shouted, hurling a smoke-bomb vial. Astrid launched into the sky, distracting the demonspawn as the vial hit the ground with a satisfying smash. Mirell sprinted forward as thick gray smoke curled up, enveloping the demonspawn in seconds.

The erebian veered left, Danika and I close behind. I flung the second potion across the street. Silver sparks shot into the air, crackling like miniature fireworks, loud enough to cover our movements and buy us a few precious seconds.

Astrid perched on the landing and lowered the ladder with smooth precision. Mirell scooped Danika into her arms in one fluid motion, lifting her to Astrid before climbing up after her.

I skidded, fumbling on the first step of the ladder in my panic. Cold metal scraped against my palms as I scurried up the rungs, smoke swirling below.

Astrid lowered herself, and I clasped onto her wrist, pulling myself upward. The ladder groaned as Mirell hauled it back up, and then a shriek rang out behind us. Demonspawn clawed at the air, snarling at losing their feast.

As much as I hated heights, I scurried up the stairs, ignoring the creaks of metal and shrieks of hungry demonspawn.

When I stepped onto the rooftop, the moon broke through the clouds, easing some of the tension in my shoulders. But I didn't lower my guard. While Mirell moved to inspect the rune at the center of the roof, the rest of us took our positions, monitoring the dark night.

Streetlights cut through the city below, but this district felt muted. Beyond it, Arkirith pulsed with life and sound.

The back of my neck prickled, the undeniable weight of eyes tracking me. I scanned the nearby rooftops, every shadow a threat, and loosened my hold on my magic, letting it bleed into the air.

Something was wrong.

The air rippled, thick with warning. Power flooded my hands, eager to obey, and with a flick of my fingers, a shimmer sparked—my shield flaring wide to protect us all.

Half a breath later, an arrow slammed into my shield right in front of me and then skittered across the roof. I only took my eyes off the skyline for a moment to assess the arrow. White fletching and a crescent moon etched into the blunted tip. A test. If I'd been too slow, the hit would've hurt, but that would've been my fault.

Neither Astrid nor Mirell drew their weapons, but that didn't mean this was over. Danika's tail swished as she padded around, restless energy rolling off her. At least I wasn't the only one on edge.

"Come and look at this," Mirell called out.

We closed ranks, not that I dropped my guard or my shield.

Mirell frowned down at the rune and lowered herself to one knee, fingertips brushing the etched lines. The rune was about a foot wide, its intricate, flowing grooves dulled to the faintest shimmer. A deep gouge cut straight through the design, marring the flow of magic. Even now, a faint glow still bled across the rooftop where the stored lunar magic had spilled free, seeping like a wound that refused to close.

"Think that's pretty self-explanatory," Astrid said.

"As to why the rune isn't working, sure," I replied. "But not regarding who would destroy a rune meant to protect the city or why."

Mirell tilted her head, urging me to continue.

"It's a single, clean strike through, which means deliberate—and likely made by a blade. A demonspawn claw would've left three marks. And the area's clear, meaning there wasn't any blowback."

Only after I'd said it aloud did the weight of my words sink in. Someone hadn't just sabotaged our protective rune—they'd done it with precision, cutting it without triggering the surge of magic its destruction should've unleashed. I doubted that was caution for anyone's safety, but rather a strike meant to go unnoticed.

"Good, anything else?" Mirell asked.

I frowned. What was I missing? And then it clicked, the magical residue I'd sensed. "They likely used a blade enhanced by lunar magic."

From the perplexed looks Astrid and Mirell shot me, that hadn't been what they'd expected.

Astrid glanced at the rune again. "What makes you think that?"

"The rune recharges at night under direct moonlight. Even at its weakest, the power stored inside should've exploded outward if the rune was destabilized. But this . . ." I gestured at the faint glow clinging to the rooftop, shimmering brighter wherever the moonlight touched it. "The magic feels like it bled out, saturating the area instead of bursting free. The only way to make that happen is to alter the rune with the same energy it was built to hold."

"You're right," Mirell murmured as she studied the rune again. Her irises flickered silver as she gathered her magic. "Someone with a lunar blade is sabotaging our runes."

A chill ran down my spine. Since the attack by Aegis and our discovery of the first Lunar Order Headquarters below the city, numerous Order members had been relocated here to establish a presence. Which meant that the number of people with such blades had greatly increased.

But could there be a traitor within the Order?

Then, her words clicked. "Wait, this isn't the only one?"

"Two more were damaged last night, but we just assumed it was those aligned with the demons." She shook her head and stood up. "I'll call it in. We will need to create a new rune to cover this area, as this one isn't salvageable."

"Where were they located?" I asked. Danika's awareness sharpened, and I could sense the weight of it through our bond.

"North Spindle."

Dread coiled through me as alarm spiked in Danika. "I helped to create and power all of those."

"There are no lingering traces of other magic here, nothing for me to track." Agitation laced Danika's words. Her hackles rose as she scanned our surroundings for threats, followed by a low, rumbling growl. My throat constricted, her own emotions echoing my fear. Someone was targeting my energy signature.

"We should report in," Astrid said, unease radiating from her. Which was code for let's not talk about this in the open. Danika shot me a look. No one bothered to suggest that these incidents might be a coincidence because at this point, nothing was ever a coincidence when it came to me.

Want to find out what happens next? Grab *Sworn in Twilight* now!

<u>From The Author</u>

Thank you so much for reading the story of Nyssa's journey!
If you enjoyed this book, please consider leaving a review to help more readers discover it.

Originally when I sat down to write the opening of book 2, I wanted to jump right into the action and get back to this fun high stake but cozy world. Only Nyssa had other plans. Out tumbled the story that she wanted me to tell, where her hopes and dreams were drowning under her fear and trauma.

No matter what you are going through in life, you are not alone. There is always a spark of hope, even in dark times.

If you would like to keep up-to-date about my next books and all other fantasy filled information you can sign up for my newsletter to keep in touch. Find it at **sfhenne.com**

Big shout out to my amazing street team for helping share Nyssa's story with the world. And a big thank you to my fantastic beta and ARC readers! I couldn't have done it without you.

A big hug and thank you to my author BBF's who are always there to encourage and support me when I need it. Laura, Jay, Poppy, Konstance, and Marsha, I love you guys.

And last, but not least, **thank you** to my family for all of their support and understanding. Thanks for putting up with me.